"Come away, O human child
From the waters and the wild;
Take a fairy by the hand,
For the world's more full of weeping
                    than you can understand. . . ."

—William Butler Yeats

Magic Tales Anthology Series From Ace Fantasy Books

UNICORNS! edited by *Jack Dann and Gardner Dozois*
MAGICATS! edited by *Jack Dann and Gardner Dozois*
FAERY! edited by *Terri Windling*
MERMAIDS! edited by *Jack Dann and Gardner Dozois*
(forthcoming)

FAERY!

EDITED BY
TERRI WINDLING

ACE FANTASY BOOKS
NEW YORK

FAERY!

An Ace Fantasy Book / published by arrangement with
the editor

PRINTING HISTORY
Ace Original / January 1985

ISBN: 0-441-22564-0

Ace Fantasy Books are published by
The Berkley Publishing Group,
200 Madison Avenue, New York, New York 10016.
PRINTED IN THE UNITED STATES OF AMERICA

For Regi,
a frequent traveler in the land of Faery

Special thanks to Mark Arnold, Robin McKinley, Jane Yolen, Patricia McKillip, and Beth Fleisher for their aid in putting this collection together.

Contents

A Troll
and Two Roses

By Patricia A. McKillip

Once upon a time there was an old troll who lived under a bridge. He was an ugly, sloppy old troll named Thorn, who liked to flip fish out of the river with his toes and eat them raw, and to leap out at travellers on the road above and collect whatever valuables they dropped before they ran. Like all trolls, he had a weakness for beautiful things. He kept his treasures in an iron chest hidden under tree roots along the bank. When the moon was high and full, he would open the chest and look at them: all the lovely things he had stolen. He had rings and ribbons, lace handkerchiefs, jeweled knives, delicate veils, pouches of gold, silk flowers, feathered hats, and even a stray velvet shoe that a young girl had lost in her terror. He never harmed anyone; he was too lazy, and so ugly he didn't need to. One glimpse of his huge, warty, hairy face peering up over the side of the bridge was enough to make anybody drop whatever they had. "Troll toll!" he would bellow, and collect it, laughing, from the dust.

Almost anybody.

One night he looked over his treasure box and a restless, discontented feeling stirred through him. It was a familiar feeling: it meant that his eyes were tired of all his old things and wanted something new to delight in. He shut his box and hunkered down under the bridge to wait. He didn't expect anyone, for it was late and the gates of the city the road led to were long closed. But he heard in the distance solitary hoof-

1

beats, and he grinned a troll grin, making fish dive out of the reflection of his teeth.

He waited until the hoofbeats thumped and echoed over the center of the bridge. Then he leaped up, all snarled and dank in the moonlight, with his eyes crossed and a frog in his beard. "Troll toll!" he boomed. An edge of pure silver sliced out of the dark at him so fast it trimmed his hair as he ducked. He yelped. A black horse with yellow eyes bared its teeth and lunged at him. A voice snapped irritably,

"Troll toll, indeed! I'll give you troll toll, you frog-eater—" The silver whistled about Thorn's ears again, and he dove into the water and swam away into the night. But not before he had seen what the rider was carrying, and that the moon shadow in the white dust was crowned.

He was consumed with longing from that moment. He could not eat, he could not sleep. The fish were safe, the travellers were safe. He sat under his bridge, chewing his beard, smoldering with desire, not, as he had done in his youth, for a troll-woman, but for the rose he had glimpsed in the dark rider's hand.

It was white as hoar-frost; it was carved out of winter. Yet it was alive, and the dew clustered on it like diamonds. He knew a little of the world: that kings and princes went on quests for such things, and that they generally gave them away to their true loves, not to untidy trolls. But this prince had been alone, in no great hurry. He had not returned in triumph; he had come back at night, riding slowly, and, even allowing for the unexpected appearance of Thorn, in no good humor. Had his true love not wanted the rose? Well, Thorn did, and finally, at dusk one evening, he dragged himself from under the bridge and went mumbling and thumping through the forest, in no good humor himself, for he hated the world. But there was no other way to possess that rose.

He reached the walls of the city before dawn. He dragged himself up over them, and wound through the cobblestone streets, shambling and snorting and giving city folk bad dreams. He found another wall and went over that, and another and went over that. And another—and then he dropped onto a smooth velvety lawn that was covered with rose trees.

A hundred peacock eyes stared at him and folded; the birds went screeching away. He stood in the dawn, smelling of river water, looking, with his little muddy eyes and his clumsy bulk, like something not even a dog would bite. But his thoughts and eyes were full of roses. He walked among the trees finding roses but never the rose he wanted. Scarlet roses, gold, pink, orange, lavender, blue-white, ivory white, snow-white, but never crystal white, ice-white, so white he could have buried his big nose in it and smelled the wintry peaks of his birthplace. He stood beside the last tree, scratching his head and wondering where to go next. He heard a sigh.

It was the prince, standing in the garden gate with the magic rose in his hand.

Thorn studied him a moment, warily. He was a burly young man, unarmed and barefoot, with tousled yellow hair, a morning beard, and black, black eyes. His shirt was loose, his crown was off; he had apparently just gotten out of bed. Thorn ducked behind a row of bushes, and crept silently, step by step, up to the prince's back. It hadn't worked the first time, but it might a second. He raised himself on his toes and yelled at the top of his lungs: "Troll toll!"

The prince dropped the rose.

He gave Thorn a furious chase through the rose garden, but Thorn batted at him once with his huge hand and the prince tumbled among the flowers. Thorn climbed back over the walls faster than he had come. When the sun rose, he was outside the city gates; when the sun set, he was back under his bridge, gazing with utter delight at his rose.

It was whiter than the moon, it was more delicate than an elvish smile. It had no root, but it was alive, caught in some spell that kept it always perfect, with no sign on its tender petals of decay. It smelled of snow and apple blossoms. A diamond of moistness balanced on the very tip of one petal. Thorn touched it with his horny finger and it dropped, dissolving. As he berated himself for his clumsiness, another diamond formed at the heart of the flower and rolled slowly across its crystal petals like a tear.

Then Thorn heard the galloping.

The prince was not alone this time. Thorn winced at the clatter of hooves over his head. He was just wise enough to duck himself down, instead of demanding a toll, and move a little faster than he had ever moved in his life. The dusk enveloped him, blurred his swift bulky form among the river reeds and trees. The prince sighted him, but his army had hard going along the soft tangled banks. The prince's horse, the black, wicked-eyed mount, seemed to melt like night through brambles and thickets. Thorn, glancing back, could see its yellow eyes burning in the dark long after the shouts and splashes of the prince's army had faded away.

Thorn was fast and tireless. His feet gobbled miles the way he gobbled fish. His leathery soles never felt a sharp stone; they could flatten a wall of brambles without hesitation. The prince's horse followed like a bolt of black lightning. It could never quite catch up with Thorn, but it never fell behind, and all night long its baleful, sulphurous eyes smouldered into Thorn's back. Finally, near morning, Thorn began to tire a little. He wanted to sit down quietly and contemplate the rose in his hand. He wanted breakfast. A dawn wind rose, puffed the last stars out. The sky turned grey as iron. In front of Thorn, massive grey peaks of stone began to separate themselves from the sky.

Thorn ran toward them with relief. He could find an opening, duck inside, and hide himself in the meandering veinwork of caves through which the lifeblood of the mountains flowed. Thorn had been born in a cave; he could see in the dark. He was no more afraid of a mountain than he was of a minnow. So when he bolted into one dark crevice among the boulders, he wasn't prepared to hear the mountain speak with a roar like a thousand cannon. The dark tore away in front of him like a curtain. Light hurt his eyes. He stumbled on wet grass. He stopped, bewildered, blinking. The mountains had vanished. He was standing on a flat plain, watching the sun rise from the wrong side of the world. There was another thunderclap. The prince and his horse leaped out of a slit in the air into the wrong morning.

The horse snorted and refrained, in its astonishment, from biting Thorn's ear off. The prince slid off its back slowly. The three stood silently, troll, horse and prince, all with the same expression on their faces. Then, faster than a fish sliding out of Thorn's fingers, the prince's sword was out of its sheath and threatening to burrow into Thorn's troll-heart.

"Give me that rose."

There was something in the black eyes more compelling than the meager blade. Visions of an endless chase made Thorn yield the rose. His small eyes blinked; he sighed. The rose passed out of his grasp.

The deadliness faded from the prince's eyes. He held the

rose gently to his cheek and said, with a tired, angry sorrow, "It is my wife."

Then Thorn wanted the rose back. The dream-woman entrapped within such a wondrous form made him snort with longing; he took a step toward it, his hand outstretched. The horse's big yellow teeth snapped at his nose. The prince ignored him.

"Look, she's crying. She never cries." He coaxed a tear onto his fingertip and touched it to his lips. Then he became aware of Thorn, his troll chest heaving, his eyes tiny and red with yearning. The prince's hands enfolded the rose, held it close to his heart.

"She loves me," he said coldly. Then he glanced around the empty, cloud-tossed sky. "Look what you did."

"I didn't!" Thorn protested.

"Where are we?"

Thorn's feet shuffled among the grass. He was hungry, he wanted the rose, he wished the prince with his bad-tempered eyes and tidy, gleaming armor would leave him alone to dangle his feet in a river and nibble toads. He was half again as tall as the prince, and twice as burly, and he was bewildered by his own submission. He said pleadingly, "I have a secret treasure box of beautiful things; if you give me the rose—"

"Forget it," the prince said brusquely. "She is a highborn lady, she is not for you. You would make her miserable, and then she would make you even more miserable."

"She could never make me miserable."

"She'd find a way." He looked around the plain again, then, and added briskly, "You led us here. Lead us back."

Thorn scowled. "If I knew how to get back to my bridge, prince, I'd be there now." He felt cold and grumpy, for the spell of the rose was aching in his heart. Yet even as he glanced at it again, his throat swelled and his eyes softened. Then at last he thought to ask, "What turned the lady into a rose?"

The prince slid his helm back and scratched his head. "I don't know. An evil spell, but who the sorcerer is, I can't guess. We were up in the mountains alone; she was sitting in my lap, we were dallying among the wildflowers, counting birds, making up riddles—and suddenly she was this rose. I waited, I searched. I shouted and pleaded and argued with the wind. She was still a rose. I came back home. Whereupon," he

added dourly, "I was assailed by an ugly old troll." Thorn
snorted. "And now, I'm here with the troll and the weeping
rose in the middle of nowhere." He turned suddenly and
mounted. "Well. You can stay here picking at grass with your
toes, but I'm going to find the door back." The great black
mount whirled. Thorn cried, "Wait! Wait for me!"

And then the entire plain rumbled. Darkness fell over it,
thick and murky, until Thorn could not even see the horse's
yellow eyes. The rose began to glow. It was a piercing, ice-
white light in the utter black. The plain was shrieking now. Or
was it wind? Thorn couldn't tell. He squeezed his eyes shut,
put his hands over his ears, and wished with all his heart he
were back under his bridge. The wish didn't work. He heard a
startled, anguished cry from the prince. Then the plain burned
with daylight and Thorn opened his eyes.

He stood staring stupidly, his mind working very slowly.
The white rose was now red. The prince was now a princess.
The horse was still a horse. The princess was sitting on the
ground with the red rose against her cheek. Her brown hair
was braided, her cheeks were freckled like apples, she was still
crying. It was by her tears that Thorn finally realized who she
was.

He fell in love. He forgot his visions of a frosty maiden with
diamonds on her smooth pale skin. He wanted to braid and
unbraid the honey-brown hair; he wanted to count all the
freckles on the princess's round cheeks. He wanted to catch
her tears and carry them in his pocket. His finger moved tentatively toward her face. She noticed him finally.

She scrambled to her feet, staring at him in horror. "Troll,"
she breathed. "What have you done to my husband?"

He broke grass stems between his toes. "I have a nice
bridge," he said shyly, looking hard at the end of his nose. "I
can catch fat red salamanders for you to eat. I'll give you a
box of beautiful things." He had to wait a little, then, while
she shouted and wept and commanded the reluctant horse to
consume various parts of Thorn. When she finally ran out of
breath, Thorn continued enticingly, "I'll bathe your feet every
day myself among the water-lilies. I'll bring you little furry
bats for pets—" He stopped, for the princess was now on the
back of the horse. "Wait! He's nothing more than a rose now;
I'll bring you a vase to stick him in. You'll like me—truly.
Wait for me!"

He began to run again, only this time it was he in pursuit of the horse.

The horse led him across the plain, up low lumpy hills, into a deep and shining forest. The forest was ancient, dark; the trees were tall and hoary. Their tangled branches linked to net the sun; their trunks were knotted with boles. Occasionally, within a bole, an eye would flick. A thick root would gesture and be still. Spider webs gleamed in the shadows as though they were woven of white fire. The shadowy air itself seemed to glint with an eerie brightness. Thorn, preoccupied with catching the horse, didn't notice the forest until the horse slowed. Then he leaped forward, caught the black tail and yelled, "Ha!"

He picked himself out of a bramble-bush a moment later, hearing little sniggers of derision all around him. He scowled, but there was nothing to scowl at. The princess was gazing at him expressionlessly. Her eyes, he saw then, were green as the rose stem.

"Troll," she said, "where are we?"

He looked around. He sighed deeply, for he was very far from his bridge.

"I would think," he said glumly, "in an enchanted forest. Inside a magic land. No place I've ever seen before. Where," he added, "there's enchantment, there's always an enchanter. I don't like them, myself. I prefer being comfortable. Now, take my bridge, that's—" The princess told him what he could do with his bridge. "Oh. Well," he explained, "it's a bit big to stick in my ear."

"Troll," she said loftily, waving the prince like a scepter, "you will lead me to this enchanter."

"I don't know where one is."

"You will find one."

His eyes grew a little smaller. "What will you give me if I do? I'd rather go home and eat breakfast. What will you give me?"

"My embroidered shoes."

"No good."

"The twelve gold ribbons in my hair."

"No."

"My lace petticoat."

"What's that?"

"Never mind," she said crossly. "I'll give you all the jewels

I'm wearing. My earrings, my silver swan pin, my gold and sapphire chains, my six rings—"

"I count seven."

"All but one."

"That," he said shrewdly, "is the one I want. That, and your hair and a kiss."

She was silent. She touched her hair, swallowing. "All of it?"

"I want your shiny braids to put into my box."

"You can have that," she said unhappily. "And my wedding ring. But no kiss."

"Yes."

"No."

"Yes."

"All right," she said, while the color ran like wine into her face. "Ouch!" She sucked her thumb, glowering at the rose. Thorn smiled a great yellow smile and nodded happily.

He plodded in front of the horse, tearing down giant luminous spider webs and mumbling to himself. "Enchanter . . . where enchanter? Who? Witch? Wizard? Fairy? First princess into rose, then prince into rose. Prince with princess-rose, then princess with prince-rose. Why not both together? Rose, rose. Then I put both in my box." He lifted his head suddenly, scenting the wind like a horse. "Troll? No. Troll magic small, small . . . this is a complicated magic." He stopped mumbling then and listened. Then he bent toward the great old hollow root of a tree and yelled, "Ha!"

"Shut up," a voice hissed.

"Little troll in the tree roots, I see you. Where is the enchanter of this forest?"

"Sh!" The voice in the roots sank to a breath. "Sh . . ."

"Where?" Thorn whispered. "I have a present for you."

"I want that red rose."

"You don't want that. It's an enchanted prince with a bad temper."

"Oh. Then what present?"

"Twelve gold ribbons to weave together into a soft bright hammock for you among the roots."

"H'm," said the voice with interest, and the princess unbound them one by one from her hair. They slid gently through the air, striped Thorn's hand with gold. "H'm," said the little voice. "Bend closer."

Thorn straightened after a few moments. He blinked; drops of cold sweat rolled into his beard. The princess said uneasily, "What?"

"Um."

"Well, what?"

He shuffled his big feet among the leaves. The horse's head turned very slowly; one eye regarded him evilly. Thorn stared back at it, transfixed. He forgot, suddenly, what he was going to say. He scratched his head. Was it about something to eat? The princess urged the horse forward impatiently.

"Oh, Troll."

Deeper they went into the forest. They crossed a stream as cold and feathery white as moonlight. Ivory-pale frogs croaked on its banks, their starting eyes of various colors full of some strange pleading. Thorn shied away from them. Magic. He had no desire to eat them. A grove of trees with leaves made of pearls and diamonds made the princess stop and stare. Thorn growled deep in his throat and stretched out both hands. Trees trembled; leaves flashed down like tears.

"No," the princess said, as Thorn bent toward them.

"No." Her face was pale; he saw the glint of a jewel on her cheek. When she wasn't looking at him, Thorn slipped a pearly leaf into his pocket.

They crossed the grove of weeping trees. Beyond it roared a wild blue river. They stopped on its mossy bank. On the other side of the water rose a great glassy black cliff. Their eyes lifted higher, higher. . . . On top of the cliff, so high the birds could scarcely reach it, stood a rose garden.

The princess's eyes fell from it to the rose in her hand. She looked again at the garden, again at the rose. The troll heard her breathing quicken. He was musing . . . Something? Fish in the river . . . twelve gold ribbons . . . the black horse, standing so quietly, still as the black cliff. Yellow ribbons, yellow eyes . . .

"Ah." He remembered what he had been wanting to say. "That's it. You might want to get off that horse."

The princess's face turned as white as the rose she had been. Thorn stopped sidling away from the horse, transfixed again by love. He heaved a sigh. The princess screamed. The black horse laughed, and with a mighty thrust of its haunches, soared into the sparkling, blue-white air, leaping upward toward the roses. Thorn, dangling from the horse's tail, which in an exuberance of love he had clutched, shut his eyes and howled.

He thumped like a bad apple among the rose trees. The horse was no longer a horse, but a sorcerer with terrible yellow eyes. The prince was a prince again. Every time he moved toward the sorcerer, a bramble would snake out of the earth and catch his wrist or his boot. The princess was becoming a whole rose tree. The prince, still struggling, was becoming a bramble man, thorny with anger, with blood-red blooms here and there on his body. The sorcerer was staring into his eyes. Thorn decided it was a good time to go fishing.

He began to sneak away behind the sorcerer's back. But diamonds were showering out of the crystal-white rose tree. Scent wafted from it of distant snowy peaks. Lovely, perfect roses, made for touching, beckoned to him, and he thought of the shiny braids the princess owed him, and the kiss. He hummed silently and waffled. Thorns were sliding through the prince's yellow hair. The sorcerer was enthralled by his spell. Thorn thought again of the kiss.

He thrust his hairy, warty face in front of the sorcerer's nose and bellowed, "Troll toll!"

The sorcerer jumped. The spell tangled in his mind. Brambles reached toward him, tangled within his powerful confusion. The prince drew a hand loose, a foot. His sword slashed at the thorns, then at the troll who was about to pluck a blossom from his lady-love.

"Just one!"

The prince snarled. His sword flashed toward the sorcerer, who was two yellow eyes in a mass of brambles. The flash kindled a fire in the sky which shouted the instant before it disappeared. The roses, the ensorcelled sorcerer, the cliff, the forest, vanished in a well of darkness. Thorn heard a slow drip of water in the night. He smelled limestone. Then he could see again.

"Where are we?" the princess said. She had a white rose petal in her hair, and rose leaves on her skirt. The prince had lost his sword, and his clothes looked as though birds had been pecking at them. "It's so quiet. Are you here? I can't see. . . ."

They were sitting on damp limestone inside a mountain. Thorn crept toward them. The princess started, and her hand went to her cheek.

"Did you do that?"

"What?"

"Never mind. . . . Troll. Lead us out, and I will give you everything else I promised."

The troll smiled.

He led them back to his bridge. It was dusk. The quiet river smelled like a good thick stew of frogs, toads, little bulbous-eyed fish. The prince and the princess, entwined, were murmuring peacefully together.

"Is he dead? What became of your true horse? He cast so many spells. Are all the roses and diamond trees and frogs back in their proper shapes?"

"I don't know, I don't know."

"Where was his land?"

"Inside the mountain. . . ."

"No, the mountain was inside the land."

"Could you see me when you were a rose?"

The troll sighed. Their voices wove together, made a private tapestry of events that no one else could see in just their way. "Ah well," he said, and thumped down underneath his bridge. The iron box was safe; bats circled his head; the river-voice welcomed him home. The princess called, surprised,

"Troll, you may have my hair now."

"I don't want it."

"My ring?"

"Keep it."

The princess was silent. Thorn heard her step from stone to stone. She came to him beneath the shadow of the bridge. She leaned over him as he sat glumly. When she left him, he was smiling.

Their footsteps died away. He reached into his pocket for the leaf of pearls he had stolen, to put into his chest. But he only found a thread of fiery hair.

The Thirteenth Fey

By Jane Yolen

In the middle of a stand of white birch on a slight rise is a decaying pavilion, inferior Palladian in style. The white pilasters have been pocked by generations of peashooters, and several kite strings, quite stained by the local birds, still twine around the capitols. The wind whistles through the thin walls, especially in late spring, and the rains—quite heavy in November and April—have made runnels in the paper. It is very old paper anyway. As a child I used to see different pictures there, an ever-changing march of fates. My parents once thought I had the sight until they realized it was only a vivid imagination supplemented by earaches and low grade fevers. I was quite frequently ill.

I was born in that pavilion, on the marble and velvet couch my parents used for the lying-in for each of my twelve brothers and sisters and me. And I was hung on my baby board in the lower branches of the trees, watched over by butterflies; the mourning doves to sing me to sleep, a chorus of crows to wake me. It was not until I reached my thirteenth year that I understood what my dear mother and her mother before her knew and grieved for but could do nothing about. It was then that I discovered that we are tied to that small piece of land circling the pavilion, tied with bonds of magic as old and secure as common law. We owe our fortunes, our existence, and the lives of our children to come to the owners of that land. We are bounden to do them duty, we women of the fey. And during all the time of our habitation, the local lords

13

have been a dynasty of idiots, fornicators, louts, greedyguts, and fools.

As the last of thirteen children I was not expected to be of any special merit. It is the first and seventh whose cranial bones are read, whose palms are searched, whose first baby babblings are recorded. Yet I had been marked with a caul, had been early to walk, early to talk, early to fly. And then there were my vivid dreams, my visions brought on by ague and earache and the peculiar swirling patterns of moldy walls. I was, in my father's words, "ever a surprise."

My father was a gentle soul. His elven ancestry showed only in his ears, which he was careful to hide beneath a fringe of greying hair, so as not to insult his wife's innumerable relatives who dwelt nearby in their own decaying whimseys, reposes, and belvederes. They already believed my mother had married beneath her. But my father, though somewhat shy on magic, lived for his library, stocked with books of the past, present, and future. He was well read in Gramarye, but also in Astrology, Philosophy, and Computer Science, an art whose time was yet to come.

My mother was never so gentle. She came from the Shouting Fey, those who could cause death and consternation by the timber of their voices. She had a sister who, on command, could bring down milk from dried-up cows with one voice, or gum it up with another. There was a great-aunt, about whom little else was said except that she could scream in six registers at once and had broken windows in all of the Western Counties as a child when bidden to do so by a silly prince one vivid day in spring.

My sisters and brothers and I were a mix, of course, both gentle and loud. But I, the thirteenth fey, was supposed to be the gentlest and loudest of all.

The events I am about to relate really began nine months before the princess was born. Her birth had been long awaited. The queen, a wart-ridden harridan, was thought barren. Years of royal marriage had produced nothing but promises. Yet one steaming hot day, so the queen said, she had gone bathing in a mountain stream with her young women. More for the sake of cooling than cleanliness, I imagine. Humans are, for the most part, a disgustingly filthy lot. And a frog had climbed upon her knee and prophesied a child.

Now I have known many frogs in my time and though the peepers especially are a solipsistic tribe, believing they alone bring spring up from the edge of the world, frogs have no magical talents and they do not have the gift of prophecy. The queen was entirely wrong. It was not a frog at all. It might have been a Muryan. Tiny, dressed in green, one might be mistaken for a frog by a distraught, hot, and desperate queen. But Muryans are a mischievous lot and their natterings are never to be taken seriously.

The queen had rushed home, trailed by her still dripping handmaidens, and told the king. He was well past believing her promises. But much to everyone's surprise (except my father, who expressed the gentle judgment that, according to a law to be enacted years hence called Probability or Murphy's —I forget just which—occasionally a Muryan prophecy might be accurate) the queen gave birth some nine months later to a girl.

They named her Talia and invited—or rather insisted—all the local feys come and bring a gift. We who were so poor as to be forced to live on moonbeams, the free fare of the faery world, had to expend our small remaining store of magicks on that squawling, bawling human infant whose father owned a quarter million acres of land, six rivers, five mountains, and the tithing of all the farms from the Western Sea to the East. It was appalling and unfair and Mother cried about it for days. But Father cautioned her to keep her voice low and, as she knew he was right, she did.

The family gathered to discuss the possibilities but I was sick again with a fever and so had no part in the family council. Who would have believed that a bout of ague brought on by dancing one starry night in a wet field should become so important to the fate of us all.

Father portioned out the magicks at that meeting, one to each child and something for Mother and himself. But he forgot me, sick abed, and so left nothing but an old linden spindle, knotted about with the thread of long life, in the family trunk. The instruction sheet to it was in tatters, mouse-nibbled, shredded for nests. Besides, the spindle lay on the very bottom of the trunk and was covered with a tatty Cloth of Invisibility that worked only occasionally and, as it happened to be one of those occasions, Father hadn't even noticed it. Besides, having decided on gifts of beauty, riches, and wit—all appropriate and necessary gifts for that particular human princess—he wasn't likely to think of giving a newborn the end of life spun out on a wooden distaff.

So the family went to the christening without me, though Mother laid a cool cloth on my head, left a tisane in our best cup by my bed, and kissed both my cheeks before leaving.

"Sleep well, little one," she whispered. It was always special when she was careful to modulate her voice and I knew then how much she loved me. "Sleep well and long."

I expect her admonition forced itself into my fever dreams. I woke about an hour later, feeling surprisingly cool but parched. I had drunk up the tisane already and so cried out for some weak tea. When no one but the doves answered me with their soft *coo-coo-co-roos* from the rafters, I remembered where the family had gone.

Rising from my sickbed, I slipped a silvery party dress on over my shift. The dress was well patched with spider webbing, but the stitches scarcely showed, especially in moonlight.

I looked in the glass. My hair seemed startled into place and I combed it down with my fingers, not feeling up to searching for my brush. Then I pinched my cheeks to bring a blush to them.

The doves *coo-coo-co-rooed* again, nannylike in their warnings. Their message was clear.

"A gift!" I reminded myself out loud, beginning to shiver, not from fever but from fear. What if I had arrived *without* a gift? The king, a fat slug who was so obese he had to ride his charger sidesaddle, would have had my father exorcised by his priests if I forgot to gift his child. Exorcism on a male fey is very painful for the essence is slowly drawn out and then captured in a bottle. Imagine my dear, gentle father corked up for as long as the king or his kin liked. It was too horrible to contemplate. One of Father's brothers had been exorcised by a Kilkenny abbot and was still locked up in a dusty carafe on the back shelf of the monastery wine cellar and labeled *Bordeaux, 79*. As that was a terrible year for wines, Father does not expect anyone will ever uncork him. Father visits once a year and they shout at one another through the glass. Then Father returns whey-faced and desperate-looking. But only a human can free Uncle Finn. Father, alas, cannot.

Is it any wonder that I turned right around and ran back into the pavilion to the storeroom in which the trunk stood?

The oaken trunk was locked with a fine-grained pinewood key but the key was only for show. The trunk was bolted with a family spell. I spoke it quickly:

> *Come thou, cap and lid,*
> *Lift above what has been hid,*
>
> *All Out!*

The last two words were done in the shouting voice and the whole, as with all magic, made my head hurt. But as the final note ended, the top of the trunk snapped open.

I peered in and at first thought the trunk was empty for the tatty Cloth was working again. Then, as I looked more closely, the Cloth suddenly failed around the edges and I saw the tip of the spindle.

"Blessed Loireg," I said with a sigh, praising my great-great-aunt, a patroness of Hebrides spinners. I reached down and the spindle leaped to my hand.

Clutching the spindle to my breast, I ran out the door and along the winding forest paths towards the castle. Since it was morning, and I being still weak with fever, I could not fly. So of course I was very late. The christening, begun promptly at cock's crow—how humans love the daylight hours—was almost done.

I had wrapped the Cloth about my shoulders for warmth and so, on and off, I had been invisible throughout the trip. A cacophony of crows had noticed me; a family of squirrels had not. A grazing deer, warned by my scent, had seemed puzzled when I did not appear; a bear, pawing honey from a tree, was startled when I popped into view. But by the time I reached the castle the Cloth was working again and so the guards did not question my late entrance for they did not know I had come in.

I stopped for a moment at the throne room door and peered around. The king and queen were sitting upon their high gilded chairs. He was—as I have noted before—fat, but Father said he had not always been so. Self-indulgence had thickened his neck and waist and the strong chin that had marked generations of his family repeated itself twice more, the third chin resting on his chest. On the other hand his wife, unsoftened by childbirth, had grown leaner over the years, vulpine, the skin stretched tightly over her cheekbones and marked with lines like a plotter's map.

Before them was a canopied cradle, its silken draperies drawn back to reveal the child who was, at present, screaming in a high-pitched voice that demonstrated considerable staying power. My father and brothers and sisters were encircling the cradle where Father, having just conferred his gift, was still bending down to kiss the squawling babe.

I stepped into the room and had passed several bored courtiers, when the Cloth suddenly failed, revealing me before I had time to recomb my hair or straighten my bent wings or paste a smile across my mouth. I had two bright spots of fever back on my cheeks and my eyes were wild. I looked, my eldest sister later told me, "a rage". But at least I did not shout. In fact, it was all I could do to get out a word, what with all that running. Stumbling forward, the spindle thrust out before me, I almost fell into the cradle. I accidentally stepped on one of the rockers and the cradle tilted back and forth. The infant, its attention caught by the movement, stopped crying.

Into the sudden silence, I croaked, "For Talia—a present of Life." And I pulled on the black thread that was wrapped around the spindle. But I must have pulled too hard on the old knotted thread. It broke after scarcely an inch.

Everyone in the court gasped and the queen cried out, "Not Life but Death."

The king stood up and roared, "Seize her," but of course at that moment the Cloth worked again and I disappeared. In my horror at what I had done, I took several steps back, dropping the spindle and the snippet of thread. Both became visible the moment they left my hand, but no one could find me.

Father bent down, picked up the thread, and shook his head.

"What damage?" whispered Mother. Or at least she tried to whisper. It came out, as did everything her family said in haste, in a shout.

"Indeed," the king cried, "what damage?"

Father took out his spectacles, a measuring tape, and a slide rule. After a moment, he shook his head. "By my calculations," he said, "fifteen years, give or take a month."

The king knew this to be true because Father's family had a geasa laid upon them to always tell the truth.

The queen burst into furious sobbing and the king clutched

his hands to his heart and fell back into his chair. Baby Talia started crying again, but my eldest sister surreptitiously rocked the cradle with her foot which quieted the babe at once.

"Do something!" said the king and as it was a royal command, my mother had to obey.

"Luckily I have not yet given *my* gift, Sire," Mother began, modulating her voice, though she could still be heard all the way out to the courtyard.

Father cleared his throat. He did not believe in that kind of luck.

But Mother, ignoring him, continued. "My gift was to have been a happy marriage, but this must take precedence."

"Of course, of course," murmured the king. "If she is dead at fifteen, what use would a happy marriage be?"

At that the queen's sobs increased.

Father nodded and his eyes caught the king's and some spark of creature recognition passed between them.

Mother bent down and retrieved the spindle. Father handed her the bit of thread. Then she held up the thread in her right hand, the spindle in her left. With a quick movement of her fingers, she tied the thread back, knotting it securely, mumbled a spell which was really just a recipe for bread, then slowly unwound a much longer piece of thread. She measured it with a calculating eye and then bit it through with a loud, satisfying *snick*.

"There," she said. "Talia shall have a long, long life now. But . . ."

"But what?" the queen asked between sobs.

"But there is still this rather large knot at her fifteenth year of course," Mother explained.

"Get on with it. Get on with it," shouted the king. "You fey are really the most exasperating lot. Say it plainly. None of your fairy riddles."

Mother was about to shout back when Father elbowed her. She swallowed hastily and said, "It means she shall fall asleep on her fifteenth birthday . . ."

"Give or take a month," my father inserted.

". . . and she shall sleep for as long as it takes for the knot to be unraveled."

The queen smiled, smoothing out many of her worst wrinkles but adding several new ones around the mouth. "Oh, that should be no time at all."

Mother smiled back and said nothing, but the smile never reached her eyes. She had had no geasa laid on *her* tongue.

Father, ever honest, opened his mouth to speak and Mother elbowed him back. He swallowed hastily and shut his mouth. Lies take spoken words, at least according to the restrictions of his fate.

Just then I became visible again, but at that point no one really cared.

Fifteen years can be a long or a short time, depending upon whether one is immortal or not. Princess Talia spent her fifteen as though she had an eternity to enjoy, learning little but how far the bad temper she had inherited from her father could take her. She had the gifts of beauty and wit that we had conferred upon her and they stood her in good stead with the company she kept. But she was rather short on gratitude, kindness, and love, which take rather longer to bestow than a morning's christening.

I spent the fifteen years reading through the L section in Father's library. I discovered I had an aptitude for Logic, which surprised everyone but Father. I also studied Liturgy, Lepidoptery, and Linguistics; I could do spells in seventeen tongues.

My eldest sister seriously questioned this last accomplishment. "If you can never leave this land, why do you need more than one language?" she asked.

I could not explain the simple love of learning to her, but Father hushed her. "After all," he said, "when fifteen years are up . . ."

"Give or take a month," I added.

" . . . Things may be very different around here." He smiled but would say no more.

On her fifteenth birthday, Talia summoned all the local fey to her party except for me. I had been left off of every guest list since her christening. My sisters and brothers were jealous of that fact, but there was nothing they could do about it. Even fairies cannot change the past.

Talia called her party a "Sleep-Over Ball" and announced that everyone was to come in nightclothes. Talia herself ordered a new gown for the occasion that resembled a *peignoir*, with peek-a-boo Alençon lace and little pink ribbons sewn in strategic places. She was much ahead of her peers and had a positive genius for seduction. There was not a male member of the peerage who had escaped her spell and several fowlers and a stable boy were languishing for love of her. Even my oldest brother Dusty, who had rather common tastes, was smitten and planned to go to the party with a handful of crushed pennyroyal in each pocket, to keep the magic—as he put it—"close to the seat of his affection."

"Affliction," I said.

Dusty smiled and tousled my hair. He was smitten, but not without a sense of humor about it all.

Father and Mother were allowed to beg off since this was to be a party for young folk.

We three watched from the pavilion steps as the twelve flew into the moonlight, the wind feathering their wings. As they passed across the moon, like dust motes through light, I had a sudden fit of shivers. Father put his arm around me and Mother fetched me a shawl. They thought it was the cold, you see.

But it was more than that. "The fifteenth year," I whispered, "give or take a month." My voice was thinned out by the night air.

Father looked at Mother and they both looked at me. Whatever I had felt, whatever had made me shiver, suddenly communicated to them as well. Mother said not a word but went into the pavilion and emerged moments later with a hat and a long wool scarf for me, an Aran Island sweater for Father, and a muff for herself. She had bad circulation and flying always leaves her with cold hands.

We closed our eyes and spoke the spell.

> Far frae earth and far frae barrows,
> Up to where the blue sky narrows,
> Wind and wildness, wings and weather,
> Allie-up together.
>
> Now!

As I lifted into the air I could feel the beginnings of a magic headache coming on, and my shoulders started to hurt as well. I have always had weak wings, but they are adequate for simple travel. We landed at the palace only minutes behind my brothers and sisters, but we were already too late. The sleeping spell had begun.

There was a cook asleep with her hand raised to strike the scullery and she, poor little wench, had been struck by sleep instead. It had happened at the moment of her only retaliation against the cook, which she got by kicking the cook's cat. The cat, unaware of the approaching kick, was snoring with one paw wrapped around a half-dead sleeping mouse.

Along the hall guards slept at their posts: one had been caught in the act of picking his teeth with his knife, one was peeling an orange with his sword, one was scraping his boot with his javelin tip, and one was picking his nose.

The guests, dressed in nightgowns and nightshirts, snored and shivered and twitched but did not wake. And in the midst of them all, lying in state, was Talia, presents piled at her feet. She blew delicate little bubbles between her partially opened lips, and under her closed eyelids I could see the rapid scuttling of dreams.

My brothers and sisters, immune to the spell, hovered above the scene nervously, except for Dusty who darted down to the bed every now and then to steal a kiss from the sleeping Talia. But, as he later admitted, she was so unresponsive, he soon wearied of the game.

"I am not a necrophile, after all," he said petulantly, which was a funny thing for him to say since right before Talia, he had been in love with the ghost of a suicide who haunted the road at Miller's Cross.

Mother put her fingers to her mouth and whistled them down.

Father announced, "Time for a family conference."

We looked in every room in the castle, including the garde-robe, but there were sleepers in every one. So we met on the castle stairs.

"Well, what now?" asked Mother.

"It's Gorse's spell," Dusty said, his mouth still wet from Talia's bubbly kisses. He hovered, pouting, over the steps.

"Of course it is Gorse's spell," said Father, "but that does not mean it is Gorse's *fault*. Don't be angry, Dusty. Just shake out your pockets and sit down."

Dusty did as he was told as Father's voice was very firm and not to be argued with. As soon as the grains of pennyroyal had touched the ground, his mood lightened and he even sat next to me and held my hand.

In fact, we all held hands, that being the best way to augment a family conference. It aids the thinking, it generates energy, and it keeps one's hands warm as well.

Mother looked up. "The knot," she said. "We must remember the knot in the thread."

Father nodded. "The Laws of Correspondence and Balance . . ." he mused.

And then I knew what to do, my reading in Logic having added texture to my spells. "There must be a similar knot about the palace," I said. I let go of Dusty's hand and stood, waving my hand widdershins. A great wind began to blow from the North. It picked up the pennyroyal, plucked seeds from the thorn, gathered wild rose pips and acorns and flung them into the air. Faster and faster the whirlwind blew, a great black tunnel of air.

> *Blow and sow*
> *This fertile ground*
> *Until the knot*
> *Be all unwound,*

I sang. One by one everyone joined me, Dusty immediately, then my other brothers and sisters, and at the last Father and finally Mother. We spoke the spell a hundred times for the hundred years and, in the end, only Mother and I had the voice for it. My voice was husky and rasping but Mother's was low and there was a longing in it compounded of equal parts of wind and sea, for the Shouting Fey came originally from the Cornish coast, great-great-great-grandfather being a sea sprite with a roving sailor's eye.

And then I dropped out of the spell with the worst headache imaginable and Mother ended it with a shout, the loudest I had ever heard her utter. It was so loud, the earth itself was shocked and opened up hundreds of tiny mouths in surprise. Into every one of those tiny mouths a seed or pip or nut popped and, in moments, they had begun to grow. We watched as years were compressed into seconds and green shoots leaped upward towards the sky. By the time the last echo of Mother's shout had died away, a great forest of mammoth oak and thorny vines surrounded the palace. Only one small passage overhead remained open where the moon beamed down a narrow light. Inside the rest of the knotted wood it was as dark as a dream, as deep as sleep.

"Come, children," said Father.

We rode the moonbeam up and out and, as the last of us passed through the hole, the thorns sewed themselves shut behind us over the deathly quiet. We neither spoke nor sang all the way home.

Having read through the Ls in Father's library, I turned my attention to the H's, my choice dictated by the fact that the wall with those books has a window that overlooks the orchard. The gnarled old trees that manage to bring forth their sweet red gifts every year fill me with wonder. It is a magic no fey could ever duplicate. And so now I have a grounding in Hagiography, Harmonics, Hormones, and History. It has been a lucky choice.

One of the books I read spoke about the rise of a religion called Democracy which believes in neither monarchs nor magic. It encourages the common man. When, in a hundred years, some young princeling manages to unravel the knot of wood about Talia's domain, I plan to be by his side, whispering the rote of Revolution in his ear. If my luck holds—and the Cloth of Invisibility works just long enough—Talia will seem to him only a musty relic of a bygone era whose bedclothes speak of decadence and whose bubbly breath of decay. He will wed the scullery out of compassion, and learn Computer Science. Then the spell of the land will be broken. No royal wedding—no royal babes. No babes—no inheritance. And though we fey will still be tied to the land, our wishes will belong to us alone.

Father, Mother, my sisters, my brothers, sometimes freedom is won by a long patience, something that works far better than any magical spell.

Lullaby for a
Changeling

By Nicholas Stuart Gray

To begin with, no one noticed that the baby had changed. A few days passed, after his birth, during which it seemed that Hewit was a perfectly ordinary, fairly cheerful, human infant; fair-haired, blue-eyed, round-faced; crying sometimes, but not too often. Contented to lie cosily in his mother's arms, or those of his father, his sisters—even those of his elder brother. And then—the strangeness showed.

His mother first noticed. She saw the blue eyes had green glints. She saw the chubby face thinning. And Hewit cried more often, screaming ill-temperedly. He was still loved and cuddled, fed and kept warm, but these things no longer contented him. One terrible morning, three weeks after his birth, his mother looked down into the cradle and saw so great a difference in Hewit that she gave a cry.

This brought her husband quickly. Also the rest of the family. Eighteen-year-old Alin; pretty Phemie, who was sixteen; and Nettie, not-quite-ten. They clustered round the cradle, and stared in growing dismay.

The gray-faced baby lay there, wailing thinly. He looked miserable and spiteful, and his tiny face was lined, and ugly, and shadowed. Even his hair had lost its colour, and was like dead ashes.

"He's ill!" cried Phemie.

And so they all thought. The farmer sent Alin to fetch the Spaewife. So the boy rode across a couple or three hills to the glen by the sea where the wise woman lived. She was old, but hale and hearty, and much respected for her knowledge of herbs and healing. In some other parts of the world, she might have been considered a witch. Anyway, back she came with Alin, full of foreboding. The last time she'd been there, to help the farmer's wife when the baby was born, she had seen the infant well and strong.

Now she knelt beside the cradle, watched anxiously by all the family—except Phemie, who had gone to milk the cows. Whatever the emergency, the beasts could not be kept waiting.

"Oh, oh . . ." said the Spaewife, after a while. "This is a terrible matter!"

The farmer's wife sobbed that she knew the child was very ill; and her husband put his arm about her shoulders.

"Not ill," said the old woman, grimly. "Changed. This is not your baby."

"What do you mean? He has a fever—or a chill . . ." whispered the mother.

"Worse. Oh, much worse. This is not your son at all."

And so the trouble was on them.

When the family outcry died down a little, the Spaewife took charge of the situation.

"It must have happened on the night he was born," said she. "The People of the Hills came slipping into the house in the dark, and took your child away. They left this—thing—in his place. One of Their own brats."

There was a noticeable drawing back from the cradle where the pale, whining infant lay, wrinkling its old-looking face, and twisting its mouth as though life tasted bitter.

"Surely not!" cried Nettie. "Who could be so cruel? And what would Those Ones want with our little Hewit? Besides, whatever sort of mother would leave her own son with strangers!"

The Spaewife got to her feet, with a helping hand from Alin, and went to the fireside.

"It's the way They go about things," said she. "Who can know Their reasons? I've heard it said that the Hill Folk, having no souls, leave their babies with humans so that the creatures can get them. I do not know the truth of this. But always there have been changelings left in cradles, and true babies stolen, since the dawn of time."

"What can we do?" cried the mother. "We must go to the

Hill, and beg Them to be merciful! Oh, they must give back my Hewit."

"They never will," said the Wise Woman.

Then she told them to let her think for a few minutes. And she sat in a big wooden chair, and the farmer brought her a hot drink. There she sat, sipping and thinking, and thinking and sipping, for what seemed like an hour to Nettie, but probably was only five minutes. At last, she put down the bowl.

"You must drop that creature in the fire," said she.

There was a horrified general outcry. The old woman waited until silence fell again, and then said it was the only way she knew to go about things.

"Burn the Hill baby," she said, firmly. "Beat it—starve it. Make it yell and scream! And They will hear, no matter how far away the Hill may be. And They'll come like the rush of the wind, to snatch back Their own to safety. And They'll have brought little Hewit for exchange."

"It's too horrible," said the farmer's wife. "We can't do it."

The Spaewife said there was no other way. And she added that the fairy baby would scarce be hurt at all.

"He'll not have time to suffer much before They come for him. And he'll not feel pain the way a human does."

"How can we be sure of that?" said the farmer, doubtfully.

"Take my word, man."

The old woman scooped the little creature from the cradle and took him to the great fireplace. There, the peats were glowing and hot, sending their scented smoke up the chimney. The infant gave a shrill cry, and one claw-like hand came groping from his shawl. Somehow, that sound and that sight seemed to release Nettie from a sort of spell. She gave a shriek that made everyone jump, and leaped to the old woman's side.

"You're not to do it!" she shouted.

"Don't interfere, child! You know nothing of magic. This that I'll do is not cruelty, but necessity. Think of your own wee brother, alone and helpless in the Hill . . ."

"I *am* thinking of him. And thinking of someone putting *him* on a fire!"

"They'd never do that, Nettie."

"Nor should we. It would make us less human than They are. This is a baby, when all's said, just as alone and helpless in our hands as—as . . ."

"Oh, my Hewit," wept the farmer's wife.

"Leave the house, Nettie," said the Spaewife, "if you've no heart or courage to save your brother."

"Oh, I'll save him," said Nettie, unexpectedly. "I'll take this one back to the Hill, and tell Those Ones they must—"

"*Must?* The way you talk, child! Who dares to tell Them what They must or must not do! We must burn this creature—whip it—starve it till it screams. Anything, so that They'll hear and come."

But now the farmer took a hand. He told the Spaewife, kindly but strongly, to leave the family alone to talk it over.

"For it's a very hard matter to decide," said he. And he lifted the baby from her arms and gave it to Nettie.

The old woman began to protest, to talk of sorcery and elves and fairies. But the farmer guided her towards the door, and said Alin would take her back home, with a basket of eggs . . .

" . . . And some bacon and butter," he soothed. "Ah, and a crock of cream? And, of course, our true thanks for all your trouble and advice."

The Spaewife went, grumbling that some people were soft and silly, and deserved to have their children changed—but she went. As Alin and the farmer took her out, Nettie caught a glint from her father's eye, and hoped it expressed approval. But all he said to her was:

"Do nothing daft, girlie. You'll talk this over with your mother and myself. Now, mind what I say."

Nettie carried the strange infant to her mother.

"Look at its poor face," said she, "so sad and old. Who could hurt him?"

But her mother turned aside, and would not look at the creature. She just went on sobbing Hewit's name, over and over.

So Nettie wrapped the baby in a soft plaid, and went very quietly from the house with it. As it felt the cool air on its face, it kicked and struggled a little. The girl told it sharply to be quiet.

"Whatever you are," she said, "you're only three weeks old. Do as I tell you. I'll try to get you home, if you're good. But be careful! You only escaped the fire by the skin of the teeth you haven't got."

Though she would not be ten for another week, Nettie was

a sensible, resolute, and intelligent girl. She was certainly frightened by what she was doing, but quite set on doing it. The thing in her arms felt almost like a real baby, if she did not look too closely. It was heavy and warm, and made small mewing noises from time to time. How could anyone really *know* if it felt pain or not, she thought crossly. She went to the cowshed, where her sister was setting new milk in wide crocks to be skimmed tomorrow for cream.

"What are you doing with that?" gasped Phemie. "Father came and told what the Spaewife discovered about it."

"I'm taking it home, of course. Give me some of that warm milk, Phemie, in a covered crock."

"What for?"

"For the baby."

The elder sister eyed her cautiously. Nettie's family often eyed her with caution. For one thing, she had bright red hair, where theirs was soft brown; her eyes were hazel, and theirs were blue; they were gentle folk, and easily swayed in small matters, but young Nettie could be as fierce as a wild-cat when she felt like it. Knowing her power over her people, she seldom used it, so they all loved her dearly in spite of the differences between them.

Phemie now made a tutting sound. But she put some creamy milk in an earthenware jug, wrapped it in clean muslin, and handed it to Nettie. She began to ask where her sister was going, but Nettie said she'd best not know.

"Well—be careful, lassie," said Phemie. "And—and don't go talking to strangers. . . . "

She stopped. She was being silly, she thought. So she just contented herself with wishing Nettie good luck and a safe return.

"I'd come with you, my heart—"

"No, Phemie. It's I who must do this, and on my own. I'll be fine," Nettie told her, "and back before nightfall, most like."

Away she went. Through the farm-gate into some fields; over dry-stone dykes, until she came at last to open moorland. She passed a few stands of pine-trees and silver birches, and into a wide plain of heather and bracken, with a few sheep grazing, some big hares that fled, and, overhead, larks, hawks, gulls all crying and wheeling.

The baby squirmed, and Nettie paused to look down at the

thin face and screwed-up eyes.

"I wonder what your name is?" said the girl.

The eyes went wide, unfocused, watery and green. The mouth opened, too, and for a moment of terror, Nettie thought it was going to tell her. But it only gave a whimper, and seemed to fall asleep. Nettie straightened her back, took a good grip on the creature, and marched off in the direction of some low, faraway hills on the skyline. As she had no idea where she was going, it hardly seemed to matter which way she headed first.

The tough stalks of the heather scraped her bare ankles as she went through it. The wind was strong and cold, with neither trees nor buildings to break its force. She came to a small glen, where a stream ran, and saw a blur of movement as some deer dashed away. And, far off to the right, where the sea was, she had a glimpse of choppy water. Nettie marched steadily on towards the hills.

The day went by. Several times she sat down to rest, to comfort the creature she carried, and to offer it milk. Her efforts were not successful. It whined miserably at her, and dribbled the good milk from its mouth.

"Don't be naughty, dear," said Nettie. "I'm trying to get you home, aren't I? There, you'll get whatever you like to eat. . . ."

Mistletoe-juice? Dandelion-milk?

"Whatever," said Nettie, firmly.

The baby made a noise like the hiss of a small cat; and Nettie shook her head at it, wrapped it carefully again, and trudged on through the scratching heather.

She was very tired by now, and the creature seemed to get heavier by the minute. She had to keep telling herself that she *must* go on, *must* find the Hill, *must* complete her task—or lose her brother for ever.

"And this one will be lost, also," she thought.

When she was about ready to cry for weariness, weakening with effort and worry and hunger, the day turned briefly to green twilight. Then it was dark. A thin sickle-moon rose brightly in a sky that seemed largely to consist of stars. And Nettie suddenly sank down beside a big round boulder, to catch her breath. Her head drooped. Dream-like thoughts invaded her mind, and she shook them away angrily. This was no time to drowse. Then came fear. She found herself listening intently. The silence was too complete. No bird called. No small animal scurried or squeaked. No distant sheep bleated. Even the changeling lay very still, though its eyes were open. The wind had died to nothing. And then—there was noise and movement.

A patter of light, quick hoof-beats made Nettie stiffen and shiver. Yet, perhaps, it was her father—her brother—searching for her, on one of the farm horses. Could any of the horses she knew gallop so fast, so delicately? She saw a white glimmer coming towards her. The horse drew near. And now she could see a mane and tail like snowy silk, rippling with the speed of the beast, and shining with light that did not come entirely from the moon. The silver hoofs were barely touching the ground. The horse had long thin legs, a white and glowing coat, and it was now so close that Nettie could see the green eyes—the glittering harness—the rider. . . .

She blinked in amazement, almost in disbelief.

The rider was tall, young—rather, without sign of age. He had a face of starlit beauty. His clothes were as green as his eyes, and as brilliant, sewn all over the arms and breast with jewels. He wore a circlet of silver on his silver hair. He was not Nettie's brother, nor was he riding a farm horse.

"We are here!" he shouted, in a wild, clear voice.

"That's obvious!" snapped Nettie. She did not like feeling so frightened.

Then it struck her that she ought, perhaps, to rise and curtsey. But the baby was too heavy, and she was far too tired for formal politeness. Besides, the horseman had a sneering sort of smile on his incredible face. He reined in his horse.

"Do you know what I am?" he called.

"I can guess. A prince of the Hollow Hills."

"She's clever, too," gibed the rider. "And she's right. I've come seeking you, farm-girl. Give me my nephew."

"Well—no," said Nettie.

A jerk on the rein made the great horse rear high into the air, where it seemed to hang over her for a full minute, neighing shrilly. She shut her eyes in terror, and the changeling gave a wail. The rider swung his beast away, and it stood shaking its mane and stamping.

"You dare to challenge me! You—what is your name?" shouted the prince.

"I'm Nettie McColl. What's yours?"

"That I will never tell. It would place me in your power—as you are now in mine. If a name is known, spells can be set."

"If you know any spells," said Nettie. "Which I do not. So you need not be afraid."

"Impudent, as well," said the prince.

He began to flick his golden rein against the palm of one gloved hand, frowning. He seemed suddenly at a loss, and Nettie wondered if he was unused to dealing with humans. She decided to help him.

"I'm taking this—er—your little nephew—home," said she.

"I know. And I intend to take him back to *your* home."

"But—we don't want him there."

"And we don't want yours!" snapped the prince. "But it's the rule. My sister's weeping her eyes out. She wants her own baby. She says he won't be looked after properly in the dull outside world. He'll not be happy there. . . ."

"And what about my brother?" demanded Nettie. "What about my mother weeping *her* eyes out?"

"There's no sense in the whole business," said the prince. "But there's nothing to be done, except obey the rule and the tradition."

"We'll see about that. Can you take me to the Hollow Hill, sir?"

"Are you daft?"

"Maybe."

"Why, if you entered the Hill, you'd be trapped in there for seven times seven years. Did you know that, girl?"

"It's a tale I've heard, sir."

"A true tale," the prince said, eyes flashing sparks of green fire in the moonlight and starlight. "You would return to the world you know, after all that time, unaged and unaltered. What would be left of the people that you love? The home you expected to find? After—"

"After forty-nine years," supplied Nettie. "I can count. Take me to the Hill, and let me worry about all that when it happens."

"You are quite impossible!"

He stopped speaking, dismounted, swept up Nettie and the baby, set her on the tall horse, and sprang up behind. He clasped her securely, and gave a high and singing yell. The whole sky appeared to fall sideways, and Nettie shut her eyes.

When she dared to open them again, a great shudder of terror ran over her. Before them stood the Hill.

It was huge and black, a rounded mountain against the starry sky, with the sickle moon over its left shoulder, and a flourish of flowering thorn in front. Flowering thorn? In July. May was the time for the thorn to flower. Fear swept again through Nettie's heart. Echoes of old tales and ballads came to her like warnings.

"Change your mind?" said the prince, jeeringly. "Return to your farm with the child, and forget this night venture?"

"Just take me inside that Hill," said Nettie.

"On your own head, girl."

He shook the rein, and the horse leaped forward. On either side, the thorn-bushes leaned away from them, as though blown by a gale of wind. The Gates of the Hill opened. From inside, light was shimmering, with spangles of green fire and sparks of scarlet. And into this great, flaring archway plunged the horse and his riders. The Gates closed in silence. Nettie was in the Hollow Hill.

She scarcely dared to breathe, let alone look about her. She was trying to remember all the old, old legends of Middle Earth—the Land of the Sidhe—the ancient names—fairyland, elfland, land of the Fair People. Her scraps of memory swelled into nightmares. Because this was no old tale; it was really happening. To Nettie, the farm-child, without knowledge of magic to aid her. She gave a gasp. And, to her surprise, she felt the prince's hand press her shoulder, reassuringly.

"It has not happened, yet," said he.

This remark was not really comforting, yet the tone of his voice was kind.

The blaze of light that had shone through the Gates had now become a cold, strange colour that was neither moonlight nor starlight, but had the quality of both. Tree-branches hung low above their heads, thick with green and white flowers that seemed to hold precious stones in their centres, as Nettie and the prince carried the baby deeper into the Hill. The air was cool and scented. From somewhere, not far off, came the sound of running water. This made Nettie feel thirsty; she began to long for the taste of it; she wanted to cup it in her hands, drink deeply, and to bathe her face in it. Yet, when the horse splashed through the stream, his legs were stained and clotted stickily to the knees with red.

"Like blood," whispered the girl.

"It is blood," the prince said. "All the blood that's shed on Upper Earth flows through the springs and streams of this land. Didn't you know?"

"It's horrible!"

"It is not we," said the prince, "who shed that blood."

Nettie was silenced.

Now the horse paced into a beautiful and narrow lane. The banks were covered with flowers, white, mauve, blue, and greeny-yellow; some were like lilies—but not quite; some like wild roses—but not quite; like crocus, hyacinth, honeysuckle —but different. The scents that blew in the air were not those of Upper Earth, but stronger and subtler. Some of the branches hung so low that the prince had to push them aside as the hose passed under them.

They came to another stream. Nettie could hardly bear to look at it. Yet she did so, and saw a fast-running burn of clear water. She felt thirsty again; and her lips were hot and dry, and slightly cracked—as though the lights at the Gateway had scorched them.

The prince reined in his mount, and slid to the ground. He looked up at the girl, and there was something in his eyes that made her shiver. A heartless gleam of laughter? A veiled threat? A warning?

"I'll be your servant," said he, lightly.

He broke a flower from its stem by the waterside, and it gave a faint scream. A round, white flower, bowl-like, with thick petals, and as large as a porringer. He held it for a moment in both hands, then filled it with water from the stream, and lifted it to Nettie. Trickles from it fell coolly on her wrist, and the scent made her head spin. She knew that one mouthful would ease her thirst, heal her sore lips, and taste like dew and honey . . .

"No, thank you," she said.

His face darkened alarmingly. He threw back his beautiful head, and glared at her. The changeling made a curious, tiny, chortling noise.

"You tried to trap me, sir," said Nettie, reproachfully. "I've heard about the false gifts of the Sidhe. But I always thought of—oh, jewels, wine, marvellous food—not just a drink of water. That wasn't fair!"

An odd expression slid like a shutter over the prince's face. Had he not been what he was, it might have been one of embarrassment. He murmured something about being bound by custom. He then flung the flower into the stream, where it was swirled out of sight, wailing thinly. He looked up at Nettie, and the cold sparkle was back in his eyes.

"Are you not tired of lugging that heavy creature about?" he said. "Oh, I'm not offering to carry him for you! I know you'd never trust me, farm-girl. But surely you'd let the horse do it? Fasten him safely to the saddle, and walk this mossy pathway with me. The least touch of it will ease your scratched and aching feet."

The idea was a very pleasant one.

"This child will not leave my hands," said Nettie, "until my brother takes his place there."

"Oh, very well!" snapped the prince. "What an obstinate little creature you are."

He led the horse onwards in silence.

A little later, there was a shrill cry from overhead. As Nettie looked up, a bird swooped to her shoulder. It was quite small, with a beak of ivory-white, blue eyes, and long wings and streamer tail like those of a tern. Its feathers were silver, and it had a coppery crest.

"Let him not kill me!" it shrieked.

It was staring upwards, and Nettie did the same. She saw the plunge of the red falcon.

"Say I belong to you!" shrilled the little bird. "Then he cannot harm me. Quickly!"

"No," said Nettie. "You're not mine. I take nothing from this land."

The bird fluttered away, and the falcon struck. Being too near the ground to check its stoop, this brought both birds crashing to the path with a fearful thud. Feathers blew softly away from the still heap. And Nettie wept.

"Oh, cruel," said she. "Another trick to bind me to Middle Earth! To make me take a gift."

The prince laughed softly. He lifted his hand. The heap of feathers stirred and rose into the air—a flurry of blossoms, nothing more.

But now Nettie was conscious of being watched from the sides of the pathway. There was stealthy movement among the bushes there, a glint of eyes, some malicious whispering and tittering. Once—twice—three times, she saw thin-legged white deer go leaping across the path, vanishing into the mists that had begun to swathe the trees beyond. Another young hind came—and, this time, two baying black hounds followed close at her heels. Nettie covered her eyes with one hand. She knew it for a trick—an illusion—but dreaded to see the killing. A death she could prevent, at the cost of her own freedom. Luckily, whatever happened, happened somewhere in the mists and shadows, and Nettie was spared the sight.

Then the track divided. It curved away in two different directions. The horse halted, and Nettie looked down into the bright eyes of the prince.

"Now you must go on alone," said he. "I've brought you as far as I may."

He lifted her from the saddle, and got up in her place. He shook the rein, and moved off a few paces. Then he halted the beast abruptly. He was frowning.

"Mistress Nettie—" And he hesitated, then said, "If you continue to deal with things as you've done so far, you just might—"

He gave a sudden, flashing smile.

"My name," said he, "is Bartclet. You are ignorant of spells to use on me—as, remember, I've used none on you—but the knowledge of my name gives you the power to call on me if you need my help. Nothing may come of it," he added, "but it's worth trying."

And he whirled his horse in a great caracole on the path, and went cantering past Nettie, back the way they had come. The girl felt very lonely without his company.

She looked carefully at the two paths ahead. They seemed alike. Narrow, dark-green rides, flanked by high banks, roofed with trees whose branches were starred with impossible flowers. Sad, nostalgic scents blew over; and Nettie was suddenly reminded of her home, so that she found herself crying. The changeling stirred in her arms. She looked at it through a blur of tears, and it almost seemed a real child, though its face was peaked and white. It smiled vaguely, and the shadow of a dimple showed.

"You *are* a baby, not just a Thing!" exclaimed Nettie. "And you're nearly home, my honey. If only I knew which of these paths—one must be right. . . ."

She gave a surprised chuckle. She had told herself the

answer. She gave the baby a hug, and started down the right-hand track.

Soon it seemed she had made a serious error of judgement. Rough pebbles replaced the moss underfoot; the scent of flowers gave way to a reek of damp and decay. Toadstools clustered the wayside. Creepers hung from leafless branches —no, they did more than hang—they grabbed! Nettie began to run. Rounding a bend, she halted in terror and dismay. Grey webs were stretched across the path, between the trees: sticky swags that undulated, with disturbing glimpses of hairy black bodies in the corners of them.

"They'll never let me by!" gasped Nettie, with a whimper of fear.

A small, chilly hand touched her chin uncertainly. The girl started, then bit her lip, clasped the baby firmly, tucked its hand warmly under the plaid, and said loudly:

"Prince Bartelet! What shall I do?"

There was rather a long pause.

"Oh, well," said Nettie. "He warned me not to expect . . ."

She heard the ghost of a laugh somewhere inside her head, and the whisper of a voice. She listened carefully, and then repeated aloud what she had just heard:

> "Hairy-scary, see me wary!
> Leggy-dreggy, can't catch me!"

The webs shrivelled, melting slowly into horrible green ooze that dripped on to the path. The shadowy things inside them hissed, and vanished. And down the wind, that was suddenly sweet-scented again, came a sound of singing.

Behind the webs, hidden by them before, gradually a clearing was revealed. It was a complicated place, full of mists, and colours, and stars. Thin white columns encircled it, seeming to hold back the trees, and prevent them from encroaching. People were moving about; and there were dogs among them, and deer, and birds flew overhead singing. And everything there was so beautiful that Nettie stood dazzled by the splendour.

At first, it seemed a smallish glade. Yet more and more people were coming in, from all sides, or just appearing casually in some empty space. Many were marvellously dressed, in flowing silks, embroidered with jewels; others wore green rags and tatters, yet were no less magnificent to see. Some rode gaily-caparisoned horses, and some rode stags or hinds. There were garlanded girls, with long green hair; and children. There was singing, playing of pipes and harps, and talking and laughing.

In the very centre of all this was a ring of blunt-topped boulders, into which no one set a foot, circling a throne of green stone. On this sat a personage who could only be the Old Man of the Hill himself. There was a crown on his head, beginning as a circlet of gold, then becoming a sparkle of gems where its spikes rose, and turning to glass that held pearls imprisoned like bubbles, and then smoking dimly at the topmost points, and blending with the mist that coiled overhead.

The beard of the Old Man behaved in much the same way as his crown; for it flowed down his breast, his knees, his feet, becoming half-transparent as it reached the steps of the throne, and flowing like fog inside the ring of boulders.

The Old Man's hands rested on the arms of the throne, long, pale, ancient and strong; with a blue stone on the left fore-finger, and a green stone on the right.

Nettie was afraid. This was the Old Man of the Mound—the Lord of the Sidhe—Master of Middle Earth—King of Enchantment and Night. . . .

She saw that his eyes were shut.

"Come, then," said a voice at her elbow.

It was Bartelet, and he looked extremely grave; and tight-lipped as if he was under some sort of strain. He began to move through the throng, with the girl at his heels, and it drifted aside to let them pass.

Near the centre of the glade, Nettie saw something that made her pause. On one of the boulders by the throne sat a most beautiful lady. She wore some sort of garment that rippled and flowed all round her long, slender body, as though it were made of water; and where the hem lay in folds on the ground, it was sewn with silver discs and roses made of moonstones. Her head was bowed, so that her pale-green hair swept down straightly, half hiding the baby in her arms. Tears were pouring down her face, although she made no sound.

"My sister," murmured Bartelet. "Grieving for her child. That one," and he nodded carelessly towards the changeling.

"Well, she's got ours!" said Nettie, indignantly.

"Ssh!" said several people, nearby. "You'll wake the King."

"And why not?" said Nettie.

She shook off Bartelet's hand, and hurried to the weeping lady.

"Here's your child, princess," said Nettie, rather too loudly. "Take him back. And give me my brother."

The lady of the Sidhe gave a small scream, looking at Nettie with slanting, drowned, green eyes. Then she stared at the changeling, and delight broke over her face like day breaking. She rose.

"It is my Jenico!" she said.

"That's done it!" said Bartelet. "She has power over him, now."

"I do wish you wouldn't keep on about power!" snapped Nettie. "I've no wish for any. I tell you, I only want my brother."

But now the princess was weeping again, and through her tears she said it was against the rules to give back a mortal child. . . .

"What nonsense!" said Nettie. "Rules? If we'd listened to the Spaewife's rules, we'd have put your baby in the fire."

There was a cry from all the listeners in the glade. The princess opened her mouth as if to scream, and then stood transfixed.

"What seems to be the trouble?" asked the Old Man of the Hill.

No one moved or spoke. Even the birds were suddenly hushed. A cold breath of disquiet held everyone rigid. And Nettie, as terrified as any human girl has ever been, heard a faint whisper inside her head. Without taking time to think, she obeyed its command. She went right into the circle of boulders, and spoke to the King of the Sidhe.

"I'll just take my brother," she said, "and then be gone, and trouble you no more."

Looking into those white-lashed, emerald eyes, she felt her blood running chill. And then another voice spoke from beside her, faint but firm.

"Sir, I implore you, have mercy," said the princess. "Just for once."

"Bartelet," said the Old Man, "as you seem to have involved yourself in this business—rather foolishly—just make yourself useful. Bring me both those children."

"No!" cried Nettie. "I won't give this one up, until . . . "

"Let's not have shouting and stupidity, girl," said the King. "You have my word and you will not be cheated. Has it ever been said or sung that we of the Hills have at any time taken *both* babies for ourselves?"

Nettie thought a moment. Then she shook her head. She let Bartelet take the changeling from her arms. He had the other baby, too, and now he took them to the King. There was a movement of the old hands, a glint of the green ring, a flash of the blue, and the children were lying on the knees of the Old Man, all among the misty coils of his beard. Prince Bartelet stood back, and lifted a hand to his mouth as though to hide its expression.

"Come now," said the King. "Mortal girl—my daughter—come here and take your own."

Nettie and the lady of the Sidhe moved forward together.

They stood looking at the babies.

Both of these were wide-eyed and awake; their unfocused gaze was on the mists overhead. But, in this curious and shifting light, it was hard to tell which infant had blue eyes, and which had green. Both looked white and peaked, as though they were unhappy, or, perhaps, uncomfortable.

"*Wet!*" thought Nettie. "Och, which is Hewit? Ah, surely, he was in the King's right hand. . . ."

She glanced at the lady, and saw her wondering gaze go from one baby to the other and back again.

"Why are you hesitating, my dears?" said the Old Man. "Surely you know your own?"

There was a bit of a pause. The People of the Sidhe were clustered about the circle of boulders, watching breathlessly.

"Well!" said the King. "Speak to them. Maybe *they* will know *you!*"

"Hewit," said Nettie, uncertainly.

"Jenico . . . " said the lady of the Hill.

They both went nearer, to stoop over the little creatures. It was strange to see, but these were now so much alike that they might have been full brothers. Nettie looked up into the face of the King.

"You muddled them to confuse us," said she accusingly.

"Confuse you? So easily?" said he. "I've had enough of

this nonsense. Take each your own, or both will become birds and fly off into—"

"No!" shrieked Nettie and the princess, in unison.

Something happened. One of the babies stretched out a groping hand towards Nettie, and smiled so that a dimple showed. It gave a little chuckle, as though it was pleased to see her. At the same time, the other child lifted its arms to the hairy lady, and mewed happily like a kitten.

"Jenico!"

"Hewit!"

The babies were lifted, and cuddled close, each by the one who knew her own, and was thankful to have him back in her arms.

"Not before time," commented the King. "Take this girl home, Bartelet, and let's all have some peace. Do, please, think twice before you play this silly trick again. It never seems to do anybody any good."

He shut his eyes.

And Nettie opened hers just outside her own farmhouse door. It was ajar, spilling firelight and lamplight, and the sound of voices.

"She must be found!" Nettie's mother was saying. "How can she have strayed so far that none of you can track her? Go out again. Search. Look everywhere. . . ."

Nettie took a step forward. Then she stopped. She felt very uneasy. She thought that everything would now depend on her mother's instant recognition and acceptance of the child. For her own part, she was not at all sure. . . .

There had been a moment when the King of the Hills had swung his hands, his sleeves, his beard—swirling the fog and mist—so that the children might, or might not, have been moved to opposite sides of his knees. Was this one truly little Hewit? Or had she the elf-child still? Yet it had known her, stretched out its hands, smiled. . . .

"Oh," thought Nettie, confusedly, "even if it *is* the changeling, it's known me since it was born! For three whole weeks, it knew only us. Why would it *not* smile at me? And, if for three whole weeks, Hewit knew only the lady of the Sidhe, why wouldn't he cling to her?"

She stared at the baby. It gave her what looked like a wink, but might merely have been a blink. She hugged him tightly.

"And maybe," she thought, "it always *was* Hewit—with a cold! And I've just been running the moors till I've driven myself daft. And a baby is a baby. If you have one for the first three weeks of its life, it's yours, anyway!"

She went into the lamplight and comfort of her home.

"Hewit!" cried her mother. "You've brought him back. Oh, my dear! My darlings!"

Brat

By Theodore Sturgeon

"It's strictly a short-order proposition," said Michaele, tossing her searchlight hair back on her shoulders. "We've got to have a baby eight days from now or we're out a sweet pile of cash."

"We'll get one somewhere. Couldn't we adopt one or something?" I said, plucking a stalk of grass from the bank of the brook and jamming it between my front teeth.

"Takes weeks. We could kidnap one, maybe."

"They got laws. Laws are for the protection of people."

"Why does it always have to be other people?" Mike was beginning to froth up. "Shorty, get your bulk up off the ground and think of something."

"Think better this way," I said. "We could borrow one."

"Look," said Mike. "When I get my hands on a kid, that child and I have to go through a short but rigorous period of training. It's likely to be rough. If I had a baby and someone wanted to borrow it for any such purpose, I'd be damned if I'd let it go."

"Oh, you wouldn't be too tough," I said. "You've got maternal instincts and stuff."

"Shorty, you don't seem to realize that babies are very delicate creatures and require the most skilled and careful handling. I don't know *anything* about them. I am an only child, and I went right from high school into business college and from there into an office. The only experience I ever had with

43

a baby was once when I minded one for an afternoon. It cried all the time I was there."

"Should've changed its diapers."

"I did."

"Must've stuck it with a pin then."

"I did not! You seem to know an awful lot about children," she said hotly.

"Sure I do. I was one myself once."

"Heel!" She leaped on me and rolled me into the brook. I came up spluttering and swearing. She took me by the neck, pulled me half up on the bank and began thudding my head on the soft bank.

"Let go my apple," I gasped. "This is no choking matter."

"Now will you co-operate? Shorty, quit your kidding. This is serious. Your Aunt Amanda has left us thirty grand, providing we can prove to her sister Jonquil that we are the right kind of people. 'Those who can take care of a baby can take care of money,' she used to say. We've got to be under Jonquil's eye for thirty days and take care of a baby. No nursemaids, no laundresses, no nothing."

"Let's wait till we have one of our own."

"Don't be stupid! You know as well as I do that that money will set you up in a business of your own as well as paying off the mortgage on the shack. *And* decorating it. *And* getting us a new car."

"*And* a fur coat. *And* a star sapphire. Maybe I'll even get a new pair of socks."

"*Shorty!*" A full lip quivered, green eyes swam.

"Oh, darling, I didn't mean—Come here and be kissed."

She did. Then she went right on where she had left off. She's like that. She can puddle up at the drop of a cynicism, and when I apologize she sniffs once and the tears all go back into her eyes without being used. She holds them for when they'll be needed instead of wasting them. "But you know perfectly well that unless we get our hands on money—lots of it—and darn soon, we'll lose that little barn and the garage that we built just to *put* a new car in. Wouldn't that be silly?"

"No. No garage, no need for a car. Save lots of money!"

"Shorty—please."

"All right, all right. The fact that everything you say is correct doesn't help to get us a baby for thirty days. Damn money anyway! Money isn't everything!"

"Of course it isn't, darling," said Michaele sagely, "but it's what you buy everything with."

A sudden splash from the brook startled us. Mike screamed. "Shorty—grab him!"

I plunged into the water and hauled out a very tiny, very dirty—baby. It was dressed in a tattered romper, and it had an elfin face, big blue eyes and a golden topknot. It looked me over and sprayed me—*b-b-b-b-b-br-r-r*—with a combination of a mouthful of water and a Bronx cheer.

"Oh, the poor darling little angel!" said Mike. "Give him to me, Shorty! You're handling him like a bag of sugar!"

I stepped gingerly out of the brook and handed him over. Michaele cradled the filthy mite in her arms, completely oblivious to the child's effect on her white linen blouse. The same white linen blouse, I reflected bitterly, that I had been kicked out of the house for, when I pitched some cigar ashes on it. It made me feel funny, watching Mike handle that kid. I'd never pictured her that way.

The baby regarded Mike gravely as she discoursed to it about a poor drowned woofum-wuffums, and did the bad man treat it badly, then. The baby belched eloquently.

"He belches in English!" I remarked.

"Did it have the windy ripples?" cooed Mike. "Give us a kiss, honey lamb."

The baby immediately flung its little arms around her neck and planted a whopper on her mouth.

"Wow!" said Mike when she got her breath. "Shorty, could you take lessons!"

"Lessons my eye," I said jealously. "Mike, that's no baby, that's some old guy in his second childhood."

"The idea." She crooned to the baby for a moment, and then said suddenly, "Shorty—what were we talking about before heaven opened up and dropped this little bundle of—" Here the baby tried to squirm out of her arms and she paused to get a better grip.

"Bundle of what?" I asked, deadpan.

"Bundle of joy."

"Oh! Bundle of joy. What were we talking about? Ba— Hey! Babies!"

"That's right. And a will. And thirty grand."

I looked at the child with new eyes. "Who do you think belongs to the younker?"

"Someone who apparently won't miss him if we take him away for thirty days," she said. "No matter what bungling treatment I give him, it's bound to be better than what he's used to. Letting a mere baby crawl around in the woods! Why, it's awful!"

"The mere babe doesn't seem to mind," I said. "Tell you what we'll do—we'll take care of him for a few days and see if anyone claims him. We'll listen to the radio and watch the papers and the ol' grapevine. If anybody does claim him, maybe we can make a deal for a loan. At any rate we'll get to work on him right away."

At this juncture the baby eeled out of Mike's arms and took off across the grass. "Sweet Sue! Look at him go!" she said, scrambling to her feet. "Get him, Shorty!"

The infant, with twinkling heels, was crawling—running, on hands and knees—down toward the brook. I headed him off just as he reached the water, and snagged him up by the slack of his pants. As he came up off the ground he scooped up a handful of mud and pitched it into my eyes. I yelped and dropped him. When I could see a little daylight again I beheld Michaele taking a running brodie into a blackberry bush. I hurried over there, my eyelids making a nasty grating sound. Michaele was lying prone behind the baby, who was also lying prone, his little heels caught tightly in Mike's hands. He was nonchalantly picking blackberries.

Mike got to her knees and then her feet under her, and picked up the baby, who munched contentedly. "I'm disgusted with you," she said, her eyes blazing. "Flinging an innocent child around like that! Why, it's a wonder you didn't break every bone in his poor little body!"

"But I—He threw mud in my—"

"Pick on someone your size, you big bully! I never knew till now that you were a sadist with an inferiority complex."

"And I never knew till now that it's true what they say about the guy in the three-cornered pants—the king can do no wrong! What's happened to your sense of justice, woman? That little brat there—"

"Shorty! Talking that way about a poor little baby! He's beautiful! He didn't mean anything by what he did. He's too young to know any better."

In the biggest, deepest bass voice I have ever heard, the baby said, "Lady, I do know what I'm doin'. I'm old enough!"

We both sat down.

"Did you say that?" Mike wanted to know.

I shook my head dazedly.

"Coupla dopes," said the baby.

"Who—What are you?" asked Mike breathlessly.

"What do I look like?" said the baby, showing his teeth. He had very sharp, very white teeth—two on the top gum and four on the lower.

"A little bundle of—"

"Shorty!" Mike held up a slim finger.

"Never mind him," growled the child. "I know lots of four-letter words. Go ahead, bud."

"You go ahead. What are you—a midget?"

I no sooner got the second syllable of that word out when the baby scuttled over to me and rocked my head back with a surprising right to the jaw. "That's the last time I'm going to be called that by anybody!" He roared deafeningly. "No! I'm not a . . . a . . . what you said. I'm a pro tem changeling, and that's all."

"What on earth is that?" asked Mike.

"Just what I said!" snapped the baby, "a pro tem changeling. When people treat their babies too well—or not well enough—I show up in their bassinets and give their folks what for. Only I'm always the spitting image of their kid. When they wise up in the treatment, they get their kids back—not before."

"Who pulls the switch? I mean, who do you work for?"

The baby pointed to the grass at our feet. I had to look twice before I realized what he was pointing at. The blades were dark and glossy and luxuriant in a perfect ring about four feet in diameter.

Michaele gasped and put her knuckles to her lips. "The Little People!" she breathed.

I was going to say, "Don't be silly, Mike!" but her taut face and the baby's bland, nodding head stopped me.

"Will you work for us?" she asked breathlessly. "We need a baby for thirty days to meet the conditions of a will."

"I heard you talking about it," said the baby. "No."

"No?"

"No."

A pause. "Look, kid," I said, "what do you like? Money? Food? Candy? Circuses?"

"I like steaks," said the child gruffly. "Rare, fresh, thick. Onions. Cooked so pink they say, 'Moo!' when you bite 'em. Why?"

"Good," I said. "If you work for us, you'll get all the steaks you can eat."

"No."

"What would you want to work for us?"

"Nothin'. I don't wanna work for you."

"What are we going to do?" I whispered to Mike. "This would be perfect!"

"Leave it to me. Look—baby—what's your name, anyway?"

"Percival. But don't call me Percival! Butch."

"Well, look, Butch; we're in an awful jam. If we don't get hold of a sockful of money darn soon, we'll lose that pretty little house over there."

"What's the matter with *him*? Can't he keep up the payments? What is he—a bum?"

"Hey, you—"

"Shut up, Shorty. He's just beginning, Butch. He's a graduate caterer. But he has to get a place of his own before he can make any real money."

"What happens if you lose th' house?"

"A furnished room. The two of us."

"What's the matter with that?"

I tensed. This was a question I had asked her myself.

"Not for me. I just couldn't live that way." Mike would wheedle, but she wouldn't lie.

Butch furrowed his nonexistent eyebrows. "Couldn't? Y' know, I like that. High standards." His voice deepened; the question lashed her. "Would you live with him in a furnished room if there were no other way?"

"Well, of course."

"I'll help you," said Butch instantly.

"Why?" I asked. "What do you expect to get out of it?"

"Nothing—some fun, maybe. I'll help you because you need help. That's the only reason I ever do anything for anybody. That's the only thing you should have told me in the first place—that you were in a jam. You and your bribes!" he snapped at me, and turned to Mike. "I ain't gonna like that guy," he said.

I said, "I already don't like you."

As we started back to the house, Butch said, "But I'm gonna get my steaks?"

Aunt Jonquil's house stood alone in a large lot with its skirts drawn primly up and an admonishing expression on its face. It looked as if it had squeezed its way between two other houses to hide itself, and some scoundrel had taken the other houses away.

And Aunt Jonquil, like her house, was five times as high as she was wide, extremely practical, unbeautifully ornate, and stood alone. She regarded marriage as an unfortunate necessity. She herself never married because an unkind nature had ruled that she must marry a man, and she thought that men were uncouth. She disapproved of smoking, drinking, swearing, gambling, and loud laughter. Smiles she enjoyed only if she could fully understand what was being smiled at; she mistrusted innuendo. A polite laugh was a thing she permitted herself perhaps twice a week, providing it was atoned for by ten minutes of frozen-face gravity. Added to which, she was a fine person. Swell.

On the way to the city, I sat through this unnerving conversation.

Butch said, "Fathead! Drive more carefully!"

"He's doing all right," said Mike. "Really. It surprises me. He's usually an Indian." She was looking very lovely in a pea-green linen jacket and a very simple white skirt and a buff straw hat that looked like a halo.

Butch was wearing a lace-edged bonnet and an evil gleam in his eye to offset the angelic combination of a pale-blue sweater with white rabbits appliqued on the sides, and fuzzy angora booties on which he had insisted because I was wearing navy-blue and he knew it would come off all over me. He was, I think, a little uncomfortable due to my rather unskilled handling of his diapering. And the reason for my doing that job was to cause us more trouble than a little bit. Butch's ideas of privacy and the proprieties were advanced. He would no more think of letting Mike bathe or change him than I would think of letting Garbo change me. Thinking about this, I said:

"Butch, that prudishness of yours is going to be tough to keep up at Aunt Jonquil's."

"You'll keep it up, son," said the infant, "or I'll quit working. I ain't going to have no women messin' around me that way. What d'ye think I am—an exhibitionist?"

"I think you're a liar," I said. "And I'll tell you why. You said you made a life's work of substituting for children. How could you with ideas like that? Who you trying to horse up?"

"Oh," said Butch, "that. Well, I might's well confess to you that I ain't done that kind of work in years. I got sick of it. I was gettin' along in life and . . . well, you can imagine. Well, about thutty years ago I was out of a job an' the woman was changing my drawers when a half-dozen babes arrived from her sewin' circle. She left off workin' right where she was and sang out for them all to come in and see how pretty I looked the way I was. I jumped out o' th' bassinet, grabbed a diaper off th' bed an' held it in front of me while I called the whole bunch of 'em what they were and told them to get out of there. I got fired for it. I thought they'd put me to work hauntin' houses or cleanin' dishes for sick people or somethin', but—they cracked down on me. Told me I'd have to stay this way until I was repentant."

"Are you?" giggled Mike.

Butch snorted. "Not so you'd notice it," he growled. "Repentant because I believe in common decency? Heh?"

We waited a long time after we rang the bell before Jonquil opened the door. That was to give her time to peep out at us from the tumorous bay window and compose her features to meet the niece by marriage her unfastidious nephew had acquired.

"Jonquil!" I said heartily, dashing forward and delivering the required peck on her cheek. Jonquil expected her relatives to use her leathery cheek precisely as she herself used a napkin. Pat. Dry surface on dry surface. Moisture is vulgar.

"And this is Michaele," I said, stepping aside.

Mike said, "How do you do?" demurely, and smiled.

Aunt Jonquil stepped back a pace and held her head as if she were sighting at Mike through her nostrils. "Oh, yes," she said without moving her lips. The smile disappeared from Mike's face and came back with an effort of will that hurt. "Come in," said Jonquil at last, and with some reluctance.

We trailed through a foyer and entered the parlor. It wasn't a living room, it was an honest-to-goodness front parlor with antimacassars and sea shells. The tone of the room was sepia —light from the background of the heavily flowered wallpaper, dark for the furniture. The chairs and a hard-looking divan were covered with a material that looked as if it had been bleeding badly some months ago. When Butch's eye caught the glassed-in monstrosity of hay and dead flowers over the mantelpiece, he retched audibly.

"What a lovely place you have here," said Mike.

"Glad you like it," acknowledged Jonquil woodenly.

"Let's have a look at the child." She walked over and peered at Butch. He scowled at her. "Good heavens!" she said.

"Isn't he lovely?" said Mike.

"Of course," said Jonquil without enthusiasm, and added, after searching her store of ready-made expressions, "the little wudgums!" She kitchy-cooed his chin with her sharp forefinger. He immediately began to wail, with the hoarse, high-pitched howl of a genuine baby.

"The poor darling's tired after his trip," said Mike.

Jonquil, frightened by Butch's vocal explosion, took the hint and led the way upstairs.

"Is the whole damn house like this?" whispered Butch hoarsely.

"No. I don't know. Shut up," said Mike. My sharp-eared aunt swiveled on the steps. "And go to sleepy-bye," she crooned aloud. She bent her head over his and hissed, "And keep on crying, you little wretch!"

Butch snorted and then complied.

We walked into a bedroom, austerely furnished, the kind of room they used in the last century for sleeping purposes only, and therefore designed so that it was quite unattractive to anyone with anything but sleep on his mind. It was all gray and white; the only spot of color in the room was the bedstead, which was a highly polished pipe organ. Mike laid the baby down on the bed and stripped off his booties, his shirt and his sweater. Butch put his fist in his mouth and waited tensely.

"Oh—I almost forgot. I have the very same bassinet you used, up in the attic," said Jonquil. "I should have had it ready. Your telegram was rather abrupt, Horace. You should have let me know sooner that you'd come today." She angled out of the room.

"Horace! I'll be—Is your name Horace?" asked Butch in delight.

"Yes," I said gruffly. "But it's Shorty to you, see, little man?"

"And I was worried about you callin' me Percival!"

I helped set up the bassinet and we tucked Butch in for his nap. I managed to be fooling around with his bedclothes when Mike bent over dutifully to give him a kiss. I grabbed Butch's chin and held it down so the kiss landed on his forehead. He was mightily wroth, and bit my finger till it bled. I stuck it in my pocket and told him, "I'll see you later, bummy-wummy!" He made a noise, and Jonquil fled, blushing.

We convened in the kitchen, which was far and away the pleasantest room in the house. "Where on earth did you get that child?" Jonquil asked, peering into a nice-smelling saucepan on the old-fashioned range.

"Neighbor's child," I said. "They were very poor and were glad to have him off their hands for a few weeks."

"He's a foundling," Mike ingeniously supplemented. "Left on their doorstep. He's never been adopted or anything."

"What's his name?"

"We call him Butch."

"How completely vulgar!" said Jonquil. "I will have no child named Butch in my house. We shall have to give him something more refined."

I had a brain wave. "How about Percival?" I said.

"Percival. Percy," murmured Jonquil, testing it out. "That is much better. That will do. I knew somebody called Percival once."

"Oh—you better not call him Percival," said Mike, giving me her no-good-can-come-of-this look.

"Why not?" I said blandly. "Lovely name."

"Yeah," said Mike. "Lovely."

"What time does Percival get his dinner?" asked Jonquil.

"Six o'clock."

"Good," said Jonquil. "I'll feed him!"

"Oh no, Aunt J—I mean, Miss Timmins. That's our job."

I think Jonquil actually smiled. "I think I'd like to do it," she said. "You're not making an inescapable duty out of this, are you?"

"I don't know what you mean," said Mike, a little coldly. "We *like* that child."

Jonquil peered intently at her. "I believe you do," she said in a surprised tone, and started out of the room. At the door she called back, "You needn't call me Miss Timmins," and she was gone.

"Well!" said Mike.

"Looks like you won the war, babe."

"Only the first battle, honey, and don't think I don't know it. What a peculiar old duck she is!" She busied herself at the stove, warming up some strained carrots she had taken out of a jar, sterilizing a bottle and filling it with pineapple juice. We had read a lot of baby manuals in the last few days!

Suddenly, "Where's your aunt?" Mike asked.

"I dunno. I guess she's—Good grief!"

There was a dry-boned shriek from upstairs and then the sound of hard heels pounding along the upper hallway toward the front stairs. We went up the back stairs two at a time, and saw the flash of Jonquil's dimity skirts as she disappeared downstairs. We slung into the bedroom. Butch was lying in his bassinet doubled up in some kind of spasm.

"Now what?" I groaned.

"He's choking," said Mike. "What are we going to do, Shorty?"

I didn't know. Mike ran and turned him over. His face was all twisted up and he was pouring sweat and gasping. "Butch! Butch—What's the matter?"

And just then he got his wind back. *"Ho ho ho!"* he roared in his bullfrog voice, and lost it again.

"He's laughing!" Mike whispered.

"That's the funniest way I ever saw anyone commit side-ways," I said glumly. I reached out and smacked him across the puss. "Butch! Snap out of it!"

"Ooh!" said Butch. "You lousy heel. I'll get you for that."

"Sorry, Butch. But I thought you were strangling."

"Guess I was at that," he said, and started to laugh again. "Shorty, I couldn't help it. See, that ol' vinegar visage come in here and started staring at me. I stared right back. She bends over the bassinet. I grin. She grins. I open my mouth. She opens her mouth. I reach in and pull out her bridgework and pitch it out the windy. Her face sags down in the middle like a city street in Scranton. She does the steam-siren act and hauls out o' here. But Shorty—Mike"—and he went off into an-other helpless spasm—"you shoulda seen her *face*!"

We all subsided when Jonquil came in again. "Just tending to my petunias," she said primly. "Why—you have dinner on the table. Thank you, child."

"Round two," I said noncommittally.

• • •

Around two in the morning I was awakened by a soft thudding in the hallway. I came up on one elbow. Mike was fast asleep. But the bassinet was empty. I breathed an oath and tiptoed out into the hall. Halfway down was Butch, crawling rapidly. In two strides I had him by the scruff of the neck.

"Awk!"

"Shut up! Where do you think you're going?"

He thumbed at a door down the hall.

"No, Butch. Get on back to bed. You can't go there."

He looked at me pleadingly. "I can't? Not for *nothin'*?"

"Not for nothin'."

"Aw—Shorty. Gimme a break."

"Break my eyebrow. You belong in that bassinet."

"Just this once, huh, Shorty?"

I looked worriedly at Jonquil's bedroom door. "All right, dammit. But make it snappy."

Butch went on strike the third day. He didn't like those strained vegetables and soups to begin with, and then one morning he heard the butcher boy downstairs, singing out, "Here's yer steaks, Miss Timmins!" That was enough for little Percival.

"There's got to be a new deal around here, chum," he said the next time he got me in the room alone. "I'm gettin' robbed."

"Robbed? Who's taking what?"

"Youse. You promise me steaks, right? Listen, Shorty, I'm through with that pap you been feedin' me. I'm starvin' to death on it."

"What would you suggest?" I asked calmly. "Shall I have one done to your taste and delivered to your room, sir?"

"You know what, Shorty? You're kiddin'." He jabbed a tiny forefinger into the front of my shirt for emphasis. "You're kiddin', but I ain't. An' what you just said is a pretty good idea. I want a steak once a day—here in this room. I mean it, son."

I opened my mouth to argue and then looked deep into those baby eyes. I saw an age-old stubbornness, an insurmountable firmness of character there. I shrugged and went out.

In the kitchen I found Mike and Jonquil deeply engaged in

some apparently engrossing conversation about rayon taffeta. I broke it up by saying, "I just had an idea. Tonight I'm going to eat my supper upstairs with Bu . . . Percival. I want you to get to know each other better, and I would commune with another male for a spell. I'm outnumbered down here."

Jonquil actually did smile this time. Smiles seemed to be coming to her a little more easily these days. "I think that's a lovely idea," she said. "We're having steak tonight, Horace. How do you like yours?"

"Broiled," said Mike, "and well d—"

"Rare!" I said, sending a glance at Mike. She shut up, wonderingly.

And that night I sat up in the bedroom, watching that miserable infant eat my dinner. He did it with gusto, with much smacking of the lips and grunting in ecstasy.

"What do you expect me to do with this?" I asked, holding up a cupful of lukewarm and sticky strained peas.

"I don't know," said Butch with his mouth full. "That's your problem."

I went to the window and looked out. Directly below was a spotless concrete walk which would certainly get spattered if I pitched the unappetizing stuff out there. "Butch—won't you get rid of the stuff for me?"

He sighed, his chin all greasy from my steak. "Thanks, no," he said luxuriously. "Couldn't eat another bite."

I tasted the peas tentatively, held my nose and gulped them down. As I swallowed the last of them I found time to direct a great many highly unpleasant thoughts at Butch. "No remarks, *Percy*," I growled.

He just grinned. I picked up his plates and the cup and started out. "Haven't you forgotten something?" he asked sleepily.

"What?" He nodded toward the dresser and the bottle which stood on it. Boiled milk with water and corn syrup added. "Damned if I will!" I snapped.

He grinned, opened his mouth and started to wail.

"Shut up!" I hissed. "You'll have them women up here claiming I'm twisting your tail or something."

"That's the idea," said Butch. "Now drink your milk like a good little boy and you can go out and play."

I muttered something impotently, ripped the nipple off the bottle and gulped the contents.

"That's for telling the old lady to call me Percy," said Butch. "I want another steak tomorrow. 'Bye now."

And that's how it came about that I, a full-grown man in good health, lived for close to two weeks on baby food. I think that the deep respect I have for babies dates from this time, and is founded on my realization of how good-natured they are on the diet they get. It sure didn't work that way with me. What really griped me was having to watch him eat my meals. Brother, I was earning that thirty grand the hard way.

About the beginning of the third week Butch's voice began to change. Mike noticed it first and came and told me.

"I think something's the matter with him," she said. "He doesn't seem as strong as he was, and his voice is getting high-pitched."

"Don't borrow trouble, beautiful," I said, putting my arm around her. "Lord knows he isn't losing any weight on the diet he's getting. And he has plenty of lung power."

"That's another thing," she said in a puzzled tone. "This morning he was crying and I went in to see what he wanted. I spoke to him and shook him but he went on crying for almost five minutes before he suddenly sat up and said 'What? What? Eh—it's you, Mike.' I asked him what he wanted; he said nothing and told me to scram."

"He was kidding you."

She twisted out of my arms and looked up at me, her golden brows just touching over the snowy crevasse of her frown. "Shorty—he was crying—*real tears*."

That was the same day that Jonquil went in town and bought herself a half-dozen bright dresses. And I strongly suspect she had something done to her hair. She looked fifteen years younger when she came in and said, "Horace—it seems to me you used to smoke."

"Well . . . yes—"

"Silly boy! You've stopped smoking just because you think I wouldn't approve! I like to have a man smoking around the house. Makes it more homey. Here."

She pressed something into my hand and fled, red-faced and bright-eyed. I looked at what she had given me. Two packs of cigarettes. They weren't my brand, but I don't think I have ever been so deeply touched.

I went and had a talk with Butch. He was sleeping lightly when

I entered the room. I stood there looking down at him. He was awful tiny, I thought. I wonder what it is these women gush so much about.

Butch's eyes were so big under his lids that they seemed as if they just couldn't stay closed. The lashes lay on his cheek with the most gentle of delicate touches. He breathed evenly, with occasionally a tiny catch. It made nice listening, somehow. I caught a movement out of the corner of my eye—his hand, clenching and unclenching. It was very rosy, and far too small to be so perfect. I looked at my own hand and at his, and I just couldn't believe it. . . .

He woke suddenly, opening his eyes and kicking. He looked first at the window, and then at the wall opposite. He whimpered, swallowed, gave a little cry. Then he turned his head and saw me. For a long moment he watched me, his deep eyes absolutely unclouded; suddenly he sat up and shook his head. "Hello," he said sleepily.

I had the strange sensation of watching a person wake up twice. I said, "Mike's worried about you." I told him why.

"Really?" he said. "I—don't feel much different. Heh! Imagine this happening to me!"

"Imagine what happening?"

"I've heard of it before, but I never . . . Shorty, you won't laugh at me, will you?"

I thought of all that baby food, and all those steaks. "Don't worry. You ain't funny."

"Well, you know what I told you about me being a changeling. Changelings is funny animals. Nobody likes 'em. They raise all kinds of hell. Fathers resent 'em because they cry all night. Mothers get panicky if they don't know it's a changeling, and downright resentful if they do. A changeling has a lot of fun bein' a brat, but he don't get much emotional sugar, if you know what I mean. Well, in my case . . . dammit, I can't get used to it! Me, of all people . . . well, someone around here . . . uh . . . loves me."

"Not me," I said quickly, backing away.

"I know, not you." He gave me a sudden, birdlike glance and said softly, "You're a pretty good egg, Shorty."

"Huh? Aw—"

"Anyway, they say that if any woman loves a changeling, he loses his years and his memories, and turns into a real human kid. But he's got to be loved for himself, not for some kid he replaces." He shifted uneasily. "I don't . . . I can't get used to it happening to me, but . . . oh oh!" A pained expression came across his face and he looked at me helplessly. I took in the situation at a glance.

A few minutes later I corralled Mike. "Got something for you," I said, and handed her something made of layette cloth.

"What's . . . Shorty! Not—"

I nodded. "Butch's getting infantile," I said.

While she was doing the laundry a while later I told her what Butch had said. She was very quiet while I told her, and afterward.

"Mike—if there is anything in all this fantastic business, it wouldn't be you, would it, that's making this change in him?"

She thought it over for a long time and then said, "I think he's terribly cute, Shorty."

I swung her around. She had soapsuds on her temple, where her fingers had trailed when she tossed her bright hair back with her wrist.

"Who's the number one man around here?" I whispered. She laughed and said I was silly and stood on tiptoe to kiss me. She's a little bit of a thing.

The whole thing left me feeling awful funny.

Our thirty days were up, and we packed. Jonquil helped us, and I've never seen her so full of life. Half the time she laughed, and once in a while she actually broke down and giggled. And at lunch she said to us, "Horace—I'm afraid to let you take little Percy back with you. You said that those people who had him were sort of ne'er-do-wells, and they wouldn't miss him much. I wish you'd leave him with me for a week or so while you find out just what their home life is like, and whether they really want him back. If not, I . . . well, I'll see that he gets a good place to live in."

Mike and I looked at each other, and then Mike looked up at the ceiling, toward the bedroom. I got up suddenly. "I'll ask him," I said, and walked upstairs.

Butch was sitting up in the bassinet trying to catch a sunbeam. "Hey!" I said. "Jonquil wants you to stick around. What do you say?"

He looked at me, and his eyes were all baby, nothing else.

"Well?"

He made some tremendous mental effort, pursed his lips, took a deep breath, held it for an unconscionable time, and then one word burst out. "Percy!"

"I get it," I said. "So long, fella."

He didn't say anything; just went back to his sunbeam.

"It's O.K. with him," I said when I got back to the table.

"You never struck me as the kind of man who would play games with children," laughed Jonquil. "You'll do . . . you'll do. Michaele, dear—I want you to write to me. I'm so glad you came."

So we got our thirty grand. We wrote as soon as we reached the shack—*our* shack, now—that no, the people wouldn't want Percy back, and that his last name was—Fay. We got a telegram in return thanking us and telling us that Jonquil was adopting the baby.

"You goin' to miss ol' Butch?" I asked Mike.

"No," she said. "Not too much. I'm sort of saving up."

"Oh," I said.

Wild Garlic

By William F. Wu

My last ride of the day dropped me off in a little mountain town. The next town down the winding blacktop highway was Eminence, but I'd missed the sign for this one. I just knew I had thumbed myself to some place deep in the Missouri Ozarks, and that night falls quickly up in the hills.

The air was cool and damp at this altitude, even in July. Springs and creeks fed rivers all over the area and I had stuck a big batch of wild garlic in my belt, held by the greens. This wild stuff is much stronger than the storebought kind and I thought maybe I could use it to break the ice with someone I met. It grows commonly up here, though, so I wasn't sure if anyone here would appreciate it.

I walked up the steep slope of the main street, sloshing my boots in the puddles of the gutter. The town showed few signs of recent growth, but it had life. The store windows were well-stocked and, unlike some of these little burgs, people even walked around inside them.

One storefront had the word "Cafe" painted on the inside of the glass in red letters. They were slightly crooked. It was a good place to start, but I paused outside, just sort of getting ready. These mountain folks see plenty of strangers from spring to fall, and remain cool to all of them, but they don't see many Chinese faces any time. I stuck one hand in my pocket to feel the two dollars there and then walked into the place.

It was a plain little joint with black and white linoleum on the floor and pink formica tables. An old iron coatrack stood in the corner and a current Coca-Cola calendar hung on the wall. The glass counter was dirty around the edges. No one stood behind the cash register, so I went to a table and sat down.

A middle-aged woman in a gray uniform and a white apron brought me a menu and a glass of water. As soon as she had gone, a hulking shadow fell across my old and dented silverware.

" 'Scuse me, mister," muttered a shy voice in a hill twang.

I looked up. The man was huge—big-boned, muscular from the rough hill life, and paunchy with age. His hair had been buzzed close to his scalp, making his craggy face look even larger. He wore a plaid flannel shirt and twisted his hands nervously.

I chose my response carefully. "Howd'ya do, sir," I said, standing.

"M' name's Boley, John Boley. Uh, the wife and I were wondering if you'd like to sit with us."

That was just the sort of invitation I loved to accept, except for the way he offered it. He really wasn't sure he wanted me, and I figured his wife had developed some missionary complex when she'd seen this poor heathen walk through the door. It had happened before.

"Thank you, sir, but I can't put you out none." Not enough drawl, I told myself. "Don' wanna be no bawther. Thank ya innawhy." That was better.

"Uh—" He hesitated, now aimlessly twisting the front of his shirt. Despite his size, he had all the commanding presence of a stewed rabbit. Lost, he looked back over his shoulder and I followed his gaze.

His wife sat alone at a corner table, surrounded by empty tables. She was an Asian woman with black hair curled into a 1957-style permanent. If she had worn glasses, they would have been those absurd, up-tilted cat's-eye monstrosities. I figured she was about sixty. She had the ageless sort of appearance that Asian women have sometimes, but her husband looked at least sixty-five. The real clue was her presence here at all. They belonged to the generation that had fought World War II, and I guessed that she was a Japanese war bride. This big country boy had brought her from a bombed-out land here to a quiet mountain town that had aged ten years in the last thirty.

"I'd be honored to join you," I said, forgetting my drawl entirely. I picked up my glass of water and followed him over.

"I am Mrs. Amy Boley," said his wife, extending her hand. Her foreign accent was strong, but no problem. "Do you speak Chinese?"

She was a Chinese war bride, then. Maybe from Chongqing.

I smiled and sat down. "No, ma'am. My ancestors were Chinese many generations ago." Actually, I knew a little Toisanese and a bit of Cantonese—household phrases and family stuff—but those wouldn't be her dialects, anyway. The waitress came to take their order and I looked them over.

Mrs. Boley was short and rather slim considering what I guessed to be her age. Her hair, in those stupid curls, was mostly black but streaked with gray. The lines of her face seemed to show primarily loneliness, which I expected, but something else was there, too. It was something in the brightness of her eyes and the sharpness of her mouth.

Boley looked infinitely older. The deep lines of his face seemed like the scars of his life in these hills, and loneliness was displayed in everything about him. He had no sharpness, though; instead he conveyed a sense of weariness unjustified by his years and health.

I ordered liver and onions.

When the waitress had gone, Mrs. Boley said, "I knew you were coming."

"Uh—I, uh . . ."

"She got a way about her," said her husband, running a gnarled, callused hand over his short bristles of hair.

"My name's Jack Hong. Maybe you mixed me up with—"

"No." She smiled pleasantly, but her glance was quick and piercing. "I have seen the qi-lin."

I gasped slightly, and stared at her. Qi-lin—"chee lin," as she pronounced it—was Mandarin Chinese for the Cantonese kei-lun, or the Chinese unicorn. It has the body of a deer, the tail of an ox, a fleshy horn. I had followed it a long way, and lost track of it more often than I had seen it. Until now, though, I had never met another flesh and blood person who even believed in it.

"The bringer of great tidings," she said. "When I saw the

qi-lin, I knew that help was coming for us. When I saw you, I knew it had arrived.''

"I . . . uh, well, I'm . . . following it. The—the Chinese unicorn. There's not much story behind it. I saw it one night and . . . just took off after it. Silly, I guess.''

"You must be a great young man, to follow the *qi-lin*. I sense that you have a way about you. Unafraid.''

"I'm always afraid.'' I looked at her closely, trying to figure out what was happening. The gray streaks in her hair gave back some of the dignity her hairstyle lost.

"Mr. Hong, since the *qi-lin* led you to me, I believe you probably have some acquaintance with the spirit world. Some people would ridicule us for saying it and others would be scared away. However, you may speak freely with me. Remember, I have seen the *qi-lin*.'' She enunciated carefully, to minimize her accent.

"We need help,'' said her husband, digging into a plate of spaghetti and meatballs. "We can pay fifty do—''

His wife kicked him under the table and he shut up. "We can pay you a very small token. Our real offer is this. If you will help, I will tell you the direction the *qi-lin* took.''

I was still in a kind of shock. *I* believe in the *kei-lun*; *I* believe in the spirit world. Generally, no one else I meet does, or admits it, anyway. This woman spoke with the same casual conviction that I had.

"Tell me about it,'' I said, starting on the liver and onions.

Boley glanced at his wife and spoke up. "Our girl inherited a cabin. I raise some hogs and chickens, that's all, up in the hills a ways. Wife hangs up the hams and all. Ain't far.'' He paused to take a swig of Seven-Up. "My pa, our girl's granddaddy, died off and left her a nice little cabin up on the south slope from here. Ain't nobody lived there for years.''

Mrs. Boley took over, still speaking carefully. "We are very poor. Our home is falling down. This cabin would be a solid place to live. It can be improved, and the land is better for the stock. But it has a spirit—a ghost. If we could move there, a man has offered to buy the site of our present home for several hundred dollars. We can give fifty to you.'' She cleared her throat. "I am sorry for my accent. Language is everything.''

I couldn't help smiling. "You want *me* to scare away a *ghost*?''

"Yes." She was calm and serious. So was he.

"*Oh.*" I leaned back in my chair and tried not to laugh. "How? I'm just an ordinary guy who wandered down the pike. I can't—"

"I knew help was coming when I glimpsed the *qi-lin*," she said quietly. "You are the man who followed it here."

"Yeah," said Boley. "We been hangin' around town every evenin' for two weeks, squanderin' what money we got. Couldn't afford to eat out every night, though." He shoveled in more spaghetti.

I thought a moment. A guy who admitted to chasing a unicorn could hardly refuse to help on the grounds of logic and pragmatism. Then another thought occurred to me. Most likely, I was the first new guy of my generation, or maybe of any, they had ever seen up here. "Just how old is your daughter, exactly?"

Mrs. Boley laughed and shook her head. "Twenty, but she is not the object we have in mind."

I was perfectly willing to meet her; I just wanted to avoid matchmaking traps. "What do you want me to do?"

Mrs. Boley put down her fork and leaned forward. "Just want you stay in cabin all night. We stay outside, wait for you. Somebody stay inside all night, haunting will end." Her English was disintegrating as she became more anxious. "You do it?"

"I just have to stay there?"

"Uh—not quite." Boley sat up and rubbed the back of his neck, grimacing. "I tried it myself. That ghost is downright mean."

"Hold it," I said. "Mean?"

Boley stopped rubbing his neck, though he left his hand there. "I'll tell you all about it. When I—"

"Anticipation will make it worse," said Mrs. Boley. "With courage and compassion, this extraordinary young man will not suffer. He follows the *qi-lin*."

I smiled weakly. This adventure fascinated me, as did the Boleys. I could use the money, and besides, most ghosts aren't real anyway. "All right. If I, uh, get rid of your ghost, you pay me fifty dollars and tell me which way the *kei-lun* went."

Mrs. Boley smiled and nodded once, briskly. "You betcha."

When the checks came, Mrs. Boley snatched up mine and gave it to her husband. As I followed them to the counter by the door, I saw that the handful of other people in the place all shied away and became very attentive to each other as we passed. The Boleys must have lived in a subtle isolation all their lives here, probably only tolerated at all because he belonged to the town. The reserve of mountain people toward strangers can be unshakable, but so can their loyalty toward their own.

Boley's mammoth frame didn't hurt any, either.

Rain was falling outside. People scurried past us as we stood under an awning, looking into the near darkness. Cars and pickups were leaving town, with their headlights cutting into the night.

"I'll bring it around," said Boley. He lowered his head and started across the street.

"Wait." His wife caught his elbow and pulled him back. "I'll be faster." Then she hurried around the corner of the building we had just left.

Boley looked at me, anticipating my question.

"Is she getting the car?" I asked. "You were going that way."

Boley nodded. "She got her ways, is all."

Apparently one of her ways was running fast and messy through the rain. In just a minute, she pulled up in a white 1960 Rambler station wagon from the direction Boley had started to take. He slid into the driver's seat as she moved over. I got into the back seat. Mrs. Boley's shoes dangled around her neck, tied by the leather straps. Her feet and hands were coated with slick, shiny mud and her dress looked like it had just been dragged through the gutter in the rain.

I looked at Boley, who seemed not to notice. Trying to be unobtrusive, I looked at her again. Yes, I had seen right.

I kept my mouth shut.

I watched the rain-drenched scenery as we drove out of town on a small winding road. It was graded but unpaved. As darkness fell completely, the sense of time slowing down here grew stronger. It seemed like a place where the *kei-lun* might be visible for a fleeting moment.

The night was black by the time we arrived at their home. The rain had almost stopped. Light showed in the windows of a small house as I stumbled up a dirt path after my hosts. In the darkness, I couldn't see any hogs or chickens, but I could sure smell 'em.

Inside, I blinked in the bright light. The wooden floor was clean and had been varnished at one time. A ragged couch of purple velvet with white lace doilies on the back and arms apparently doubled as someone's bed—I assumed the daughter's. A table with two chairs stood at the far end, positioned to suggest that the third person sat on the arm of the couch at mealtime. The house had one real bedroom and a kitchen, with an outhouse through the back way.

As Mrs. Boley had said, the house was coming apart. Great vertical cracks had opened in the walls and were now stuffed with newspaper. A fine white dust from the ceiling plaster lay over everything and I could feel it falling on me as I stood there. The foundation of the house had been moving for some time—maybe the whole side of the mountain had been sliding. Anyway, the house was beyond repair and the site had probably never been fit for a building in the first place.

"Sit down, Mr. Hong," said Mrs. Boley, brushing plaster dust off the couch. "John, heat water for tea."

"Call me Jack," I said, sitting down.

They both went into the kitchen without answering. The floor creaked under Boley's weight. I looked around some more.

I peeked under the red oilcloth on the coffee table. The coffee table was actually a green military footlocker with "PVT. J.H. BOLEY" stenciled on the side over a serial number. On the wall across from me, someone had taped up a photograph of a red fox cut out of a magazine. On the floor by the couch, a jumble of clothes seemed to serve as the daughter's closet.

Boley's quiet voice drifted out of the kitchen. "Amy, that boy looks as tough and lean as a 'seng hunter, but I still don't know. You sure he's right for this?"

"He follows the *qi-lin*," she said simply. "Did you see his face when I told him I had seen it?"

I felt like an eavesdropper. Clearing my throat, I rose and pulled the garlic bunch from my belt. "Mrs. Boley?" I walked into the kitchen. "I'd like to give—" I stopped, surprised. Boley was alone, standing quietly watching a pan of water on a single-burner gas stove.

"Wild garlic," said Boley, reaching over to close the back door. "Say, them's big ones." He accepted them.

"You know," I said. "Despite what she said about anticipation, I'd like to know what this is about."

Boley rubbed the back of his neck. "There's been a haunt in that cabin for years. Must be five or six folks who tried to last the night. They all ran out in a fright, including me. Wife'd been workin' on this even before my pa died. She even tried some old Chinese exorcism up there. It didn't work, but if anyone knows the supernatural, it's Amy."

He paused to shake the pan of water. Bubbles came loose from the bottom and rose. "The ghost is an Oriental, see."

"Asian," I muttered, but he didn't hear me.

"Her folks moved from New York, where she was born, to St. Louie in, oh, maybe '21. My Aunt Lily. My uncle, pa's brother, went to work in St. Louie and met her there. He was just over twenty. She was seventeen, and her folks frowned on him."

I nodded.

"So, she ran off with him. Came back here and got some land with the city money he'd saved up—they was boom times, the '20s. They built this cabin and lived there. I just barely remember her. She gimme rock candy once."

"She was younger then than your daughter is now."

"Well, the folks up here looked at her about like her folks had looked at him. Wouldn't speak to either of 'em lest they had to. Thought she was a pickled snake in a jar. She got to where she wouldn't come into town, and he started leavin' her for longer and longer stretches. He was drinkin' out of frustration. Should of moved back to St. Louie, but before they got to that, he drank himself silly one night and fell off a mountain. Still she wouldn't come out. My pa finally went up there, but he couldn't find her."

"Then he inherited the place, and left it to your daughter."

"We never moved up there. She was dead—prob'ly killed herself or starved—and haunted the place ever since." He sighed. "My pa taught me a little different from most folks around here. Felt bad about her, I guess. Anyway, I never planned to fall for Amy overseas, but maybe I had the curiosity about Aunt Lily planted in me early. And the city boys in my outfit never thought twice about it. I thought things would be different when we got back, but . . ." He shrugged.

"You didn't leave her," I said quietly.

"Yeah, well. That's the story, 'cept for Amy understands the haunt part better. All I know is, she's sure you can put that girl to rest."

The door banged and Mrs. Boley came in pulling a tall slender young woman wearing a ragged red t-shirt and smudged white underpants. Her clothes were drenched and dirty. She tugged the shirt down low as soon as she saw me. Her short hair was plastered against her head and her bare feet and hands were muddy.

"Jack, this is Tracey. This is Jack."

Tracey wiped a hand on her shirt and held it out.

"Hi," I said, as we shook. She was very pretty, reflecting her mixed genes in even measure. Her hair was straight and brown, and her eyes slanted. She combined some of her father's height with her mother's grace. Also, she shared the indefinable quality of her mother—something sharp in her appraisal before she turned away uninterested, the way a carnivore regards a salad.

"Excuse me." She glided out of the room, feeling with her hand to see if the t-shirt covered her crotch.

"It has been hard," her mother said apologetically. "She has no friends." She slid a lid onto the pan of water.

I nodded. The house had a feeling of ingrown solitude, as if no other guest had ever been there. That might account for the strange sharpness in the women and his soul-weary manner.

Mrs. Boley and her daughter washed mud off themselves and Tracey put on a plain blue skirt. Then Mrs. Boley poured tea at the table. "You must eat before you go. Later I will cook something with the garlic you brought."

I accepted a cup of Chinese tea and blew on it. The silence grew, and the light seemed too bright. "Maybe I should rest," I suggested. "How 'bout if I stretch out for a while and freshen up?"

"Very well," said Mrs. Boley. "I'll cook up some vegetables for you later. In fact, I have garlic of my own here, too."

Boley vacated the couch and I lay back on it, genuinely tired. I felt the white dust from the ceiling falling on my face and covered my eyes with one arm. Mrs. Boley went into the kitchen and Boley went into the bedroom. I heard the back door bang and guessed Tracey had gone back outside. What she was doing, and why they let her run around at night like that, was a mystery. I dozed off wondering if she had shed her skirt again.

I awoke to the sound of garlic sizzling in hot oil and the smell of it filling the little house. Tracey was sitting at the table, wearing her skirt, yawning with her head in her hands. She looked more like she was fifteen than twenty.

I got up and went into the kitchen.

"Three hours. You slept. Midnight already. Eat quickly, okay?" Mrs. Boley smiled.

"Smells great," I said groggily.

She dumped a plateful of chopped green vegetables into the hot oil. "We can't afford spicy oil. For hot Siquan-style seasoning, I use onions and wild garlic."

When it was ready, I sat down at the table with a pitcher of cold water. She gave me the entire skillet-full of vegetables and then went into the bedroom to change into warmer clothes. Tracey dug a blanket out of the pile of clothes by the couch to wrap around herself. Boley was standing by the door of the bedroom putting on another flannel shirt. They were going to keep a sort of watch outside the cabin to catch me if I ran out screaming, or came staggering out as Boley had.

Mrs. Boley came back when she had changed. "You like it?"

"Great." I gasped. "A little hot, though." My entire digestive tract was on fire by this time and I could hardly see the plate on account of tears. "Yeah, I love it."

"I'm glad. You must go on a full stomach."

I smiled and guzzled a cup of cold water. If this kept up, I would have no stomach at all. Still, I was hungry and bound to get hungrier.

By the time I had finished, nothing in the spirit world was more frightening than the thought of more spicy food. I wondered if she had planned it that way. She had intended to use plenty of onions and garlic even before I had contributed to the pile.

Mrs. Boley came and stacked the dishes, but instead of taking them away, she stood looking at me. "The girl in the cabin is lonely—my husband says he explained to you how she was abandoned. She needs reassurance—to be put to rest, she must feel that someone cares about her once again. You can convince her."

"I don't follow you."

"I went to the cabin. Tracey and I. We made a mistake, burning incense and preparing herbal charms and calling upon Guan Yin to grant peace to her. Instead, the ghost began to scream. She attacked us, wailing whole—*the* whole—time."

"But what can I do that you—"

"Please wait. I asked John to go next because he is the nephew of her husband. Perhaps, I thought, she would remember and respond to him. She attacked him, too. But you are different."

"Your ancestry is Chinese, like mine, and your husband is a grown man, like me. How am I different?"

"You are different because you are her kind—neither mine nor John's. You and she are both Chinese of this land. Chinese rites could not put her to rest. A *bai*—neither can John put her at ease. I wish you could speak Chinese, but that cannot be helped. She needs only to know that someone has returned for her."

"Pardon my asking, ma'am, but how do you know that?"

She picked up the dishes and started into the kitchen. "That is the way of hauntings, Jack. You know that."

Maybe I did. Anyhow, that was all the answer I was going to get.

Boley tossed me an extra flannel shirt. "Half hour walk," he said. "I'm ready."

"So am I," said his wife. She looked at me and smiled reassuringly. "You are prepared. We'll go."

We went out the back way without a light. They did not seem to own a flashlight and the night had neither stars nor moon. The rain had stopped.

Tracey led the way through the forest and obviously had learned something from her late-night wanderings out here. She was smooth and confident. Her mother went second, and held my hand as though I were a small child. The two of them slipped through the night forest sure-footed and quick, dragging me along as I crashed into wet tree trunks, fought through dripping branches, and stumbled over slippery rocks and roots. Behind me, Boley had none of their grace, but as a man born and bred to these hills, he had a hill man's natural footing. I felt like a fool the entire trip.

We broke into a clearing that was just as dark as the forest. I knew it was a clearing only because I quit running into things. Mrs. Boley spoke quietly to me.

"John will take you to the cabin door. We will be here at the edge of the meadow with a small fire. I hope you can stay until dawn, but if you must run, we will take you back to the house. Remember, the sun rises early—you only have four hours to wait."

Boley put a big warm hand on my shoulder. "Okay, Jack?"

For the first time, I began to realize just exactly what I was doing—marching alone into a dark room at the request of total strangers. I would never have done that in a city. Now that I was helpless out here, though, I had no choice.

"Steps. Step up," said Boley.

We walked up three wooden steps and thumped across a wooden porch.

"Okay. It's just one room, real big, and the only furniture is a cot on the left wall—somebody left it behind in a hurry one night. Here's a couple matches to get you that far." He put my hand on a cold metal doorknob and walked away, his feet echoing on the wooden porch and stairs and then going silent.

Matches. Two. I had never imagined that I would have to stay in the dark all night—having a light was so basic that I had never asked about one. I should have known that a haunted, neglected cabin would not have electricity hooked up.

Matches.

I lit one and opened the door, feeling my hands start to shake. The flickering flame showed a plain, good-sized cabin with a wooden floor and assorted junk lying around—a rusted can, several rags, plenty of dust. Streaks in the dust marked Mrs. Boley's exorcism rites. I pushed the door open all the way and kicked a hunk of wood under it to hold it. I kicked it twice to jam it in well. Without light outside, either, the open door made little difference, but I felt better. A green army cot stood against the far wall and I reached it as my match burned down. The last thing I saw before the flame died was that all the windows were heavily shuttered.

Darkness. A lonely cabin lost in the hills. Solitude.

What a sucker I was.

I wriggled slightly on the cot to see if it would creak. It did. Gingerly, not wanting to disturb any ghost that preferred to stay dormant, I pulled my feet up and stretched out. The canvas was dusty and cold.

I lay quietly. The night was so dark that I could not even tell that my eyes had adjusted to the darkness, as they must have by that time. I lay motionless in complete silence—even the night sounds of the forest were missing. After a while, my mind began to wander and I lost track of the time.

I was caught between two feelings. After the story Boley had told me, I did care about the young wife who had died up here—her being abandoned like that horrified me. On the other hand, I wasn't entirely convinced that the place was haunted at all. I do believe in spirits—but I don't believe every silly story I hear.

Yet Mrs. Boley had seen the *kei-lun*, and had mentioned the creature before I had.

Tracey came to mind, also bothering me. Something very specific was odd about her. I didn't consider myself anything special, but I was a guy just a few years older than she. I might have expected almost any response from a young woman: fear, curiosity, shyness, hostility, flirtation, humor, criticism. Tracey, after her first appraisal, had shown no response at all—she was totally neutral. This response seemed even stranger when I considered that I must have been one of very few people, if any, she had ever seen of her mother's race. I wondered—

The door slammed shut with a bang like a rifle shot. I stiffened, gripping the sides of the cot so hard my fingers hurt. The air in the cabin had not stirred at all and I knew I had wedged the door fast against the wall.

Darkness. Silence.

I stared into the blackness, not wanting to turn my head toward the door. From across the room, a low creaking sound began. It was not the sound of a hinge, but of wood bending and squeaking against other wood. It sounded like a board in the wall, or maybe the floor. I forced myself to keep breathing evenly, waiting for the creaking to stop. Instead, it continued, growing higher in pitch, slowly climbing and climbing. It rose quietly, like a solitary distant scream, on and on.

Then it stopped.

I forced my head to turn, eyes wide and straining into the darkness. Carefully, I relaxed my grip on the cot and listened to my own breathing. I could hear nothing else.

Darkness. My heart was pounding. My breath rasped in my throat.

Light took shape across the room, directly in front of me. A faint amber luminescence swirled into a vertical column and glowed white. It became a naked young woman.

Relief flooded over me. "Hoax," I whispered to myself. The sound of my voice was another relief.

I peered forward, trying to recognize Tracey under phosphorescent paint. I figured one of her parents had slammed the door to make me jumpy and the creaking sound had been a hidden door someplace. The only question now was why. I swung my legs over the edge of the cot and stood up.

The glowing figure in front of me stepped forward slowly. She had flat stringy black hair and eyes sunken into her head. Her cheeks were hollow and her mouth hung slack, showing teeth that were chipped and broken. Narrow ribs showed clearly. I figured Tracey had been out back earlier to prepare her make-up.

I smiled, lifted one hand, and flicked my second match into her face.

It sailed through the center of her translucent head and fell soundlessly behind her.

Shocked, I watched her come closer. Her eyes were wide and bloodshot. The pleading face had no resemblance to Tracey's at all. She looked like she'd been crying every night since Boley was a boy.

"Look," I muttered. "I, uh—" I couldn't go on. My throat was dry and I had nothing to say.

She came forward, searching my face. I drew away and backed into the cot. She grabbed my shoulders in a solid grip with fingers so cold they hurt my skin through the flannel shirt. A moment ago she had been an image without substance; now she was as hard as stone. She stared at me by the light of her own glowing form, and when she was sure I was not her husband she screamed in rage. Her breath struck me full in the face, as an icy, tearing wind.

"Wait—" My words were cut off by a hard slap in the face. I reeled from the cold sting of her palm.

Hard fingers grasped my shoulders again and yanked me up.

"I came for you," I gasped, saying the first words that

came out. "Don't you understand; I want to see you—"

She pounded on my chest with the palms of her hands, like a small child in a tantrum, shrieking and sobbing.

"Lily! Listen, Lily—"

At the sound of her name, her eyes widened and she suddenly drew back.

"Lily—Lily, I've come here for you, to—to—" To what?

Rage held her gaunt features in a contortion. She leaned forward again and the sunken, slanted eyes came shining toward mine. Tears glistened and brimmed in them. She hissed harshly through her teeth.

"Wait, Lily—"

She blew on me. I shut my eyes against the cold and felt it sting my forehead and cheek as I twisted away. She grabbed my shoulders and held me firmly. Her graveyard breath blew again and I turned my head, taking the cutting cold on my exposed neck. The pain weakened my knees and the chill crept across my neck and into my spine. I jerked once, but her grip was solid. She blew on me again and I rocked backward, loose in her hands like a broken doll. I whimpered faintly and felt her fingers loosen for a moment.

I yanked myself to one side, but she recovered her hold and blew into my face once more. Her own face was a hideous blur. I let out an involuntary breath from the shock of cold.

She winced and averted her face.

Before I could act, though, she turned back to me again. I saw her coming and twisted away in time to take the cold breath on my neck. It felt like a blade.

When she paused to inhale, I turned and exhaled as fully as I could. A full dinner's worth of onions and garlic hit her and she dodged her head away. When she faced me again, I took my turn to duck and take her breath on my neck.

Abruptly, I remembered a phrase from Mrs. Boley—"herbal charms," she had said. This garlic charm seemed more organic than mystic, but I was suddenly sure it was no accident. She had sent me up here prepared, in a way.

I drew in the most air I could and steeled myself. As I blew into her face, I leaned in close and gripped her shoulders to keep her face toward me. Her flesh felt like cold slimy clay and I nearly retched. She pulled away with a soft cry and stumbled back.

"Lily—*moy moy*." I said it without thinking.

Lily staggered away and stopped, standing turned from me.

"*Moy moy*," I repeated. That was Toisanese; I didn't know if she understood it or the similar Cantonese, so I tried that, too. "*Muy muy, nei laile*. C'mere, sis."

She was weeping softly now and did not move as I reached her. I pulled her by one elbow and she fell into my arms, sobbing against my chest. The night around us was silent.

I smelled the dust in the cabin and stroked her sticky, matted hair. She held my torso in an embrace as tight and cold as her earlier hold, but it was the grip of relief and hope this time. I stood there in the dark without moving, holding a crying woman who wasn't there.

"Little sister—*siu-muy. Moy moy*. Our bloodlines don't matter—tonight you have me, and you are my *moy moy*."

Lily wept all night in my arms—what was left of the night. Her fingers burned me with their cold. Eventually I realized that I could see a tiny creak of dim light across the way. It was the first light of false dawn, grown bright enough to shine in through cracks around the shutters.

Finally, she drew away from me reluctantly, with my hands still on her shoulders. She searched my face with wonder and curiosity this time. Her eyes were clear.

Tentatively she turned to a far corner of the cabin. A plank was missing from the floorboards. She looked at the hole, then back at me. Very slightly, she shook her head.

Beneath my hands, her shoulders began to change and shift.

"Goodbye, *moy moy*," I whispered.

In a moment, I held only a swirl of light without substance, twinkling away in the growing morning. A rooster crowed the arrival of dawn and hard substance filled my hands again. I looked down to find a narrow plank of old wood in my grasp.

I hesitated, then took one hand off the board to open the door. The piece of wood seemed no different from an ordinary plank. I walked out onto the porch, squinting in the dawn sun's rays shooting across the mountain slopes.

I walked down the steps and entered the lush green clearing. More roosters were crowing up and down the hills. Across the way, at the edge of the forest, I could see a tiny fire glowing. Tracey was curled up on top of her blanket fast asleep against the base of a large tree. Boley sat before the fire with his knees drawn up and his head fallen forward in a fitful doze. Mrs. Boley's bright eyes saw me.

I held out the piece of wood as I approached, too tired and shaken to speak. She smiled tightly and indicated the fire. I laid it down carefully across the flames and stood looking at it. She awoke Tracey and Boley and hurried us all away from the fire into the clearing.

Tracey yawned and stretched gracefully. Boley inhaled deeply and rubbed the back of his neck. The flames curled around my piece of wood and it began to darken.

Immediately, the fire gave off black smoke and the sweet scent of pine, with just a hint of sandalwood—surely a finer fragrance than my breath that night. The black smoke billowed up from the fire and swirled into nothing in the bright dawn air.

"She starved herself to death," I said. "She crawled into a space underneath the floor to die."

Mrs. Boley smiled faintly. "Pardon my asking, Jack, but how do you know that?"

I shrugged and tried to smile. "You got me."

"Well, thank you, in any case. You are fearless. John will have your money by noon. In the meantime, Tracey and I will track the *qi-lin* for you, and put you on its track at noon. Tracey?"

"Track it?" I asked. "You can track the—the unicorn?"

Mother and daughter walked to the cabin, throwing long sharp shadows across the clearing. They walked up the steps and went inside, almost closing the door, but not quite. I stood with Boley on the grass at the edge of the clearing.

"Ain't none of my business," said Boley. "But why do you follow that critter, anyway?"

I shrugged. "Its appearance is auspicious—means that something wonderful will happen. Maybe I'm crazy, but I think it's leading me somewhere. Even if I'm wrong, I had a boring existence until I began following it, and life has never been dull since."

The cabin door opened wider. A large fox with brown fur and a grizzled muzzle trotted out and down the steps. It was followed by a smaller, sleek young fox that overtook the first. They slipped into the forest and vanished.

Boley turned his great, craggy, tired face toward me with the tiniest hint of a wry smile. "I know what you mean."

I grinned weakly and rubbed the back of my neck.

Shape-shifters. Shape changers. Chinese fox fairies.

No wonder Boley was so weary.

No wonder his wife knew the supernatural.

No wonder Tracey had looked right through me—in the centuries-long life of a fox fairy, she was still a child.

The Stranger

By Shulamith Oppenheim

There came to the door of a cottage one winter's night a solitary traveler.

"Enter, enter quickly," cried the woodsman as the snow swept through the door he held open against the wind. "Enter and share our fire."

The stranger gave a shake of his cloak on the doorstep and walked in.

Immediately the woodsman relieved him of the heavy outer garment and drew him toward the hearth where two women sat, the younger with a book on her lap, the older working a piece of coarse linen.

"Wife." The woodsman, an expansive, good-natured person, smiled broadly. "Here is one who has lost his way. I have asked him to share our fire. And to stay the night." Then he turned to the younger one. "And this, my daughter," he said, addressing the stranger who stood rubbing his hands before the fire, "Sylva, pour our guest a hot drink, for he is surely bone-chilled and used to warmth and comfort, especially on such a night."

The girl stood up and closed the book, a Bible, inserting a piece of red wool to keep the place. The stranger glanced at her. For one fleeting moment he drew her eyes to his. Two bright pink circles appeared on the girl's cheeks. She gathered up her skirt and fled to the cupboard at the far end of the room.

"A drink, my host, would be welcome." The man spoke for

the first time, his voice deep and full. Then looking at the wife, he straightened his black velvet jacket and bowed.

"I would be honored, Madame, if you would keep me for the night. How I came this way, far off the main coach road, is a long tale of little interest or consequence."

The woman smiled and put out her hand.

"It is for us to thank you, Sir. We seldom have visitors. But here is Sylva back." The girl's mother looked up at her daughter and the pride glowed openly in her face.

Sylva carried a large steaming pewter mug.

"Sylva." The stranger took the drink from her. "Sylva," he repeated softly to himself.

The girl looked at him curiously.

"Do you find my name strange, Sir?"

The man seemed not to hear her. He was staring down into the cup. Then he looked up.

"Curious? Not at all. I was simply repeating it. I like the sound. I approve of it." And he turned to her parents who were watching the two. "I approve of it, my friends. I approve the name Sylva. I approve of your daughter. I would say she is a beauty among beauties."

The wife, made uneasy by the man's tone, looked anxiously at her husband. But he appeared completely at ease, and much taken with the compliment to his only child.

"Come, wife." He put a hand on her arm. "Come, we will drink a toast to the health of our guest."

Mugs were filled and raised. The toast was made, to the health of all, as the stranger insisted. Only Sylva, standing next to him, noticed his trembling hand as he put the mug to his lips.

"Stay a while and talk," the stranger addressed his host. "We will keep our voices low, the women won't be disturbed. Stay." And he settled himself into a low wooden chair before the fire. For the first time the woodsman noticed how thin and wiry the man's legs were in their tight black stockings and high boots, how thin and wiry his arms. His hair was long, well below his shoulders, thick, and the russet color of a fox.

"Another log on the fire, then." The woodsman tossed a fine piece of cherry on the hearth. "We are set for an hour or so."

The stranger's hands drummed on the floor behind him,

long fingers thickly covered with russet-colored hair.

"Your daughter," he began slowly, choosing, it would seem, his words with care. "Your daughter. Tell me about her."

Delighted to speak of his jewel, the woodsman drew another chair up beside his guest. "With pleasure, Sir." Then he dropped his voice. "But I must speak softly, for my wife is very close-mouthed." He laughed nervously. "At least about this. It is a tale she has never told to a living soul. Nor I, for that matter. But to you"—the woodsman hesitated—"yes, to *you* I will. I feel I am able to speak." Pausing, he repeated the words, as if to reassure himself. "Yes, I feel it." And he put a finger to his lips.

The stranger raised his brows, and a light smile played about his eyes as he too put a finger to his own mouth.

"You understand?" the woodsman peered at him.

The man nodded.

The woodsman looked to the door of the sleeping chamber.

"Many years we waited for a child. We prayed. My wife drank herbs, followed charms, wore amulets, but never did it happen. Then . . . " The man leaned forward in his chair. "It did."

"*It* did?"

"We came outside, a morning in early spring it was, after a rain, and the child was there. Wrapped in a fox skin, lying in a cradle of woven twigs. Sixteen years last April. Can you imagine it?"

"And?"

"And?" The woodsman appeared perplexed. "Sir, that was it. We found her before the cottage. Rosy and smelling of musk, a bit smoky, but that soon disappeared. And as good-natured a baby as one could ask for."

"You wondered where she came from, no doubt?"

"Wondered? That's a mild way to put it, Sir. My wife listened to market gossip. She asked the priest each Sunday. She lingered outside the church before and after Mass. But not a word. Not a word of a lost child, abandoned, forgotten, missing. Nothing."

"Nothing else?" The stranger's tone was casual, but he had sat up in the chair and pulled himself closer to the woodsman. "Nothing else?"

The woodsman scratched his head. "With all respect, I

can't imagine what else. It was beyond explaining. We never found out where she came from. And for years, my wife didn't let her out of sight, for fear, whoever"—here he shook his head—"or whatever left her by our door would take her back as silently as she came. Now of course it's been sixteen years." The woodsman put his hands under his wide leather belt. "Sylva's a bright girl. She's quick, she's mindful, and she's as hardworking outdoors as in. She's perfect in . . . well, almost perfect, that is." The woodsman pulled at his moustache. "Well, almost—you see, she's . . . but it's no matter."

"Well *what*, for God's sake, man, say it. I must . . . " Then seeing the man's astonishment at his outburst, he drew a hand across his forehead.

"Forgive me." The stranger took in a sharp breath. "Forgive me. When I am interested in someone or something, I become a bit overwrought. What were you saying, my friend? Your daughter is *almost* perfect?"

"SSSHHH. Quietly *please*." The woodsman glanced again at the chamber door. "That's right. She's almost perfect." He leaned over till he was nose to nose with his guest. "Her ears are pointed."

"Pointed? Pointed you say?" The stranger shut his eyes. He seemed calm, but the trembling was back in his hands. This time the woodsman noticed it.

"Are you ill, Sir?"

In an instant the stranger flung his arms tightly across his chest.

"No, no. Take no notice. Go on, go. . . ."

"Well yes, we noticed it soon after we brought her into the house. I dropped my axe. It made a terrible clatter. My wife came running up; she had Sylva in her arms. She put a finger to the child's head. There, coming up through the curls—she had a crop of reddish brown curls, the color of leaves in autumn, the color . . ."

"Go on, go on. . . ."

The woodsman scratched his head again. "Where was I? Oh yes, coming through the curls were two ears, perked up, listening you might say. Perfect they were, but small and pointed." The woodsman slapped his knees. "And that was that. We've had her ever since and she's our joy, I'll tell you. Though she can be a little vixen if she takes something into her head."

"Vixen indeed." The stranger gave the woodsman an intense look of deep approval, bordering on pleasure.

"I'm glad to see you're partial to spirit." The woodsman rose and with a twig broom brushed the ash close up to the new smoldering log.

The stranger stood up suddenly.

"Good host, I am dead with sleep. Where would you put me?"

The woodsman indicated a door by the left of the hearth.

"In there is a boxbed with down coverlet. You will be comfortable, I'm sure." Stretching out his hand, he added, "What a pleasure to have you this night. And to have shared our story. You seem to care." And once more he put a finger to his lips.

The stranger started to walk toward the door, then turned on his heel.

"She is of an age to marry, woodsman."

Something in the stranger's voice sent the statement into a challenge, yet it was said quietly, even gently.

The woodsman shook his head, regret written over his broad face.

"True, good friend, but where are we to find a husband for such a prize in these parts? Who will take the daughter of a penniless woodsman, beautiful and well-spoken as she may be?"

The woodsman came close up to his guest.

"*You* will understand this, he must be a gentleman, and . . ."

"And what?" The stranger lowered his eyes.

The woodsman pulled at his moustache, a gesture now familiar to the other as the inability to express a thought clearly.

"He must be . . . understanding. That's it, he must have an understanding nature. One never knows the future, Sylva is young. Yes, that's it, if you take my meaning."

Putting out his hand, the stranger smiled for the first time since his arrival.

"I take your meaning, good host. And I bid you a very good night."

Only the sound of sleepers deep in dream filled the cottage. The wind had died away; an owl's lonely hoot cut the night's silence. Silently the stranger opened the door and stepped into the darkness. His fingers twitched by his side. He stood, his face whipping sharply from side to side, this way and that, picking up scents and sounds on the night air.

"I take your meaning, good host. *We* will remember it, in future years." He threw the words onto the black stillness. Then he re-entered the cottage and took his cloak from off the wall peg. He arranged it nest-like before the dying embers. Then warily circling it three times, he dropped onto his belly and with head between outstretched arms, the stranger slept.

Spirit Places

By Keith Taylor

In those days the southern continent was unknown to men with pale skins. The Dreaming surrounded day-to-day time as a cocoon surrounds a caterpillar. The tracks of the beings who had shaped the land as they wandered were still plain. In the Dreaming, the time that surrounds time, they were always present. In the life-giving land they were commemorated by this gorge, that rock shelter, that waterhole . . . spirit places which spawned their own kind of beings.

Three such ran through the desert. One had the shape of a human child, except that her legs and arms were too long. Her skin was the grey of ash, banded with the black of charcoal; white hair capped her head. One of her companions, shorter, pot-bellied but elsewhere thin, had the face of a fish without scales. He breathed arduously and lurched. The other hopped along like a wallaby.

"Not far now!" the girl said. Her voice crackled like a fire. As she waved her hand forward, a red glow appeared along her fingers' edges.

The fish-being stumbled and flopped. "I can't move!" he gasped.

After waving her hand through the air again, the girl poked his backside with hot fingers. "You will!" she spat. "You will or I'll roast you for *them* to eat! They won't stop!"

"Here they come," the other said, looking back. "Goanna brothers! Fly eaters! Best you move, Fish. A little more and you can lie in water."

The figures racing after them bulked twice their size, manlike, with scaly skins pied black and yellow. Their slate-coloured tongues ran in and out, tasting the air. The two carried spears and narrow hardwood shields.

"Fly eaters!"

Fish stumbled up the dune through tufts of spiny grass. Ashfire, the girl, ran conspicuously along the crest, stopping once to make a taunting gesture. The goanna brothers hissed their rage. Being somewhat stupid, they followed her instead of the slower prey.

She led them in a wide circle and gave them the slip at last in a shimmer of hot air. She would see them again, she knew. They were as persistent as ugly. Still, they would not come to the sacred place.

It lay in a tumble of great angular rocks. Grass, small thorny acacias and a couple of coolabahs—sure signs of available water—grew there. In the shadow of a huge leaning slab, a pool gleamed. It had never been dry since the Maker in his wanderings had scooped it out to ease his thirst. Some of the *djinganarani* had been spawned from the pool, others by the Rainbow Snake, Ashfire, when lightning struck a boulder. Fish had come an unknown distance at a time of big floods; now he could not go far from the pool until, in some other year, the wet season should again be outstandingly wet, and set him free to travel.

None of them knew whence the goanna brothers had come. They had simply appeared one day, vicious, unendingly angry, and a menace. Because they never came near the sacred places, they could be endured.

Ashfire perched on the slanting top of the rock to bask in the burning sunlight. Below her, Fish lolled in the water with equal pleasure. He had changed his shape; he now sported gills, his legs had dwindled and a finned tail grown from the end of his spine. It waved slowly, making ripples which shone.

Wallaby hopped up the fissured rock. Some disturbed finches flew out of a bush as he passed, their wings whirring in the desert air. He possessed the legs and tail of his totem animal, but the belly, upper body and limbs of a dark-skinned boy.

"They have nearly speared me twice," he said, aggrieved. "Another time, they may eat me."

"I scorched one of them," Ashfire chuckled, and kicked up

her long legs. "Aroora, yes! If I could catch them in thick
scrub, I'd roast them in their fat! But there's none here-
abouts."

She rolled over on her belly, elbows on the rock, face in her
hands. The desert stretched afar, huge tawny ridges crested
with grass. Little grey mesas rose out of it at intervals. Northward, the way Wallaby was looking, it gave place to scrub
with rock escarpments, gorges and more fertile country
beyond. It was all the territory of one tribe.

"They aren't like us," Wallaby complained. "They don't
know our land. They don't belong here."

"They are here," Ashfire said, "and none of us have the
strength to make them go. Maybe the Rainbow Snake spewed
them."

Wallaby shivered, for he was timid. The long barbed spears
of the phantom brothers threatened pain, terrible pain, and
what else they might do to him he did not know, or wish to
discover. He wondered if he could be killed when he had not
yet been born.

"It should eat them again!" he said with bravado.

Looking all about him as he said it, to be sure the goanna
brothers were not nearby, he saw other *djinganarani* approaching from the desert. These four were much alike, tex-
tured like earth, the colour of red ochre, their hair running to
their shoulders like loose sand. They could swim through the
ground as through water, or walk on top of it, as they wished.
However, they could not speak. For that gift they must wait
until they were born.

Filing through the rocks, they waved to Ashfire and
Wallaby. Fish drew himself streaming out of the water; his tail
became legs. As the three watched, the earth-children began to
speak in their own way.

Two vanished within a boulder. The others mimed with
their red child-bodies. They walked about. One stood on his
right foot, the left raised, resting on the inside of his knee,
while he used the butt of an imaginary spear for support. Suddenly he was poised on both feet, the spear aloft for throwing
while he glared at his target.

The second performer mimed the use of a digging stick, and
filling a bag with seeds.

Man and woman.

They pointed to the northwest, then danced a journey of

days. It involved a lot of love-making, to judge by the number of positions they assumed and the amount of buttock-moving that was done during the "halts."

Fish gurgled, "They will fall down and die before they get here!"

The other earth-children entered the dance. They rose stealthily out of the ground, squirming on all fours like lizards. At a distance, they followed the man and woman, drawing closer at the night halts, watching intently. At other times they rose on their hind legs, running as big lizards sometimes run. The depiction was so true that even Ashfire bit her hand.

The goanna brothers. They were following, tracking two tribe-folk, probably a married couple on a journey to the spirit waterhole. All the *djinganarani* knew why they would be making such a trek in the dry season. They wanted to conceive a child. Maybe a child of a particular totem.

If the mimed report of the earth-children was true, they were doing their part mightily. It would be for nothing unless one of the *djinganarani* entered the woman's body and quickened what was there—and of course the *djinganarani* were known to frequent the spirit places.

"Why are the goanna brothers skulking after them?" Fish wondered.

The question was in all their minds. Typically, Ashfire reached a decision first.

"I'll go and see. Who wants to come?"

"Not I. Too far from water; I'd dry out like a cicada case."

"If *they* are coming here," Wallaby declared, "I'm going the other way."

"All right." Ashfire sprang up, flaunting her swift thinness. "They'd catch either of you anyway. They won't catch me." She yawned. The inside of her mouth glowed red, like the inside of a tree stump after a brush fire was passed. "And you?"

The earth-children didn't hear. She danced her intention before them, swift and crackling; two agreed to go with her. Ashfire, who did not like mysteries, was finding the goanna brothers more and more puzzling. What could they want?

Being Ashfire, she moved to find out, not to sit and wonder like Fish, or flee like Wallaby. She needed no water. She needed no food, aside from an occasional tussock or bush to devour with her flames.

Walking into the desert with her red ochre companions, she

followed the track of the ancestral Makers. Long ago, they had made the desert waterhole, plants and trees, an enclosure of cliffs where game was still trapped and speared—and at last one had killed the other for an unforgivable crime. The place where he had turned to stone was still known.

The survivor had given shape to the first human beings, who had been formless until then. He had made laws and ceremonies for them too. Then he had left the region to do more wonderful deeds in other places.

Ashfire knew the route he had taken. So did the brown men and women of the tribe. To follow it from place to place was to re-enact the rites of creation—but here, in the southern part of its territory, the tribe only came together when the brief light rains made the desert flower. At no other time could several hundred be fed there.

Ashfire and her friends travelled until nightfall. As warmth left the desert surface, the red earth-children slipped below it where some heat remained. There they curled up together like burrowing things.

Ashfire made her own heat. Finding a grass-tree, she climbed its ridged stem to the ball of long foliage at the top. She sucked in great breaths of the cold night wind till the inside of her mouth glowed yellow, then blew little outward breaths into the foliage. Soon she sat in a ball of roaring fire, feeding gluttonously. When the grass-tree was consumed, she was strong enough to travel on for three days and nights without feeding again.

The earth-children were better at tracking than Ashfire, and far harder to see in the desert. Not that much tracking was needed to find the man and woman again; they were following the ancient, sacred trail of the Makers. The *djinganarani* came upon them near a dry creek bed, sheltering among rocks from the noonday heat.

While the earth-children watched them, Ashfire climbed a long tree (contorted, leafless, white as bleached bone) and pressed herself into a fork to watch for the goanna brothers. She hoped she would seem from the ground like a remnant of bark.

She didn't see them. Banking herself like a camp fire, she waited until twilight, then rejoined her friends. She wanted to see these people, and now she could do so without her ash and charcoal colours giving her away.

The man and woman sat by a tiny fire which was mostly coals. Ashfire saw by that as clearly as the pair would have seen by daylight. The man, lean and sinewy, wore raised ceremonial scars on his skin, and a braided headband around hair like curled black wire. His beard jutted forward, gleaming.

The woman was perhaps a dozen years younger, though Ashfire knew little of human growth and ageing. She saw someone sleek and almost plump, with hair wavy rather than curly. Across a distance and at first glance, Ashfire gained an impression of good humour.

"Another day and we'll reach the spirit place," the man said.

"Good," his wife replied positively—perhaps too much so. "The *djinganarani* are often there?"

"Thick as midges. That's a thing you should know. How many of your friends have come with child there?"

"Enough. My mother did too. Many times she told me how she knew she carried me; she saw a crow in a dream, and it spoke to her, so my totem is the crow." She gave a harsh caw, and laughed.

"It should be the kookaburra," her husband said. But he smiled too, and reached for her.

Ashfire watched with fascination what happened next. Flesh and blood was as much a wonder to her as her own constitution to a human, and this act would someday be her gate to a life in the flesh.

She was so involved that she didn't hear the goanna brothers creeping behind her.

A scaly grip on her feet yanked her backwards. She whipped around and bit. The hot inside of her mouth branded a mottled arm. Ashfire pulled free, flashed to the top of a rock like a whirling spark, glimpsed the second brother holding an earth-child by an arm and a leg, and jumped on his mottled back.

He sprawled. The earth-child vanished underground, merging with the soil. The goanna brothers turned upon Ashfire. She was trapped, confined among rocks, and could not intermingle with their solid substance as her friends could. She would have been smothered, crushed out.

Boneless lizard-fingers were almost touching her when the first earth-child emerged from the ground. The leading goanna brother tripped over him. Ashfire jumped back, striking a rock, and thrust herself forward away from it with both hands. She trod on the fallen brother and brushed the second, moving with desperate quickness. His hand ripped through her hair and was left streaked with white ash. Then she was gone.

There was no more sign of the earth-children, either. Hissing in rage, the goanna brothers tried to dig for them, without success. Blind below the ground, the earth-children felt the lightest footstep and knew where their enemies were.

"Stupid fly eaters!" Ashfire shrieked from the desert.

Her they might find, but probably could not catch.

After a time, they went away.

Ashfire lurked warily for a while thereafter. Then she approached the camp fire, still treading with care. Firelight glowed on the woman's skin, and a long mounded shape lay under a possum cloak near her.

Ashfire called, "Coo-eee!"

The woman's head jerked up. "Who? Who's there?"

"I'll not harm you. See, I'll come closer and you can look. I've a word you should hear."

The man's head lifted from under the cloak.

"Come forward, then."

Ashfire did. The woman threw a stick or two on the fire, to make more light. It flickered on the grey and charcoal child-form, striped limbs, banded face, the pale fluffy hair in which sparks stirred as the wind brushed it . . . and the woman's eyes and mouth rounded.

"Spirit," she whispered.

"I heard things. Was that you?" the man asked.

"I and others, being chased by goanna men. They must be out there yet, somewhere. Can I sit by your fire?"

"Come."

The matter-of-fact speech was for lack of anything fitting to say. Spirits were everywhere, in the rocks, the night, the trees, the wind, but seldom did they announce themselves in voices. Man and woman gazed at Ashfire while she sat. They were greatly afraid and not willing to betray it.

"You came looking for me, or one of those like me," Ashfire said. "*Djinganarani*. The trouble is with what else you may find. There are bad things here."

"The goanna men?" asked the husband huskily.

"Two. I don't know why they are here. They don't belong

in this country. They don't know it. They wander about, and never come near the spirit places although they are spirits, and they're always angry. They have chased me more than once. And they blunder across the sacred tracks as if they meant nothing."

The man felt a little more at ease now. Talk of his beloved tribal lands gave him something in common with even a spirit child.

"Strangers, eh?" he said, rubbing his beard.

"No *djinganarani* ever saw them until the last two moons," Ashfire told him, and added, "They have followed you for days."

The woman shrieked.

"Quiet, Neera!" The man frowned and rubbed his beard some more, to show that he was thinking hard. "My name is Baramul. I heard of two men who came to our country to steal women . . . Yanilbin men. They tried it with another band, not ours, and they were killed. I didn't hear what their totem was, but it might have been goanna. Surely if they died away from their own tribal lands, their spirits would be crazy. They can't find their way home."

"And their ghosts turned into goanna men," Neera said. She shivered. "I do not want to meet them."

"They are following you," Ashfire assured her. "They were prowling just now, but they've gone away. I think they'll be back. But why would they follow you?"

"I don't know." Baramul frowned. "Why would they chase you?"

"Oh, that's nothing. They chase all *djinganarani* they see. They're always angry, always eager to kill—but they forget quickly. Except you. They keep coming back to you, yet they haven't hurt you yet. I was hoping you'd know why. Can I have something to eat?"

"We have nothing tonight but seeds and a lizard."

"Not that. I'm a fire child. I eat wood."

Startled, Neera passed her a stick from the little pile of fuel. Ashfire gnawed on it contentedly, as a dog would gnaw a bone. Although not truly hungry, she was like fire and like a human child, always willing to eat. Besides, she wanted to astonish this pair.

Although neither commented, they both stared as the stick

began to smoulder. Ashfire nibbled and chewed, waiting, and Baramul furrowed his brow in fresh concentration upon her question. At last he said: "They were killed trying to steal women. Maybe they are still trying." He glared his rage at the thought.

"What tribe did you say they were?"

"Yanilbin. Their country lies south of here."

"What would happen if they went back there? On their own land, would they know who they are, and that they are dead, and go where the dead are supposed to go?"

Baramul considered this. He had only lately been initiated to that degree of knowledge and was not sure of it. Still, he answered with the steady gravity of one who had lived as long as the rivers and mountains, and possessed the knowledge of death for every day of it. Unseen by him, Neera grinned.

"They would, surely; but who's to take them by the hand and lead them there? They attack on sight, you say."

"You could lead them," Ashfire said. "That is, Neera could. They would follow her. You would not have to go far into Yenilbin lands. We'd be rid of them, and you could come straight back."

"Huh!" Neera said, provoked into speaking her mind, even to this disconcerting little spirit. "Suppose they seize me instead? *I* don't wish to be carried off by ghost goanna men!"

"You won't be," Baramul said grimly.

"You won't be," Ashfire agreed, "for we *djinganarani* would stop them. We'll protect you flying and walking, and from under the earth. And when the thing's done, and they are gone, we'll give you whatever you want from us. Your womb quickened by any totem spirit you like."

It was the way. Man's white semen and woman's red blood went to make a child, bone and flesh—but only a spirit of the land could enter her body and make it live. Which spirit, and where in the tribal country it happened, could mean much. It governed whom a child might marry when grown, for instance. These were things Ashfire did not comprehend, born as she was of a lightning stroke. Matters of mother and father, totem and moiety, clan and skin, meant nothing to her. Yet she comprehended enough of what they meant to Baramul and Neera.

"Can you speak for all?"

"They will tell you themselves if you come to the spirit place. You can name any bargain that will send the goanna brothers away. Dare you come?"

"We walked here for this!" Neera said.

Ashfire smiled then. "It's good. Tomorrow you will see."

The next day they saw many things. They set out in the early morning, through the scrub and hummock grass growing between immense sand ridges. Neera gathered sticks of fuel as she went, and in a couple of hours that afternoon she foraged enough food for several people, in a desert where a woman from the northern wetlands would have been baffled. From a supposedly dry waterhole she dug sand frogs bursting with liquid, and although Baramul might have hunted he did not go more than five paces from her.

Ashfire needed no food, and the red earth-children who blended so perfectly into the landscape looked after themselves. Neera watched them with fascination and unease. She had known about them and other spirits since she could understand words. They were not among the very mighty powers like the Rainbow Snake, or the two Makers. Nonetheless she feared them.

So did Baramul. She could tell. He was too curt, too much on his dignity. They had planned this journey together, and it would be something to talk about until they were old, but first it had to be successfully over.

Once the spirit called Ashfire cupped her hands and cried shrilly at the sky. The long warbling call of a quarrion answered her, but what flew down was no bird. About as tall as Baramul's waist, boy-bodied and slim, it had a beaked yellow face and crest. Brown and white feathered wings grew where arms should be.

Ashfire talked with him for a while, and he took flight again to carry her message. His swift, steady wing-beats bore him out of their sight.

"Now he'll tell as many as he can find, and they will be at the spirit place before we are," Ashfire said. "You may take your pick."

"It's a grey wallaby child we seek," Neera said.

"I know one." Ashfire felt a pang. Wallaby was a pleasant playmate . . . maybe they would take another. "He's dear, but he's not brave."

"After he grows to a new shape in her belly, he will be,"

Baramul said proudly. And unexpectedly.

The spirit place put on splendour for them. Every bush flowered with finches and wrens. Water shimmered green among the ancient rocks. Everywhere the *djinganarani* waited.

Most looked like children, yet always there was something uncanny, like Ashfire's colour and glowing mouth, or the dry texture of the earth-children. One had spiny grass for hair and rootlike toes, another a dingo's golden fur. Some were not remotely human in form. Baramul jumped and bit back a yell when he saw a green ant large as a yabby near his foot.

Fish lolled in the water and Wallaby stood shyly back. However, he heard the terms of the bargain with all the rest, and standing face to face with Neera he agreed to meet them—and bargains made in the spirit places were not broken.

The next morning, only a dozen *djinganarani* remained.

"Uh! Where have they gone?" Neera asked.

"You won't see them. The goanna brothers won't see them either." Ashfire chuckled. "All they will see is you and Baramul and me—and our other friend, if it comes to that. Do you have him?"

Neera held up her dilly-bag as if it contained a sorcerer's curse. The thought of what she must do frightened her. If she had not wanted a child of the right totem so much—but she did, and she had heard the conditions and agreed. Although she liked all the ease and comfort she could get, she was very stubborn when her heart was set on something.

"He's here," she said. "Do we set out now?"

"Yes." Baramul looked southward.

They followed the timeless trail of the Maker between the sand ridges. Tough, dry country scrub gave shade and cover which might conceal anything. Baramul killed a snake or two with his long club as he walked, and was ever watchful for goanna men.

"You won't see them until they are here," Ashfire told him. "They can travel unseen if they wish. All we have to do is lead them home. Maybe they won't attack first."

"All *I* have to do is lead them home. It's me they want." Neera put on a wicked smile. "How I'll tell the story when we return . . . how the spirits followed me through the desert, their spears dragging low when I was out of their sight, pricking high whenever I was in view. Minirrip and Garmai are always bragging, but let's hear them match that!"

"So?" Baramul was interested. "What do they brag about?"

"If I told you or any man, there would be duels and death curses. Do you tell women about the love magic you work?"

"I haven't done any of that since I was a boy," Baramul said loftily. Then he stared beyond her in sudden dread. "There! Goanna men!"

He crouched, narrow shield lifted, one barbed spear ready to fly, the hardwood club tucked through his belt of human hair. His lithe muscles moved slowly under their coating of dust.

"Where?"

"Oh," he said innocently. "I was wrong."

Neera berated him. They both knew better than to joke about spirits, but on the other hand playing the fool raised their own spirits. They travelled throughout the day, husband and wife and the spirit girl. They dug for water at one of the land's many hidden waterholes, and found it. They ate, slept close together, and the next day moved on.

In the distance, the desert slowly gave place to mulga, plains covered with dry yellow grass, scrub and an occasional low acacia tree. In the dry season there was little to choose between them for the birds and wallabies, but for Baramul it stank of danger. In Yanilbin country he would be killed on sight by its men, just as the goanna brothers had been killed on his tribal land.

" 'Ware!" Ashfire suddenly screamed, pointing into the sun. Baramul, walking ahead of them all, went flat with unquestioning speed. A spear hissed above his prone back.

A black and yellow shape came leaping down the side of a dune. Baramul fitted spear to wooden launcher and threw powerfully. The goanna man struck it aside with contemptuous skill.

His brother rushed from the rear. His boneless, nailless fingers seized Neera. Shrieking, she dropped her dilly-bag, bit, scratched and struggled. The ghost creature slung her writhing across his shoulder. She pummeled; she bit.

Meanwhile, the spirit with the form of a great green ant had crawled out of her dilly-bag. Making for the goanna man's shifting, stamping feet at the risk of being trampled, it climbed his toes, his instep, and reached his mottled calf. Serrated jaws stripped away flesh; the sting pierced hotly.

Neera's captor dropped her with a rasping scream, first of a series. She moved away from him. He stumbled after her, but Ashfire pushed him sprawling.

"Go!" she cried to the woman. "Run!"

Neera fled in long bounding strides towards the mulga. Baramul did not see her go, for he was battling the other goanna man. It knocked him down, shield against shield, and stood over him, swinging a club.

A slim red form rose out of the earth, holding a stone. It threw with wonderful aim and sent the club hurtling yards from a helpless hand. Two more earth-children appeared to throw other stones, fast and irresistibly hard, until the goanna man backed away from his fallen victim. Seeing Neera's clenching, driving buttocks vanishing through the haze, he rushed in pursuit. A last stone struck him behind the knee with wicked force. He fell, spraying sand, rose and blundered on.

Half limping, half crawling, his brother struggled in the same direction. Although winded, Baramul followed.

As he recovered his breath, bit by bit, the first goanna brother's limp grew worse. The second went hopping, stumbling, lurching, dragging a leg bloated by the green ant's sting. Looking back, Neera slowed her own desperate pace lest they give up the chase short of their own tribal lands, now so near.

There was little risk of that. Glaring, obsessed, they kept their reptilian gaze on her, making amends for lack of speed with endurance and purpose. On and on they pursued her. The second brother crawled now, scrambling on all fours like a true goanna. His swollen foot throbbed with pain.

Suddenly his will broke. He curled in a circle, biting his own leg in agony. Baramul had known intense pain himself, at his manhood initiation among other times. He did not pity the spirit. Still, he ground his teeth involuntarily at the sight.

The goanna man crept into a thicket of saltbush which covered one side of a dune. Ashfire did not share even Baramul's degree of empathy; she clapped her hands in delight.

"I'll rouse him out of there," she promised. "You follow Neera! She may need you."

That was wholly true. Baramul ran, closing the distance between himself and the leading goanna brother a little, so that he could catch him swiftly if Neera's wind failed. She was still running strongly, though, to Baramul's relief.

Behind him, he heard a fiery crackling. The spirit girl had

ignited the thicket. It blazed along one side, the flames driving
the second brother into the open. Ashfire went through the
center of it like a gleeful swimmer through waves, and came
out with a burning branch in her hands. She beat and lashed
the goanna man with it until he moved, and Ashfire made sure
that he did not stop. But his progress was so slow and painful
that she danced with impatience.

At last he paused, looking about him in a daze. Ashfire let
him pause, not knowing why, but somehow aware it was not
from pain or exhaustion that he halted this time. Recognition
stirred behind the reptile eyes; comprehension showed in the
lift of the head. Baffled, senseless rage distilled into something
else.

His puffy foot had touched Yanilbin tribal ground. The
swelling lessened with each halting step the goanna brother
took, and some way further on he rose to walk upright like a
man again. Bemused yet glad, he paid no attention to Ashfire.

She left him gazing around at his own country. The goanna
men were a danger no more. Here they belonged, and here
they would stay.

She saw no sign of the other. Baramul and Neera were close
together, brown figures under the seared, faded blue of the
desert sky, but the monitor shape which had run between them
had vanished.

"It's done," she said.

"*Our* part of it is done," Baramul answered pointedly.

"And Wallaby will do his! Now let's go back before some
man spears *you*, and it begins all over again."

The bargain was kept. As Baramul and Neera made their
way back across the desert, north to the hills, they saw a grey
wallaby. Baramul killed it and gave it to Neera to eat, as he
had been advised to do.

The child she bore nine months later had furlike grey hair
which only slowly turned black as it grew. He also had a red
mark on his skin where Baramul's spear had gone into the
wallaby. In the desert, Ashfire missed her playmate, and in the
camps of Neera's band, he lived to become a noted songman.

The Box of
All Possibility

By Z. Greenstaff

At the dawn of things, the Shining Ones caused a great tree to grow at the crossroads of the worlds. They called it the Tree of All Possibility, and so it was, for its roots reached to the core of the earth where the dreams of all peoples yearned to take form.

Now this tree was marvelous.

Its wood was glistening green and smelled of things wet and wild and pungent. And at the end of every Age when the East Wind blew, the uppermost branches tinkled like emerald glass and bloomed. In a time of their own choosing, these blossoms would spin free and cast a sweet perfume of possibility across the land. And so in this way was civilization eternally renewed.

Then one day the youngest and most curious of the Shining Ones had a wily idea. He would fashion a small box from the glistening wood of this great tree, and he would fill it with the most powerful of all magicks, the Giving Green. And then, just because he felt like it, and because he was the Trickster, he would give this marvelous box to the Two-Leggeds—just to see what would happen, you understand. Just to see.

And for a time things went very well indeed.

Until Sigrinne. But let us start the story properly.

Once there were two sisters. The elder was a dreamer, and her name was Sigrinne. The younger and more favored by their mother was practical, and her name was Hilda. Now, because Sigrinne was the elder, she started her bloodcycle first, and on that day all things became possible.

It was a custom of Sigrinne's people to hold a celebration for any daughter of the new blood, and give her special gifts. Sigrinne, however, was such an odd child that no one was quite sure what to give her, and so Sigrinne's mother took charge.

"For heaven's sake," she said, "give her something practical. Something for the kitchen, the bath, or the bed. *Don't* give her books, and *don't* give her paints."

So nobody did and Sigrinne was sad. After she had put all the new pots and pans away, and folded the towels and sheets, she took a walk by the stream which ran between her mother's modest house and the Old Fey Forest. Now Sigrinne had a lovely voice and when she was alone she would sing strange little songs to herself. Her mother had asked her once who in the *world* had taught them to her, and Sigrinne had replied:

"The East Wind."

"Oh," said her mother and rolled her eyes at Sigrinne's sister, who shrugged demurely and shook her head.

But Sigrinne hadn't cared what they thought then, and didn't care now. The East Wind had taught her, and that was all there was to it. Still it was difficult to be so different than her sister and mother, and sometimes late at night Sigrinne would cry silently into her pillow, and wish she could be practical.

Sigrinne sat on an old tree stump, and watched the stream slip and wind over mossy stones. To cheer herself up, she hummed a little tune about horse whiskers and moonlight. As she started the second verse, she heard an answering harmony from deep within the forest. Startled, she got to her feet.

"Hello?"

The music stopped. Disappointed, Sigrinne returned to her tree stump and continued to watch the stream. Then, without realizing that she had started again, she began to hum. And just as before, a sweet harmony lilted toward her, all dappled with green shade and summer sun. Sigrinne could stand it no longer. She must know who sang so sweetly. So she got to her feet once more, but this time she continued to hum. She crossed the stream, and entered the Old Fey Forest.

After she had walked for some while, she came to a small clearing. In the center of the clearing sat an old woman dressed in a tunic the color of evergreens. She had flyaway gray hair and rosy cheeks, and in her hand she held a corn-cob pipe. As soon as she saw Sigrinne, she stopped humming and lit the pipe. The tobacco smelled of things familiar and far away and caused Sigrinne's heart to yearn. The old woman smiled at her now, and motioned her over.

When Sigrinne reached the old woman's side, she pointed to the grass at her feet and bade her sit. Sigrinne did so, her eyes wide and full of wonder.

"Child, there is one more gift that comes to you today. It is something that has been passed from mother to daughter for centuries."

"But you're not my—"

"Shush," said the old woman with a sharp gesture of her wrinkled hand. "There are mothers, and then there are mothers. And then there is the Earth. And she is mother to us all. Be silent, and do not insult her with your forgetfulness. Understood?"

Sigrinne nodded, red-faced.

"Good," said the old woman. Then she reached into one of her pockets, and her hand seemed to go a very long way in before she found what she was looking for. Now she pulled her hand out, and opened it.

Sigrinne stared, speechless. She reached with trembling fingers, and took the gift from her Feymother. It was a small, marvelous box. It glinted green like glass in the morning sun, a thousand diminutive faces carved into its glistening surface, each one strong with individual purpose and history.

"Child," said the old woman softly, "this is your soul inheritance. This is the Box of All Possibility, and there is no greater gift a mother can give her daughter. Receive it then, with my blessing."

Tears welled in Sigrinne's eyes.

"One more thing," said the old woman leaning forward and staring deeply into Sigrinne's eyes. "Do not open the Box of All Possibility until you are ready to seek your way in the world. If you should open it before your time, great harm may befall you. Understood?"

Sigrinne was silent. She swallowed. "But Feymother, how will I know when it's my time?"

"The same way that Spring knows when Winter has ended. It knows. And so will you."

"But—"

"Shush," said the old woman sharply. Then she smiled,

and disappeared. And Sigrinne was left alone in the small clearing, the marvelous Box clasped tightly in her young hands. Then the East Wind blew, and led her back to her mother's house.

When Sigrinne returned with an idiot grin on her face, it was clear to both mother and sister that something very peculiar had befallen Sigrinne, and they resolved to watch her closely.

Now, having the Box of All Possibility produced some remarkable changes in Sigrinne. She became more confident of what she perceived, and the odd things that she heard or knew—without knowing how she knew—she accepted as real, and trustworthy. And the more she believed, the more charmed her life became. Soon the village took notice and people came from far and near to hear Sigrinne speak. And, as Sigrinne's dreams grew, so did her sister's envy.

Hilda complained daily to their mother about Sigrinne's good fortune, and begged her to use village magick and discover Sigrinne's secret. Finally, tired of her younger daughter's badgering, she agreed—though she did not expect to find out anything, for in truth, Sigrinne and Hilda's mother did not believe in the power of the Giving Green, nor in the time-honored traditions that made up the lore known as village magick. So, of course, since she did not believe—she failed.

"It didn't work," she told her youngest daughter.

Hilda was silent. Then her eyes turned cold.

That night, Hilda went into the Fey Forest and caught one of the silver snakes that lived there. Then, when she was sure her sister lay sleeping, she put the snake on the bed. The snake slid across Sigrinne's breasts, and crooked its shining head at her ear. There it tickled her with a delicate red tongue.

"What do you want, Earth Crawler?" muttered Sigrinne.

"What is the secret of your good fortune?"

"The Box of All Possibility."

The next morning, Hilda reported what she had found out to her mother. Neither of them could make any sense of Sigrinne's answer. But now Sigrinne's mother was curious, so the following night she hid behind the curtains in her daughter's room. Hilda came again to her sister, this time brewing a nasty potion of bitter herbs which fouled the room but did not wake Sigrinne. When Hilda was sure her sister had breathed deeply of them, she sang a spiteful little song over her.

> *Hominy, nominy no more misery,*
> *I take the Box of All Possibility!*

But since the Box was a gift from the Giving Green, it could not be taken, and Hilda went to bed empty-handed again. The following morning, Hilda told her mother what had happened. Now of course her mother had heard and seen it all the night before. She was silent for a few moments. She was thinking. She was thinking about how practical a Box of All Possibility would be—for a practical girl. Sigrinne was a sweet child, but a dreamer; a talker, but not a doer. She put her butter-knife down, and turned to her youngest daughter.

"I think you should try again."

So, on the third night, Hilda and her mother came together to Sigrinne's bed. Hilda, who was rapidly turning into a very unpleasant girl indeed, leaned close to Sigrinne's peaceful face, and muttered some ugly words. Now this incantation was a bad magick—one designed to strip and pry and cause only the deepest harm. Sigrinne groaned, and struggled to wake. To her horror she found she couldn't. She heard her mother's voice, and wanted to cry for help like a child suddenly frightened of the dark, but her tongue rested like cold stone against her frozen lips. Then she realized her mother was part of the night's terror. A scream burned in her throat.

"Sigrinne," said her mother sternly. "Sigrinne, you're a very selfish girl—keeping the Box of All Possibility to yourself. You've been very greedy, but that time is past. It's time to share with your sister. Now tell me where it is."

Tears squeezed from Sigrinne's eyes. "In the hope chest," she whispered brokenly. "At the foot of the bed."

Hilda shrieked in triumph. Her mother said it was most unseemly to do so, but nonetheless she helped her younger daughter rummage through Sigrinne's hope chest until they found the Box of All Possibility. Angry and sad, Sigrinne watched her mother and sister cluster like carrion birds around the Box of All Possibility.

"Don't open it!" Sigrinne screamed.

But she was too late.

Smiling, Hilda lifted the lid of the small, marvelous Box. She did not notice the change that had come over the thousand carved faces; she did not see their teeth nor their cruel smiles. Hilda peered beatifically into the Box of All Possibility, her face lit from below by a seething mass of glimmering things—a mass which had a life of its own, and perhaps resented her intrusion. Now Hilda paled. She clutched at her throat, and shielded her eyes.

"There's too many!" she cried.

"Close it!" shouted Sigrinne.

"Shut up—both of you," said their mother. Then she turned to her younger daughter. "Don't be such a ninny, Hilda. Just go on and pick one."

"It's not her time!" cried Sigrinne.

"Of all the ridiculousness!" snapped their mother. And then she did a terrible thing. She reached into the Box of All Possibility, and chose a dream for her younger daughter. When she withdrew her hand, she held a shining green thread. She thrust it at her trembling child.

Now as soon as Hilda touched the thread, a peculiar transformation took place in both Hilda and Sigrinne. Hilda lost all fear, and indeed seemed to lose all character as well. Her smile turned waxen. Sigrinne's change was more subtle. Suddenly all things were *not* possible. Sigrinne could not bear to live with this new knowledge, nor could she bear to live in her mother's house one moment longer. She left within the hour, though neither her sister or mother understood why.

As Sigrinne prepared to cross the stream between her mother's house and the Old Fey Forest, she felt a hot and hungry wind at her back. She turned around in time to see the upper floor of her mother's house lit as though with green fire. She remembered her Feymother's warning:

"If you should open the box before your time, great harm may befall you."

Sigrinne sprang toward the house, but before she had gone three steps the building exploded. Green fire roared, consuming everything within moments. When the smoke cleared, only the blackened bones of her sister and mother remained. The Box of All Possibility was nowhere to be seen, and Sigrinne was afraid to look for it. Choking on smoke and fear, she ran into the forest.

Sigrinne wandered without recall for many days, eating berries when she could find them and drinking water from clear streams. It was a time of emptiness and great grief. And it seemed to her as she walked that her thoughts grew more tangled by the day. She had no money and no shelter. Worse, she had lost her soul inheritance—how was she to survive? How could she ever find her way in the world without the Box of All Possibility? These questions made her young head hurt, and finally when she could think no more, she lay her head down on a mossy hill and went to sleep. Two gentle hands lifted her, cradled her against soft wool, and walked in silence into the heart of the forest.

And while Sigrinne slept, she dreamed—over and over she saw her mother reach into the Box of All Possibility, and her sister accept the shining green thread, and over and over Sigrinne was helpless to stop them. She woke with a cry, her eyes wild, her palms wet.

"It was only a dream," she whispered to herself.

"True," said a voice behind her. "But in my house dreams are more true than the bed you lie on."

Sigrinne sat up abruptly, and realized she was no longer outside in the forest. She whirled around.

Her Feymother smiled calmly at her.

Sigrinne's eyes filled with tears, and all she could think about was how she had failed the Box of All Possibility. How she had abandoned it; how if she had been a little bit stronger, she could have saved her mother and sister's lives. How she could have—

"Do you think," said the old woman slowly, "that you're the only one with a Box of All Possibility?" She lit her pipe. "Do you think, for instance, that I'm without one?"

Sigrinne frowned.

"Listen carefully. I shall say this only once. You believed in the Box of All Possibility only so long as you could touch it. Now you think it's gone, and you're without inheritance. False. Everyone is given this inheritance, though most do not depend on a box in order to find their way in the world. They simply believe themselves capable of it, and that is enough."

"Look," said Sigrinne, swallowing hard. "I don't want the Box—"

The old woman chuckled. "You can't get out of it that easily."

Sigrinne could feel her face turning red. "I don't want the

Box," she cried. "It killed—"

"Would you abandon your dreams?" snapped the old woman.

"But my mother. My sister."

There was a long silence.

"Your mother and sister," said the old woman softly, "abandoned their own dreams. Would you do the same? Would you someday give birth to a daughter, and then because you have no dream of your own that you are loyal to, would you slip your hand into your daughter's Box of All Possibility, and take what is not yours to take?"

Sigrinne flushed. "Well—no—I—"

"Good," said the old woman, standing up. "Now go along with you, Sigrinne. Go back to the rubble of your past, and pick up your Box of All Possibility."

"I looked for it—it wasn't there."

The old woman rolled her eyes. "How could you expect to see something that you did not believe was there, hmmm?" Here she frowned at Sigrinne, her eyebrows a thick ridge of reproving bristles.

Sigrinne nodded hastily, and backed out the old woman's door. When she looked back over her shoulder a few moments later, the house had vanished. Sigrinne shivered, and headed out of the Fey Forest.

In a few hours, she arrived at the charred remains of her mother's house. To her surprise, she found a series of charms set here and there to protect passers-by from harm. Then she found a plaque with a written description of what had happened. Sigrinne frowned. The brass on the plaque was tarnished. Just how long had she been gone? As she rubbed the brass clean, the face reflected was the face of a young woman.

She picked slowly through the rubble, and found the Box buried under a shattered window. She cradled it in her hands, and her fingertips began to tingle. Then she felt the Box stir in her hands. She took a deep breath, and opened the Box of All Possibility. It spoke to her gently.

"Those who hurry the ripening of the spirit are doomed. Those fortunates who bloom at the proper moment are blessed, and all heaven rushes out to meet them. Choose your heart's desire, and add your joy to our own."

And there were a thousand smiles, on a thousand faces.

Sigrinne peered into the swirling interior of the Box. Wonderful scenes and faces opened before her. For a moment, she thought she caught a glimpse of the Fey Old Woman smoking her corn-cob pipe in the center of a clearing, and then the picture folded in on itself, and vanished. Sigrinne let the images flow over her, and refused to be drawn in until directed by her heart to do so. And then it happened. Sigrinne saw herself seated beneath a large tree, children and grown-ups alike gathered at her feet. She appeared to be telling them a story as much with her hands as with her voice. She could not put this scene from her, and with trembling hand, she reached for it. A green thread danced in her palm. It shimmered briefly, then straightened like an arrow of Love, and pierced her heart and mind. Suddenly her mouth was filled with the most wonderful tales all clamoring to be told.

This was one of them.

The Seekers
of Dreams

By Félix Martí-Ibañez

My host, as tall as a tower and as tightly knit as the kernels on an ear of corn, lifted high his glass of champagne.

"To *her*!" he toasted, emphasizing the last word, as if it were spelled in capitals with the initial letter illuminated in gold.

I took a sip from my glass. It was good champagne but as warm as a convalescent's chicken broth. Besides, two o'clock on a July afternoon in Maritecas, close to the steaming Paraguayan jungle, is hardly the most appropriate hour for drinking champagne. The air was hot and humid and heavy with the buzzing of flies. The golden bubbles rising to the surface of my glass contributed to the impression that it contained a simmering brew.

"It's a strange tale but not altogether incredible," my host, Arnaldo, continued. "Anyway, it is siesta time. Either we sleep or we chat, and what I have to tell you is a fulfilled dream, and that is better than sleeping."

He drank the rest of his champagne and filled his glass again. The sun sparkled on a fine crack in his glass while he stared intently at the tiny bubbles dancing their merry ballet.

The porch where we were seated was littered with old boxes, empty baskets, broken furniture and odds and ends. The table was as old and discolored as a tired peasant. In the midst of all the junk, the champagne bottle with its bright gold foil neck stood out like a *grande dame* visiting her poor relatives.

On the other side of the porch there was a small orchard

with a few wilted vegetables; farther on, a wooden fence separated the orchard from the beehives. In the silence of the siesta hour, the snore of an asthmatic cat, sleeping in the sun and all covered with green flies that shone like spangles, blended with the soft buzzing of the bees.

"See this crack in my glass?" Arnaldo asked me, wiping the sweat off his forehead with the back of his hand. "I dropped it. I'm glad it didn't break. Right now it contains champagne, but at the bottom of it there sparkles the story of a dream."

Finally, I felt angry at my host, whom I had met only a little while before. Instead of the porch, where the heat had the fierceness of a wild fire, I would have preferred my room, which was higher up and where I could stretch out naked on my bed to sleep or read. But I had no choice. His words, like stones in a tightly set wall, left no chink through which to insert the knife of escape. This middle-aged man with sandy hair and faded blue eyes, who had forsaken a successful law practice after his wife's death over ten years ago and had buried himself on this farm alone with his bees, was now opening a deep well of long-suppressed words. And though, being a writer, I am a bad talker and a worse listener, I resigned myself to listening to him and even resolved not to offend him by yielding to the temptation of shutting my eyes. Who knows, he might fall asleep in his rocking chair before I did.

I had come to his lonely bee farm, which had been recommended by mutual friends, in search of documentation for a chapter of the novel I was writing. When I arrived, after two days of hot and dusty traveling, I found Arnaldo in a state of great nervous excitement. He did not even inquire about our mutual friends, who had kindly given me a letter of introduction, but immediately offered to share with me the fried chicken he was having for lunch. When I refused, he brought out the champagne, which I accepted, without suspecting that with the bottle went the obligation to listen to a story.

"I'll show you the stuff my tale is made of," he said, smiling.

He opened a large old box standing on the table and took out one after the other a folded letter, a lump of dry mud, a red ribbon with tiny silver bells, a photographic plate, a little cage that looked like a mousetrap and a broken crystal ball. When all his treasures were lined up on the table, he drank some more champagne.

"Strange collection," I commented halfheartedly.

He seemed not to hear me. His eyes stared straight ahead, as if trying to pierce the mystery of the forest slumbering under the sun in the distance. The buzzing of the bees was as soft as the brush of a silk skirt across a polished floor. Each crack in the parched earth was a thirsty gullet begging the heavens for a drop of rain. A lizard wriggled lazily along the porch rail. The flies seemed permanently pasted to the slimy glasses. Sweat rolled down my back under my soaked shirt. Arnaldo's face, studded with drops of perspiration, reminded me of a Toledan jug sprinkled with dew.

Suddenly my host pointed to the cracked champagne glass.

"All these things," he repeated, "are the proof of my tale. But the main thing, what gives life to my story, is this cracked glass."

I felt very hot and tired and my irritation mounted. A madman can be as annoying as a drunk. Still, my host was neither. The man facing me seemed to be under the spell of a strange memory. His face reminded me of passport photos, in which one always looks as though one were mesmerized by a ghost.

"I don't understand what you're talking about," I said impatiently.

"No one can, no one will—ever," he said.

"Why don't we leave it alone then?"

"Perhaps that would be best. Still, I *must* talk to someone, or I shall go mad. What the devil! I am not asking you to believe me. Only to listen. It all began with this letter," he continued. "When it arrived I was happy here, all alone with my fifty beehives, which yield all the honey I care to sell. Here, read it."

As he handed me the blue wrinkled note, a vague whiff of perfume reached me. The handwriting was long and slanting like the delicate dance of a spider's legs. I skipped through the first lines:

" . . . At the café in Asunción where my husband and I have our breakfast every day, many people use your honey in their coffee. I myself do not care for things so sweet. The owner of the restaurant told us about your bee farm.

"My husband's great passion is photography. Some of his pictures have been published in various magazines in Argentina, one of which is now interested in color photographs of bees. Won't you please let us spend a few days at your farm?

We won't be any trouble. We shall be outdoors all day. All we
require is a room with a bed and a table. We'll pay you whatever
you think is fair for room and board. I cannot cook—and
don't care to try—so we'll be happy with anything you care to
prepare. We both thank you. Please answer us in care of this
café."

The signature, Dolores de Gaviria, was adorned with little
rings like a schoolgirl's curls. There was a postscript:

"There is so little time before our deadline that we have
decided to take a chance and not wait for your answer. We are
starting out immediately."

"The letter," continued Arnaldo, "arrived twelve hours
before they did. Late that night their old car came to a halt in
front of my door after breaking the fence. The crash made me
jump out of bed. Before I realized what was happening, they
had already made themselves comfortable in the room you
now occupy and I had in my hand an advance of one hundred
pesos and a fearful headache from the sudden awakening and
the commotion they made.

"Early next morning they knocked on my door. Gaviria was
a big man with thin gray hair, a moustache like the horns of a
bull, and eyes the color of muddy water. The condescending
look he gave me irritated me. His wife, on the other hand, immediately begged me to call her Dolores. She looked about
thirty and was perhaps fifteen years younger than her husband. She was tall and slim, with sleek, black hair, and her
eyes were the color of the honey from my bees.

"They struck me as pleasant people but rather eccentric.
They both were very impressed by my having changed my law
practice for beekeeping. Dolores talked continuously and
Gaviria drank a lot. He had brought a trunk full of champagne. He had the easy, pleasant but artificial familiarity of
politicians and country priests.

"I showed them around the farm but, to my surprise,
Gaviria showed no interest at all. Dolores, on the other hand,
went into raptures over my omelettes and butter cakes, and
turned the house upside down, not only because she loved
making a fuss over everything but because her exuberant
nature required constant action, just as my bees must work all
day. I must say that I found her frivolous chatter and little
whims delightful, for since my wife's death I had not had a
woman near me.

"Gaviria snapped dozens of photographs of my bees but he was mortally afraid of them, while Dolores' chubby pink fingers fluttered merrily around the golden clusters of my bees.

"Two days later he announced that he had enough pictures of my bees and that he would now take photographs of the jungle. When I ventured that there was nothing unusual to photograph in the woods, he abruptly turned his back on me and walked away.

"That night at dinner we hardly spoke to one another. Gaviria was completely absorbed in his own thoughts and I was annoyed by his bad manners. By the light of our acetylene lamp, he ate his stew and drank his wine in silence, while Dolores, beautiful in a white dress, toyed with a bread crust, dipping it in the gravy and leaving it untouched on her plate. By the time we came out here to take the air, I had decided to ask them to leave the next day.

"It was hot and dark outside. Gaviria, drenched in perspiration, was smoking a cigar, and every time the tip glowed the tense lines on his face stood out in scarlet aggressiveness. For a while, the only sound audible was that made by the mosquitoes and our rocking chairs. Suddenly Gaviria began to speak, and his voice rang with a mordant tone.

" 'Do you know what I used to do before I came to Paraguay?'

" 'The same thing you do now, I suppose,' I replied coldly.

" 'You're wrong,' he said. 'Tell him, Dolores.'

"In the prevailing darkness, softened only by the pale glow of the stars, her pale face looked like a delicate mask modeled in wax.

" 'My husband,' she said, 'was a bookkeeper for a textile house in Bolivia for twelve years.'

"Gaviria's laugh, short and sarcastic, interrupted her.

" 'That is an appalling understatement, my dear. What she means is that for twelve years I slaved ten hours a day in a commercial office that was a veritable prison, so that I could eat meagerly and sleep fitfully under a peeling roof hung with cobwebs in a revolting boarding house.'

" 'Two years ago, quite unexpectedly,' she continued, 'my husband inherited some money, which has made it possible for him to travel and to indulge in his favorite pastime—photography. I shared his last two years as a bookkeeper. We have been married four years.'

"There was a pause. I could think of nothing to say, but he kept the conversation going.

" 'Perhaps that may explain,' he said, 'my strange manners. You have always lived in the open, close to the sky and the stars. I wasted my entire youth piling up mountains of numbers in the heavy ledgers of a rotten company. Let Kant and his caboodle of philosophers rave about the "sublimity" of mathematics. They can have it! I prefer the beautiful.'

"His hand sought Dolores' in the darkness.

" 'It might never occur to anyone,' he went on, 'that a near-sighted bookkeeper with threadbare clothes, dandruff on his shoulders and a calculating machine forever at his fingertips, can harbor dreams of the beautiful for twelve whole years. Yes, one must eat, and work is hard to come by. But I was a coward. I was afraid to quit the security of my prison. I didn't have the courage to seek the fulfillment of my dreams.

" 'When I was notified of my inheritance, I went to bid my pious and pompous employer good-by. He examined the books and found an error of one peso and seven cents, which he promptly asked me to correct. Humble and obedient, as I had always been in the past twelve years, I was about to begin my last task, when outside the window a street organ broke out into a romantic tune. The warm May air wafted the sweet notes through the open window. I thought of beautiful Dolores waiting for me. I thought of the years crammed with numbers and empty of hopes. And calmly, quietly, I broke the calculating machine, I upset the inkwell over the last sheet of the debits and with its corresponding credit sheet I made a paper bird. I drew monkeys in red ink over the black figures and donkeys in black ink over the red figures. And then I went out and with a happy smile stood near the organ grinder, whom I had ignored for too many years.'

"Gaviria's story," Arnaldo said, "made me forget my decision to ask them to leave. He said good night and I wished him luck with his pictures. Dolores remained behind and looked at me with tearful eyes.

" 'Thank you,' she said. 'Were it not for what he told you, I myself would have no patience either.'

"From then on our relations were smooth and even pleasant. I was busy with my bees, while they devoted their entire day and even part of the night to photographing the jungle.

Dolores explained that they wanted to take unusual photographs of birds and insects in the night. I thought it all very strange, but they paid me well, and besides, I liked having Dolores under my roof. If her husband was as unbending and gloomy as a pine, she was as graceful and gentle as a palm tree.

"One night—it was really almost dawn—I heard them returning to the house. Their voices were high and excited. When I came downstairs, they were in the dining room drinking coffee.

" 'Did you take a picture of the moon retiring to its mansion?' I asked them jokingly.

"Gaviria's little mineral eyes shone maliciously. In a mysterious tone he answered, 'Better than that. We have discovered the stuff dreams are made of.'

" 'Signed, Gaviria and Shakespeare,' interrupted Dolores, licking the coffee from her full scarlet lips.

"That was all they said before they retired to their room in the olive light of dawn. On the table lay a piece of wrinkled paper and as I picked it up something fell out. It was a lump of dry mud. Here it is. Look."

Arnaldo handed me the piece of hard dry mud. It bore several thin marks, as if traced by a sharp point, triangular in form. They did not resemble the footprint of any bird or insect I knew.

"I was examining the piece of mud under the light, which I immediately realized came from far away, from the other shore of Lake Mariana, when Gaviria entered noiselessly and angrily tore it from my hand. We didn't say a word. I was too astonished and he too indignant, or vice versa. I can still remember the look in his eyes. A priest would look that way if he saw his holiest relic profaned.

"Two nights later there occurred the second of the series of incidents in this tale. I was sitting out here when Gaviria and Dolores returned late as usual. We exchanged an indifferent greeting, for since the episode of the mud our relations had again been strained. I detected an air of excitement about them and heard them muttering excitedly while having the cold supper I had left for them in the kitchen. Later, I went in for a drink of water. They were seated at the table excitedly discussing a photographic plate, which Gaviria repeatedly held against the light of the lamp and then compared with some

drawings in books lying open on the table. The untouched
salad in their plates had already turned the color of copper and
the wilted rice looked more like paste. They never noticed my
presence, and out of the corner of my eye I read the titles of
two of the books. They were the tales of Grimm and Ander-
sen, and *Tom Thumb*. I can assure you that a cold sweat ran
down my back. No one likes to shelter two lunatics under his
roof.

"I came out here again, and my pipe went out while I
wondered how to get rid of them. Suddenly Gaviria stepped
out on the porch and sat down heavily next to me. A strong
odor of brandy trailed after him. I heard Dolores fussing with
the dishes in the kitchen.

"Gaviria's big hot hand gripped my knee.

" 'What do you know about the country around here?' he
asked me.

"I was already accustomed to Gaviria's unusual questions.

" 'Nothing,' I answered, 'except that it provides the heat
my bees require.'

" 'Damn your bees!' he snapped. 'Can't you think of
anything else but bees?'

" 'One has to make a living,' I replied, trying to control my
indignation.

"He laughed derisively and somewhere a frog croaked as if
imitating his laugh.

" 'That's exactly what I thought for twelve years,' he
returned, 'but one has to dream too.'

"I told him that I very much enjoyed taking care of my
bees.

" 'You're blind!' he shouted. 'There is a whole world of
dreams right under your nose and all you have eyes for is
bees!'

"I got up angrily. I had no desire to argue with a barrel of
brandy. Dolores' voice behind me tried to be conciliating. Her
gentle, forever-smiling face now bore the same hardness that a
pencil drawing acquires when one passes a crayon over it."

" 'My husband is obsessed by the idea of recovering his lost
dreams,' she said.

" 'Let him learn first to respect the dreams of others,' I
retorted angrily, and dashed into the house and up to my
room. Through the open door I heard them arguing for a
short while. Later I heard them moving around in their room

next to mine, and finally I heard Gaviria leave the house.
From my window I saw him enter the dark forest.

"A moment later there was a knock on my door. Dolores,
fully dressed and pale as a tallow candle, smiled wanly at me
when I opened it.

" 'What you must think of us!' she said.

" 'Not "us," just him,' I answered.

" 'Don't be too hard on my husband,' she pleaded, tears
trembling in her eyes. 'He is excited. He is working very hard
and he is on the point of an extraordinary discovery.'

" 'I know of nothing extraordinary around here other than
the secretions of my bees,' I remarked ironically.

"A strident whistle, cutting through the night like a diamond through glass, interrupted us.

" 'That's my husband calling me,' Dolores explained. 'I
must bring him some tools. Good night. Thanks for being so
patient.'

"I saw her scurry across the clearing made by the lemon
moon and disappear in the darkness beyond. I went to bed
vaguely uneasy, suspicions buzzing inside my head more
fiercely than the mosquitoes outside.

"Some time later I woke up with a start. There was a
metallic clinking, as of tiny bells, somewhere in the room. A
second later I heard it again very clearly. It came from my
guests' room. From my window I could see their window wide
open. Suddenly I heard a chair crash to the floor, a stifled cry
from Dolores and an exclamation from her husband. Then
something dropped to the ground from their window, but it
was too dark for me to see what it was. I did hear the clinking
of bells again, but this time it was moving away from the
house.

"I went out into the hall and knocked at their door. Gaviria
opened it.

" 'Is there anything wrong?' I asked him.

"I had never seen such a hard metallic brilliance in human
eyes.

" 'No, nothing,' he replied.

" 'But the noises I heard,' I insisted. 'Something like
a—like a rattlesnake.'

" 'Here is a part of the rattlesnake,' he guffawed, showing
me this spangled red ribbon hung with miniature bells. 'As
you can see,' Gaviria continued mordantly, 'it can neither

crawl nor sting.' And he shut the door in my face.

"A few minutes later I heard them go out. From my window I saw them disappear into the woods, their lantern projecting a silver thread on the ground.

"I could not go back to sleep. It was four o'clock in the morning. I sat down and wrote them a letter asking them to leave by the end of the week and left it in their room.

"All that day while I did my work I watched the woods. In the evening I sat out here still watching the woods. I have lived on this farm many years and the woods are part of my life. At first the eerie silence and the mystery that forever hovers about them disturbed me, but as time passed I became accustomed to them, just as one becomes accustomed to having a dark, dusty attic in one's house. But now I began to look at the woods with different eyes. A man and a woman were deep in the green shadows looking for something; I didn't know what. Slowly, as it grew darker, the forest swelled like a giant green cat arching its back. The noises of the night began to creep through the air. I waited for a long time and then, just as I was about to go back into the house, they emerged from the woods. I held the door open for them. When they approached and the light through the open door shone on their faces, I gasped. I was looking at two strangers.

"Have you ever seen pictures of Indian swamis when they emerge from a trance? That is what Gaviria looked like. His face was lighted by a joy so intense that it was not of this world, while Dolores, at his side, was but a wasted shadow with waxen face and lifeless eyes. Not even a trace remained of the sparkling woman who, only a day or two before, had filled the house with her gay prattle.

"Gaviria greeted me with a joy so ferocious that it was offensive.

" 'We are all worn out,' he said, 'and famished, but it was worth it. This is the happiest day of my life. We'll eat anything you have and we'll drink champagne together, lots of champagne.'

" 'Your dinner is in the kitchen and I don't feel like drinking,' I answered coldly.

" 'Come! Come! Don't withdraw into your foolish pride again,' he said. 'We must drink a toast—you, Dolores and I. Dolores likes champagne. It is the drink of dreams.'

"From the staircase came Dolores' voice, 'You will have to

drink without me. I have a headache and I am going to bed.
Good night.'

" 'Just like a woman,' Gaviria said scornfully. 'But you
and I will drink together. Do you know what I have here?' he
asked, patting a package wrapped in coarse paper. 'A little
cage no bigger than a mousetrap, and inside . . .'

"He didn't finish. Instead he burst into laughter and then
said, 'Even dreams can be imprisoned behind bars. But let's
have some champagne.'

" 'Don't bother, Gaviria,' I said. 'I don't want to drink
with you.'

"He looked at me with angry eyes.

" 'What's this?' he snapped. 'Are you and Dolores in a
conspiracy against me? But today no one can make me angry.
If you change your mind, knock on my door.'

"He went up the stairs mumbling. I heard him say, 'I don't
want any supper. It would ruin the champagne.' And then he
said aloud, 'Dolores, what's the matter?'

"Dolores was coming down in her robe, a blanket over her
arm. 'You may have the room all to yourself tonight,' she
said, her voice as cold as frost at dawn. 'I'll sleep downstairs.'

" 'But why?' he asked her.

" 'Because I am sure you will enjoy your work far more if
you are by yourself.' She hissed the last word like a snake.

" 'Forgive me for intruding,' I interrupted them, 'but
Dolores may have my room and I shall sleep down here. Just
let me fetch some things from my room.'

"Before they could answer me I ran up the stairs. When I
returned a few minutes later, Dolores, pale as a ghost, stood
alone in the dining room.

" 'My husband was angry and locked himself in his room,'
she said.

" 'What the devil is the matter with him?' I asked her.
'Can't I help?'

" 'No one can.' She nodded sadly. 'I read your note. Don't
worry, we shall leave tomorrow.'

"I started to apologize but she interrupted me.

" 'Please don't apologize. You have been most patient and
there is no earthly reason why you should understand. He and
I have known much happiness together, but the lost twelve
years keep coming between us.' She sighed and her sigh was
charged with tears as a cloud with rain. 'His dreams are all

that matter and I am no longer one of them. Now I am only *reality*.' And she ran up the stairs sobbing.

"I stood alone in the dining room surrounded by shadows. Little white moths danced around the flickering light and their daring shadows licked my hands as gently as a dog's tongue. From the rooms above there came no noise. Gaviria's window cast a square of bright yellow light on the orchard. Farther on, the woods were rendered sinister and menacing by the darkness. I put out the light and lay in a hammock.

"I had dozed off when an explosive noise brought me to my feet. Almost at once I realized that it was only the uncorking of a bottle of champagne. Everything lay in deep darkness except Gaviria's window. From his room came the tinkling of glass against glass.

"A moment later I heard the noise of breaking glass. Evidently he was having an orgy all by himself. Then came the noise of another uncorking, more broken glass and peals of laughter that echoed weirdly throughout the silent house.

"On tiptoe I made my way up the dark stairs. I listened for a moment at the door of my room and heard stifled sobs. Then I moved on to Gaviria's door and holding my breath, I listened. He was pacing up and down, muttering all the while. The keyhole shone in the dark hall like a cat's eye. I stooped down and peeked into the room.

"At first the light on the table, in direct line with the keyhole, blinded me, but soon I was able to make out three bottles of champagne on the table, two of them empty and one still corked, and two empty glasses. Gaviria, his features distorted by a satanic smile, was staring at something in his cupped hands. He finally put the object down on the table, uncorked the third bottle and, after pitching the cork viciously at the wall behind which his wife was quietly weeping in the darkness, filled a glass. He then sat down at the table and pushed the object directly under the lamp. It was a tiny cage.

"At first I could not see clearly what the cage contained, but it was something white that fluttered like a bird. Just as I was about to abandon my uncomfortable position, irked by the ludicrous scene of a man drinking in the company of a bird, I saw him put his hand inside the cage, take the bird out and drop it gently in the empty champagne glass. I saw the thing then. It was not a bird. It was a woman! A tiny nude woman! A tiny naked woman, with flowing golden hair and pink flesh.

A beautiful little woman no bigger than my forefinger.''

With trembling hands the beekeeper filled the cracked glass with champagne and quickly gulped it down. In my eyes he must have read disbelief and even the doubt about his sanity that quickly crossed my mind. Mockery sparkled in his faded eyes, but, wiping the sweat off his brow, he went on with his story.

"I have read many a novel where in even the most extraordinary circumstances the hero reacts with a great presence of mind and goes on to face the situation and master it. In H. G. Wells' stories the heroes, often country folk, are surprised by nothing but simply proceed to come to terms with the inexplicable. In my case, I could not think clearly but I was not frightened either. It never occurred to me that I might be drunk or mad or dreaming. From the first moment I just knew that what I saw was true. Here was something that I had thought existed only in fairy tales. A fairy, smaller even than James Barrie's Tinker Bell, had been captured by a fanatical seeker of dreams.

"I remember getting up, my nails digging into the palms of my hands, my knees shaking. The house was dark and still, except for Dolores wailing monotonously in her room like a child sent to bed without dinner. Sweat poured down my face and my eyes smarted. Again I bent down and peered through the keyhole. The tiny woman or fairy was twisting inside her crystal prison under Gaviria's inflamed eyes and flustered face.

"Tiny though she was, the fairy was perfectly proportioned. Have you ever seen the shrunken heads done by South American Indians? Though shrunk to half the normal size, the features preserve a perfectly harmonious proportion. So it was with the canary-sized figure in the glass prison. Every single feature of her face and body was perfectly formed. Her long yellow-colored hair was abundant and glowed like a polished metal under the light, the delicate pale face might have escaped from a Fra Angelico miniature, her mouth was the size of a hemp seed painted red, and her eyes were two bright dots of deep blue sky. But it was her body that fascinated me, her exquisite little body with its tiny supple limbs and flesh that shimmered like fine silk. As she moved I saw on her little shoulder blades two tiny wings with the iridescence of mother-of-pearl and the texture of gossamer.

"Gaviria began to poke at the little woman with his bony finger, laughing coarsely at her fright. The tiny figure, threatened by her captor's long finger, was like a butterfly in danger of being impaled by a telegraph pole. When he finally got tired of pushing her, he grabbed the bottle of champagne and poured a little of the foaming liquid over her. And then the most enchanting thing happened. The little fairy was at first startled by the liquid gold shower but soon began with much glee to frolic in the bubbling wine. When she stood up she was all pink and gold, a rosebud sprinkled with dew.

"Suddenly seized by the desire to see closely the beautiful little creature, I stood up and thrust open the door to the room. Gaviria jumped up from his seat.

" 'What the devil—' he began angrily, but I quickly interrupted him.

" 'You said that if I changed my mind I should come to your room. Well, here I am.'

"Gaviria, instead of attacking me as I had expected, pushed me toward the table saying, 'Go ahead, take a good look. You are not dreaming. It is a fairy. And she is mine, mine to do with as I like! I have the power of life or death over a fairy!'

"He abruptly took the tiny creature out of the glass, her body streaming with champagne, and was about to put her back in the cage, but then changed his mind. Instead, he took out of a box a crystal ball, like those with little figures inside and miniature snowflakes that whirl around when the ball is shaken, only this ball was empty and had a wooden base that he proceeded to unscrew. He then lifted the little nude fairy by the hair, transferred her to the crystal ball, screwed back the wooden base and held it up to the light. Never in my entire life have I seen anything so lovely! The tiny naked figure reclining on her bed of glass was indeed a dream imprisoned in a crystal ball. Gaviria placed the ball on the table, covered it with a handkerchief, took my arm with one hand and the champagne bottle with the other and said firmly, "Let's go downstairs.'

"We left the light on and the door ajar. As we went down the stairs I heard Dolores moving about in her room. We sat down in the kitchen and in silence finished the bottle of champagne. Finally Gaviria said sardonically, 'You are as excited as I am. Who wouldn't be? A fairy! A real fairy! No one would believe it. It's a dream, a dream I have made come true. It is my reward for twelve years of drudgery. No one, not even

Dolores, knew what I did in my spare time. They would have thought me mad. But not now, not anymore, not when they see the crystal ball, not when they *see her*!

" 'As a child I was fascinated by fairy tales. I read them again and again, until I knew them all by heart. When I was older I began to delve into books that explained the psychological meaning of fairy tales. The subject soon absorbed me completely. Do you know that Puss in Boots is a cat with sadistic and criminal instincts? Yes, and the witch of the forest is a result of a projective mechanism, and the Sleeping Beauty a symbol of a pathoplastic mechanism of flight through suspended animation. It all sounds crazy to you. Well, I was far from satisfied. I read every book in existence on cyclopes and gnomes and hobgoblins and witches. Do you know that cyclopes really existed? They were just people with hypertrophy of the epiphysis, and gnomes were hypotrophic people, and hobgoblins and witches mentally supranormal beings. I also avidly read every book on fairies I could get hold of. The hours I spent reading about sylphs, sprites, gnomes and naiades! From the dwarfs of Paracelsus to the *Willys* in the *Florentine Nights* of Heine. And especially Arthur Conan Doyle. The day I read one of his autobiographical accounts and saw the photograph he himself took of "A Girl with a Gnome," as he captioned it—that day I found the road to Damascus. What he could do, I too could do. People, of course, laughed at Conan Doyle's picture, but I believed in it. A girl in a forest with a tiny gnome at her side!

" 'No sooner had I received my inheritance than I began to hunt fairies with a camera. Dolores followed me meekly, but she never understood. How could she understand what this meant to me? I came here to photograph your bees. Your bees! You have lived here for years and yet never knew that only a few yards away from you there is a marvelous world of fairies and gnomes!' "

"He paused for a moment and I heard the creaking of wood on the top of the stairs. Gaviria, oblivious to everything, continued talking.

" 'Last night Dolores and I saw them at the foot of the tree where we were hiding. Several days before in the same spot we had found a piece of dry mud with their footprints. In the codex where I discovered the legend that a colony of fairies existed in this region of Paraguay it said that they antedated the founding of Paraguay. After waiting for hours, we saw, exactly at midnight, gnomes scurrying through the darkness toward the giant mushrooms growing around the tree. In the darkness they looked like mice, but when they emerged from under the mushrooms to dance about in the moonlight, I distinctly saw their tiny white beards, their little red suits and caps, and their funny little pointed shoes with bells.

" 'We watched them dance for a while. Then the fairies arrived, with their little silver-sequined bodies, their wings shimmering like tears in the moonlight. Dolores was shaking with fright and I with excitement. There, at my feet, fairies and gnomes, real and tangible, were dancing. This was not a dream. This was reality. The flash of my camera dispersed them like magic, but I have a plate in my pocket with over a hundred tiny figures cavorting around the mushrooms. Nobody has ever taken a photograph like this one. It outdoes even Conan Doyle's.

" 'When we returned to our room I could not go to bed. I knew that the gnomes would follow us, for they are reputed to be even more curious than women. I was right. At dawn one of them climbed to our window and I tried to grab him, but he dropped down to the ground, leaving behind, caught in the window, one of his little ribbons with bells. You saw it. After that, it was not difficult to track them down to their underground caves. You saw the result upstairs. I captured a fairy!'

"The air in the kitchen was hot and unbreathable. A livid dawn was creeping through the window.

" 'And now what?" I asked him.

" 'And now what!' He turned the question into an exclamation. "How can you ask me that? I shall have the entire world at my feet. I, who all my life was utterly ignored by everybody, shall have the eyes of every man, woman and child fixed on me. But even that is not important. Upstairs I have what I want. A fairy! And she is mine, all mine! I can look at her for hours on end. I can watch her pink body splashing in a glass of champagne. I can caress her broken wings. Who knows? I may even come to learn her language and she mine. Don't you see? I am in love with her. I feel such love for her as even the greatest poet could never conceive, a love not of the flesh, not of this world. Between us there can be only dreams."

"The noise of breaking glass on the floor above startled us. We ran up the stairs and into Gaviria's room. By the table stood Dolores, fierce reproach imprinted in every line of her chalk-white face. On the floor lay the broken pieces of the crystal ball.

"Gaviria and I dashed to the window and simultaneously uttered an anguished cry. From the windowsill hung fine, glittering, crystal-like threads, and down below, across the orchard and toward the forest, ran hundreds of little figures, their silver-bell-studded garments bright red in the pallid light of dawn. I saw them clearly. I swear it. I heard their bells merrily tinkling, and I saw her, white and naked amid her rescuers, her hair waving like a tiny golden flame, her iridescent wings shining rainbow-hued in the first rays of the sun.

"Gaviria, cursing wildly, reached the door in three leaps, knocking Dolores down on the way. I heard him dash downstairs like a madman as I helped Dolores up.

" 'He knocked me out of his way to run after this wild dream of his,' she said with a sob in her voice.

"When we came out here Gaviria, his face distorted with fury, was staring at my beehives. The gnomes had disappeared.

" 'I saw her run into the beehives,' he shouted. 'The bees will kill her.'

" 'If she is a fairy,' I replied with irony, 'the bees are her friends and will not harm her.'

"Gaviria's eyes darted wildly from Dolores to me, and then suddenly he ran toward the hives. Dolores screamed and started to run after him, but I held her back.

" 'That would be mad,' I said, holding her firmly.

"Gaviria reached the bee fence and wildly began to kick the hives. What happened then happened so fast that it takes longer to tell. From under a beehive the tiny naked fairy emerged, white and unharmed, and majestically walked away, surrounded by a buzzing escort of bees like a cloud of gold. A dense cloud of angry bees swooped down on Gaviria, who, uttering bloodcurdling screams, darted from place to place, his arms waving wildly about his head, and finally fled into the woods, the humming cloud around him so thick that I could not see his head. Dolores, shaking herself loose from me, ran after him, disappearing into the forest.

"That was two days ago. I don't think they'll ever come back. If the bees succeeded in their attack on him, he couldn't have lived. What Dolores did then, only God knows."

Arnaldo picked up the cracked glass and drank the rest of the champagne. I hardly felt like drinking a wine so closely linked with the hunter of fairies. The heat rose from the parched earth in waves. The bees dozed under the implacable sun. The dense forest hummed with sounds. On the table, the handful of objects, the shattered pieces of a dream, struck me as the remains of some weird sacrifice.

"What are you going to do now?" I asked Arnaldo. He stared at the cracked glass he was swirling between his fingers.

"Wait," he replied. "Maybe *she*'ll return."

"Dolores?"

"No, the fairy. I would gladly give my life to see her bathing once again in this champagne glass."

Bridge

By Steven R. Boyett

Luce looked up from his morning paper as Roger came into his office.

"Have you heard, Mr. Luce? About the fairies?"

Luce closed the front section and set it aside. Roger glanced at the headline, which read:

Soviets Threaten to Enter West Berlin
Demand Removal of Pershing III Missiles

"They marching again?" Luce shook his head. "What is it this time—they want a gay Pope?" He snorted.

"No, Mr. Luce, it's—"

"That the Nimsloe account?" He nodded at the brown file in Roger's hand.

"Yes, Mr. Luce. They're thirty days delinquent as of today." Roger set the folder on Mr. Luce's precisely ordered desk. "I also thought you might want to look at their Workmans' Comp claims for the last two years."

Mr. Luce opened the file and began leafing through it. "What about them?" he asked, not looking at Roger.

"Well, there've been a lot of them, for one thing. And most of the claims have been for substantial amounts for substantial injuries, for another. Either their employee safety is awful, or—"

"Or they're trying to screw us." Mr. Luce frowned. "Thirty days late, you say?"

"Yes, sir. They—"

"All right, let me go over this. Bring me another cup of coffee and see that I'm not disturbed. You can take the morning paper, if you want." He leaned back in his chair and looked up at Roger. "On second thought, never mind. Leave it here."

Roger shrugged, smiling, and Luce realized that Roger had been positively beaming since he'd entered the office. Luce's frown deepened. "That's all, Roger. Don't forget my coffee."

"Right away, Mr. Luce." Roger turned and left, still beaming as he softly shut the door behind him.

Luce scowled. For some reason that smiling, beatific, positively *angelic* expression made him furious. Driving to work he'd passed a knot of people waiting at a bus stop, all bundled up against the morning chill, steam issuing from mouths, noses, and (though he had noticed it, he had not really realized it until now) all of them *smiling*, and looking at each other and nodding and *smiling* as if they shared some secret, some private joke.

Later, on the freeway, someone in a new Porsche had cut right in front of him, and he'd had to stomp on his brakes to avoid an accident. At first opportunity he'd changed lanes and sped up until he was beside the Porsche. Red-faced, he rolled down the window and turned to shout at the driver.

—and stopped cold at the expression on the man's face. It was . . . it was rapture. Rapture, and no other word for it: distant eyes; serene expression, beatific smile—the exact joymask worn by Roger as he had left Luce's office. Luce had rolled his window back up and turned on the radio, just to have some noise in the car, listening dully to the latest on the Soviet ultimatum on West Berlin.

Luce sighed and looked down at the Nimsloe folder on his desk. What was it with people nowadays? Was everyone turning into a Moonie, for Christ's sake? He ran his fingers through the long strands of hair he habitually combed across his bald spot.

A few minutes' perusal through the file convinced him that, sure as shit, Nimsloe was trying to screw Luce & Hutches on the insurance payment schedule. It happened every so often with mid-sized corporations—or rather, with some accounting manager in the mid-sized corporations, since blanket checks were sent to cover gross Workers' Comp owed—and Luce was both appalled and amused that they thought the patterns of fudged accident reports wouldn't surface sooner or later. He rubbed his hands, anticipating the letter he would send. He pressed the intercom button. "Roger? I thought you were bringing coffee."

"Yes, sir. Peggy didn't come in this morning and I've had to cover for her. I'm making a fresh pot now; it'll be ready in a few minutes."

"Peggy. She call in sick?"

A few seconds' hesitation. "Well, Mr. Luce, actually she didn't call in at all."

"Well, when she does deign to phone in, let me speak to her. And send in Miss Reeves to take a letter."

"Yes, sir. Oh, uh, I'm afraid . . . Miss Reeves hasn't come in yet, either."

Luce glanced at the digital quartz clock in its clear Lucite rectangle on one corner of the desk. "It's eight forty-five."

"Yes, sir. I know that, sir."

"Mr. Whittaker, is there anybody in the office capable of taking dictation? If it isn't an imposition, of course."

"I suppose I could, sir, if you don't mind—"

"Never mind. I'll type it out myself."

"Certainly. Oh, your wife called a few minutes ago."

"Was it urgent?"

"She didn't say, Mr. Luce."

"All right. If she calls again, tell her I'll call her back before lunch." He released the "talk" bar and cursed under his breath, then turned to his IBM Selectric and switched it on. It hummed to life and he inserted a sheet of Luce & Hutches stationery, closed his eyes, and began mentally composing the letter to Nimsloe & Co. In a few minutes Roger brought in coffee. "Peggy's on line two for you, Mr. Luce," he said, setting the mug of steaming coffee on Luce's desk. On the cup was written, in gothic letters, *Illegitimi non carborundum*. Luce nodded and waved him away. He lifted the cup and set it atop a cork coaster on the right side of the desk, turned to the phone, pressed the button with the winking light, and lifted the receiver. "This is Mr. Luce."

"Mr. Luce, this is Peggy."

"Yes, Peggy. I imagine you are calling to tell me you aren't coming in today."

"That's right, Mr. Luce."

"I assume you have some medical reason? We're already

short-handed today, you know."

"Well, it isn't a medical reason, exactly, Mr. Luce."

"Yes?"

"I'm just . . . not coming in."

Luce watched a number on his quartz clock shift silently to the next minute. "You have been with this company how long, Miss Lindley?"

"A long time now, Mr. Luce." She chuckled. "An awfully long time."

"And you're just not coming in, are you?"

Peggy laughed outright this time. "That's right, Mr. Luce. It's. . . . Well, I fell pretty silly just saying this outright, but . . . it's the fairies. They're taking me home. They're taking everyone home."

There was a prolonged, uncomfortable silence while Luce simply stared as his clock shifted to the next minute.

Peggy giggled. "They look just like Tinkerbelle, but with green eyes. Can you believe it?" Another giggle. "No, of course you can't."

"Miss Lindley, are you drunk?"

"I'm sorry, Mr. Luce." The disturbing good humor drained from her voice. "Not for leaving, but for you." And the click of a replaced receiver sounded in Luce's ear.

Luce stared at his receiver a moment before returning it, gently, to its cradle.

A brief knock on the door, and Roger walked in. He stopped just inside the office and cleared his throat. "Mr. Luce? Um, there's still fresh coffee in the pot. Your wife wants you to call her. Miss Reeves called to say she isn't coming in anymore. Just about everybody else is gone, sir, and I'm afraid I have to hurry if I'm going to get out in time. Is there . . . anything I can do for you, Mr. Luce?"

Luce stared dumbly. He glanced about his desk, as if a proper reply might be written on a notepad, or scribbled on his dull gray blotter. "What do you mean, just about everybody else is gone. Gone where?"

"I tried to tell you, sir. This morning. It's—" He shrugged, and he smiled. "It's the fairies."

Luce stared out his window at the city streets twenty stories below before looking back to Roger. "Will you please tell me what is going on?" he said finally, and in his own voice he heard a sound he had never heard before, a sound he did not like at all, the sound of an old man who really was out of it, who truly had no idea what was going on. "Is there some sort of rally, some kind of political—"

But Roger was shaking his head. He came closer to the desk until he stood just before it with his hands clasped in front of him like a self-conscious schoolboy called before his headmaster. "Look at the headlines, Mr. Luce. It's here; it's really here. There's just no way to explain it any clearer." He laughed a small laugh. "Either it works for you or it doesn't, Mr. Luce."

"I don't know what you're talking about."

"I know." The smile became pitying. "I'm sorry." Roger turned and opened the door to the office. Just before he left, he said, "Goodbye, Mr. Luce. I hope . . . " He raised a hand, dropped it, and shrugged. "Well, goodbye." Roger shut the door softly behind him.

Luce stared at the door in a confusion that quickly grew into anger. After a moment he snatched up the telephone receiver and punched his home number. The call was answered on the first ring.

"Hello, Robert."

"Polly. Listen, I—"

"I'm not home right now, so I've left a message on the machine."

Roger slowly lowered the receiver from his ear until he was staring at the holes from which his wife's tinny voice emerged.

"To tell you the truth, Robert," Polly's voice continued, "I doubt I'll be home again at all. There's a lot of that going around. I'd bet even money you don't know anything about it, though."

She sighed. "Robert Junior called. He and his wife are meeting me here, and we're going together. We're going home. Everything's sorting itself out, it seems. I suppose there's a chance you'll end up going with the rest of us, but Robert Junior and I aren't banking on it, and there isn't really enough time for us to wait, so . . . I'm afraid I have to sign off. Robert sends his love, and of course I do, too. I'd say it's been wonderful, dear, but . . . oops—I have to run; they're here. Good luck, Robert. I love you."

And the hissing of tape and the click of the broken connection, and then the dial tone, and not until the braying of the signal that the phone had been left off the hook did Luce replace the receiver and stare at the brown walnut veneer of his telephone, afraid to breathe. He looked at his desk. He closed the folder containing the minutiae of the Nimsloe account and centered it on the blotter, reached for his coffee, took a sip (it had been perfectly sugared by Roger; no cream), replaced the mug precisely on the cork coaster, and then stood up and looked out the window at the stillness of the city.

The clock read 10:00 when next Luce noticed it. In an hour of staring at the city, and at the interstate knifing east-west just beyond downtown proper, he had seen perhaps three dozen cars, perhaps two dozen pedestrians.

He glanced again at the newspaper headline. Had there been an alert? Surely the air-raid sirens would have sounded.

Could he have missed hearing them?

Mr. Luce grabbed his overcoat from the rack in the corner, put it on, and looked around his office. Then he turned off the lights and locked the door behind him.

The typing pool was empty; the machines were all turned off and covered. There wasn't a person in sight. Mr. Luce unplugged the coffee pot and left the offices of Luce & Hutches. His footsteps echoed in the corridor as he walked to the elevators. He jabbed the "down" arrow, which stubbornly refused to light. Luce waited ten minutes for the elevator before giving up and taking the stairs.

At the tenth floor he met a cleaning woman. She was radiant, filled with a joyous kind of fervor that made Luce quicken his steps.

"Now hold on," called the cleaning woman behind him. "Jus' you hold on there."

Luce hesitated. The woman caught up to him, smiling. "Where you goin' in such a hurry? They be comin' anyhow if you go fast or slow." She had a rasping voice that made Luce want to clear his throat.

"Who's coming? The Russians?" Luce felt the blood draining from his head. "My God, have the Russians launched a strike?"

The woman shook her head. "Don' know 'bout no Russians. I'm talkin' 'bout the angels, the *angels*! They's pure white, filled with the light of the Lord, and come on their wings to take us home." She caught the sleeve of Luce's overcoat. "Ain't you seen the angels?" She peered closer at Luce.

He felt as though she were reading the lines on his face. "Oh, Lord, I can tell jus' by lookin' you ain't."

Luce tugged his arm from the woman's grasp. "Let me go," he said unnecessarily. He stared a moment at the deep pity forming in her dark brown eyes. "Let me go," he whispered.

"I'll pray for you, Brother," she said. "I surely will."

Luce fled down the stairs and through the lobby of the office building, pushing through the revolving door and blinking in the sunshine. The cold hit him in a wave.

He thought he saw something move in the corner of his eye and he turned to see, but there was nothing. He shivered. Far away, up the avenue, a car horn blared twice and then stopped.

Fred Sandesky was still watching the gate from his booth at the parking lot. Fred always looked as if he needed to take a good long shit. He seemed to blame the world at large for the limp in his step and the constant pain in his back, but Luce greeted him in his booth like Crusoe sighting a distant sail. "Fred! Fred! What are you still doing here? Where is everybody? I don't know what's going on here, not at all."

Fred regarded him sourly. In his right ear was a plug leading to a small transistor radio. "God damned communists," he said. "I'm tuned to CONELRAD right now—"

"CONELRAD?"

Fred looked annoyed. "Emergency broadcast system. They don't know what the hell's going on."

"Why are you still here? Why weren't there any sirens?"

Fred shrugged. "Nowhere else to be. Ain't time to go no place else."

"But where is everybody?"

The guard spread his hands. "People get crazy, you know? Been running around all day, screaming nonsense. It's the goddamned communists, is what it is. People don't even know who the real bad guys are anymore." He snorted. "Where you going?"

"I'm going to drive home," said Luce. And suddenly he felt afraid.

"You do that, Mr. Luce. You just do that."

Getting in his car, Luce caught movement at the edge of his vision. He glanced around and, again, saw nothing. He started his car and drove from the lot. Fred waved him through, one hand on his earplug.

Half the traffic lights in the city were out. A magazine stand on the sidewalk stood open and unattended. Driving on Brantley Boulevard toward the interstate, Luce encountered only three cars. Two were driven by men, the other by a woman. All three drivers wore tight, unyielding expressions. They glanced at Luce as he passed them, then looked away.

He switched on the radio and began turning the knob to find a station but there was nothing but static.

Something appeared in the road in front of Luce's car. He hit the brakes and swerved. The back end of the car skewed; Luce fought to retain control as the car screeched to a halt.

He sat a moment, staring through the windshield at the nearly deserted boulevard. He opened the door and stepped onto the road, a lump at the back of his throat. It had looked like a little boy. . . .

He swallowed, forcing down the lump.

It had *not* been a little boy. He had gotten just a glimpse, just one frozen moment as a lithe figure darted in front of his car, but the instant was embedded in Luce's brain.

It had been . . . thin, horribly thin, with long legs and arms, and flowing yellow hair, and a porcelain face into which were set the most shockingly green eyes. . . .

Luce turned about, scanning the road, but there was nothing. Just that single, flash-frozen instant behind his eyelids. Finally he went back to his car, switched off the ignition, and pocketed his keys. He locked the door and left the car.

He scanned the buildings on either side of the street as he walked: on the left the welfare housing, looking old though built only five years ago; on the right a laundromat, a deli, a pawnshop.

Luce clenched his hands. "I saw you!" he shouted suddenly. "Damn you, *I saw you!*" His voice reverberated down the street. A dog barked. "Come out!" His voice, gravelly from shouting, lowered. "Please come out."

The dog ran out from around a corner. Behind it came a girl with long, dirty blond hair. She wore a pair of leather sandals, ragged blue jeans, and a yellow halter top. The dog, a black terrier, halted in front of Luce, growling and barking.

"Albert!" called the girl. "Bad dog! Be nice." She looked at Luce. "It's okay. He doesn't bite." She bent down and thumped the dog on the head. "Come on, boy."

"Wait a minute," said Luce. "Please. Where is everybody? Where are you going?"

The girl regarded him a moment. "We've found shelter," she said. "I came back for Albert. They said I could bring him."

"The shelters? Then there was an alert?"

She shrugged. "I don't know. I just came for Albert." She patted her thigh and the dog put its front paws on her leg, licked her jeans, and dropped down again.

"Can I . . . can I come with you? Will they let me in?"

She shrugged again. "Sure. Why not? The bridge is right over there, anyway, back the way you came. Didn't you see it?"

"The bridge?" Luce frowned. The girl was very pale, and her expression serene—was she high on something?

"Come on," she said. "I'll show you. We probably better hurry, though. Come on, Albert."

They retraced Luce's steps along the boulevard. When they reached his abandoned car the girl turned right, toward the alleyway between the deli and the pawnshop. Luce labored to keep up. The dog, barking excitedly, darted ahead of the girl and ran into the alley. The barking stopped.

"Oh, hi," said the girl to someone Luce could not see. "Thanks for waiting. There's someone behind me, okay?"

Luce stepped into the alley. A gust of cold air washed over him, parting his hair to reveal his bald spot. He saw garbage cans, stacked newspapers, beer cans, wine bottles, potato-chip bags, broken concrete blocks. Nothing else. He stepped forward, intending to call out, but turned at a sound behind him.

A fairy stepped into the alley.

It stopped when it saw him. If there was an expression in the huge, green eyes—green as emerald, huge enough to fill a third of the angular, delicate face—the expression was fear. Its membranous wings unfolded and quivered, as if the creature was poised on the edge of flight. Luce felt huge and awkward in front of it, for it was only as tall as his sternum.

He stepped toward it. The dragonfly wings twitched.

He took another step. The fairy glanced past Luce at the alley wall. It spoke. "Please," it said. "Let me by." Its voice was light, with a faint ring like a fingernail flicked against a crystal goblet.

Luce tried to speak, cleared his throat, and said, "I'm not stopping you."

The creature nodded uncertainly. It took a step forward, never taking its eyes from him, then stepped again. It moved as though buoyant, as if it barely weighed enough to keep it on the ground. Luce held his breath as it rounded him—giving him as wide a berth as possible in the narrow alley. Just as it edged past him and turned to run, Luce's arms shot out and grabbed it by the shoulders. It did not struggle, as he'd expected, but stood still while its double wings fluttered wildly. The fairy smelled of mint and gardenias. Luce held fast and the fairy cried out. It felt fragile beneath his hands, as though its bones were hollow like a bird's.

"Please," it said, and its voice was calm. "Let me go."

"No," said Luce.

"I have to go *now*, or the bridge will close."

"You're taking me with you."

"No."

He tightened his grip and the fairy cried out again. "Take me with you," he repeated.

"It isn't my choice. It's yours. Please—the bridge is closing, can't you see?"

"No, I can't. I see an empty alley where a girl and a dog disappeared not two minutes ago."

"If you see nothing else then there is nothing I can do!"

"Then you stay here with me."

The wings stopped beating. The shoulders went rigid beneath his hands and Luce could hear it crying. "Please," it whispered. "In a few seconds it will be too late. I don't want to die here."

"Neither do I."

"But you can't do this. You can't force your way through. Don't kill me because you are blind."

Luce hugged the fairy close to him, as he would a child. Its wings fluttered against his stomach with a sound like crackling cellophane, and Luce felt the creature's fear and realized that it was his own. He looked to the end of the alley where the fairy yearned to go, but could see only brick walls. His palms grew wet on the smooth shoulders of the impossible thing he held. His heart beat loudly, his breath quickened. . . .

And he let go.

He dropped his arms to his sides, where they hung as if made of wood. The fairy glanced back at him. Luce bowed his head, unable to meet its gaze.

The fairy nodded slowly, and then it turned and ran. Its wings straightened and beat like a hummingbird's, and its feet left the ground and it sped head-first toward the brick wall, and through it, and as it passed through Luce blinked his eyes, for suddenly he could see—vaguely, distantly, where the creature had gone—the misty contours of a country landscape, of people, and what looked like houses, all colored brick red by the wall in front of him.

It looked like *home*.

The vision blurred. Luce wiped tears from his eyes and stepped forward.

Crowley and
the Leprechaun

By Gregory Frost

Well, *begob* it's yourself now, isn't it?

I should hope so.

Ah, now, there's me pint, have you heard about the fella they're holdin' down at the station? No, I thought not, an' you bein' a loyyer no less. Struth, if ever there was a man needed the experteese of a counselor, it's your man down at the station. The brother is one of them, you know.

Beg pardon? Do you mean to say your sibling is a lawyer, too?

I mean no sucha thing, God forgive me if I did. The brother's a Sergeant don't you know. Likes to be called that, too. Big on the titles he is. And he told me about this fella they nicked. An American. Would you care to be hearin' about him?

As my glass is far from empty, it seems that I have little choice short of flight.

Fine. Well, first off, the name's a quare one. Calls himself Cornelius Crowley. Says he came over here to spend his holliers, of which he had three weeks, and he was about lookin' up his family records, claimin' that his people departed the shores for America back in 1858. Now, what family records could he be wantin' do you suppose? The Sergeant thinks the story smells of fish cakes and proposes the name's an alias, too.

Well, I don't know. This is Cork, there must be thousands of Crowleys about.

That's just what I tells him, but once the Sergeant has his

mind made up, there's no workin' with it. He says that's exactly *why* he's after thinkin' it's an alias if you please. A man
of logic, the Sergeant. Right. If the fella Crowley's to be
believed, he comes over "to search for his roots." Roots,
begob. The man's tall and thin as a willow whip but still looks
nothin' like no tree to me. As you can see, it's a perplexin'
matter.

It is?

Wait now. So, wan night this Crowley's drinkin' in the pub,
pourin' down the stout like he's got a funnel for a mouth. The
fags get passed around and your man starts talkin' how he
loves it here so much but, he says, seein' things out of the window of a Bed-and-Breakfast is not like livin' in the heart of the
country. Well, the Sergeant happens to be there, sippin' a
pint, and he overhears this and he goes up to your man an'
tells him about a place to rent up in the Nagles and would your
man be carin' to rent it for a bit, say through a week arter
Frida which is when the man's flight back to America is pro-
fessed to leave. An' do you know what your man says?

I presume he answered in the affirmative.

That I couldn't say, but he did agree to it. So they went on
swallyin' stout and smokin' the fags an' colloquin' until the
pub shut down. Then it's my opinion an' the Sergeant's as well
that some suspicious character pulled out a jar and started in
on that with your man. The Sergeant reports that the poor
fella must have drunk enough posheen to set his teeth
wobblin', though the Sergeant only knows this third hand as
himself would never stoop to drinkin' such an illegal concoc-
tion as that. The Sergeant did see him back to his digs, but
once inside, who can say how things went.

*Just a minute. I thought your brother was a policeman.
What is he doing renting out this house?*

Just what the others at the station wanted to know, especially in light of the outcome of it. But the Sergeant had an
answer for the lot, and he barked out at 'em like a seal—a
fierce man, the Sergeant—that he had every right to work a bit
of the real estate if it suited him as there's absolutely no law
against it. Mind you, he said no word further about the jar to
them after that, his mood was so black. O there's no dealin'
with him when the shiv's up his bung.

Ah, my, yes, what happened to this fellow, Crowley?

You know they say as patience is a virtue. But I'll tell you, seein' as you're losin' your foam. The next mornin' the Sergeant picks up your man, who looks like he spent the night under the wheels of a caravan that was stuck in a bog. He barely remembers the night before, he says, but climbs in with his baggage and lets himself be taken off. For a time he sits there, his eyes closed and his skin the color of milk as the Sergeant tells it. Then he opens his eyes a bit and asks after the Sergeant has he ever seen one of them big rabbits.

How's that?

Just the reaction your man received to his question. So he clearifies it by explainin' about this movie what stars Jimmy Stewart and has this great six-feet-tall rabbit in it called Harvey, only the rabbit's invisible don't you see.

I suppose I wouldn't, eh?

Drink your stout. This rabbit, he says, is called a pookah. The Sergeant explains that pookahs are "normally depicted" as horses, not rabbits, and that he himself has never laid one eye upon such a thing, though he knows a few as have claimed to see them arter a dozen pints o' porter. Well, the Crowley explains then that he's been readin' Yeats an' knows all about them fairy rings and banshees an' ghosts an' things of that like. An' the Sergeant starts eyein' him as you'd expect be now and says to him, "You Americans are a superstitious lot, ain't you?" Well, your man had nothing more to say after that. The Sergeant claims that was the moment he became suspicious of the fella.

So, the house used to belong to this fella Kilpatrick what moved his family into the city some years back. Not much to look at, but Kilpatrick's wife does go up there now and again to trim the rosebushes and brings her goats for to trim the grass. It's got a chimbley and a fair amount of wood, too. Ould Kilpatrick'd been tryin' to get something for it for a long time, which was why by his claim he had turned to robbery in the first place and how he had met up with me brother. He was so happy about havin' a tenant that he went up there the night before and seen that all was ready if you understand me.

I'm not sure I do.

I mean the ould man had left some bottles of Black Bush and some bottles of stout to help his tenant pass the time. The Sergeant says that your fellow tried to give him a five pound note for drivin' him up there.

No, not really.

I just told you. That was the last the Sergeant seen of the fella until yesterday when he went to pick him up and give him a ride to the train up to Limerick. And it was at the train station that all the trouble they're hollerin' in the papers came to light. Course, even that's not half as unlikely on the face of it as this tale Cornelius Crowley's tellin' for his defense.

And what tale would that be?

THE ONE I'M ABOUT TO TELL YOU. Here, now, sit back down an' drink your pint, you want to hear this, you've no idea how much. There's nothin' for your like to do just now anyways as no ambulances pass here at this time of the day.

Really. All right, continue.

Fine. Well, your man's story goes like this. When he sees the place he thinks to himself what a joy it'll be out in the country, away from all the skerryin' and rushin' about of the city, and don't we know just what he means? Now he knows there's no phone or radio in the place. The Sergeant told him as much an' told him as well how far down the hill to Toorgarrif he'd have to walk if he wanted anything more than what the ould man had stocked in the pantry. No, said he, that was fine by him. He's plainly in love with the place, *The Cottage* he calls it. *Quaint* he calls it. So, left alone, he settles right in, starts a fire and sits there before it, throwin' the odd block of peat on it every now and again. The next morning he's up at dawn, ready for a refreshing day. Looks out the back an' sees someone down the slope, wan of the locals with his sheep about. Out goes your man, pullin' on his jacket against the chill of early morning. He follows the little stone walk round the back an' discovers a well beside the wall. Bucket, cover, rope an' all, your man hasn't the slightest notion yet what it's for besides the "atmosphere" of the place. Dim if you ask me, but the matter of his faculties will be brought up again.

I'm sure.

Right. So Mr. Crowley, he starts to climb over the low wall, swings up wan foot to climb over and steps down right into somethin' that Mrs. Kilpatrick's goats left behind. Straddlin' the wall as he is, his foot slides out from under him and he twists his ankle bad enough that he doesn't dare continue down the hill for fear of hurtin' hisself fierce. Back he hobbles inside. Well, it looks as if it's bound to swell, so he thinks he'd better be soakin' it. Goes up to the cupboard to search for a pan, an' that's when he notices there's no tap water. It's shut off. He goes into the bathroom an' that's shut off as well. That's when he sees the well in a new light as it were. And he sees too that there's nothin' for it but to be goin' back out there to acquire water for his foot. He has to hop around the back with a bowl under one arm, and by now it's begun to rain and he's left his coat inside. So he gets soaked through while gatherin' enough water to get his foot wet. He takes the water in and heats it. While he's soakin' his foot he starts thinkin' of how he's going to shave an' take a bath, and the more he dwells on this the more down in spirits he becomes until he finally breaks open the Bush and has a nip.

Perfectly understandable under the circumstances. For the pain if nothing else.

Exactly. Your man claims he spent four days be the fire in whiskey-sodden bliss with nothin' to do and no one comin' by to see him.

But, good heavens, why didn't he try to go out? Surely the sprain wasn't so severe as to keep him inside all that time.

I'll give you a laugh. Your man says that he tried to go out every now and again, but that the skies opened up on him every time like he was cursed. He gave up finally trying to go out because the last time he had gotten a quarter mile from the place when the rain spilt, and wasn't it a downpour fit for Noah? After that he stays in until, like I said, his four days are up. By then he can't stand himself anymore, he's raised whiskers that itch and his hair has flakes ridin' on it. He says he felt like he'd doused in bacon grease. Begob, it was only *four* days he'd gone, but you know how Americans are about washin'. Have to have a bath every day they do. Personally, I think it's their diet what does it to them.

Too much grease?

Indeed. And wasn't it the grease that finally made him put on his cold wet coat and go out to the well to fetch some water to boil for a bath? Again, your man claims it was pourin' rain outside, worse still than anything he'd yet seen, so much rain that he couldn't make out the valley where the sheep had been the first day. So he's shieldin' his eyes with one hand and reaching up for to release the catch on the handle with the other. But before he can lay his fingers round the handle itself, the thing spins like a tango dancer, smacks him in the shoulder hard enough to send him slippin' up to the wall where he falls down. And what does he hear as he's clutchin' for his balance? He hears somethin' inside the well cry out. Then he hears the bucket splash down. He sits there muddy in the rain, waitin'. All of a sudden someone down in the well begins to shoutin' all sorts of curses like would broil your ears. Even though your man doesn't understand a single word of it he knows that's what he's hearin'.

Remarkable.

Yes, isn't it. So, Mr. Crowley, he gets up and starts windin' the bucket back up to the top, all the while peerin' down into the depths to see what it is he's caught. The bucket was a weighty subject too he says. He sees two eyes gleamin' up at him. Then the voice surges up arter, sayin', "I hope you're satisfied wit' yerself as now yeeve done the dairty deed." Talkin' just like that if your man's got any gift for speech to match his gift for obfuscatin'. It surprises him so much he puts up his hands an' the bucket with its contents goes careerin' down again. The voice, angrier than ever, cries out "Muise, I've fallen prey to an idiot. WILL YOU PULL ME UP, YOU GREAT TOADSTOOL." Your man gathers his wits about him and cranks the handle with both hands as hard as he can turn. And up comes the bucket into the light. Now what do you suppose is inside it?

I dare not guess.

Course not, you'd be daft to even submit the proposition. What's inside the bucket is a little man with a white beard and his face all puffed up red with anger and his white hair all shaggy like a goat's but all stuck out in points now 'cause of the water drippin' from his crusher.

Do you mean to tell me that this Mr. Crowley the American claims to have encountered . . . to have brought forth a leprechaun?

On the face of it that would seem to be the case now wouldn't it? And that very fact dawns on him and he says the same in great surprise. The little ould man stares at him with eyes bulgin' from a near seizure and says "AN' WHO ELSE WOULD BE TAKIN' REFUGE IN A BUCKET?" He grabs onto the rope with his little hand, tryin' to pull himself out of the situation before the handle gets thrown again. It's not a ride he's enjoyed. But the bucket sways, "precariously" as the Sergeant would say, and the leprechaun ends up wrapped over the rim for fear of takin' the plunge. He screams at your man to lock the handle, but the Crowley sees the situation in a new light all of a sudden. He cries, "O no, I've read about you." The leprechaun looks a bit on the nervous side but tries still to bluff it out. "O have you," says he, "an' I wasn't even aware dat I was particularly well known." Your man replies, "But you are, and now I've caught you." Well, the leprechaun tries to argue that, but your man just lets go of the crank for a second, long enough to drop the bucket a foot or two, which in turn causes the little man to bleat like a stuck sheep. Again the question's put to him, is he caught or not. And he says, "Well now, *caught* is a trifle indelicate to me ears. I was tinkin' more like *experiencin' a setback*." So your man offers him one more chance else he's going to drop him back down in that hole and leave him for a few hours in the dark till he's had time to reconsider how things are. That's the final blow to the leprechaun's dignity. He agrees to being caught and in return gets lifted from the perils of the drink. Once your man has his hands on the little fella, though, he's not about to let him go. He carries him back inside the cottage and sets him down by the fire, suggestin' to him that he could dry off. The ould man squints up at him and replies, "It's kind you are, *terrible* kind." Then the leprechaun removes his coat and tosses it up over his head as casual as that. It soars up like a bird as the testimony goes and hangs itself on a wood peg that sticks out from the mantel. Your man's sittin' there with his teeth chatterin', trying for all the world to get warm and he takes a screw at his prisoner and finds the quare little man as dry as kindling.

This is quite utterly impossible to believe.

Oh no, this is the believable part of the tale. The little man asks for something to drink, something that would warm his insides like the fire warms over his outsides. Your man goes and gets the bottle of Black Bush, pours two glasses of it and sets the bottle between them. Meantime the leprechaun's lit up a little clay pipe using a cinder of peat from out of the fire no less. If your man's to be believed, the leprechaun just reached right through the flames and plucked it out, glowin' and smokin', without so much as a blister to himself. If your man's to be believed.

Not by me, he isn't, I assure you.

Well, now, how are you going to defend him if you don't even trust him this far?

Who said I had the slightest intention of counseling the gentleman? And I am still awaiting elucidation on what charge they arrested him. The telling of tales is hardly a criminal act, except perhaps in this pub.

Sure and the Sergeant could argue that with you. But if you'll let me finish, I'll be "elucydatin' " what he got nicked for. As I was sayin', the two of them were sittin' by the fireside, the little man smokin' as idle as you please an' the big man shiverin' like a wet hound. The leprechaun says, "I expect now ye'll be wantin' yer reward." Your man takes a swig of the Bushmill and nods his head. The leprechaun takes the pipe from his mouth, taps it to his head and says, "An' I suppose it's the gold ye'll be havin' of me, it always is." To which your man replies, "And what's wrong with gold? Do you have any idea what the world gold market is like these days?" Well, the leprechaun hasn't a clue to that mischief any more than I do, but he gets all serious and says, "I've been honest with ye till now and I'll go on that way, so what I'm tryin' to tell ye here is that it's goin' ta take me a wee bit a' time to get yer gold." Well, your man begins splutterin' and squawkin' like a budgie about what the devil does he mean, "a wee bit of time"? To which the leprechaun replies, "I see that ye've got a head full of the printed lies about pots of gold an' the like, but the truth of it is, me treasure's up in Loch Sheelin, barried in the mud an' it'll take a bit of doin' ta get it out before next week." Now, do you suppose your man believes that?

I shouldn't think so.

Absolutely right. He says that he's got just three days left till the Sergeant comes to collect him for the train to Limerick and he'd better have his gold by then or else. He leans up close to the little man and asks as to whether or not the leprechaun knows what happens to fairy people who welsh on an agreement.

That's an interesting point. What does happen to them?

You'd know by now yourself if you hadn't interruptioned. What happens is that they're supposed to wither up and die, only this leprechaun's got half a notion to disregard to whole matter as stuff an' nonsense. But the other half tells him he's never been in this soup before and would he care to find out first hand if there be any truth in back of it. He agrees to do everything in his power to fulfill the wish of Crowley by Frida. Hearing that, his grateful host picks him up an' tosses him out on his ear. Between you, me, and Kevin O'Domnaill, it's there I'm thinkin' that he made his fatal mistake as the mystery writers say.

I still fail to see any transgression.

Well, luckit and you will.

I am looking.

Bedamn, you put a man in flitters on the way to your edificatin'. Now, as I was sayin', three more days go by, by which time your man is in terrible shape. He still hasn't bathed proper, a fact readily supported by anyone at the station. He has a terrible cold up in his head and his bag does be out of order from improperly eatin' and drinkin' so that he's spendin' most of his time seated openly in the cringin' position if you follow.

Thank you, too well.

The Sergeant comes to pick him up and finds him lookin' like he's already gone to the wall. Your man is half in and out and does be babblin' all sorts of things, mostly curses at the leprechaun, though at first the Sergeant thought they was directed at him and took great offense. But your man kept repeatin' things like "little bastard" and "snot-nosed shrimpy little fart" so that the Sergeant came round to understandin' it couldn't be him, seein' as how he's ten stone or more. The poor miserable wretch has had the presence of mind to pack his bags at least, although he can't even remember doin' it and starts to look around to gather up his belongings. The Sergeant decides to leave him alone for a bit then, gathers up the bags and puts them in the boot. He's all ready to go when suddenly your man lets out a shriek and goes screamin' round the side of the house. The Sergeant gives chase and is just in time to see your man leap over the wall like a champion jumper all the while shakin' his fist at the sky and spewin' out the curses. The Sergeant testifies he was stricken dumb by the sight.

I would share in his astonishment.

It's sure I am you would. All of a sudden, the hillside's empty. Your man has disappeared, bang like that. The Sergeant creeps up to the wall, not knowin' just what he's into. He leans over and takes a screw at the hillside below, mutterin' to himself all the while that there are some people in the world who have swallyed too much civilisin' to be left out on their own. They just don't have the complexion for it. He looks down and sees two great gouges in the sod like two sled

runners would be makin', two lines runnin' right straight as
you please down the hill. He says that one of the man's shoes
had come off and stuck in halfway down and the sock had finished the path so that it was not as distinct from that point on.

Yes, but what had happened to Mr. Crowley?

Oh, he was lyin' at the bottom, flat on his face, kickin' and
beatin' at the ground, his clothes all covered in sheep's
manure. I can tell you that the Sergeant had a moment of
serious doubt over going down there to retrieve him.

Personally, I would have called for a straightjacket.

You might at that, but the Sergeant can handle three or four
on each arm, even on a Saturdah night.

Well, no wonder he became a police officer.

I'm going to overlook that remark for your sake.

Excuse me?

Exactly so. Now, the Sergeant hauls his smelly bundle up
the hill and drops him in the front seat, as I said, much against
his better judgment. And all the way back your man's sneezin'
and blowin' and callin' out names and curses somethin' fierce.
The Sergeant ignores it but does hurry his speed to get to the
train, but what he can't ignore is the smell. So he keeps the
windows rolled down all the way despite its being a chilly
morning, the only way, he says, to "minimize" the effect. He
might have cleaned him up, but that would have made him late
for the train and the Sergeant was in no way desirin' to be
responsible for the Crowley any further.

Who could blame him?

Not me. The Sergeant took him to the station, put him in
front of the window and wished him luck before escapin'. You
understand that your man wasn't somethin' you could hide at
that point. The Sergeant thought he'd seen the last of that bit
of trouble.

I gather he had drawn an erroneous conclusion.

Quite a mistake. Seems that your man was actin' so quare
that they decided to look into his belongings. Normally, of
course, they'd never as do that, but your man was mutterin'
all sorts of vile things at them and causin' a scene and makin'
enough trouble in a general way that they couldn't help
themselves from givin' him more than a polite once over. The
Sergeant hadn't gone two blocks from the station when he got
the order to turn around and go back.

So they arrested the man for being a nuisance? I should

think a phone call to the American Embassy ought to solve that problem.

A nuisance? Hardly that. Do you know why they arrested him? Can you have the slightest notion of what they found in his luggage when they opened it up?

Not the slightest, no.

Gold is what they found.

Gold?

And not just any gold at that, but gold crosses and spoons. Chalices covered in gems and some of them rare pieces with centuries on 'em. All gold, every bit, not a speck of silver in the take.

You don't mean to say . . . surely not.

I *do* mean as to say, and yes it was the treasures stolen night before last from the tourin' show of the National Museum that resided in the luggage.

Incredible. What have the police done?

See? I knew you'd be interested in the matter. Well, they're holdin' your man nice an' tight, especially once the story about the leprechaun came out, with the accused tryin' to point the finger at the little man because he must have run out of time and took what gold was at hand.

They're not believing that claim.

No, no. But do you know what really has the Sergeant convinced that the man's story is off?

What?

What's got him convinced that it's a "tissue of lies" as he puts it is your man's complaints about the terrible rain keepin' him inside when everybody knows that the most we've had in the past week has been a few days of the heavy dew—certainly not more than three inches.

Ah.

Ah, indeed. So, I'll be lucking forward to hearin' of your handlin' of the case. Gob, there's me bus pullin' up. Well, cheers!

The Antrim Hills

By Mildred Downey Broxon

The spring sunlight on Maire's face brought her back from sleep. She reached across the bed, then sat up, frightened. The blankets on Tadhg's side lay smooth; he had not come to bed last night. Maire knew where he must be.

Better, far better, if he were with another woman; after the Beltane fires not all men slept in their accustomed beds, nor did the women wait alone. But the desire that drove Tadhg was different, and more dangerous. If she were right—and she knew she was—The dread was upon her.

The green hills, sun-touched, rose above the misty valleys, but Maire was blind to any beauty. Barefoot and uncombed, she ran from the house. Stones bruised her feet, and nettles stung her ankles. *He has been Taken,* she thought, *for last night he went to hear the music of the Sidhe.*

She took the path by the boggy lowland, where mist hovered even on the hottest days. Those who ventured there on moon-lit nights saw gaunt armies of barrow-folk creep from their graves, saw the gleam of bronze weapons, and armies meeting in ancient, silent battle. No weapons clashed, and no wounded screamed; the horror was greater for that. At dawn the dead crawled home again to sleep.

Turf-cutters once had found a golden collar in the bog, but those who handled it soon died, and the collar was cast again into the sticky blackness. No one now worked in the haunted place.

151

This morning the air was sweet-sharp with the smell of peat. The sun glanced off the sheet of mist, and the ground itself was hidden. One fog-tendril crept up the next small hill. As Maire reached the top she paused. Never before had the mist spread like this; the dead were reaching out, and the dense whiteness filled the next hollow too. The fairy-mound with its single hawthorne tree rose from the haze, and on the mound lay Tadhg, his harp by his side. His ear was pressed to the ground, as if he were listening. Maire hesitated a moment, then stepped through the fog, trying not to think of what might wrap around her ankles and drag her down. She had more to fear, for Tadhg had heard the music.

She knelt on the wet grass and touched his cheek. His skin was cool, not like the flesh of a living man. She shook him; he was slow to waken. She shook him again, roughly, and he opened his eyes.

His eyes.

Blue they once had been, and bright, but they were now milky as the eyes of the old and the blind. He did not seem to see her. He sat up with one smooth boneless motion. His fingers dug into the ground, his hands and the roots of the hawthorne tree.

Maire released his shoulder. "Tadhg, do you remember me?" She expected no answer.

Bewildered, he looked at her with his old-new eyes. He sat a moment as if listening for something, then rose, picking up his harp. Maire led him home.

She fed him bloodwort, and burned bunches of remember-me, but no steams, no tea, no sacrifice was any use. Leechcraft, no matter how skilled, could not restore a stolen soul; Dian Cecht the Physician did not hear her prayers. Through sleepless nights she watched Tadhg as he lay, but never once did he remember her. Whatever lived in him sat dreaming; through the month of Beltane, while the Springtime sun woke the sleeping land, Tadhg huddled near the fire. He took no notice of those who came to Maire for healing; cattle-tending and hunting went likewise unnoticed. This was right, for his harpist's hands were not for labor. But day and night he sat, shaking with chill, plucking eldritch melodies on his brass-stringed harp. His fingernails broke, and his fingers were cut and bleeding, but he would not stop clawing out the music.

Maire watched Tadhg's pale shadow in despair. He was lost, as lost as she had been in that terrible time. . . .

. . . She had not minded the long months of pregnancy, nor the hours of labor, but the endless moments before her baby cried— And when it did, the cry was weak and wrong. Then she rose, bloody from childbed, forcing back the women who tried to restrain her, until she stood over her child as it gasped a last few times.

Whatever soul was reborn in her child was not ready to return, the women said, trying to comfort her. She would have more children, she was young. But she stood silent, looking down at the small pale form until she fought her way through them, out of the house. They found her by the lakeshore, crawling toward the water, they said.

For a time, all was darkness, dim dreams and walking nightmares. Through the dark Tadhg sang to her, calling her back from the grey land with his songs, for he spoke best with a harp in his hands. When she grew strong again he walked the hills with her, in sunlight and in storm, until at last the violence of forest and sky left her at peace, and she could speak again, even laugh, and hope. . . .

But Tadhg was not this thing that shivered by the fire on the warmest days, his strange eyes vacant. Tadhg was as lost now as Maire had been before. He had brought her back from darkness; could she do less for him?

She did not know where to search, but she knew where she might begin.

The Christians now claimed the holy pool by Lough Neagh; they said a saint dwelt there, whatever sort of god a saint might be. Maire had not visited the spot in a year or more. She wondered if the holy trout were safe.

She need not have worried. The pool in the sacred place lay clear and calm, though the path to it was narrower, choked by taller crowding grass. Narrow or not, the path was worn by centuries of pilgrim feet, and a few tokens still fluttered from the tree. Among them was the woolen cloth she had hung in offering for another child. The red fabric was tattered now, faded by sun and wind and rain. Still she had no answer. Children came, or did not; it was not hers to question. She knelt beside the pool.

But now I do question, she thought. *Tadhg is taken beyond all healing, and that at last is too much to bear.*

The pool was small, and white stones gleamed on the bottom. Through interlacing branches Maire could see a wind ruffling the lake, though the pool itself stayed still. Across its surface an insect walked, its hairlike feet dimpling the water. A shadow rose, and the insect disappeared.

Maire leaned forward. She had never seen the trout in all the times she had come here. It turned and faced her; its eyes were not the flat blank eyes of fish. They glowed amber, and were unafraid.

Soundless, it spoke. "You would be Maire ní Donall?"

"I am she."

"You are searching for Tadhg MacNiall, your husband." The trout hung in the water, effortless, its gills opening and closing, its fins waving gently.

"It seems he is mine no longer," she said. "He was to play for the High King, and slept on the fairy mound to hear the music of the Sídhe. Since then he is changed, and in no way can I heal him."

"He played for the King of the Cruthini, and wished to play at Emain Macha," said the trout. "But now he plays for the King and Queen of the Sídhe, while another wears his body. The Queen of the Sídhe is very beautiful; perhaps, in the court beneath the lake, Tadhg has forgotten you."

"It was years we had together; for beauty he would not forget me," Maire said. She grew angry. Was Tadhg a man, or a bull to be captured by the Queen? "I will go after him," she said.

"Come back, then," said the trout, "bringing your changeling with you, if you can." It flicked in a circle, then disappeared. Maire could not see how it left the pool, but the pool was empty.

She led Tadhg to bed that night—he would not leave the fire willingly—and lay awake beside her changeling-man. Through the window she watched the silvered tree-tops moving in the wind, the cloud-wisps streaming across the sky. If Tadhg would scarcely leave the fire, how then could she lure him to the pool? Only his breathing showed him to be alive.

"There is a treasure of amber by the lakeshore," she

whispered, thinking of the trout's eyes. "Come with me, I will show you."

Tadhg put one arm over his eyes.

She lay watching the stars march overhead, pale and bright, a sleepless company. After a long time she said, thinking of the water, "I have heard music by the lakeshore. Come with me and hear it." Tadhg turned his back to her, covered his ears, and slept on.

The night passed. When the sky was paling toward dawn, Maire said, "Those who sleep under the hills ask you to play for them, for their sleep is long and dreamless. Bring them dreams."

Only then did Tadhg rise from their bed. He stood in the grey morning light while she dressed him and herself.

Maire led him by the hand, for he cringed from sunlight, always seeking the shade. His clouded eyes blinked until he closed them and allowed himself to be guided like a blind man. He could not have known where they were going, but still he held his harp in one bleeding hand.

Something of Tadhg still dwelt in him, unless the changeling had once been a harpist too.

The trees stood ghostlike in the morning mist as Maire and Tadhg approached the pool. The trout was waiting.

"Well done, Maire ní Donall," it said. Tadhg sat on the ground, his eyes blank. "I can guide you now to the palace under the lake, if you would go."

"Others have seen things under the lake, but not I. I do not have the Sight," said Maire.

"The palace is there, nonetheless, and there also is your husband. But if you go, eat nothing and drink nothing, or you must stay there forever." The trout's amber eyes gleamed.

"If I go beneath the waters of Lough Neagh I may well stay there forever, drowned," Maire said, "for I cannot breathe water."

"Death and age have never entered the crystal palace." The trout flicked in an impatient circle. "Go now, or go home."

Maire hesitated, thinking of the Tadhg-changeling. "What of him? He is like a child, and I brought him here by trickery."

"Go," said the trout, and vanished.

• • •

Maire stared for a long time at the empty pool, then at Tadhg. She could not leave him sitting there. The form of Tadhg was still on him, and something of Tadhg still was left in him. She took him by the hand and led him to where a boat was beached, on the lakeshore. Sitting him in the shade of a boulder, she pointed to the nearby hills and said, "The sleepers wish you to play dreams for them. Play now, while I go out in the boat."

He took up his harp, playing the strange melody she had heard so often in the last month. Somehow, hearing it strengthened her.

The boat was heavy, and smelled of fish. *I am sorry,* she thought to Connor the fisherman, *but I need it more than you.* Maire wrestled it across the gravel beach and into the water. Once water-borne it bobbed, light and at home. She waded out and climbed in.

She looked back once to where Tadhg sat playing the same melody over and over again. Already he was pale, greying like the rock. She took the oars and rowed.

Through the shallow water she could see pebbles gleaming on the brown lake-bottom; a few submerged logs lay massive and dead, but there was nothing she had not seen in other lakes and streams. Lough Neagh was the greatest lake in Ireland. It grew deeper, and the bottom disappeared. She rowed, and watched, and saw nothing.

She was far from shore, and the sun was warming her face and hands, when she heard a splash and saw a silver trout flash into the air. Not *a* trout; *the* trout, for its eyes were amber. It swam up to the side of the boat.

"Look back to shore, Maire," it said. "What do you see?"

She looked. "Nothing but the rocks and the trees," she said. "And a harp gleaming in the sun."

Tadhg was faded and gone.

"What do you hear, Maire?" asked the trout.

"Nothing but the wind in the trees, and the lapping water, and the music of a harp," she said.

The music stayed.

"Look into the lake, Maire," said the trout. "What see you there?"

She looked. Beneath her, in the depths—she had never seen such a palace. Not even the King of the Cruthini had buildings like this. It glowed with its own light, burning through the water, beckoning—

"Go to your husband, Maire," said the trout. "Go find him in the palace under the lake."

Maire looked at the breeze-ruffled water. The sun was high now, but she was cold. Her mantle would hamper her, and her belt was heavy with jewels. She unfastened her shoulder-brooch, folded her woolen mantle on the bottom of the boat, and laid her belt and sandals atop it. *Someone will find it,* she thought, *and know where I have gone. Will they think I drowned myself for shame?* She sat in her saffron linen gown, looking down into the water.

"Go," said the trout, as it swam away. Maire looked back once again to shore. Could she still see the harp gleaming in the sunlight, or was that a bright rock on the far beach? She pulled the oars into the boat, stood, shakily, and plunged overboard.

She had never swum; as the cold greenness covered her she choked and thrashed. The trout returned, then. "Do not struggle," it said. "Flow with the water, until the water is no more to you than the air."

Maire was already deep in the lake, too deep to reach the surface. Overhead the world of air gleamed far away. She gasped, and lakewater filled her lungs with burning pain. She tried to cough, to expel the water, but the trout hung before her, motionless, its gills waving. Maire looked down to the lake-bottom, to where the palace lay, and all of a sudden she was drifting like a snowflake, like a feather, and she no longer needed breath.

Slowly she sank through the waters of Lough Neagh; slowly the building became more distinct. The walls were like glass—not the wavy white-streaked glass of the High King's goblet, but as clear as the small patches through which one could see the wine.

The palace walls gleamed green and red and yellow. From nearby, golden-haired folk in rich garments looked up at Maire and laughed. The sound of their laughter was sharp and clear as bells.

She touched bottom beside the palace wall; behind was the lake-bottom of stones and weeds and logs. She struggled for footing, and her hair drifted upward in an unruly cloud. Here, beneath the lake, her dress was drab, and she herself felt plain and clumsy, though on land she was considered fair. But she was all too clearly human, and those who dwelt here were no kin to her. Ageless, unchanging, immortals, their faces pale, their eyes a milky blue, their forms clothed in moonlight and mist; she dared not look at them too closely, lest she forget why she had come, and even who she was. With eyes downcast she approached the palace.

In all the crowd of fairy-folk she did not see Tadhg; nor did she see any old ones to tell stories by the fire, or any young ones to listen. All were aged the same, and their age was no age, but ageless.

Maire stood on golden pavement by the palace. Green towers leapt upward, fairy-bells chiming on their tops; the music caught at her heart, and she knew how Tadhg had been trapped. Through small windows clouds of fish swam in and out. The palace had no entrance; the fairy-folk melted through its walls like ice in water.

As the last of the Sidhe entered, Maire tried to step through. The wall was solid. She stepped back, rubbing her nose. *Will they then refuse a guest?* she thought, and knocked. The sound was muffled, but in the wall a door swung open to a pearl-lined room, a giant mussel-shell. In one wall a streak of silver shone. Fish glittered overhead, and on the walls blue-lighted torches gleamed. Maire stepped inside, and the door swung shut and vanished. She stood within the curving shell-like room whose wall was broken by a silver door; the door opened at her touch. She stepped through it into a silver room where torches shone with ghastly light, and swarms of silver fish swam overhead. Set in the farthest wall, a golden door bedecked with eldritch symbols summoned her. Maire thought the carving might be words, but it was not the edge-notches of Ogham script; this writing moved and writhed across the golden surface as currents flow in water. Maire studied it, and felt it pulling her.

She woke with an effort. "Enough," she said. "Far have I travelled to be guested so. Is this the Good Folk's hospitality?" As she spoke she was afraid, for the golden door swung open into a green-lit hall, and in it were the Sídhe.

Though the great hall's roof arched high overhead, clear and green, those who sat at feasting were not dwarfed. Each pale face, every milk-blue eye in the company was turned toward

Maire. She felt more chilled than when she had first plunged into Lough Neagh. She dared not look on them, but dare she must.

The tables, laden with crystal fruits and glowing wine, stretched back toward the green-flamed fire. At the tables' head sat two who were crowned with stars. Around their necks were clasped gold collars like the one found in the bog. And behind them—

"What do you want here, woman?" It was the Queen who rose. Her gown was moonlight, her hair was morning, and her eyes were blue and terrible as a storm. "Why have you come?"

Laughter rippled round the table like a tide, though the faces did not smile. Hostile, or afraid? Maire spoke. "Queen of the Sídhe, I come to find Tadhg MacNiall, the harpist, my equal husband under Brehon Law."

The Queen set down her golden cup; the King leaned back in his chair, watching. The Queen's eyes were scalding milk, but her voice was honey. "Woman," she said, "is this your man?" She sat again, and gestured.

By the green-glowing fire sat Tadhg, playing a song. As he played, he sang.

> They rest after battle, cold silver in moonlight.
> The bright hills guard all of the bold ancient dreams.
> They will sleep through the ages, until in the dark night
> They wake, for their slumber is not what it seems.

Tadhg's voice was clear and true, and the Sídhe listened in silence.

"It is he," Maire said.

"And a fine harpist he is, to serve me," said the Queen. She smiled, and her pointed teeth gleamed like frost-spears on grass. "Come, little one, sit beside me for a time and enjoy the music."

Maire bowed, and walked toward the Queen. Her saffron dress was brown-streaked with mud, and she was coarse and human, but she had come too far for shame.

"Sit by me," said the Queen. She gestured, and a chair appeared. With one slim hand she pulled her gown aside, lest it be soiled. Maire sat and looked at Tadhg.

In the harpist's place of honor, he played his song for the

court. When the music came to a rest he looked at her, his eyes sleepy.

"A cup of wine?" said the Queen. As she spoke Tadhg turned to her, his eyes longing. The Queen smiled, poured wine, and handed it to Maire.

Tadhg's harp crashed to the floor, its chords crying. *"No!"* He reached out and dashed the cup from Maire's hand. The wine bled crimson on the tablecloth, and the Queen laughed.

Tadhg turned away from the fairy-woman. "Go, Maire, go while there is still time," he said. But as he spoke his gaze sought the Queen again. The wine had not touched her dress. The King was silent, still watching.

"And if I do not go?" said Maire.

"Then you are bound here forever, as am I." Tadhg looked at the lofty walls, at the gleaming floor, and once more at the Queen. The Queen's laughter echoed through the hall, mocking.

"My lady, forgive me. My wine has been spilled," said Maire. She held out her cup, but it was the King, not the Queen, who filled it. Maire looked at none of them until she had drunk it all. After that, she had nothing left to fear.

"Play, harpist," said the Queen. Her voice was a sigh. Tadhg picked up his harp and sang of moonlight on the hills and starlight on the lake, and the company was silent. Then, like the moon in clouds, they vanished, leaving only the green firelight to brighten the Great Hall. Maire and Tadhg were alone. The tables and dishes had vanished as well, and the empty hall was cavernous and cold.

"They come and go as they wish," said Tadhg. "Something caught their fancy; moonlight, stargleam, a passing breeze— who knows?" He set his harp on the floor and turned to face Maire, but he did not look at her, nor did he reach out to her. "Ill was the night I heard their music," he said, "and ill it was when you came after me, and drank their wine. Now you must stay as well." He picked up the harp again and stroked its strings. The chords echoed through the empty hall. Music always soothed him.

"Should I then have stayed without you," Maire said, "with the changeling they sent in your place, the poor mad driven thing? Or should I have divorced you, and you gone?"

"But you are trapped here now," said Tadhg, "and you have offended the Queen."

Maire made no reply. She had seen the Queen look at Tadhg, and he at the fairy-woman, she who was bright and ever young. She did not want to live without him; at his leaving the joy in life was gone. Now she had found him, but they were still apart, and trapped in this strange place. "I would like to see the palace," she said, "if I must indeed live here."

Tadhg smiled a little. "Come, then," he said. "It is all beauty." He took her hand and led her through the gleaming rooms.

Nothing here was twice the same, Maire saw; each chamber changed as they walked through, so when they turned it was all new again. There was no more permanence here than in rippling water or drifting clouds. She shivered; there was nothing to rely on, and it would be easy to get lost.

"How long has it been?" said Tadhg. They stood in a green-glass room; gold, purple, and amber ripples chased each other across its walls. Windows appeared and melted, doorways grew and shrank, and the floor was now gleaming metal, now pearl, now glass.

"It was a month since Beltane when I came," Maire said. "But here—" She looked at the ever-changing room. "Here, who knows how time passes?"

"There are no days or nights, no months or years," Tadhg said. "At the banquets no one goes hungry, yet no one is filled. They do not sleep, except to dream. Nothing changes, but nothing is ever the same."

High overhead bells rang, and a song floated down to them. "Their music," said Tadhg, and his voice was sick with longing. "If I could play and sing like that—"

"But they admire your own playing," Maire said. "Or the Queen does."

"I am a novelty," said Tadhg. "Perhaps they laugh at me."

Maire thought of the still white faces, and the silence. "No," she said, "they were not laughing. You speak to them."

"If so," said Tadhg, "I wonder what I say." The bells rang again, closer. He looked upward, his eyes alight with yearning. The Sídhe were coming back. He hurried to return to the Great Hall.

It was as if they had never gone. The great lords and ladies stood pale and slim, almost transparent, their blue-white eyes focused on nothing, their long slender hands clasped. But some sadness, Maire saw, had touched even them. The Queen whispered something about alien gods, then forced a laugh. The King, beside her, looked into the distance. "Play for us, harpist!" the Queen called. "Fill the hall with music!"

To crowd out what? Maire thought.

Tadhg stepped forward and played, but Maire saw the Lady from time to time lose her brilliant smile. At those times her pale hands gripped the arms of her chair, and she looked up toward the ceiling, toward the surface of the lake, where a dimness was spreading; then, quickly, she would look down again, as if afraid. "Play something merry," she commanded, and rose to dance. The company rose with her; around the chamber they danced, rising from the floor, whirling near the ceiling, and Tadhg played faster and faster, until the frenzied circle broke and, like thistledown, all drifted toward their places, whatever troubled them forgotten. Indeed, the dimness was gone.

There was much eating and drinking; Maire and Tadhg shared in the strange food that did not fill. Then, two by two, the company drifted off, until only four remained: Tadhg and Maire, the King and the Queen.

The Queen rose. "Go," she said. "Leave us." Maire wanted to protest, but found she could not speak. She looked toward Tadhg, but he avoided her eyes. The King and Queen sat rigid, waiting.

Maire left the green-lit chamber, headed she knew not where.

If I were on land I would train up soldiers to fight beside me, Maire thought, *and go forth to meet her in honest battle. But here I stand alone, no family, no clan, not even Tadhg.*

Her anger cooled. *He is enchanted, and cannot help himself.* Why then did she want to cry, and why did she wish she had never come to find him? *I am young, I have property, I could have divorced him and taken another. But it would not be the free marriage of equals, for I would not want another; I still want Tadhg.*

Her sight blurred; the rooms were shifting, always shifting, so that she stumbled blindly. Somehow she found the pearl anteroom, but the wall where the door had been was blank and solid. She had made her decision, and for her there could be no going home.

She turned and went back through the two doors, the silver and the golden, until she stood again in the Great Hall. The thrones were empty. The King and Queen and Tadhg were gone; where, she did not know. The palace walls rippled around her. Somewhere in those ever-changing chambers Tadhg was with the Queen, and for her there was no one. She could not bear to stay inside.

She ran through chambers of garnet and amethyst until at last she found a door that led, not to another room, but to an enclosed garden.

The plants that bloomed there chimed like bells, their leaves and flowers sharp and crystalline. Bright clouds of fish swam through the branches, avoiding the knifelike edges. Maire sat on a stone bench and watched the palace walls wavering—or was it the water-currents that shifted? The green light made everything unreal. She looked up to where the lake surface must be, but overhead the green glow faded to darkness. Had it been this dark before?

Through the dimness a glowing man-tall shape approached; she saw it was the King. He drew closer, and Maire stood in respect. He was, after all, a great lord. But the King, too, was looking at the darkness overhead.

When finally he looked at Maire, his eyes held sadness and some other thing. "You have travelled far, woman," he said. His voice was like the wind in the trees, bending all before it.

The words echoed. "Far . . . far . . . " Maire knew she was indeed a long way from the land of the living.

"Too far to come, to be left alone, and you so bold," said the King. He put out his hand and touched her shoulder.

"Alone . . . alone . . . " Indeed she was alone. Was the Lord of the Sídhe mocking her helplessness?

He towered over her, his eyes like mist and moonlight, mist that stole across her memory. She could not recall Tadhg's face. Instead she saw the Lord of the Sídhe, immeasurably aged, yet brilliant and undying, he who had the shape of a man, but was not human. He wore the gold collar of the barrow-folk, the ancient ones who now were memory. She knew he desired her, and she was lost. She opened her arms.

First he held her fiercely, and her body sang with joy. Then his cool white hands ran through her hair, his fingers caressed her face, his gentle lips touched her eyelids. He took the collar from his neck and placed it about hers. *Cold, dead*, a part of

her cried, then was still. His arm closed about her again. He
lifted her as if she were a cobweb and carried her into the
palace. She lay in his arms and forgot mortal men.

She walked dressed in moonlight, like a woman of the Sídhe,
though such gossamer made her mortal flesh seem dull. The
Queen saw her golden collar, and her eyes narrowed, but she
said nothing. Maire lived in a dream, though when the Sídhe
danced through the air she could not join them, and she could
never sit by the King's side. The Queen still sat beside him,
while Maire crouched at his feet, hoping for a glance.

When she looked at Tadhg he was nothing more than the
Queen's harpist, even when the ghostly company, bent on
other revelling, left them alone.

They sat once in the empty Great Hall, and Tadhg plucked
at the strings of his harp and sang.

> *The hills of this kingdom will bear no more battles,*
> *No more will the rivers run red to the sea,*
> *For the folk of the loughs and the hills in the moonlight*
> *Now dream in the arms of the Sidhe.*

Maire wondered, for a moment, of what folk Tadhg sang. She
remembered vaguely that they two had once lived on land, and
she had loved him, another human, as an equal, not adored
him as a god. She looked at him, bewildered; he stopped
singing and looked back at her. For a brief sharp moment she
remembered love, and pain; there had been a child, and after
that this man had walked the hills with her, sung to her,
brought her from darkness back to sunlight. The walls grew
dim. She tried to remember her fairy-lover, and for one cold
moment she could not. Tadhg, too, looked stunned, as if half-
awakened from a dream.

"How long has it been?" he whispered.

Maire shook her head; she did not know. But then she
sensed the fairy-host returning, and her memories faded into
adoration.

It was Maire who found the strangely-dressed child in the
garden. He sat with his hands folded, his feet together, his
small face pinched and still. Only his eyes moved, and they
followed every wall-ripple, every fish-flash.

Like a mouse, thought Maire, *afraid to move.* She circled to the front, not wishing to startle him; she stood a moment in his field of vision, then approached. He cringed, and put his hands up to shield his face.

"A greeting to you," said Maire, for even in her dream some part of her remembered children, and this boy looked no older than nine.

"You are not one of them," the child cried.

His speech was odd; Maire wondered if she might be forgetting human language. "That I am not," she said. "But I will gladly take you to them if you wish. What is your name, and how came you to this place?"

The child looked suspicious. "Would you be a Scot, then? You do not talk like me."

"I am of this very land," said Maire. "If we speak slowly, perhaps we can understand each other."

"Would you be a Protestant, then?" The boy looked frightened, and began to edge away.

"Child," said Maire, "I am not understanding half your words."

"Is there anyone," he said, "that does not know of the killing and burning and shooting done by Cromwell's men?"

Maire shook her head. "I know of no such thing," she said. "I came in time of peace. Are the Cruthini attacked? How came you here? Who is High King now? Reigns he in Emain Macha, Cashell, or Tara? And where are your people?"

The child began to cry again. "There is no High King in Ireland, and my people starve on the roads and are slaughtered by Cromwell. I have no people left." He could say nothing more, but wept.

"Come," said Maire, "I will take you to the folk of the palace."

The boy stopped sobbing and stood, but he would not take her hand. "What kind of flower is this?" He touched one of the crystal blooms; it shattered, cutting his fingers. A small curl of blood eddied out, darkening the green twilight. He watched it in silence.

Maire led him indoors, and the Sídhe took him to themselves. When Maire asked, they would not tell her what the child's words signified.

The boy sat always in the hall and was made much over; he spoke little to Tadhg or Maire. It was as if he wished to forget he was human, though he, too, was left behind when the Sídhe danced their wild dances, or vanished. At those times he would sit, small and lost, until they returned.

Tadhg and Maire, ensorcelled, paid him little heed, though something in Maire yet reached out to him when she was not bedazzled by the King.

As the twilight grew slowly darker, the Sídhe went less often to the lakeshore. When they did go they returned, not star-sparkled, but dimmed somehow, and faded. Even the King grew grey, and Maire began to realize that time and change were passing overhead.

It happened when they sat in the Great Hall. Tadhg was playing the harp to a silent company. The darkness thickened, and a thin crimson tendril curled through a window to twist across the ceiling. Harpsong died; the Sídhe covered their ears as if to block out screams.

The Queen snapped the stem of her golden goblet. In a moment the metal sprang together, mended, but its shape was distorted, its shining surface marred. The company froze, watching as more tendrils writhed across the ceiling. At last Maire saw the source of the growing darkness. She threw herself before the King, pleading, "What is it, lord?"

He stared upward. When finally he looked at her his misty eyes were blank. "Blood," he said.

The child screamed and ran for the Queen's lap; she stroked him absently, watching the stain spread across the crystal ceiling. Where it touched the clouds of fish they shuddered away.

Maire studied the inhuman faces. Was it fear she saw there, or sorrow, or some nameless alien emotion? Their milky eyes were wide, and their gleaming features became pale masks. Enchantment was fading.

Maire and Tadhg looked at each other, and at the swirling crimson stain. It was Tadhg who spoke first. "What is happening?" His eyes were bright, no longer dreamy. He sprang to his feet, and his golden harp fell to the floor. It made no sound.

Maire realized she was lying on the floor. *Why?* She rose to her feet, looking at him who sat the throne. He was pale and fading now. She shivered. Was this water that surrounded her? The company was shadowy as ghosts. Where was their merriment, their endless joy?

Tadhg spoke. "It was not a dream, then. The stories were true—I was—I have been—" He turned toward the throne, where the Queen sat frozen, the child in her lap. "I loved—"

"I know," said Maire, looking at the King. "I know." She felt the collar on her neck, heavy and cold. *Barrow-treasure!* She flung it from her, trembling.

Tadhg and Maire touched; their hands were warm human flesh. They felt cold water-currents against their skin.

"All is fading, all is gone," said Tadhg. "And only we are left."

From the throne the King spoke. His voice was weak. "This will be the end of all we knew. Hatred has poisoned the land, and magic is dying."

The ceiling was bloodier now, and the tendrils were descending. "Is there then nothing you can do?" said Maire. Her flesh was solid still, as was Tadhg's and the child's. "You are fading, but we remain. Return us to our people and let us live again."

"Your people are gone," said the Queen. "The world is different now."

"But it is our world yet, and we are yet human. Must we die down here, helpless before that?" Tadhg pointed to the blood. "Whatever else happens, music still lives."

"As does healing," said Maire. Her hands had done no work for many years; she wanted toil again, even fatigue. She was free of enchantment, and she should be triumphant, but she considered the pale company, the choking crimson cloud, and instead she pitied them. Even the Queen. "Release us; we will see what we can do."

The faces of the King and Queen were sad and strange. "You are free, then, both of you," said the Queen. She held the child close, then glanced upward again and shuddered. The King touched her hand; for the first time in aeons, their slim white fingers interlaced.

"What is done cannot be undone," the King said. "But you are free. You may return to whatever you find—" he hesitated, "up there." He said to the Queen, "The boy is human too. Send him with them."

"No," the Queen said fiercely. "Let him decide. He came to us for refuge from his world." She smoothed his hair and said, "Open your eyes, little one. Which do you choose?"

"You can come home with us," Maire said.

The child shook his head. "No. I have no home but here, no folk but these."

"If you stay, child," said the King, "we cannot know—" He looked up again at the spreading stain. "The land is in torment. How can you humans live, knowing always you will die?" He was almost transparent now. "You belong with your own people, child."

The boy clung to the Queen. "*You* are my people. I will never go back to that."

"He has decided," said the Queen. Somehow she looked glad. "But we cannot hold you two here longer." She beckoned Tadhg; slowly he approached. "I give you the Sight," she said, touching his eyelids, "and the Understanding." She placed one hand on his forehead. Lastly she leaned forward and kissed him; he drew back. "And I give to you the Speech. Music I cannot give you, for that you always had."

The King beckoned Maire. She stepped toward him and noticed the golden collar on the floor. She picked it up.

"A parting gift," he said. "The Sight, the Understanding, and the Speech." He kissed her; the touch of his lips was cold, and he was nothing to her now. She held out the collar.

"I will return your other gift," she said. He did not reach out for it; she placed it on his lap and watched as it sank through him, as if he were nothing but water. She stepped back beside her husband. "We are free to go?" she said. The royal pair nodded, and Tadhg and Maire walked swiftly from the hall. Maire looked back once, at the child. The Sídhe were almost invisible; the boy sat with his eyes closed.

Out through the gold door into the silver room, and through the silver door into the pearl room, until the wall opened for them and they stepped outside. The pavement was tarnished, and the palace no longer glowed. The water was very cold now, and they felt the need to breathe. In the distance Maire saw a flash of silver.

"My harp," said Tadhg. "I forgot my harp." His hands hung empty at his sides.

"We have no time," said Maire. The silver flash drew closer. It was the trout, its eyes shining amber. It turned and flicked toward the surface. Tadhg and Maire felt themselves drawn after it, and suddenly they were swimming, rising to the surface from deep water, their lungs bursting. The trout led

them onward, giving them strength, until at the last moment
before they would have to breathe water and drown they
broke surface into a half-cloudy night.

Gasping and air-starved, they floundered.

"Ho! Who's there?" They heard the splashing of oars. A
brilliant light swept the water like a wand and came to rest on
their faces. "What are ye' doing out here, so far from land?"
a voice said. "Like to drown, ye are. Here, hold on to the
side."

They clung to the wooden boat; it rocked. "Come on,
now," the man said. "Ladies first." He pulled Maire into the
boat. "Well, it's not dressed for company ye be, either," he
said. "Have ye no shame at all?" He took off a rough wool
jacket and handed it to her. "Cover yerself, girl."

"An' now you, young fellow." He helped Tadhg aboard
and looked at him. "Another one? A pretty pair ye are,
the both of ye. Wha' happen, then? Swamp yer boat?" He
skimmed the light along the lake surface. "Ye must ha' sunk
it. Luck for you I came along."

Tadhg and Maire sat in the boat, still gasping.

"Quiet, aren't ye? Ah!" The man set down the light and
reached for a pole propped under the seat; the end was bobbing and jerking. "Think I got somethin' at last. Besides fool
swimmers, that is." He reeled in the line. At the end of it,
fighting for its life, was a trout—a fish whose eyes glowed
amber, even in the darkness. "Ah, a fine large one, too." The
man began to reel in the line.

"No!" said Tadhg. "Let it live!" He reached out; his
strong hands snapped the line. The trout vanished into the
deep.

"So what possessed ye to do that?" the man said. "A fine
fish he was, and fine thanks I'm gettin' for fishin' ye out." He
shipped the oars and doubled up his fist. In the distance there
was a roar and a dull-red flash.

"They're at it agin, the bloody IRA bastards," the man
said. He picked up the oars, rowing with long, angry strokes.
"Blew off me brother's leg, and he going to post letters. All
through the War, and he buys it right in front of his own
house with a bloody car-bomb." He stopped rowing and
looked at them, suspicious. "And where would you two be
from, traipsin' shamelessly about this time of night?"

Maire cleared her throat. "Here." The word was strange on

her tongue. "We've lived here a long time." She wondered how long.

"Never seen ye before, wench," the man said. "Yer no decent Antrim woman. Sure you dinna come up from the Republic to make trouble?"

Tadhg leaned forward. "Truly, we are not understanding you," he said. "You can see I am a harpist, not a warrior." He held out his hands; the fingernails were long, and only the fingertips were calloused. "Do these hands wield swords, or drive horses?"

The man shook his head. "Swords and horses? It's daft ye both are, or drunken, and that's for sure. I shouldna fished ye out o' the lake." He rowed again toward shore.

Far in the distance there was a rattling noise. "They're shooting now, the bastards," the man said. "Hope it's them, not us, gets hit." The boat scraped on stones. "It's been a bad week. Out wi' ye. They'll be needin' me at home. The wife takes fright, these days."

Maire and Tadhg helped him drag the boat on shore. They stood at last on dry ground.

"Keep the jacket, Miss," the man said. "Ye need it for decency." He walked away, his boots scrunching on the stones. Tadhg and Maire watched him go. As clearly as they saw him, with the new Sight they saw the land. Wounded by war, weakened by famine, burned by hatred, the land lay before them, sick, old, and in pain.

They knew then why the Sídhe grew pale and weak. In the distance was another rattle of sound. Suddenly Maire understood what the child had meant when he spoke of shooting.

"Is everything gone, Tadhg?" she whispered in the Old Speech. "The land has the wasting illness; I can hear it cry in pain."

Tadhg was looking farther up the beach. Maire, too, looked and saw something gleaming there. Tadhg went to pick it up. It was his harp, not the golden harp he had played for the Sídhe, but his brass-stringed willow harp of old. It had hidden there, waiting through the years. He strummed a few chords.

If Ulster's old memories sleep in the moonlight
And, faded like phantoms, the Sídhe walk no
*   more—*

● ● ●

He stopped singing and looked out over the empty moonlit water. "The trout lives, but the trees are gone from the hills, and evil memories walk the land."

"Yet we have the Sight, and the Understanding, and the Speech," said Maire. "Perhaps we can put the hatred to rest, to dream under the hills with the other ancient things."

Tadhg plucked a few strings on his harp. The music was clear, and a few dark clouds fled the moon. "Perhaps." He slung the harp over his back.

The harpist and the healer set forth toward the darkened hills.

The Snow Fairy

By M. Lucie Chin

In the last month of the year, when the dragons have retreated beneath the seas, the handle of the "Drinking Gourd" points toward winter and the sky becomes heavy with clouds dark as rust. Then the fairy Chou Ch'ung-i, whom the Heavenly Jade Emperor placed in charge of Hibiscus Village, home of the fairies and lowly Earth spirits, summons those of her subjects in charge of winter. They leave their caves and dwelling places and dutifully gather at the great hall of her mansion in the center of the village.

The white tiger of the winter wind appears from his lair. The Fairy of One Hundred Flowers presents the spirits under her care; Wintersweet and Plum Blossom and all the others who will bloom before spring comes. The Fairy of One Hundred Trees brings the spirits of the evergreens. The Frost Fairy and the Lady of the Winter Moon present themselves as do the fairies Tung Shuang-ch'eng, keeper of the crystal Snow-vase, and the Fairy of Ku-She, keeper of the Golden Chopsticks. These two appear riding upon the White Mule which is the spirit of snow.

When the summons is received, all the fairies so called don their finest clothes and ornaments and prepare to leave their caves and homes bearing small gifts as tokens of respect, for Chou Ch'ung-i is the greatest fairy of all. She alone must answer to the Heavenly Jade Emperor for the conduct of her subjects, and it is she who decides where and when and how much of the efforts of the lesser fairies must be applied to the world of Men.

In the great hall, Chou Ch'ung-i receives her subjects who perform obeisances, swear allegiance to the Heavenly Jade Emperor and present their tokens. Chou Ch'ung-i instructs them in their duties to the Emperor and their responsibilities for the coming winter. The formality is observed with all due pomp and ceremony. She tells each how he or she must prepare for the coming season and gives her written order to those whose duties commence most immediately. Then all withdraw to a fine and sumptuous banquet where they sit feasting and drinking, talking and playing games, dancing and singing for the amusement of their hostess for a day and a night. At the rise of the next dawn they withdraw to their proper places to prepare for the winter now at hand.

The winter tiger walks the earth and cold winds rattle the bamboo and freeze the water in the buffalo wallows. The fairies of One Hundred Trees, One Hundred Grasses, One Hundred Plants and so on, call home the spirits of summer and growing things, and the land becomes brown and withered. Leaves fall and nothing new is born in the earth. Then the Fairy of Frost walks the land by night, chasing after the Lady of the Winter Moon, and soon becomes bold once more and sports about over fields and lakes and through the streets of towns in the day as well.

It is then that Chou Ch'ung-i summons Tung Shuang-ch'eng and the Fairy of Ku-She. They appear before her with the crystal Snow-vase and the Golden Chopsticks and are instructed in the placement and amount of the year's first snowfall. For every flake Ku-She removes from the crystal vase with her Golden Chopsticks a foot of snow will fall upon the earth. If Ku-She drops the flake delicately from atop a cloud the snowfall will be gentle, the snow fluffy, soft and beautiful. If several flakes are given to the white tiger to be carried to earth in his mouth there will be a fierce blizzard with great winds and bitter cold. Tung Shuang-ch'eng must guard the vase carefully lest it become broken or overturned, for then the world below would be buried in snow nearly to the height of Heaven itself and mankind would be in danger of perishing.

In the spring Chou Ch'ung-i calls them all together once more and reads a message from the Heavenly Jade Emperor himself, remarking on their conduct in the performance of their tasks, praising or admonishing as necessary and granting them release from their duties. Once more a feast is held and the fairies of winter go home to rest. Tung Shuang-ch'eng and the Fairy of Ku-She return to their snug cave and the crystal Snow-vase and the Golden Chopsticks are put safely away.

It came about one fine morning in early summer that a youth appeared at the gate before the caves of the two fairies of the snow and announced that Tung Shuang-ch'eng and Ku-She were summoned to appear before Chou Ch'ung-i at once.

Lady Tung and Lady Ku-She dressed quickly in summer gauze and lightest silks. Powdered and rouged, jeweled only with earrings of white jade and slim golden hairpins hanging with tiny golden snowflakes, they set out for the great house of Madam Chou. Each carried a box filled with light summer tea cakes and, in case it should be required, the scroll with the new snowflakes designed for the coming year.

When they were ushered into Madam Chou's presence they found she was not alone. Seated beneath an awning of palest green silk was a man who appeared to be of middle years with the bearing of a great nobleman. He was dressed in gold mail over a tunic and skirt of blue brocade embroidered with fish and sea serpents, and all about the hem the ocean waves rolled and crested, row upon row. His coat was all the colors of the rainbow, richly embroidered with patterns of clouds and waves and, worked as a series of medallions, the crest of the Dragon King of the Northwest.

Lady Tung and Lady Ku-She recognized the emissary of the Lung Wang at once and prostrated themselves, knocking their heads upon the ground seven times in a gesture of respect. Chou Ch'ung-i bid them rise and presented them to the emissary as tea was served. Both Tung Shuang-ch'eng and Ku-She knew, of course, why he had come, but it would not have been polite to say so.

Lady Tung bowed politely and began. "You honor us beyond measure by this audience, my lord. To what do we, your humble servants, owe the priceless treasure of your visit?"

The emissary was pleased by their humility as well as by their beauty and would have liked nothing better than to sit and exchange pleasantries but today he was not in a position to do so.

"My Lord, the Lung Wang, desires your services as you must no doubt realize. As occasionally happens, the thaw in the Northwestern mountains was unusually thorough this spring. Even the tops of the greatest peaks in the country are nearly bare of snow now, a fact which distresses my master greatly. Because of this depleted condition there is not enough moisture in the high heavens for the proper manufacture of clouds. Rising vapors from the lakes and oceans have not been as abundant as in most spring seasons and have only contributed sufficient moisture for lower level clouds and light rains. The great storm clouds must draw their moisture from both the landbound bodies of water and the vast snow caps of the highest peaks together. The Lung Wang is concerned that there is already too little moisture in the high ranges to prevent drought by the late summer. He has, therefore, petitioned the Heavenly Jade Emperor for an increase of twelve feet of snow in the Northwestern mountains within the month and the Emperor has so commanded."

So saying, the emissary took from his sleeve a scroll sealed with the huge jade and gold seal of the Emperor of Heaven himself which he handed to Chou with a bow.

Madam Chou, who was used to dealing with seasonal anomalies at the request of one major deity or another, opened the scroll with no more formality than was due, read it briefly, called for her own writing implements and set down an order for twelve feet of snow to fall upon a strictly prescribed area and only above a carefully defined altitude before the full of the next moon. Upon this document she affixed her own personal seal and handed the scroll to the two snow fairies.

Content that his master's interests were satisfactorily in hand, the emissary of the Lung Wang took his leave, having much other business of a pressing nature to accomplish before the day was out.

The fairies returned home to prepare for the journey, but later in the day, as Tung Shuang-ch'eng was overseeing the grooming of the White Mule, the Fairy of Ku-She came running to her side greatly distraught. Her hair was disheveled and her gown undone. She was obviously in a high state of anxiety and on the verge of tears.

"Oh, Sister, Sister," she pleaded. "You must come with me at once. Something terrible has happened!"

Ku-She ran through the halls of the cavern to her own

chamber where she collapsed upon her couch sobbing.

"Ku-She!" Lady Tung said sternly, partly distressed for her friend's difficulty and partly annoyed at such irrational behavior, "You must tell me what has happened or we can not decide how to remedy it. Stop crying and talk to me."

"Oh, Sister, it is the worst thing that could possibly happen and I am done for!"

Tung Shuang-ch'eng was exasperated. "This is utter nonsense," she said. "There is only one thing which could be that bad and . . ." Lady Tung abruptly stopped speaking and sat upon the couch next to Ku-She. "The Golden Chopsticks?" she said. "What has happened, Little Sister?"

Ku-She huddled against the cushions, hugging herself, looking bleak. "They are missing," she said in a very tiny voice.

Tung Shuang-ch'eng nodded. Indeed, to lose that which was in one's charge was the worst fate that could befall an elemental guardian, and Ku-She's tears were not unjustified. "How, Little Sister?" she asked gently, stroking Ku-She's hair, hoping to calm if not quite to comfort her companion.

"If only I knew. The chest is here by my couch and, until a moment ago, was still locked. I undid the latch myself. Inside, the satin cushions and the silken bag were all in place, undisturbed, exactly as I had arranged them on the last day of our service. The chest *was still locked*, but the Chopsticks are gone!"

As she spoke Ku-She sat clutching the key about her neck. All fairies whose duty included the care of an artifact wore such a key. It was suspended upon a chain of gold and silver. It had no catch and was not sufficiently long to allow it to be removed over the head.

Without thinking, as she listened to Ku-She's words, Tung Shuang-ch'eng also stroked the little key about her own neck. Then suddenly a single thought entered both minds and the two women ran from the chamber to look in the casket where Tung kept the crystal Snow-vase. With great relief they found it in place and unharmed.

"It is safe," Ku-She sighed, "but perhaps only for the moment. Whatever magic has stolen my Golden Chopsticks could surely also be used against the Snow-vase or any other object in a fairy's charge. What can we do?"

"We must go to Madam Chou at once," Tung Shuang-ch'eng said, locking the casket again. "We must tell her what has happened and beg her forgiveness for the poor quality of our guardianship. I will ask that the crystal Snow-vase and all the other fairy objects be kept safely in a guarded room in her palace for the time being and you must promise to find the Golden Chopsticks and their thief."

As Lady Tung lifted the casket and stood to go, Ku-She collapsed in a heap and looked as bleak as before. The strength of what, for a short while, had seemed to be a common problem had deserted her entirely and she sat on the floor shaking.

Lady Tung put down her burden and sat on the floor also. "Have courage, Little Sister," she said. "All is not lost. You have a month to carry out the search before any but Madam Chou and those few who must place their tools in her care must know. And an entire summer before our season of duty comes. Much can be done in that time. We will all help as much as we can."

"The great dragons are not known for their patience," Ku-She said. "And Madam Chou will be furious with me. It would be only right if I were to be banished from the Village forever."

"That will not return the Golden Chopsticks," Lady Tung said. "It is up to you to do that and if you succeed, no one can find fault with you."

"But if I do *not* . . . "

"Then you are no worse off than you are now. But if you apply yourself diligently in your search, even though you fail, your punishment could not help but be tempered by the sincerity of your effort. You must go, Ku-She."

"Yes," Ku-She replied, drying her eyes and sitting more erect. "You are right. I have no choice and it is my duty, but . . . if only I knew where to start."

Tung Shuang-ch'eng rose and lifted her casket once more. "In the Great Hall of Hibiscus Village. Once we have informed Chou Ch'ung-i of the dilemma, and you have shown a proper respect for your position and fault, we may seek her aid and council. She knows much of the ways of the gods and the world of men and it is to her advantage to help us since the Heavenly Jade Emperor will not hold her blameless for the conduct of her inferiors.

"Take heart, Little Sister. There is much to be done before failure becomes inevitable."

•   •   •

Madam Chou was not pleased, but neither was she as surprised as they had expected her to be.

"Taoist magic," she muttered into her fan. "I should have petitioned the Jade Emperor ages ago and had that fellow struck down by a dragon."

Astonished, Ku-She raised her head from the floor and stared. "You know the thief?" she exclaimed, then remembered herself and ducked her head again as Madam Chou's gaze shifted to her.

"I know of a likely suspect," she said, and her voice sounded stiff with annoyance. "A great many years ago by the lives of mortal men, our Village was accidentally discovered by a Taoist monk. As you may recall this sort of thing happens from time to time. Such events are rare, but till now, none has ever found us a second time, for, with respect to the world of men, we do not exist in any specific place. This monk was a particular nuisance and swore to me that he could find the Village whenever he wished; that he could come and go at will, unstopped and even unseen, and that he could take whatever he desired by way of proof."

"Then *surely* it is he!" Ku-She cried to the tiles beneath her nose.

"Ku-She!" Tung Shuang-ch'eng whispered. "Shhhh!"

"Nothing is certain," Chou said sternly. "Nor will your task be simple because you have the man's name. You must still find him and retrieve the Chopsticks.

"Go now, Ku-She, and prepare for your journey. Take nothing with you save what is absolutely necessary. You may take one servant, but Tung and the White Mule must stay here. Shortly I will send a servant to you with the name of the monk and what little we know of him. You must seek him as best you can, and quickly, but take care; there are many dangers in the world."

"Madam," Ku-She said, "Will I be mortal in the world of man or will I still have all my fairy powers?"

"You will be more than they are but less than you have been. How much so I do not know, but it is one of the consequences of walking among them in their own world. Were we gods it would not matter, but we are merely fairies and in some ways the Taoist magic may prove stronger than our own."

•   •   •

At dawn the next day, Ku-She bid Tung and all her other "Sisters of the Winter" farewell and set out from the cave to find most of the principal fairies of Spring, Summer and Autumn awaiting her at the gate.

"Do not fear, Little Sister," said the Fairy of One Hundred Trees. "Our spirits are everywhere in the world below, especially now that it is full summer. We will watch over you and aid you as best we can should you be in peril."

Ku-She thanked them sincerely, though she knew she must do this task alone. Then she set off into the hills with one serving maid following behind and two small bundles, neatly packed and hung on a yoke.

First she traveled to the underworld and sought an audience with the judges of the Court of Death. The monk, Wei Pan Ch'ao, had been by all accounts, an audacious man who had learned much of magic and especially longevity, but he was uncommonly fond of a good prank.

Ku-She had brought gifts, and the First Judge was very helpful.

"This monk you seek is well known to us, Little Fairy," he said. "Wei Pan Ch'ao has cheated death more times than I can recall. He is regularly on the roll of those to be summoned to court, and yet he always finds a way to avoid his fate. He is due to be summoned again in two months' time and once again I expect he will have a reprieve. Have you, perhaps, some means by which we may keep him at last?"

Ku-She bowed her head sadly. "No, Your Honor," she said, "I have nothing, and I cannot wait two months."

"Then neither of us can be of service to the other, as he can not be summoned earlier without some cause. You must seek him among the living, Little Fairy."

"Yes, Your Honor," Ku-She said, bowing deeply before the assembled judges. "But as this monk is a nuisance and a bother to find constantly upon your rolls, and as this unworthy slave will be in the world of men, it is not entirely unlikely that she may find something of use to you. I therefore humbly beg your indulgence and ask if you could but tell me where in the world I might seek him."

The judges thought for a moment and conferred among themselves. Ku-She stood still as stone and barely dared to breathe. At last the First Judge took up his brush and ink and, with a quick flourish, set down a neat row of characters.

"This is the province in which he is currently traveling," he said, handing her the note. "More than that I can not tell you. In two months' time we will know his location exactly, but for now this is all we can do for you. You must find him yourself."

Ku-She thanked them profusely, performed a great many kowtows and took her leave, finally emerging into the mortal world with her maid servant following closely at her heels.

The day had been long and hot and not at all fruitful. The two peasant women walking along the side of the road carried a sheaf over each shoulder and a small bundle in one hand. The sun was setting but they turned from the road and walked toward a large grove of catalpa trees some distance across a meadow instead of traveling the four li to the village ahead, a thing to be greatly wondered at had anyone been about to see. But they had been sure that no one would see. For women to travel alone on the open road was unusual enough. Taking the sheaves to market was a barely sufficient excuse, but to be found camping by the roadside was not only shocking, it was dangerous. That was unimportant, however, compared to the task they faced. Thus they had lived for a month and an end was nowhere in sight.

Neither woman was old, but one was clearly younger than the other. At once the younger set about making a comfortable place of repose within the grove, loosening the sheaves and arranging them so as to provide a place to sit and later serve to cushion their sleep. As darkness settled into the grove they built a tiny fire, sheltered from sight of the road by the thick trunk of an old tree, and there they settled in to quietly await another day.

From the little bundle she had carried the young maid produced a kettle which she placed upon a flat rock at the fire's edge. As she reached into the pack again and withdrew a pair of fine and delicate porcelain tea cups, the kettle began to boil at once, though she had fetched no water. She next removed a small lacquered box which contained a number of various tea cakes. She placed the box before her companion and poured the tea, sitting patiently to one side, waiting for the other to begin. They ate and drank their fill and the kettle remained warm and brimming and the contents of the little box never diminished.

When she had finished eating, the little maid reached into the bundle once more and withdrew a comb of ivory and gold and a tiny alabaster jar filled with scented oil. Settling down behind her companion, she undid the untidy knot of hair at the back of her neck and began to carefully comb out the bits of debris which had caught there. She oiled the ends of the long, night-black hair and did it up again in an elegant coil held in place with silver pins and clips.

While the maid worked her mistress gazed up into the night sky at the stars, bright among the dark branches, winking in and out as the warm breeze ruffled the leaves overhead. The moon was already up. It looked like a fat pearl, softly glowing like dragon fire. Ah, the dragons. The Lung Wang . . . in spite of the warmth of the night, Ku-She shivered at the thought. The little maid mistook the gesture, thinking she had caused her mistress pain.

"Forgive me, my lady," she said urgently, "I did not mean . . . "

"Hush, child," Ku-She said, patting her maid's knee. "It is not you. You have served me well and I am well pleased at my choice of you." Ku-She looked up into the sky once more. "In four nights' time the moon will be full and we have not yet accomplished our task. I fear the wrath of the dragons, but even more I fear the displeasure of the Emperor of Heaven, for he may find fault with Chou Ch'ung-i and all of Hibiscus Village on my account."

"Tomorrow, my lady," the maid said boldly. "The old men in the market felt sure we would find him in the city, and we will be there by noon easily."

"Yes, little one," Ku-She said. "Perhaps. But to find him is one thing. To get from him that which he has stolen is another. I have no idea how I may go about it."

The maid slid the last of the pins into her lady's hair and went to the tea kettle which grew warm again as she held it in her hands. "Have faith, my lady," she said. "When the time comes, you will surely know what to do."

At dawn the maid was up and tending to her lady's toilet. She dressed Ku-She's hair in the high and elegant style of a married woman of wealth, adorned with clips of gold and pins of silver hung with amythest and crystal. From the pack she drew forth a traveling gown of summer gauze and cloud-light silk,

richly embroidered with flowers and a loose linen coat of deep
green worked with flocks of birds and banks of chrysanthe-
mums.

The maid unrolled the tight bundles and with a slight shake
all the wrinkles fell away. Thus garbed, with jade and pearls
about her neck and gold upon her fingers, Ku-She bid her
maid be off and settled down to wait in the grove which had
suddenly grown dense and impenetrable with tall thick stalks
of bamboo.

In good time the maid returned along the road upon a litter
she had rented in the town.

"There," she said, pointing across the fields to the grove,
once more free of its bamboo fortress. "My lady awaits
within."

The litter bearers settled Ku-She among the cushions, ex-
pressing their condolences that her coachman had been such a
scoundrel as to run off with the coach and all her baggage
while she took her rest in the shade, and swearing that they
were no such rascals and that they would remove her to the
city with all due haste and great care.

Ku-She smiled into her fan and shortly they had entered the
gates of the town. She instructed the litter bearers to take her
to the best tea house in the city where she took a small private
room at the front of the second floor from which she could
watch the street from behind a balcony screen, and once more
sent the maid out into the town in search of Wei Pan Ch'ao.
While the maid searched, Ku-She, with the aid of three gold
rings from her own fingers, procured the aid of the tea house
owner to enquire of his customers who might know of the man
she sought.

Near evening, the little maid returned, a flush upon her
cheeks and a glow in her dark eyes. She immediately cast
herself upon the floor at Ku-She's feet and performed numerous kowtows, talking all the while.

"Lady," she said, "I have failed to find the one we seek; indeed, I believe he is no longer within the city walls, but I have
other news of him which may please you well enough to
forgive my clumsy and fruitless efforts."

"Rise," Ku-She said. "Your bobbing up and down dizzies
me. Speak quickly and plainly, child, for this waiting about all
day has sorely tired my nerves."

The maid sat on the mat at her mistress's feet and did not

trouble with an account of the day but went straight about her news.

"I do not know for a fact that he is not here, but those who knew of him believe him to have gone two days ago. None has seen him for that time. But there is more.

"While he was here he lodged at the house of a young scholar. The youth is of independent means, though modest ones, and is without family, save a sister, newly married. He has a small house in Black Lotus Street and it is there Wei Pan Ch'ao was lodged for a week. The monk is said to be the young man's uncle, though some say Wei Pan Ch'ao is of great age and several generations separate that kinship.

"It is also said that the young man, whose name is Wei K'e-yung, has only recently passed the Imperial Examinations with the highest of honors and that, on behalf of this achievement, Wei Pan Ch'ao bestowed upon his 'nephew' a fine and glorious gift, fit even for the Emperor himself."

Ku-She's eyes brightened and the maid looked up in excitement. "Surely it must be what we seek. I can not imagine one such as he with possessions of any value, save what he stole from you.

"Perhaps he knows we seek him and has left them behind to try to confound us."

"As this generosity does not seem to be a deep secret," said Ku-She, "it is more likely that he has simply tired of carrying them."

"I do not know the nature of the gift," the maid said. "That particular I could not discover, but . . ."

"It is enough," Ku-She said, settling back upon her cushions and sipping at her tea. "It was well done, and I agree, the gift could be little else but what we seek."

The maid accepted a cup of tea from Ku-She's own hand and trembled slightly with joy and relief until she noticed the shadow of melancholy still clinging to her mistress's eyes.

"Now," Ku-She said quietly, "it remains for me to know how I will rescue them from him."

Very early the next morning an old woman made her way slowly down Black Lotus Street to the gate of a modest house. A servant answered her knock and she enquired if this was the home of the scholar Wei K'e-yung. When the boy allowed that it was she announced herself to be Madam Feng who, because of her wisdom and skill in such matters, had been employed as go-between on behalf of a lady of means, and therefore had an arrangement of considerable merit to discuss with the master.

Astonished, the boy hurried off into the house but returned almost at once, bowing and very careful of his manners, and showed the old lady into the main hall where he offered her tea and cakes till his master, who had been still asleep, could make himself presentable and come to her himself.

She acknowledged this with a curt nod but accepted only tea and looked about the room with a sharp and critical eye.

Presently a tall, slender young man entered the room, quiet and unhurried but polite. He wore the blue robe of a scholar of the First Rank but informally, without hat and bound only with a simple sash. His hair was dressed neatly in a modest style and his demeanor was entirely that of a serious student without airs or pretentions above his station. When Madam Feng saw him she drew a quick breath and all the sharpness went out of her look, for the grace and charm of his person were considerable and his beauty was astonishing. They exchanged formal salutations and the matchmaker began the business at hand.

"Young sir," she said, "as you have no living parents nor older brothers I have come directly to you on a matter of great delicacy, one I think you will find of great advantage to you. I have taken on this employment on behalf of a Madam Ku who is herself a widow with no living relatives of either her husband's or her own. She has no children and is still quite young and, due to the circumstances of her husband's death, possessed of considerable wealth. It is not unusual for a woman in such a position, particularly one of such rare beauty as Madam Ku's, to find her virtue assailed from all sides by schemers and fortune hunters, and though she remains chaste and devoted to her husband even in the Land of the Dead, she feels it would be most wise to ensure the safety of her fortune and the perfection of her reputation against even the *possibility* of foul lies by seeking an honorable marriage with a man of unquestionable principal and talent. Since her husband was nearly forty years her senior, she feels it would be unwise to seek someone who might once again leave her estate unprotected while she is still too young to be unreproachable. Her wealth and position make a marriage as Second Wife unsuitable. Therefore she has set me the task of finding a young bachelor of proper station and skills.

"You, sir, are a most favorable candidate. For, though your means are hardly worth considering, your reputation is exceptional and your success in the recent Imperial Examinations promises much for your career in the Emperor's service. Furthermore, the lady herself has expressed a desire that I investigate your suitability as she feels you would make a good match if my enquiry proves fruitful and you yourself are willing."

Wei K'e-yung was somewhat taken aback by her forthright speech. It was a boldness he was not accustomed to in women and which would have been unacceptable from any but a professional go-between. But he listened to what she had said and realized that Fortune had, indeed, smiled upon him. Yet he was not at ease.

"Mistress Feng," he said, "I am humbled by the generosity of this offer and feel myself to be most unworthy of such a match...."

"Do not reject this match too hastily, young scholar. Further inquiry on both sides can only be of benefit right now."

Wei K'e-yung agreed and a series of formal questions were posed by both parties. Madam Feng examined him closely about the source and extent of his income, his lineage as well as the tutors who had instructed him in the classics. Finally the old woman said, "Since you qualified so highly in the Imperial Examinations why have you not been given an official post?"

"A position as First Secretary to the District Magistrate of Lanchow was offered to me. A very important district and a fine post for a first appointment, but I felt my time would be better spent applying myself to further study so that I might place well in the second degree examinations as soon as possible and hence the opportunity for higher honors while I am still young with a long career ahead. To this end I expect to commit all my energies and small resources rather than seek profit and a higher lifestyle now."

The old lady smiled slyly. "With a rich wife, young sir, you could do both and, when your second degree arrives, perhaps purchase a higher post than you could manage merely by appointment of an Imperial Minister."

"Mistress Feng," said Wei K'e-yung, "if I were to accept this proposition on those grounds I would be no better than any fortune hunter. I do not see how this can be resolved."

"It is because of this very uprightness of character which causes you to hesitate that my employer would find you such a morally acceptable candidate. In addition to which there is the lady's own preference to consider. Since her position is not a usual one, and her fortune is so great she has insisted that I urge you to an unusual course of action and, therefore, requests to meet with you personally."

Reluctantly Wei K'e-yung agreed and a time was set to meet at a tea house in New Moon Street the next afternoon. The young servant boy showed Madam Feng to the gate and bid her good day but no sooner had he barred the gate than a little maid ran up with the old lady's fan which had been left behind in the reception hall. Hastily the boy threw the bolt and ran into the street but to his surprise the old woman was nowhere to be seen.

The fairy maid poured hot tea from a cold pot and produced sweets and delicate pastries from a simple, seemingly empty straw basket which she placed before her mistress. But Ku-She neither ate nor drank. The little maid combed her lady's hair out of the matron's knot and oiled and dressed it with silver pins and a gleaming net but Ku-She seemed unaware. She laid out the sleeping mats and the silken sheets but Ku-She would not lie down to sleep.

"You must rest yourself, most excellent lady," the maid begged. "There is much to be accomplished tomorrow. There may yet be a way to prove his possession of the Chopsticks and learn where they are kept. You must not despair of this. You shall win them from him yet."

But Ku-She merely closed her eyes and bowed her head lower and a single tear jeweled her cheek.

The old woman who met Wei K'e-yung at the tea house door and led him to the private room on the second floor did not look precisely as he remembered Mistress Feng. She seemed smaller and more frail, but a woman often deceived the eye in public and he could not deny he had known her at once. In a clear voice she thanked him for the return of her fan and begged him to come upstairs to meet a young lady of her acquaintance to whom he might prove of some assistance with a small problem. Thus, well chaperoned and public propriety appeased, Wei K'e-yung followed the go-between to have a look at the lady who offered him her fortune and her person.

It required no further persuasion nor negotiation on the matchmaker's part to convince Wei K'e-yung of the wisdom of the match. The lady could have been penniless and burdened with family debt and he would gladly have taken her to wife and given over all his means, sold his house and servants and even his books to unburden her if such had been required. For, in the instant his eyes fell upon her, with one brief glance, he utterly lost his heart and much of his reason.

By the time he returned home half the night had gone and the servants had begun to fear for his life, for he was not generally given to late carousing. When he entered the gate at last their fears were only slightly diminished for he did not seem himself. Though he had drunk many pots of wine he did not seem intoxicated. He could not recall if supper had been served but he had no desire for food or tea. The old man and his wife who kept the scholar's house could barely get him to speak and he wandered about the garden dazed and distracted, smiling softly. Then suddenly he would stop and speak aloud to no one. Gazing at the moon he proclaimed its luster to be far inferior to the pale perfection of a lovely skin. Stopping by a shrub he would pick a blossom and declare the softness of its petals to be as coarse as grinding stone beside that of a tiny hand upon his wrist.

Yet the young master seemed deaf to his retainers' urgings so the boy was sent into the night to fetch the doctor. But the doctor said he could not come until morning. He sent a powder to be disguised in a pot of warm wine to make the young man sleep but they could not induce him to take it. In desperation the old woman herself went into the next lane to the house of a midwife and roused her from sleep to come look at Wei K'e-yung. The midwife stood in the shadow of the veranda and observed him carefully as he wandered about. When she left she said:

"You must give him the powder even if you force it into him and send for the doctor again at dawn. I fear he is under a fairy enchantment and will not live many days if not properly treated."

Terrified by her words the old couple heated the wine and mixed in the powder but they were afraid to try to force him and angry to discover that the boy had run off and hidden himself for fear they would require *him* to do it. In the end the old woman tricked him, saying: "This is the finest wine in the countryside. Taste it and see how its sweetness compares to a kiss."

Shortly he was asleep beneath a tree in the little garden but he did not sleep long and awoke at dawn only moments after the boy had again gone for the doctor. He seemed amazingly vigorous and called for a huge breakfast which he shared with the doctor when he arrived. While they ate the doctor asked many questions and observed his behavior closely. At last he expressed his diagnosis.

"I agree that you are suffering from an enchantment, but it is not one the fairies have cast. This is a very mortal illness and the only cure I know for it is marriage—and the sooner the better or your health will suffer. If there are no candidates I can recommend the services of a fine matchmaker who has served my own family well."

When her master only smiled the old woman said, "I believe he has already been approached on that subject and has even seen his prospective bride."

"Ah," the doctor said. "A most foolish youth. This must indeed be the cause of the affliction. He should not have set eyes upon her till all was arranged. It is well known that such indiscretions can cause fevers of the brain. I would consult a geomancer at once for an auspicious date before more foolishness compounds his illness."

In the afternoon Madam Feng came again and accepted the commission on behalf of Wei K'e-yung to arrange an acceptable wedding date and see to the traditional exchange of gifts, even though Mistress Ku had no family. In the evening he received word by messenger that the date was set. The geomancer was much distressed and had cast the bones six times as Madam Feng sat by nodding and watching each throw intently, but the results were consistent. The wedding must take place in four days. All the signs for the next two years pointed to a disastrous union. So short a betrothal was barely within the bounds of civilized behavior and, had there been families involved, would have been wholly unacceptable, but Wei K'e-yung was delirious with joy.

On the eve of the wedding, Ku-She sat in the courtyard of a small, plain house she had taken under the name of Madam Feng while the little maid once more dressed her hair, combing out the matron's coiled bun. The girl prattled as she worked and Ku-She watched the sun-colored sky fade and the lantern light tint the night air of the veranda.

"It will not be long now, mistress. They are within your reach and very soon you will possess them again. Then we will return to Hibiscus Village and all will be right with the world once more. The Lung Wang will forgive you and the Jade Emperor will reward you and all Hibiscus Village will be honored. . . ."

Ku-She bowed her head behind her fan and did not reply.

"Please forgive your stupid servant, mistress, but I still do not understand why you must actually *marry* this worthless mortal. I know it has not been sanctioned by the Emperor of Heaven and thus you cannot be bound to it, and I know I am too stupid and ugly to have played this part on your behalf, but was there not some other way? Some way that would not have required you to suffer this creature for even one night?"

"No," Ku-She said softly, the flutter of her fan hiding her face in the flickering shadows of the lantern light.

Then Ku-She fell silent and would discuss it no more and the maid fell silent also and put crystal snowflakes into the velvet black hair with silver pins.

The wedding was simple, as was proper for a woman's second marriage. At dawn the groom's sister met the bride at the gate to the go-between's house and escorted her on foot to the temple. After the brief ceremony the groom rode off on horseback to prepare the house, making the proper offerings to the door god and kitchen god and his ancestors while his sister and new wife followed on foot. But halfway home the women were met by a fine sedan chair decked in red wedding banners. The correct gestures having been made in an already unorthodox union, Wei K'e-yung was determined that his beloved bride should have all the honors he could give her.

Much to the amusement of the household and the chagrin of the lady's personal maid the newlyweds were not seen outside their room for three days and then only Wei K'e-yung emerged. He went to his study briefly and returned with the apron of his blue robe filled with books and small objects, ink slab and brush, and his lute over his shoulder. The little maid slipped into the room as soon as she noticed him below, but she found her mistress sleeping, her hair a wild tangle and a beauty upon her face that the maid had never seen before. Her smile was soft and her skin pale and cool in the summer heat. There was a tint of rose on her temples and lips and cheeks and the swell of her breasts. To look upon her sleeping so made the girl hesitate in her intent and before she could wake her mistress the young husband returned, the same rosy blush upon him, and she had to leave them.

The food and wine left at the door was brought in regularly now and twice more Wei K'e-yung emerged to run to his study and return at once with small boxes and other objects in his sleeves and apron. The maid merely waited, for it was clear that her lady was about her business. But a day passed, and another, and again Wei K'e-yung was in and out of the room several times.

Finally, on the night of the fifth day, the housekeeper summoned the maid from her evening rice saying: "Your mistress requires you. Hurry."

There was a brusqueness and indignation in the old woman that the maid had not seen before and she ran to Ku-She's room as fast as she could. On the way, she found Wei K'e-yung sitting in the garden. His head was in his hands and there was such an air of despair about him that, for once, the maid felt a tug of tenderness for him, but she hurried on to Ku-She, her heart beating wildly in her breast. What awaited her in the darkened bedroom was not what she had been prepared to find, however.

Ku-She sat on the bed, her face in her hands lost beneath the unkempt fall of black hair shrouding her head and shoulders and gathering in her lap like a dark pool. Her slender body trembled and heaved with the heavy sobs of her crying and the room possessed a distinct chill. The maid ran to her mistress and hovered about her, not knowing what to do, not daring to touch her. Finally she threw caution to the winds and embraced Ku-She fiercely, crying: "Oh, my most cherished mistress, what has he done to you? The foul mortal! If he has injured you I will tear his limbs from his body and scatter the pieces to the four corners of heaven and earth!"

"No!" Ku-She cried, throwing herself from the maid's embrace onto the bed.

"Lady, please tell me what has happened. Unworthy as I am there might still be some service I can do you. How may I console your grief?"

Ku-She did not reply at once and only sobbed on for a few
moments more, but gradually her crying lessened until she sat
upright upon the bed again and pushed the hair from her face.
Her skin was pale as a winter moon and the blush was gone
from her. Her eyes were swollen from tears and dark as the
mountain caves.

"We are lost," she said at last. "*I* am lost. It is *I* who have
failed. Chou Ch'ung-i and the Jade Emperor can find no fault
with *you*. But I am doomed. I can never be forgiven. The fault
is too great, the failure unredeemable. . . ."

"The Chopsticks," the maid whispered. "Oh, mistress,
does this mean the mortal does not *have* them?"

"No," Ku-She said softly. "He does not have them. The
foul pestilence of a monk did indeed make him a gift fit for an
earthly emperor, but it was a treasure only mortals would
regard for its age and history; a scroll of poetry by a scholar of
great learning in a past dynasty . . . but not my precious
Chopsticks."

The maid sat beside Ku-She in a quiet daze. All the spirit
had gone from her mistress and her own energy seemed to
have fled as well. She thought of Wei K'e-yung and her moment of pity for him, thinking his sadness to be over the loss
of his treasure and his new wife both at once. Now she felt
only anger toward him for having sidetracked them from their
true path and for the long days and interminable nights
through which her mistress had had to suffer his use of her.

"We will find him yet," she said quietly.

"No," Ku-She said. "We will never find him. He must
surely know we are in search of him and will continue to stay
beyond our reach. It is hopeless and I do not have the strength
to continue."

"Perhaps the judges in the court of the dead will snare him
this time," the maid said. "Did you not tell me they said his
time was near once more?"

"Yes, but he has evaded them for many lifetimes. I can not
rely upon his capture. And even if it did come to pass, that
would regain the Chopsticks for the Heavenly Emperor but
would not relieve me of my failure and my guilt."

"But, mistress . . . "

"*Enough*. It is done now. I cannot go back without them
and I can search no longer."

"Then what will you do, madam?" the maid asked in a small voice.

"I will stay here with my husband. In the mortal world. I will live as one of them, keep to this house, forego my magic and tell him I have lost my wealth. I will call no attention to myself and if he is to rise in society it will be through his own merit without my power to beguile, for I would eventually be found by the use of it. I will be a good and honorable wife to him and when the time comes I will follow him to the Land of the Dead as a mortal woman.

"The Emperor of Heaven will find a way to correct this difficulty in time. No great purpose would be served by my returning to Heaven. If I have failed I might as well stay here and make at least this one man happy. That much good I can still do."

The little maid twisted her small hands in her apron and stared at her mistress with large dark eyes, and a wondering confusion upon her brow.

"Do you care for this mortal as a true husband, my lady?"

"Yes," Ku-She said softly, and the blush slowly rose upon her temples once more. "I love him as dearly as anything I have ever known, and will gladly follow him into the Land of the Dead when the time comes. He captured my heart the moment I saw him. His manner filled me with admiration and his beauty filled me with desire. It was the grief on my very soul that I knew I would have to leave him when I took the Chopsticks from him, just as it is the grief of my soul that I will never again see Hibiscus Village, nor attend to my heavenly duty. There is no happiness for me either way, but my love for him may at least make my short mortal existence contented.

"But there is no fault in you, child. You may return to Hibiscus Village and the service of my Sister Tung Shunang-ch'eng."

"No, madam. I will stay with you. It would be necessary for me to reveal your whereabouts and I will never betray you. If you choose to remain here a mortal span, I will remain also. I desire no service but yours and will be as faithful as my miserable worthless soul permits."

Ku-She was grateful, for the burden of her secret would be great over the years. She bid her maid help her dress and ar-

range her hair and make her appearance fit and as the girl set
about the familiar tasks Ku-She began to feel some of that
burden lift just a little.

In the garden Wei K'e-yung sat beneath his tree and felt the
weight of despair upon him. Gradually, so slowly that he did
not notice it at first, the hot late summer air grew cooler about
him and when finally he became aware he also heard the gentle
liquid whisper of silk and the quiet scuff of feet behind his
tree. Looking up he saw his bride and her maid approaching
slowly. The maid stopped at the edge of the path and his new
wife came to him, kneeling by his side and placing her forehead upon the stones of the path before him. The cool breezes
surrounded her and played with the edges of her silk gown.
Even bowed to the ground her beauty was hypnotic. He was
enthralled and could think of no reproach to say to her. She
begged his forgiveness for her wicked and thoughtless
behavior and swore she would never again cause him so much
as a moment's unhappiness. He knew she had said this,
though he could not recall the exact words. He had often
found himself wondering at this lately, for at all other times he
was remarkably clear about whatever was said to him by
others. Now, however, he knew only that there was no crime
she could ever commit for which he could not grant immediate
forgiveness. Her presence made his happiness complete and in
his heart the quarrel had never happened.

Ku-She rejoiced in her husband's forgiveness, but her heart
was still troubled. She longed to tell him the truth, but in fact
her first acts as his wife and the manager of his household
were to deceive him further. She forged a document in the
form of an official notice that her late husband had offended
the Imperial Court and that a judgment had been sent down
that his lands and all his personal wealth be confiscated on
behalf of the Emperor. It further implied he should count
himself lucky he was already dead. Then Ku-She sent her maid
out to market with the document hidden in her sleeve, instruc-
ting her to find a messenger to deliver the item to the house
three days hence.

When the messenger came at last she fell into a fit of weeping and would not eat for two days. She begged her husband
not to abandon her now that she was poor and had nothing to
give him but her love and, perhaps, children. There was no

doubt, of course. He was as bewitched as ever.

The more he loved her the more her beauty seemed to increase. He longed to show her to his friends, to display her as a jewel upon his breast but she had grown shy and would not be seen. When men came to the house to see Wei K'e-yung she would keep to her room and not even speak to them from behind the screen in the reception room nor allow herself to be glimpsed passing in the halls. If men came to the house when her husband was away she bid the old man greet them and the boy wait upon them if necessary but under no circumstances would she enter their presence. Wei K'e-yung was glad to have found someone so conscientious and impeccable of behavior, but he could not help but wish that just once in a while she would allow a moment's harmless lapse.

The month turned into the harvest season and the crop was poor. The summer rains had been sparse, the lakes low, the rivers sluggish. The monsoons would replenish the coast, but inland things did not look hopeful unless the winter snowfall was heavy.

As autumn set in, the scholar's house, which had been a refuge of coolness in the summer heat, took on a chill. As winter came Wei K'e-yung applied himself more and more deeply in study; of both his books and his beautiful wife. He spent as much time in the bed chamber as he did in his study and often his wife visited the study as well, endlessly embroidering silver snowflakes on a white linen canopy for their bed. Her needlework was exceptional and Wei K'e-yung convinced her to sell it to help in their support. Reluctantly she agreed but would not work the snowflakes which were her finest patterns. She embroidered girdles and aprons and pillows with birds and flowers which fetched a high price but in the end of the twelfth month she once again began to work the snowflakes, this time onto fine lengths of swaddling clothes.

Wei K'e-yung was overjoyed. He no longer pressed her to appear in public and waited out her pregnancy with her in blissful seclusion.

That winter proved the coldest in the town's memory. Though not a flake of snow fell the temperatures were bitter and the house, which the previous year had proved sound even against the worst winter storms, could barely be kept warm. Wei K'e-yung spent a great deal of his small income on fuel

and extra clothing for, oddly enough, it often seemed colder in
the house than in the street. Concerned for his child, Wei K'c-
yung kept his wife even more bundled up than the rest of the
household and insisted a brazier be kept near her at all times,
but neither she nor her maid seemed much affected by the
cold. Often he would see her wandering about the little garden, lightly dressed and not at all distressed.

The spring was late and the early buds pushed their way
relentlessly through hard-packed earth, but finally, slowly, the
winter died and gave over to a cool planting season. The fields
were dust and the streams and ponds little more than puddles.
As the summer passed prices in the market places grew steadily
higher and the quality of goods grew poorer and finally rice
and produce became scarce. Wei K'e-yung's kitchen garden
did well enough with the help of his well, but anything they
could not grow put an increasingly heavy burden on his means
and he began to fear for the next year if things did not improve
soon.

And he worried for his family. With the coming of spring
much of the joy had left his wife and, as her time drew nearer,
her mood deepened into real sadness. The midwife came from
time to time and scolded him for not cheering his wife. It en-
dangered the child, she said. The mood of the mother during
the waiting time determined the child's personality and could
even influence gender. This melancholy outlook would no
doubt produce a petulant, unhappy girl whom they would
have trouble marrying off.

Wei tried everything he could think of and somewhat more
than he could afford. He proposed a trip to the countryside
but she refused to leave the house, even in a closed chair, and
he could not really blame her. On the few occasions he himself
had to venture outside the city walls he found the countryside
in a desperate plight. Much of the spring planting had refused
to grow and by midsummer what remained was parched and
dying. The fields looked burned, the trees and bamboo groves
bore withered yellow leaves and rattled like bundles of dry
kindling in the scorching breezes. The earth was dust and blew
entire fields away and the rivers were trickles of sludge, the
ponds and lakes were bogs. Only the mosquitoes thrived in the
slow stagnations, but soon there would not be enough water
for even them to breed.

Throughout the summer Ku-She kept mainly to her own

rooms and kept company only with her maid. Her melancholy was deeper than anyone could know for it was a true grief and a great guilt.

"It is not your fault," her maid would say. "It is that cursed Taoist magician who has done this."

And though Ku-She would nod, she knew whose fault it really was and she wept often and could not be cheered.

The child was born on the third day of the seventh month and, much to the midwife's amazement, was a loud, robust, healthy boy with bright black eyes and a quick smile. Wei K'e-yung was overcome with joy and his love for his wife grew a hundredfold. He sent word to his sister and her family, his neighbors and teachers and everyone he knew that on the third day of the eighth moon there would be the traditional month-old celebration for his first-born son and all would be welcomed with open arms. But still the sorrow hung upon his wife and this hurt him deeply.

"You should have joy in our child," he said.

"I *do*," she replied earnestly, nursing her son in her cradling arms. "Besides you, my beloved husband, he is the greatest blessing of my life."

"Then why do you sigh when he smiles at you; why do you weep when he laughs?"

More than ever Ku-She longed to tell Wei K'e-yung everything but there was no answer she could give him.

In the evening, while her husband studied and the child was laid to sleep and the servants busied themselves with preparations for the coming celebration, Ku-She sat apart with her maid and mourned the fate of the world and her small family.

"I thought I could hide here and be happy with him. I thought the Jade Emperor of Heaven would find a way to repair the damage my failure has done but I see that it is not so. The world is dying. Without the rain there is no hope and without the snow there can be no more rain. And when all the world lies dying but you and me, my beloved husband will look at me and know why I survive. He will know what I am and that I have caused this and he will hate me where he dwells in the Land of the Dead until the end of time."

The maid soothed her, but Ku-She would not be comforted.

"In five days this house will be filled with people for the first time since our marriage. It is unavoidable. This time I cannot refuse. It is the child's right and my husband deserves this much happiness. I will appear as required, even though Heaven's spies may take notice and discover me."

She turned from the window and tears stained her cheeks and a passionate despair burned in her eyes. "Then I must return to Heaven. I will confess my fault, throw myself upon the Emperor's mercy, do whatever he wishes, suffer eternal torture if he will only spare these people!"

"Forgive me, mistress," the maid said, "but the Jade Emperor has surely done all he can and only time may finish whatever great work he has set into motion. It would hardly seem likely that he would cause all the earth to perish just to get even with one lowly elemental fairy."

At once the maid fell to her knees and knocked her head upon the floor exclaiming that so foul a mouth as hers should instantly be filled with ashes or her tongue cut from her head. But Ku-She only sat upon the bed and bid the girl rise for she knew her maid was right.

On the morning of the celebration, Ku-She rose early and supervised the servants in their final preparations. She had made up her mind to confess all to her husband that evening, spend one last night with him if he still wished it, and return to Heaven. Thus resolved, though the choice had been hard and ached within her even now, she felt better than she had since the loss of her precious treasure. As she worked about the house she discovered a growing joy, for the event, for the child. She had always loved the banquets in Hibiscus Village heralding the beginning and ending of seasons and this, though smaller and simpler, was an event of the utmost importance to her. She would make it as grand and gay as she could. When she went upstairs to dress she had her maid do her hair in the grand fashion and put the crystal and silver snowflakes in its coils.

Wei K'e-yung was, without doubt, a man bursting with pride. Pride in his new son, but also pride in his wife. Lean as his budget was, poor as the items available in the markets had been, she had set before them a banquet fit for an Imperial Prince. Everyone in the neighborhood came and some folk from great distances and she received them all graciously and with perfect correctness. Everywhere she went the sun shone and the cool breeze played. Everything she touched seemed grander for having been under her hand. Of all the eyes that witnessed this wonderful event, all were pleased by what they saw but only two pairs recognized it for what it was. One belonged to the lady's maid. The other belonged to the monk Wei Pan Ch'ao.

Even before her husband presented her to him she knew him. The faint glow of magic, like infant dragon fire, hung about his person and flickered slightly as it mingled with the shadows of great age, yet he was a man not entirely past his prime and vigorous with a careless smile and a quick, sharp tongue. He had known her as well, immediately upon entering the scholar's gate, for her fairy aspect was full upon her and though her magic masked much from mortal eyes, his were no longer entirely mortal.

"He is among us!" Ku-She had whispered hastily to her maid. "What am I to do? I cannot let him slip away this time and yet I cannot reveal myself before all these people. And he knows who I am, I am sure of it. He will evade me once more unless something is done quickly."

"I will help in any way I can, madam," the maid said. "You have but to command me."

"I have a thought," said Ku-She, "but dare I call upon the aid of my sister fairies? The Jade Emperor's spies will surely know if I do, and yet I have little choice. Stay close to me, Little One. I will require you the moment there is a chance to slip away."

It was not long before her chance came. While her husband and his uncle were engaged in happy conversation, Ku-She and the maid fled to a storeroom on the second floor in the farthest corner of the house.

Ku-She knelt upon a mat and raised her voice to Heaven while the maid watched the door.

"Sisters, hear me," she said. "I require your aid. All the fairies in the Jade Emperor's service may suffer unless I succeed in this and to that end I beg your assistance."

A long moment passed in silence and Ku-She, with a sinking heart and trembling hands pressed to her bosom, cried out, "Help me, Sisters. Please!"

Wei K'e-yung had searched the ground floor of the house for his wife and no one had seen her. She was not in their bedroom but when he emerged he found her descending the stairs looking pale and tired and sadder than he had seen her all day.

His heart turned at the sight of her beautiful, melancholy face for he had believed the sorrow gone and now he knew that the joy of the day had been only temporary. But she smiled again when she saw him and he took her hand and they descended into the garden once more.

After a brief time Wei Pan Ch'ao came to pay his respects and depart. His nephew was amazed that he did not intend to stay longer and accept the hospitality of his home for the night as he usually did when he came to visit, but the monk insisted he had to be on his way. As they stood beneath the garden wall, unnoticed by all the guests or the young man at his side, a small white spider dropped onto Wei Pan Ch'ao's shoulder and hid itself in the collar of his robe.

Ku-She watched him go with a feeling of desolation. It was still early in the afternoon and the Taoist could go far before the guests left and her husband retired and she was free to slip away to search for him.

In a quiet shrine by the northern city wall, Wei Pan Ch'ao stopped and paid his respects to the priest, lit incense before the altar, took tea and sat in the shade of a sickly mulberry tree in the garden. The shrine was to a minor local god and was kept by one old man and his young novice so it was not long before Pan Ch'ao was alone, apparently dozing beneath the tree. Therefore it was surprising when he spoke aloud in a soft voice, though no one had approached and his eyes were still closed.

"You may come out now, my child," he said.

There was no response, but this was to be expected.

"Come, now," he said. "I am not a foolish old man, though I may seem so at times. You may look like a spider and hide in my robe, but I know you for what you are. You are the fairy maid of my nephew's wife. She called upon the Fairy of One Hundred Insects who enchanted you and made you into a white spider so you could follow me and later lead your mistress to me. Magic knows when other magic is present and the fairy aspect is on you even in this form. I did not hear your mistress call, but I felt the magic gathering in the upper corner of the house and realized what it must be, for I knew her at once. Come out, child. I will not harm you or your mistress. We have much to talk about."

Slowly the little spider emerged from a fold of cloth at the back of his shoulder and scurried down his arm to the ground where he saw her as a tiny glow in the dry grass.

"Can you assume your normal form at will or do you have to wait for the fairy to unbind you?"

"No," said the girl, kneeling on the ground before him, "I can restore myself as you see. But I cannot regain the spider form."

"You trust me," he said.

"I am the lowliest of fairies in the realm of Heaven," she said. "I can do little but serve others, but I can tell a lie from the truth, and though I cannot call you an honest man I do not see deception in you. Now."

The monk looked her squarely in the eye but she did not avert her gaze. "You are bold on your mistress's behalf."

"I am her humble slave and would follow her to the four corners of the great bowl of the world. I would place myself before her and any harm due her I would take upon myself if possible."

"What is her name?" the monk asked. "Is it the Fairy of Ku-She or Tung Shuang-ch'eng you serve?"

"My lady is the Fairy of Ku-She," she replied.

"Your loyalty is commendable, child. I shall tell her so. And you may serve her by conveying the message that I wish to meet with her, most urgently. I have been searching for her since the turn of the year. I will be in my nephew's garden by the kitchen wall at midnight. If she will come to me we have much damage to repair."

The maid hurried back to the scholar's house and slipped in by the kitchen garden. Ku-She was surprised to see her so soon. It was barely dusk and many of the guests were still about, the men drinking and gambolling in the main hall, the women in the garden examining Ku-She's embroidery.

"He will come to you," the maid said. "In the garden at midnight."

"How can he be trusted?" Ku-She exclaimed. "You should not have revealed yourself. You have failed me and now he will vanish again."

"Forgive your stupid slave, madam," the maid said, bowing to the floor. "But his magic is strong. He knew me from the moment my spider form touched his shoulder. He knew when you called to your sisters. And, though he is not a noble man, he has seen the error of his ways. His last encounter with the Judges of the Land of the Dead was but narrowly escaped. This drought is killing the world and, no matter how powerful his magic, it cannot place him beyond that ultimate fate. He has cheated death for many mortal lifetimes and he does not wish to face it now because of a bad joke.''

Ku-She understood the truth when she heard it too and her anger subsided. "Then he *will* come," she said.

"Yes, madam, I am sure of it."

Ku-She patted the maid's hand with a sigh. "It was well done, child. And it is nearly over." She looked into the garden from the shelter of the kitchen porch and saw her husband searching for her among the women. "Farewell, my love," she whispered. "Have great joy today, for tonight you will surely lose me. I can no longer reveal the truth to you as I planned, but you and our son will live and I will watch over you from the Land of the Fairies as best I can." Then she went out to him in the garden with her most beautiful smile and all the warmth of her love in her eyes.

Wei Pan Ch'ao felt the cool breeze of her approach before she appeared at the far end of the courtyard; and she could see him, though to other eyes he would have been but a shadow upon the wall by the kitchen corner.

"At last," she said, politely bowing her head. "The thief. The instrument of my shame. Why do you come to me, jackal? You should simply return the Chopsticks to Heaven and make my failure the more miserable. Surely that would please a jester such as you; a mean joke upon a lowly fairy. Yet you cause your people and your own kin great suffering and then you come to me. Why?"

"By the time I knew I had lost you I was far from here and did not know where you had fallen from my path. I did not intend this to go so far, but I cannot return them without your help. I can no longer enter Hibiscus Village as I used to. Heaven is too alert and I can not go before the Jade Emperor's court free of risk. At his most merciful your exalted ruler would grant me a home in the Land of the Dead rather than require me to suffer an eternity of his pleasure. It is unlikely, however, that even the return of the Golden Chopsticks would persuade him to be *that* lenient. So, as I have no wish to walk into the den of the hungry tiger, it is wiser that *you* return them, thereby fulfilling your assigned task, though somewhat belatedly."

"If *I* am to be punished for *your* jest it seems only right to me that you should be also," Ku-She said angrily.

"I completely agree," Pan Ch'ao said. "But I am concerned about my life, mistress fairy, not about what is right. Until I have your word not to reveal me to Heaven or the Judges of the Other World, *you* shall not have your Chopsticks."

"I agree," Ku-She said, furious, "because I have pity for these creatures and this leaves me no choice."

"And because you love my nephew and your son." Pan Chao smiled.

Her reply was an icy glare the monk felt to the very marrow of his bones, but he merely shrugged.

"Your promise, madam?"

"You have my word," Ku-She said slowly and deliberately, "that I will not reveal you to any Heavenly agency in return for the safe return of my Golden Chopsticks. *Now give them to me.*"

"Ah." The monk smiled. "I do not have them."

Ku-She was rigid with fury. "You *vermin*! You *tricked* me!"

"No, I never said I still had them. But I know where they are and we may retrieve them without difficulty. Not long after I took them I grew tired of carrying them with me; the hunt was of more interest to me than the bait. I gave them to an old farmer in exchange for a few nights' hospitality. They were the grandest things he had ever possessed, though he did not know the extent of that truth, and swore before his ancestors that he would never part with them."

"And where does this old man dwell?"

The monk named a district far from the city and Ku-She frowned in thought.

"My sister fairies wish me well and can be trusted, but it is dangerous for me to call upon them. I risk discovery and they risk the wrath of Heaven, but this is worth the risk. I shall call upon the Fairy of One Hundred Birds to give us the form of hawks so we may fly far and fast without fear of being preyed upon and if we keep our wits about us, men can be avoided."

"Then make haste, Small Fairy. Your goal is nearly in reach."

"Tomorrow at noon," she said, "I will meet you outside the Western Gate. I will have this final time with my beloved ones, for I shall very likely never see them again. Now go. I do not want you here."

Ku-She turned and crossed the garden and sat down upon the broad, moonlit sill of her husband's study and began to weep. From inside the maid heard her and laid open the shutters.

"There is one last thing I would require of you," Ku-She said quietly, "and then your service to me will be at an end. You must watch over my loved ones for me. Stay here and see that they are safe and as untroubled as possible. For even if I succeed I will surely never be able to return."

Then Ku-She climbed the stairs to her husband's bed-chamber for the last time and the maid bowed her head and wept also.

Shortly after noon of the following day, a pair of brown hunting hawks flew upward from the Western Gate. Even in bird shape, with few stops for hunting and resting, it took eight days for Ku-She and Wei Pan Ch'ao to reach the village where the monk had left the Golden Chopsticks. The farm they sought was two li beyond the village, and from the air, miserable as the draught had made all the land, it was clear the farm was deserted. They had to abandon their bird forms and enter the village in order to learn that the old man had died shortly after the Taoist had left him. His son, much to his surprise, had inherited a magnificent pair of Golden Chopsticks along with the wretched farm, and he had sold the farm and gone off to the city to find someone with sufficient means to purchase the treasure. With that money he planned to set himself up in business and grow fat.

Once again Ku-She called upon her sister fairies, and they flew northward into the night. It was a journey of three days to the city. There they learned that the farmer's son was in prison for his debts, for he had purchased a rice distribution firm, and as the crop failed in the spring it had fallen into ruin. It was seven more days before they discovered that the farmer's son had sold the Golden Chopsticks to an agent for the District Magistrate for twenty taels of silver and fifty strings of cash. They were, no doubt, in the treasury at the district capital by now.

The district capital was a five-day walk, for Ku-She did not dare call upon her sisters a third time lest the eyes of Heaven fall upon her. It was now the middle of the ninth month. The harvest was over for there was little to gather, and the land lay open in jagged cracks like the cracking of a glazed vase. The branches of dead trees rattled like the bones in the geomancer's bags. When they reached the capital, Wei Pan Ch'ao had no trouble slipping inside the District Treasury, but the chopsticks were nowhere to be found. Ku-She learned from one of the maids to the District Magistrate's First Wife that the master had paid a bribe to his superior in order to retain his position. Among the rare books and silks there had been a pair of magnificent Golden Chopsticks.

Above the District Magistrates were the lower ranks of the Imperial Bureaucracy. It would be necessary to travel to the Imperial Capital at Peking which surrounded the Imperial City like a tea cozy and the Forbidden City deep within that. It was a journey of thirty days on foot, and the weather was turning cold. Wei Pan Ch'ao urged Ku-She to call upon her sister fairies once again, but she would not.

"Each time I call to Heaven I risk being heard by those we seek to avoid, especially you," she said angrily. "I have promised not to betray you, but *you* would give us both away."

After that he was silent on the subject and they began to walk.

Ku-She could have traveled day and night, but Wei Pan Ch'ao was still human enough that he required sleep, and food, and shelter when the nights grew cold. They took refuge in deserted cottages and roadside shrines. The peasants in the villages were not hospitable and often chased them from their gates with hoes and clubs and stones. They foraged where they could, for Ku-She was reluctant to use the magic basket. The basket would feed them, but somewhere in Heaven the fairy magic would be felt.

Finally Wei Pan Ch'ao's pace began to slacken. One afternoon they stopped to rest in the shelter of a tiny cave and Ku-She was dismayed, then alarmed to discover she could not rouse him. The old man burned with fever and presently began to mutter through clenched teeth.

Ku-She gathered wood and dry grass and built a fire to warm him, resorted to the fairy magic of her pot to keep him full of warm tea and soup. She tried not to touch him, for cold was her own most natural condition. But there was little more she could do for him, and she waited and watched as he struggled between life and death in the way of mortals. On the fifth day, she was startled to hear his voice.

"Flee . . . " he murmured. "Flee this place, Little Fairy."

"You are not well enough," she said. "If I leave you, you will surely die."

"The Judges of Death already know where I lie. When they come for me, they will find you too. Flee. You have no time now. Call upon your sister of the birds."

"Uncle," she said, "as long as you live I have a duty to you."

"Your duty is to the Jade Emperor. And to my nephew and grand-nephew. For the sake of these last two, the only things I have held dear in all this long life, I require you to go. Quickly. Obey me, *niece*."

Reluctantly Ku-She knelt and bowed her head to the stones three times.

For days the brown hawk flew north and east to the fringes of the capital of the earthly Emperor and at last into the heart of the city. The man she sought was a bureaucrat of moderate success and would live near the walls of the Imperial City within Peking itself. But his station was not high enough for him to own a villa within those walls. Nonetheless, once the district of his residence was located, word of the man himself was not hard to come by. His name was still on many lips for only six days before his daughter had married the eldest son of a High Imperial Minister and it took the fairy no time at all to learn the further fate of her Golden Chopsticks. They had become part of the girl's dowry and were now housed within the Imperial City itself, in the keeping of the Minister Fong Wen Wah.

Ku-She grew reckless with desperation, for it was rumored that Fong had a treasure of incomparable worth to present to the Emperor. Speed was imperative, for it was said, and not untruly, that even to the touch of Heaven, the most remote and unscalable mountaintop was more accessible than the Forbidden City. The Imperial City surrounding it would be difficult enough for her to breach. She would call upon her sisters one more time, and soon.

Fong Wen Wah lit the braziers in his study himself, adjusted several chunks of charcoal and began to grind ink as the small room warmed. He examined the parchment before him with great dissatisfaction. The hand itself was superb, one of his finest examples of gossamer script, but wasted on the content. The form and the verse were not in harmony. It disturbed him that recently his thoughts had not been worthy of his hand.

Dismissing his last effort he paused with loaded brush above a fresh parchment. The poetry commending such a magnificent gift as his to the Son of Heaven whom he served should be a work of the highest order and gossamer script required inspiration to capture the entirety of the thought in one single, fluid, utterly graceful line. But the poised brush never touched the parchment.

"Your Honor," an old hag said. "I beg your forgiveness for this inexcusable breach of protocol but I must see you most urgently."

Startled, Fong leapt up with a cry, brush poised like a weapon, his face darkened with rage.

"Who are you?" he exclaimed. "How dare you enter my house?" Putting down the brush he reached for his gong mallet but the old woman did not move.

"It is true," she said, "you have the right, but you will have to do so yourself. You have but one servant in the house tonight and he sleeps in the kitchen in a drunken stupor . . . with my aid of course," she said with a slight bow. "The gardener and gatekeeper are too far away to hear the gong and those maid servants who did not go to the south with your wife have gone to their own families for the night. Your household is sparse. That is why I have chosen this time to speak to you."

"You threaten me?" he said, amused now, for she was not only old, she was also small and light of bone. "I could crush you with this mallet if I chose."

"There is no threat," she said mildly.

"Then what do you want?"

"Only that which is mine."

"I have *nothing* of yours," he said, his voice full of contempt for the mere idea.

"Ah, but you do, though you do not know it."

"And you have proof?"

"You will find me convincing enough, my lord."

Minister Fong laughed. "Speak. Claim your possessions and convince me."

The hag smiled. "Through the good fortune of your son's recent marriage you have come into possession of a pair of Golden Chopsticks."

The indulgent smile left the minister's face.

"The handles are inlaid with tiny, perfect snowflakes of silver and ivory and pearl and each is capped with a snow-white moonstone. They were stolen from me and I will have them back."

"You presume too much upon my humor, hag," he said, features once more grim. "How would a creature as low and miserable as you rightfully possess a treasure fit only for an Emperor?"

"How did *you* come by them, my lord? From a man of lesser station than yourself, to be sure. And how did *he* come by them? From a country magistrate who acquired them from a peasant turned merchant. Each knowing the treasure too grand for his own station found use in passing it on to higher and higher ranks but never so high as from whence it came. I have followed the Chopsticks across the land for a long time for in the beginning they were mine and even so I was but their custodian."

"You would claim much for yourself, though I can not say precisely what."

"I am not what I seem."

"Nor am I," the minister said angrily. "For I am not a fool! Nor one to be spoken to so boldly. You tempt me to violence, hag. You dishonor my name, call me a thief. . . ."

"Not a thief, though only you can undo the theft."

"You have convinced me only that at some time you have seen the Chopsticks. No more than that."

"And that I know, as you do, what they are."

Fong regarded her silently.

"They are objects of great beauty and exquisite workman-

ship but that is not what makes them worthy gifts for an
Emperor. You have taken them from their box as the others
never did. They looked and saw a rare treasure. The lowly felt
unworthy to touch them. The more astute still preferred to
keep them pristine. But you took them into your hands and
felt the fairy magic tingle in your fingers. *This* is the gift you
felt worthy of your Emperor. A prize stolen from Heaven.''

"Yes," he said. "There is fairy magic there. And all the
more reason they would never be fit for the likes of you."

The old woman bowed slightly. "Ah," she breathed. "But I
have already told you I am not what I seem."

She turned away from him then and crossed the room to the
garden doors and as she passed a deep chill fell upon the
room. Though the braziers hissed and burned brightly all
their warmth had vanished in an instant and Fong Wen Wah
watched her with a dread growing as frigid as the room. When
she turned and regarded him from the door she looked half
her former age and as fair as any woman he had ever seen. She
smiled and invited him into the garden.

The moon was full for it was the first of the new month and
it cast a brilliant white glow on the courtyard. Had he cared to
Fong could have read a book by it.

The old woman had vanished as had the handsome woman
at the door. In the cold moonlight stood a young woman of
little more than twenty, possessed of the most perfect beauty
the minister had ever seen, though her exact image seemed to
elude him. The shimmer of her fairy aura was upon her and he
knew she beguiled him, yet he also knew her beauty was true
and it pained him to look at her. She was clad head to foot in a
shimmering white gown, ropes of pearls and white jade about
her neck and her hair was done up with jeweled silver clips and
silver pins with snowflakes falling from them.

"Do you know me, mortal?" she said. But Fong Wen Wah
was silent with wonder. Quietly, Ku-She called to her sisters
and slowly the frozen winter garden began to warm about
him. Crocus and hyacinth and azaleas put forth buds and
bloomed and the fruit trees blossomed as well. The air grew
soft and the night sky lightened for in another season at that
hour it was barely dusk. The trees greened and the grass grew
long. Catalpa and dogwood threw open their flowers and all
the plants about the path bloomed riotously. The air was

heavy with a dry, itching heat and the minister found himself tugging open his gown. The greens became dark and robust and apples and cherries and loquats ripened and fell from the trees as cooler breezes ruffled leaves beginning to blush with color, then fade to brown and fall. The grass grew dry and rustled in the cold wind and the minister clutched his robe about him once more, mute with wonder.

Had he really seen an entire year flee across the face of his garden with the speed of the hand flinging forth that inspired verse he had longed for . . . only a moment ago? He felt as though a lifetime had passed in those mere moments, not just one year.

He looked at Ku-She. Her beauty no longer pained him. "Who are you?" he asked.

"I am the Fairy of Ku-She, and I have come to claim what is mine."

There was ice in her voice but not the daggers of icicles hanging from the rooftree. Rather the delicate fernlike patterns of the first glaze on a shallow pond; fragile and brittle. "Do you require more proof, mortal?" she asked.

In reply he threw himself at her feet and pressed his head to the paving stones. Then he went into the house and quickly returned with a simple ivory box. No sooner had he delivered it into the fairy's hands than a tall, pale form appeared and moved toward him across the garden. It was another strange and beautiful woman upon a white mule. In her hands she held a crystal vase, pale and translucent with a glow and flutter of movement inside.

Minister Fong was transfixed.

"Much evil has befallen the world for lack of these," said the woman upon the mule. "We thank you for their safe return."

"Forgive me!" Fong cried as he once more fell to the ground. "I should have understood at once."

"Perhaps your mortal Emperor would have, had you given them into his care. You were at least wiser than to cherish them too closely for your own sake. But I find you an honest man and to safeguard the earth against further harm of this sort I leave you with a trust."

At Ku-She's bidding he got to his feet and watched as she took the Golden Chopsticks from the ivory box. Dipping them into the crystal vase she plucked out a shining snowflake like silver lace, and then another which she quickly dropped into the ivory box. Then she placed it in Fong Wen Wah's hands.

"For each snowflake cast from the box a foot of snow will fall upon the earth. Keep them safely in the box and they will be preserved for all time. You may open the box briefly from time to time but never touch them or they will melt away as any snowflake would. If they must be released touch them only with the purest gold or silver. I give them into your keeping to safeguard and pass on to your heirs or give over to the stewardship of your Emperor as you see fit."

Then Ku-She turned and mounted the white mule beside Tung Shuang-ch'eng, and as the creature turned away they vanished.

Still numb with wonder the Imperial Minister Fong Wen Wah stood mute in his garden looking at the ivory box in his hands. He roused himself presently for it had begun to snow. He placed the little box safely in a chest in his study and once more seated himself at his writing desk, brush loaded and poised above the snowy parchment and when the moment came, with a single remarkable stroke, he wrote the finest poem of his era.

When the Season's End festivities were over and Hibiscus Village was quiet once more, the Fairy of Ku-She and Chou Ch'ung-i were summoned before the Jade Emperor of Heaven himself.

The world was again growing green and lush and Ku-She had word from her sister of One Hundred Flowers, whose agents filled Wei K'e-Yung's garden with color, that her son was strong and healthy and her husband was at peace. Knowing this, Ku-She presented herself willingly to hear the Emperor's decree. Chou Ch'ung-i had petitioned the Heavenly Court on her behalf, but the Jade Emperor was not impressed.

The fairies knelt before him on a floor paved with sky-blue jade. The Emperor's throne was made of clouds and sunlight and he sat upon the curled back of a sleeping golden dragon. Rising behind him, rooted in the misty cloud, was a willow tree of alabaster and its tiny jade leaves hung like the fringe of a canopy before him and tinkled gently in the breeze. When he spoke his voice could not be heard but the thunder of it vibrated deep within the very bones of the little fairy and its whisper touched her soft as silk.

"We are not pleased with you, child," he said. "Though you cannot be blamed for the theft, nor for failure to fulfill your duty, your conduct in pursuit of that fulfillment can be greatly criticized. You *set aside your duty* for your own pleasure and caused great suffering by so doing. You married *without the consent of Heaven*. You took a *mortal* to spouse and you brought forth a child who is half of our world and half of theirs. This flaunting of our authority can not be taken lightly and requires that you be punished severely. Yet all things must be considered. Chou Ch'ung-i declares that you have always been faithful and conscientious, that you have taken great joy in the fulfillment of your duties to your season and that your artistry is unparalleled. It has also been noted that you sacrificed your worldly pleasures when your duty was once more placed before you and in the end you succeeded. These facts temper our judgment but do not prompt us to forgive you your transgressions. Do you admit your fault, fairy?"

Lying face down upon the tiles, Ku-She acknowledged her guilt.

"And do you repent your wickedness and accept as just whatever punishment shall please me to serve upon you?"

"Oh Highest Master of All That Is," Ku-She said meekly. "I can never repent the evil which befell the world as a result of my selfishness in love's name. I was weak and unfaithful and am deserving of the harshest punishment you can inflict."

The Jade Emperor was silent in consideration for a long time. The two fairies dared not move and lay motionless on the jade tiles.

At last the Emperor spoke again.

"Where is the monk Wei Pan Ch'ao? Tell us this and I may be tempted to greater leniency."

A small smile escaped onto Ku-She's lips and she was grateful for her prostrate position. "Oh Most Exalted Ruler of Heaven and Earth," she said, "I truly can not say. I gave the monk my word I would not reveal him in exchange for his assistance but when I left him he was dying and I honestly do not know what became of him if the Judges of the Dead do not have him."

The Emperor's voice beat like a gong upon her ear. "And would you tell us if you *did* know, fairy?"

"In all honesty, lord, I could not. Would you wish to com-

promise the word of Heaven? Even so small an oath given by
so puny and miserable a fairy? No, my Most Excellent Master,
I could not say even if I knew. But in truth I do *not* know."

Again the Emperor was silent for a long time. By Ku-She's
reckoning a day and a night might have passed for such time
meant nothing to the masters of the universe. Such things were
important only to those such as she, who watched the seasons
pass. But she lay still and waited in silence.

"You are banished," the Emperor said at last. "For the
span of a mortal lifetime."

Ku-She's heart leapt at his next words.

"You will return to your husband and live out his life with
him, growing old as mortals do and suffering all the pains and
ills of their condition. You will experience death as mortals
do, but you will not be allowed to enter into the Land of the
Dead and you will bear him no more children. Once he has
entered that realm he will be lost to you for all eternity and
word of him will not be granted to you. But till then his fortunes will be his own and you must follow him however they
fall for you will not be allowed to leave him while he lives, nor
influence his fate. Your power of enchantment will also be
denied you. He will see you as you are and if his love for you
was a trick of your own making you will soon have cause for
regret.

"I cannot deny your child immortality. But it is not yet clear
if he possesses it. When he is twelve years old he will be
examined and if he is mortal he will remain with you and he
too will be denied to you after his death. But if he is fairy in
that regard he will be taken into Heaven and raised as one of
us.

"Upon your own death you will once more return to
Hibiscus Village and regain your stewardship of the Golden
Chopsticks, and you will never be allowed to venture into the
mortal world again."

At the Emperor's bidding Ku-She and Chou Ch'ung i
withdrew. Ku-She's heart was heavy, knowing she must once
more lose her beloved Wei K'e-yung, this time after the growing love of a lifetime together. But she did not fear the rejec-
tion the Jade Emperor had implied. For of all the mortals she
had met, Wei K'e-yung's eyes were the only ones she had *not*
beguiled.

The Five Black Swans

By Sylvia Townsend Warner

Portents accompany the death of monarchs. A white horse trots slowly along the avenue, a woman in streaming-wet garments is seen to enter the throne room, vanishes, and leaves wet footmarks; red mice are caught in the palace mousetraps. For several weeks five black swans had circled incessantly above the castle of Elfhame. It was ninety decades since their last appearance; then there were four of them, waiting for Maharit, Queen Tiphaine's predecessor. Now they were five, and waited for Tiphaine. Mute as a shell cast up on the beach, she lay in her chamber watching the antics of her pet monkey.

The mysterious tribe of fairies are erroneously supposed to be immortal and very small. In fact, they are of smallish human stature and of ordinary human contrivance. They are born, and eventually die; but their longevity and their habit of remaining good-looking, slender, and unimpaired till the hour of death have led to the Kingdom of Elfin being called the Land of the Ever-Young. Again, it is an error to say "the Kingdom of Elfin": the Kingdoms of Elfin are as numerous as kingdoms were in the Europe of the nineteenth century, and as diverse.

Tiphaine's Kingdom lay on the Scottish border, not far from the romantic and lonely Eskdalemuir Observatory (erected in 1908). Her castle of Elfhame—a steep-sided grassy hill, round as a pudding basin—had great purity of style. A small lake on its summit—still known as the Fairy Loch, and local babies with croup are still dipped in its icy, weedless

water—had a crystal floor, which served as a skylight. A door
in the hillside, operated by legerdemain, opened into a complex of branching corridors, one of which, broadening into a
set of anterooms, led to the Throne Room, which was
wainscotted in silver and lit by candles in crystal sconces. It
was a circular room, and round it, like the ambulatory of a
cathedral—and like the ambulatory of a cathedral fenced off
by pillars and a light latticing—ran a wide gallery where the
courtiers strolled, conversed, and amused themselves with
dice, *boutsrimés*, news from other Kingdoms and the outer
world, needlework, flirtations, conjectural scandal and tarot.
The hum of conversation was like the hum of bees. But at the
time of which I write, no one mentioned the five black swans,
and the word "death" was not spoken, though it lay, compact
as a pebble, in every heart.

Dying is not an aristocratic activity like fencing, yachting,
patronizing the arts: it is enforced—a willy-nilly affair.
Though no one at Elfhame was so superstitious as to suppose
Tiphaine would live forever, they were too well-mannered to
admit openly that she would come to her end by dying. In the
same way, though everyone knew that she had wings, it would
have been *lèse-majesté* to think she might use them. Flying was
a servile activity: cooks, grooms, laundresses flew about their
work, and to be strong on the wing was a merit in a footman.
But however speedily he flew to the banqueting room with a
soup tureen, at the threshold he folded his wings and entered
at a walk.

In these flying circles of Elfhame, Tiphaine's dying was
discussed as openly and with as much animation as if the
swans were outriders of a circus. A kitchen boy, flying out
with a bucket of swill for the palace pigs, had been the first to
see them. On his report, there was a swirl of servants, streaming like a flock of starlings from the back door to see for
themselves. The head gardener, a venerable fairy, swore he
could distinguish Queen Maharit in the swan with the long
bridling neck: Maharit had just such a neck. Tiphaine's servants were on easier terms with death than her courtiers were.
They had plucked geese, drawn grouse and blackcock, skinned
eels. They had more contact with the outer world, where they
picked up ballads and folk stories, flew over battlefields, and
observed pestilences. The mortals among them, stolen from
their cradles to be court pets and playthings, and who, failing

in this, had drifted into kitchen society, seldom lived into their second century, even though on their importation they were injected with an elixir of longevity, as tom kittens are gelded for domestication. Thus death was at once more real to them and less imposing. Every day their loyalty grew more fervent. They said there would never again be such a queen as Tiphaine, and had a sweepstake as to which lady (Elfindom inverts Salic law) would be the next.

In Elfindom the succession is determined by the dying ruler naming who is to come after her. If, by some misadventure, the declaration is not made, resort is had to divination. At sunrise half a dozen flying fairies are sent up to net larks—as many larks as there are eligible ladies, with a few over in case of accidents. During the morning the larks, one to each lady, are caged, ringed, and have leaden weights wired to their feet. On the stroke of noon the court officeholders—Chancellor, Astrologer, Keeper of the Records, Chamberlain, and so forth —wearing black hoods and accompanied by pages and cage bearers, go in torchlight procession to the Knowing Room, a stone cellar deep in the castle's foundations, where there is a well, said to be bottomless. One by one, the larks are taken from the cages, held above the well while the name of their lady is pronounced, and then dropped in. The weights are delicately adjusted to allow the larks a brief struggle before they drown. Its duration is noted with a stopwatch by the Court Horologer and when one by one the larks have drowned, the lark which struggled longest has won the Queenship for the lady it was dedicated to. The officials throw off their mourning hoods and go back to the Throne Room, where they kiss the hand of the new Queen and drink her health from a steaming loving cup of spiced and honeyed wine which recovers them from the cramping chill of their ordeal in the Knowing Room.

At Elfhame, however, all this was hearsay: Tiphaine and the two Queens before her had been named. Lark patties and the loving cup were all anyone expected.

Early in the new year the weather changed. Rain pockmarked the snow that lay in rigid shrouds over the black moorland; the swans were hidden in a web of low-lying cloud. Suddenly they reappeared; the wind had shifted into the north and there it would stay, said the head gardener who remembered Queen Maharit, through the three long months ahead—

the starving months, when shrew mice feasted underground, and deer and cattle wandered slowly in search of food, eating frozen heather, rushes, dead bracken, anything that would stay the craving to munch and swallow.

It was warm in the castle, where the walls of solid earth muffled the noise of the wind. Chess tables were laid out in the gallery: matches lasted for days on end, protracted by skillful evasions, long considerings before the capture of a pawn. From the musicians' room came intermittent twangings and cockcrowings, flourishes of melody broken off, begun again, broken off again, as the court band of harps and trumpets rehearsed the funeral and coronation marches which would soon be needed. In Tiphaine's chamber the Head Archivist sat by her bed, waiting to take down her dying command about her successor. Every morning he was brought a new quill pen. Every night he was replaced by the Sub-Archivist, who had a peculiar aversion to monkeys, unfortunate but also convenient, since it kept him reliably awake.

The monkey's life depended on Tiphaine's. Royal Favourites are seldom popular in court circles. The monkey had amusing tricks but dirty habits; few would put in a good word for it when Tiphaine's death plunged the court in sorrow. Nothing at all could be pled for Morel and Amanita, Tiphaine's latest importees from the mortal world. Strictly speaking, they were not changelings, for they had been bought with good fairy gold. This in itself was against them; but, however got, they would have been detested. They were twins, and orphans; their parents had been burned as heretics during the Easter festivities in Madrid, and the Brocéliande ambassador, on his way back from the Kingdom of the Guardarramas, had stolen them from the convent of penitents to which they had been assigned. Tiphaine had bought them from him. For a while she was devoted to them—as devoted as she had been to the still remembered changeling Tiffany, who for thirteen years she had kept as her lover. Tiffany, in his mortal way, was tolerable. Morel and Amanita were intolerable from the start. They thieved, destroyed, laid booby traps, mimicked, fought each other like wildcats, infuriated the servants, and tore out the Chief Harpist's hair. (Custom dictated that it be worn long and flowing as in olden days.)

For as in the kitchen loyalty grew daily more ardent and more undiscriminating, in the gallery it developed a sense of historical perspective. There had been some regrettable incidents in the past—blown up by scandal, of course; but there is no smoke without fire. Tiphaine was indiscreet in her choice of Favourites—the fault of a generous character, no doubt, but she was often sadly deluded. Admittedly, she was headstrong—but to live under the rule of a vacillating Queen would be far more exhausing. Beauty like hers could atone for everything—or almost everything. Perhaps her complexion had been a shade, just a shade, too florid? "You would not think that if you saw her now," retorted the Dame of Honour.

"I suppose so, I suppose so." The words sounded slightly perfunctory. The speaker was looking at the chessboard, where Morel and Amanita had rearranged the pieces.

By now, it was the end of March and cold as ever.

The Sub-Archivist had entered the bedchamber, seated himself, wrapped a fox-skin rug over his knees, taken the virgin parchment, the day's quill pen. The monkey sat hunched before the fire. Dwindled, mute, a dirty white like old snow, Tiphaine lay among her snow-white pillows, and did not notice the replacement. She was remembering Thomas of Ercildoune.

It was May Day morning, and she rode at the head of her court to greet the established spring. Doves were cooing in the woods, larks sang overhead, her harness bells rang in tune with them. She pulled off her gloves to feel the warm air on her hands. The route took them past a hawthorn brake and there, lolling on the new-grown grass, was a handsome man —so handsome that she checked her horse's pace to have a completer look at him. She had looked at him and summed him up when suddenly she realized that he had seen her and was staring at her with intensity. *Mortals do not see fairies.*

She spurred her horse and rode fast on from the strange encounter.

That night she couldn't sleep, feeling the weight of her castle stopping her breath. An hour before sunrise she was in the stables, scolding a sleepy stableboy, had a horse saddled, and rode at a gallop to the hawthorn brake. And he was not there and he did not come. She rode on over the moor. The sun was up before she saw him walking toward her. She reined in her horse, watching him approach. Keeping her pride, she looked down on him when he stopped beside her. "You're out early, Queen of Elfhame," he said. She couldn't think of anything to say. He put his arms round her and lifted her from the saddle, and she toppled into his embrace like a sheaf of corn. The dew was heavy on the grass, and when they got up from their lovemaking they were wringing wet and their teeth chattered.

From then on it was as though she lived to music. To music she followed him barefoot, climbed a sycamore tree to look into a magpie's nest, made love in the rain. Once, they came to a wide rattling bum, with a green lawn on the farther bank. He leaped across, and held out his hand for her to catch hold of. It was too wide a leap for her and she took to her wings. It was the first time in her life she had flown, and the sensation delighted her. She rose in another flight, curling and twirling for the pleasure and mastery of it, as a fiddler plays a cadenza. She soared higher and higher, looking down on the figure at the burnside, small as a beetle and the centre of the wide world. He beckoned her down; she dropped like a hawk and they rolled together on the grass. He made little of her flying, even less of her queenship, nothing at all of her immense seniority. Love was in the present: in the sharp taste of the rowan-berries he plucked for her, in the winter night when a gale got up and whipped them to the shelter of a farm where he kindled a fire and roasted turnips on a stick, in their midnight mushroomings, in the long summer evenings when they lay on their backs too happy to move or speak, in their March-hare curvettings and cuffings. For love-gifts, he gave her acorns, birds' eggs, a rosegall because it is called the fairies' pincushion, a yellow snail shell.

It was on the day of the shell, a day in August with thunder in the air, that she asked him how it was he saw her, he who had only mortal eyes. He told how on his seventeenth birthday it had come to him that one day he would see the Queen of Elfhame, and from then on he had looked at every woman and seen through her, till Tiphaine rode past the hawthorn brake. In the same way, he said, he could see things that had not happened yet but surely would happen, and had made rhymes of them to fix them in his memory. She would live long after him and might see some of them come true.

With one ear she was listening for the first growl of thunder, with the other to Thomas's heartbeats. Suddenly they began to quarrel, she railing at him for his selfish mortality, his refusal to make trial of the elixir of longevity. He flung away from her, saying she must love him now, instantly, before the lightning broke cover. A time would come when he would grow old and she would abhor him: he could tell her that without any exercise of prophecy. The storm broke and pinned them in the present. When it moved away they built a cairn of hailstones and watched it melt in the sunshine.

The Sub-Archivist woke with a start. The Queen was stirring in her bed. She sat up and said fiercely, "Why is no one here? It is May Day morning. I must be dressed."

The Sub-Archivist rushed to the door and shouted, "The Queen has spoken! She wants to be dressed."

Courtiers and women servants crowded in, huddling on their clothes. There was a cry of "Keep those two out," but Morel and Amanita were already in the room. They saw their hearts' desire—the monkey. The monkey saw them. It screamed and sprang onto Tiphaine's bed, where it tried to hide under the coverlet. The Court Physician hauled it out by the tail and threw it on the floor. While the court ladies crowded round the bed, chafed the Queen's hands, held smelling salts to her nose, urged her not to excite herself, and apologized for their state of undress, Morel and Amanita seized the monkey. At first they caressed it; then they began to dispute as to which of them loved it best, whose monkey it should be. Their quarrel flared into fury and they tore it in half.

The smell of blood and entrails still hung about the room when the Sub-Archivist took up his evening watch. Everything had been restored to order: the bed straightened, the floor washed and polished, a fresh coverlet supplied. Tiphaine had been given a composing draught, and was asleep. That deplorable business with the monkey had made no impression on her, so the Court Physician assured him. She might even be the better for it. Morel and Amanita had been strangled and their bodies thrown on the moor as a charity to crows. With every symptom so benign, they could hope she would return to her senses and name her successor.

As the virgin parchment had been crumpled during the scuffle, the Sub-Archivist was given a new one, and left to himself.

The room was so still that he could hear the sands draining through the hourglass. He had reversed it for the third time when Tiphaine opened her eyes and turned a little toward him. Trembling, he dipped the quill in ink.

"Thomas—O Thomas, my love."

He wrote this down and waited for her to say more. She grunted once or twice. The room was so still he could hear the swans circling lower and lower, and the castle beginning to resound with exclamations and protesting voices. The swans rose in a bevy, and the chant of their beating wings was high overhead, was far away, was gone.

No one at court had a name remotely resembling Thomas, so preparations for the ceremony of divination were put in hand.

Thomas
The Rhymer

Traditional Scots Ballad

True Thomas lay oer yond grassy band,
And he beheld a ladie gay,
A ladie that was brisk and bold,
Come riding oer the fernie brae.

Her skirt was of the grass-green silk,
Her mantle of the velvet fine,
At ilka tett of her horse's mane
Hung fifty silver bells and nine.

True Thomas he took off his hat,
And bowed him low down till his knee:
"All hail, thou mighty Queen of Heaven!
For your peer on earth I never did see."

"O no, O no, True Thomas," she says,
"That name does not belong to me;
I am the Queen of fair Elfland,
And I'm come here for to visit thee. . . .

"But ye maun go wi me now, Thomas,
True Thomas ye maun go wi me,
For ye maun serve me seven years,
Thro weel or wae as chance may be.

223

"Then harp and carp, Thomas," she said,
"Then harp and carp, alang wi me;
But it will be seven years and a day
Till ye win back to yere ain countrie."

She turned about her milk-white steed,
And took True Thomas up behind,
And aye wherneer her bridle rang,
The steed flew faster than the wind.

For forty days and forty nights
They rode thro red blood to the knee
And they saw neither sun nor moon,
But heard the roaring of the sea.

O they rode on and further on,
Until they came to a garden green:
"Light down, light down ye ladie free,
Some of that fruit let me pull to thee."

"O no, O no, True Thomas," she says,
"That fruit maun not be touched by thee,
For a' the plagues that are in hell
Light on the fruit of this countrie.

"But I have a loaf here on my lap,
Likewise a bottle of claret wine,
And now ere we go farther on,
We'll rest awhile, and ye may dine."

When he had eaten and drunk his fill,
"Lay down your head upon my knee,"
The lady sayd, "ere we climb yon hill
Where I will show you fairlies three.

"O see ye not yon narrow road,
So thick beset wi thorns and briers?
That is the path of righteousness,
Tho after it but few enquires.

"And see not ye that braid braid road,
That lies across yon lillie leven?
That is the path of wickedness,
Tho some call it the road to heaven.

"And see not ye that bonny road,
Which winds about the fernie brae?
That is the road to fair Elfland,
Where you and I this night maun gae.

"But Thomas, ye maun hold your tongue,
Whatever you may hear or see,
For gin ae word you should chance to speak,
You will neer get back to your ain countrie."

He has gotten a coat of the even cloth,
And a pair of shoes of velvet green,
And till seven years were past and gone
True Thomas on earth was never seen.

Prince Shadowbow

By Sheri S. Tepper

Prince Shadowbow of Faerie believed that time was fairly done for princes. "I am an anachronism," he said to his reflection in the pallid pool of stars which had the peculiar property of reflecting everything, even thoughts, whether at noon or midnight. Moons, moods, faeries, feelings—all were the same in the pool of stars, and it rippled now at the Prince's dramatic expression of despair as he turned to his companion of the court and demanded, "Am I not, Georges?"

"I am not sure Your Highness is old enough to be an anachronism," replied the old man, keeping a carefully straight face.

"One need not be old. Eighteen is quite old enough. Besides, it is the Princeness of me which is out of time, not the age of the Prince in question. I was an anachronism when I was born." This approached a forbidden subject rather more closely than was considered appropriate, and the Prince noted a slight tightening in Georges's expression. He peered out, therefore, at the limits of vision—as though seeking someone to agree with him—to the mist-veiled edges of Faerie which were tattered now, fringed with time-mould and that strange rust which eats at the delicate borders of dreams. "I see the place fading around me, Georges. Day by day it tarnishes and dwindles. The colors are not as bright as when I was very young. The songs of the nymphs are not as sweet. The whole place is an anachronism."

"It has that quality, Your Highness. However, from time to

time it can have that quality and still be restored to what it . . . was. One might say that what was, will be. One might say that the fragility is . . . intentional." The old courtier let the words trail into silence as the moody youth took them up.

"I've heard the argument, Georges. Since Faerie may have that quality intentionally, may we not say that the World outside is more truly the anachronism? Sorry, Georges. That would be a case of the flea defining the dog, would it not? I have been carefully reared not to think overmuch, but even such a mist-brain as I can see that the outside is much more . . . vital than the inside. Are we not only a drifting dream waiting to be experienced and forgotten?"

"Are we indeed, Your Highness? That would much surprise your mother, our Queen. And, who is to do the forgetting?"

The youth sighed. "Sometimes I am tempted to turn myself inside out and do it myself, just to end the agony of suspense. Oh, I know. Such moebian conduct would not become a Prince. My Royal mother would be distressed. Still, Georges, sometimes I feel this tension, this oddness, a wanting to run away, to be elsewhere . . ."

"A condition, if I may say so, Your Highness, which is not untypical of youth."

"Even in this untypical place, eh, Georges? Well, this is no time to flirt with irresponsibility. The ceremony is tonight, isn't it?"

"It is, Your Highness." As both of them knew well enough and had known well for as long as both could remember. The ceremony would take place at dusk on the ides of autumn which would occur when Shadowbow was eighteen. The season had been advancing for some time now. He could scarcely remember the springtime of his birth. Even the summer of his childhood had faded—he remembered it as a tapestry in which the colors had gone and only the lovely workmanship remained to testify to beauty long past. And now the autumn, and the ides of it upon him, and then—either spring again or . . . Either the slow rot at the borders would be stayed, the gradual paling and fading of the fabric of Faerie would be stopped, or . . .

Well, nothing could be done until the ceremony. All would be wagered, then, on one attempt. Thinking of it, Shadowbow flushed, bit nervously at his lower lip and tried to think of anything else, anything else at all.

"We'll walk back through Trollwood," he offered, turning from the pool of stars and strolling into the copses which lined the clearing. They walked on leaf-strewn paths, passing the gnarled shapes of ancient trees and the dark pits of the Trolls who leered and menaced from the entrances. Though they groveled at the sight of the Prince, he did not deign to notice them. Trolls were among the least favored of Faerie's inhabitants. They tended to snivel, the Prince thought, rather more than was necessary to be in keeping with their roles.

He turned his back on them and went down a side path to the Unicorn Glade. The single unicorn on duty was allowing itself to be used as a quoit target by three centaurs pitching wreaths of flowers.

"Pretty," called the Prince in a sarcastic tone. "Very pretty." Only one of the centaurs had the grace to flush; the other two only grinned as they galloped away.

He walked into the Glade, reaching out to the unicorn, burying his fingers in the silken mane. "Farewell," he whispered, overcome by nostalgia. "I will not be able to hold you so again, lovely one."

The unicorn sighed, rubbing her silken head upon the Prince's cheek. Then she stepped back, touched the needle point of her horn to his forehead and pressed, lightly, until the bright blood started through, falling like dew upon his cheek. "Lovely one," he sighed, fingering the mark. It would leave a tiny, puckered scar, like a kiss. His mother carried such a scar. Presumably her . . . progenitors had done so as well.

The centaurs had returned, galloping around the edges of the Glade as though the unicorn were only another like themselves. "Common," remarked the Prince with some disgust. "Common."

"It is still some time until dusk," murmured Georges, his voice soothing. "They seek to distract themselves from what lies ahead. They are only playing. . . ."

"I know, Georges. Believe me, I do know. I would sometimes prefer they they play for *me*, too. Is that selfish of me?"

"You pay no attention when the Trolls play for you."

"That's because the Trolls aren't playing. They're so dreadfully sincere. Every grovel a sincere grovel. Oh, Georges, forgive me. I'm nervous, touchy, and I know it's unbecoming. Don't pay attention to me. Ignore me."

Georges nodded, somewhat ironically, at this command as

he opened the wicket gate leading through the great hedge into the stable yard. Here a dozen grooms were currying the dragons while stable boys mucked out the stalls. A dragonet amused itself by puffing fiery breath into the dragon trough, sending clouds of steam puffing into the slanting sunlight. The grooms nudged one another to attention as the Prince walked by. He smiled, making an effort to appear pleasant and calm. Poor little sods. What must it be like to be a dragon groom and know that no matter what happened in Faerie or the World outside, one would still be a dragon groom? On the other hand, it wasn't that bad a life. At least they could stay in Faerie. There were no ceremonies hanging in their futures to make all grim and fevered with duty and despair.

"I should hurry," he murmured, not hurrying. "Did you lay out my clothes, Georges?"

"I did, Your Highness. The suit of pearl, of course, as is traditional. Your seven league boots and the cloak of invisibility. It came back from the cleaners only yesterday." Georges coughed, the dry, wry cough of a valued retainer who may indulge himself in a little carefully veiled sarcasm. "Your Highness may remember the episode during which it became . . . soiled."

The Prince blushed.

"Her Majesty, your mother, will give you your bow, of course."

"Of course."

There were murmurs behind them as they went from the stable yards into the orchards. At one time Geroges would have hurried the boy through these pleasant reaches, but he did not presume to hurry the youth. The nymphs of the trees had laughed no more seductively for the five-year-old Prince than they did now, but one did not presume to protect the Prince of the Royal Line on the eve of his great trial. Georges allowed himself one curious glance at the Prince's face, but there was no lust there. Instead, he was gazing up through the scarlet trees to the castle wall where ivory towers blossomed with pennants against the rosy sky.

"It is very beautiful," he admitted in the voice of one who would rather have criticized but could not.

"It is certainly very beautiful," assented the old man. "There is nothing more beautiful; there can be nothing more beautiful. As is intended, Your Highness."

"I know," sighed Shadowbow, with a little laugh.

That laughter was echoed by the nymphs, and that laughter in turn faded behind them as they approached the gate, open upon the solemn quiet of the courts. From one shimmering tower a bell rang, plangent and marvelous, echoing in sound the brilliance and sadness of the sunset. Along the corridors, the servitors stood in their hundreds, bowing as he passed, line on endless line, their voices following him.

"Bring us to springtime, Your Highness."

"Grant strength to Your Highness for the ides."

He nodded, smiled, smiled and nodded, coming at last to his own tower room where body servants waited to bathe him, where the suit of pearl lay inexorably splendid upon his bed.

In the largest audience hall of the castle the nobility of Faerie had gathered. The floors were tesselated in sardonyx and crysoberyl, amethyst and topaz. The lanterns were of gold, filled with exotic oils and rare resins upon which the pale flames danced. Through the tall, western windows the last light fell into the glory of the place, not more glorious than those assembled there glistening in samite, scintillating in jewels. The Queen, pale as ivory, stood upon the dais among her coterie, her laughter falling into the pool of their attention like drops of molten silver, hissing into heavy silences. Prince Shadowbow stopped this careening metaphor. He had seen her so ten thousand times, so high, so royal, so beyond his callow youthfulness. And yet, and yet they were one blood, one line, and he loved her in desperation and silence. Over her shoulder he saw the shadowy face of King Cloak-of-Mist, the Queen's father and mate, Shadowbow's father. Beyond the King stood Queen Morning-Glory, the King's mother and mate, mother of the Queen. One line, doubly mated within itself, to rule—to rule *if* . . .

"Oh, let it all pass away," he told himself, "if only she might live. . . ." She could not, of course. If Faerie passed, she would pass with it, and this knowledge alone was enough to hold him to his duty, however foul and gross it seemed when compared to her grace. He knew that if he turned quickly, he would surprise an expression of gentle concern in Georges's eyes. He sought a distraction, a bit of misdirection.

"I am thinking," he said, trying to sound lightly humorous, "that it is all very *intentionally* melancholy."

"No less enchanting for that," whispered Georges.

Somewhere a signal was given. Trumpeters filled the room with silver tumult, and the Prince walked behind tabarded escorts to the dais where his mother fixed him with a stare of oracular perspicacity. "She knows," he thought, suddenly astounded by that knowledge. "She is not so far removed from her own youth. She remembers when she turned eighteen. Did she feel this same fear? This shame?" In the fullness of that thought he was overtaken by embarrassment and chagrin. He could have borne his own feelings, but to know she had borne them as well! He knelt, which was all he could have done. Neither of them would have wished to weep before the court.

"Prince Shadowbow," cried the Queen. "We see Faerie fade around us. Our lives run chill into autumn. Time creeps upon us as the night-slugs creep upon the delphinium spires, eating them to nothing. I call upon you, heir to the Throne of Faerie, Master of the Mists, Lastborn son of the Line of Oberon, Lord of the Borderlands, Prince Shadowbow of the Golden Arrows, to say whether you will risk your very soul in our renewal, or will you remain with us, beloved . . . son . . . and dwindle with us into silence?"

Behind her on the high, marble wall hung the lip-curved shapes of the bows which the ancestors of the line had carried, a thousand shadow-kisses upon that wall. Beside the Queen upon the dais lay her own bow. The Prince looked upon the wall and choked down cowardice. What they had done, he could do. What she had done, he could do. He turned to make the affirmation.

"I, Prince Shadowbow, last of my lineage yet alive, swear unto everlasting time my joy and my duty, to venture into the World that the strength that is there shall be brought to my people and my lineage. . . ." He turned, hands held out, palms upward, to take upon them the thing he had seen but never touched until then, the great Shadowbow of the Borderlands. Even as he held it, felt its delicate weight upon his hands, he heard the glad cry of the Queen as she hung her own bow upon the marble wall, hers retired into honorable place from which she never need take it again—as her father's before her, as his mother's before him, into time past remembering.

Only the minor ceremonies remained; the incantation over the arrows, the dedication of the quiver which held them, the censing of the cloak. Then came the processional ride to the borderlands, all in company, the Prince first among his gentlemen and the Queen riding in a light carriage behind them. It hurt him to see her riding so, she who had been first in every hunt, no centaur more part of her steed than she. Now—now she had taken a new role, and he bit his lip again as she came down from the carriage at the border saying that no hands but hers should fix the boots upon his feet or clasp the cloak about his throat. There at the border she kissed him, bidding him farewell and safe return, and their eyes met in a mutual understanding at once pungent and achingly sweet.

"So we say farewell to innocence," she whispered. "My love will not be less on the morning when it is done."

He bowed before her, holding her tiny hands in his own. He could not bring himself to believe her, but doubt would have seemed discourteous. What could he have said? "Until that morning, then." Something more lengthy and equivocal? No, better to say nothing and go; go and hope to return, no matter how one dreaded it or despaired of being able at that last instant to do what one had to do. He felt weak and ill, empty. There had been no feast. Who could have eaten before this? Who could believe her love would not be less on the morrow? After this betrayal, this infidelity?

Except, he reminded himself, that in her time, she too—she, too . . .

He merely bowed, therefore, and was silent as he turned and stepped across the border into the World.

To emerge invisibly onto a grimy street in the afternoon. The evenings and mornings of Faerie did not coincide with the times of the World. He knew this, but the transition left him disoriented for the moment. The place stank of chemical fumes, which he had been prepared for, counted on. Georges had said that the disgust he felt at the smells might be his best—perhaps his only—protection. Nervously he checked the bow, the arrows. Everything he needed was with him. He stepped forward in the seven league boots, a tiptoeing step which brought him to the center of the city, motion and sound boiling around him, unquiet and impatient, full of fury and disenchantment.

He clutched the cloak high above his throat, drew it across his mouth and nose. The disenchantment was like acid air, eating away at him, draining purpose and vigor. There were stories of some who had come into the World and had not returned, who had succumbed. He could not delay. Delay would increase the danger. Summoning all his concentration, he listened for the tug—the tug.

It came, a kind of harsh pulling, a half pleasureable pain, and he went toward it, in tiny steps, stopping between them to look and listen. With each step the sensation grew stronger. He stopped at last near a green lawn to the wild cacaphony of bells where *they* poured from a building in their hundreds, their thousands.

He staggered, overwhelmed by the mad, wild pulsing of his blood, the thundering of his heart. They were all around him, in twos and threes, their arms about one another, in crowds and clots, singly, flowing away in all directions, girls, Worldly girls, the beast scent of them filling the air in clouds so that he could not breathe except of that smell.

Oh, he cried to himself, but they are graceless. Look at the things they wear upon their feet. The crude, high, clogs which cripple their walk so that they prance like the back half of a cow. Look at their hair. Like briars, tangled, like rope, frizzled. Oh. Look, look at their eyes, daubed like those of a chimney sweep. They are trolls, trolls. . . .

And they did resemble the Trolls more than he had expected, but it did not matter for the smell of them was in his nostrils. It would not have mattered if they had appeared as Afrits or Demons, as witches of the depths, with that smell in his head, he could not have let them go. Even as his body turned to follow a group of them, however, his mind said cold, harsh things to him, bending his discrimination toward them. "Pick with some sense," he told himself. "Pick with some chance of success. . . ." And he dropped behind them a little way so that he should not be so maddened by the smell of them.

There were one or two in the group who looked less Troll-like than the others. They seemed cleaner, with less soot around their eyes, with hair that was more like silk than rope. These two or three he followed with his eyes, finding the places they went, remembering them. Then he left the place, as quickly as he could. When it was dark, he would return.

He sped the boots from the city to a more rural place, one saddened with trash and indiscriminate filth, but removed from the smell which had maddened him and the noise which had disgusted him. He waited for night, brooding upon the needs of Faerie.

"I am an anachronism," he said again. "Is it worth this? Would we not do better to fade into time as the older Gods have done, forgotten and long gone? Oh, in the ancient times when the borderlands were permeable, when the World and Faerie lay like lovers at one another's sides, yes, oh, yes, then it was right. But now? Now, when one must come into a place totally strange, totally inimical? When one must risk everything to break that border so much as a hair's width—only a hair's width—to let the rude vigor flow through?"

And his memories swept over him, the loveliness and glory of his home, the beauties of the Queen, and he answered himself. "Yes. Though it is to open only a hair's width to the door of life, though I risk everything, still it would be worth it, for if Faerie fades, nothing would be left but *this*." And he put his head into his hands, summoned up a memory of the well of the naiads and their coruscating fountain and to the memory of that music he listened until darkness came.

In the town once more he was glad to see that much of the ugliness was decently hidden by the dark. He began at the first house among those he had identified, searching for the spoor Georges had taught him to recognize, holding his breath not to smell them. He moved into rooms where girls slept, searched there, left there to lean weakly upon a fence or porch railing, sick and heaving. Romance novels. Movie magazines. Rock music. Caches of dried herbs—drugs of some kind or other.

Pictures of loose-lipped, meaty boys. Records of their voices shouting in a primitive, rhythmic chant words the Prince could not understand. That, too, was Troll-like. They did a great deal of that.

Finally only one house remained. He tottered toward it, weak and febrile. Far in the east the false dawn lit the sky with a fluorescent glow, and he shivered at the sight, an omen of failure. If he could not find the traces Georges had told him to find, then he must take one of the others for he did not think he could survive another day in this place or another night of search. Almost weeping, he went into the room where the last girl slept.

He remembered her. Of the little group he had followed, she had been the silent one, the one with lips pursed tight as though they closed over a delicious secret. Her forehead was slightly bulbous under level brows, and in sleep her face was drained of the day's dross to gleam with almost porcelain smoothness. He began the search. . . .

And found them almost at once. The notebooks into which paragraphs had been distilled slow word by slow word. The verses, crossed out and a hundred times rewritten. The little box, sticky with much handling, which held yellowed newspaper clippings announcing the winners of a writing contest. Upon her bookshelves were the names he had been told to seek.

The Prince steadied himself, then took the great Shadowbow from his shoulder and notched a golden arrow. With a fervent appeal to all the strength remaining in Faerie, he shot her through the heart.

Thus enchanted she could be carried to the borderland. Thus bewitched she could be laid upon the velvet mosses while he blew his horn in signal that he had returned and was not alone. He was fighting very hard to keep from sneezing. The scent of her, even while it fevered his loins almost unbearably, was very difficult to bear. He divested himself of cloak and boots. Then, fully visible and in the glory of his youth he knelt beside her as the nymphs began the much rehearsed chorus.

Even he, who had heard their song from his cradle, was moved. Upon the heights trumpets blew, the sound of joyous bells wafted from the castle. "Play, people," he murmured to himself as he prepared to wake her with a kiss. "Play, for Faerie depends upon it."

The eyes of Elsbeth Blodge opened and she beheld Prince Shadowbow kneeling at her side, resplendent in the suit of pearl.

Thereafter it was as it had been rehearsed a hundred times.

There were declarations in enchanted forests, abductions by Trolls, Ogres, Demons. She was set free from ensorcelled towers, dungeons, caves, only to be captured again. They fled together on unicorns, dragons, on winged horses. Skies loomed dark with fantastic clouds, cleared into crepuscular twilight, dawned with roseate charm. Nymphs chorused in the background except during the more martial episodes. Only he, who knew the language of the Faerie, understood their bawdy lyrics. To Elsbeth Blodge, late of the World, it could have been a caroling of angels.

Days fled in mixed terror and glory. Romantic dusk was succeeded by passionate night until at last . . . at last only that final, ultimate act remained. Prince Shadowbow fixed his mind upon duty, brought determination to fever pitch, and accomplished that impregnation which left him exhausted and ill. He lay where they had coupled, breathing raggedly into the graying mosses.

The golden arrow which had transfixed her heart was melting. She had to be returned to the World before it was altogether gone. Georges, efficient as always, and as kind, donned the seven league boots and the cloak of invisibility to carry her home. The sound of their exit through the border was as of a delicate fabric ripped. It alerted the servitors who sought their Prince, brought a soft litter on which to carry him to the castle, stripped him of the suit of pearl, washed him in water from the well of the nymphs, and let him go on sleeping. It was all they could do to stay awake until this last duty was done. They slept. All of Faerie slept. The last strength had been used, the last enchantment spent. Now it was left to time, time and Elsbeth Blodge.

Time.

The evenings and mornings of Faerie are not those of the World. The seasons of the World are not those of Faerie. Who knows how many of the one were slept away, how many of the other shaped clangingly upon the anvil of Time. Who was Elsbeth Blodge, after all? Whose child was she? What power resided in her that all of Faerie slept on her account, knowing it might never wake again.

Until one morning.

Prince Shadowbow wakened to see the east alive with rose and amber, heard the sound of singing from the green chasms among the orchard trees, felt the blood of Faerie foil along his veins in a surging flood. On the castle roof outside his window ruby-footed pigeons danced intricate minuets. Wind scurried among the leaves, bringing a scent of flowers. High against a backdrop of cloud, dragons chased one another, and from the Troll forest came the thunder of drums and the rattle of bones.

"Oh," laughed Prince Shadowbow, "this is how it was when I was young, so young. . . ."

"This is how it is when we are young, so young. . . ." It was the Queen, standing in his door clad in boots and trousers, looking no more than fourteen in the rosy light. "This is how it is my son, my love, my husband, my Shadowbow."

"Then she . . . she did it . . . she . . ."

"Shhh," said the Queen with a moue of distaste. "We will not speak of it."

He frowned, obscurely disappointed by this. "I would like —I would like to have seen it."

She looked at him, perhaps a trifle annoyed, perhaps with only a flicker of foolish jealousy. "Very well, my love. I believe I, too, felt much the same. We will send Georges."

So, faithful Georges went out into the World once more to return bearing a small burden. He found the Prince eating pears in the orchard, his head in the Queen's lap, while they watched the dryads dance. Georges put the burden down upon the grass, swaddled as he had carried it.

The Prince looked long at it, somewhat doubtfully. "Is it really mine, Georges? You're sure?"

"Your firstborn," said Georges, fondly and sadly at once. "Your firstborn, Your Majesty."

He knelt to unwrap it there upon the lawn of Faerie, and they stared at it when the wraps came away. It was only a slender thing, a little enough thing with its name upon its cover.

" 'The Trollwood,' " read Prince Shadowbow. " 'By Elsbeth Bouvier.' Was that her name, Georges? I don't recall."

The Queen made a face. Georges, who was wise about many things, removed the book. He took it to the deep and hidden place he had taken all the others. Even the earliest lay there still. The foundations of Faerie rest upon them.

The Erlking

By Angela Carter

The lucidity, the clarity of the light that afternoon was sufficient to itself; perfect transparency must be impenetrable,
these vertical bars of a brass-colored distillation of light coming down from sulfur-yellow interstices in a sky hunkered with
gray clouds that bulge with more rain. It struck the wood with
nicotine-stained fingers; the leaves glittered. A cold day of late
October, when the withered blackberries dangled like their
own dour spooks on the discolored brambles. There were crisp
husks of beech mast and cast acorn cups under foot in the
russet slime of dead bracken where the rains of the equinox
had so soaked the earth that the cold oozed up through the
soles of the shoes, lancinating cold of the approach of winter
that grips hold of your belly and squeezes it tight. Now the
stark elders have an anorexic look; there is not much in the
autumn wood to make you smile, but it is not yet, not quite
yet, the saddest time of the year. Only, there is a haunting
sense of the imminent cessation of being; the year, in turning,
turns in on itself. Introspective weather, a sickroom hush.

The woods enclose. You step between the first trees and
then you are no longer in the open air; the wood swallows you
up. There is no way through the wood anymore; this wood has
reverted to its original privacy. Once you are inside it, you
must stay there until it lets you out again, for there is no clue
to guide you through in perfect safety; grass grew over the
track years ago and now the rabbits and the foxes make their
own runs in the subtle labyrinth and nobody comes. The trees
stir with a noise like taffeta skirts of women who have lost

themselves in the woods and hunt round hopelessly for the
way out. Tumbling crows play tig in the branches of the elms
they clotted with their nests, now and then raucously cawing.
A little stream with soft margins of marsh runs through the
wood, but it has grown sullen with the time of the year; the
silent, blackish water thickens, now, to ice. All will fall still,
all lapse.

A young girl would go into the wood as trustingly as Red
Ridinghood to her granny's house, but this light admits of no
ambiguities and, here, she will be trapped in her own illusion
because everything in the wood is exactly as it seems.

The woods enclose and then enclose again, like a system of
Chinese boxes opening one into another; the intimate perspectives of the wood changed endlessly around the interloper, the
imaginary traveler walking towards an invented distance that
perpetually receded before me. It is easy to lose yourself in
these woods.

The two notes of the song of a bird rose on the still air, as if
my girlish and delicious loneliness had been made into a
sound. There was a little tangled mist in the thickets, mim-
icking the tufts of old man's beard that flossed the lower
branches of the trees and bushes; heavy bunches of red berries
as ripe and delicious as goblin or enchanted fruit hung on the
hawthorns, but the old grass withers, retreats. One by one, the
ferns have curled up their hundred eyes and curled back into
the earth. The trees threaded a cat's cradle of half-stripped
branches over me so that I felt I was in a house of nets, and
though the cold wind that always heralds your presence, had I
but known it then, blew gentle around me, I thought that
nobody was in the wood but me.

Erlking will do you grievous harm.

Piercingly, now, there came again the call of the bird, as
desolate as if it came from the throat of the last bird left alive.
That call, with all the melancholy of the failing year in it, went
directly to my heart.

I walked through the wood until all its perspectives con-
verged upon a darkening clearing; as soon as I saw them, I
knew at once that all its occupants had been waiting for me
from the moment I first stepped into the wood, with the endless patience of wild things, who have all the time in the world.

It was a garden where all the flowers were birds and beasts;
ash-soft doves, diminutive wrens, freckled thrushes, robins in
their tawny bibs, huge, helmeted crows that shone like patent

leather, a blackbird with a yellow bill, voles, shrews, field-
fares, little brown bunnies with their ears laid together along
their backs like spoons, crouching at his feet. A lean, tall, reddish hare, up on its great hind legs, nose a-twitch. The rusty
fox, its muzzle sharpened to a point, laid its head upon his
knee. On the trunk of a scarlet rowan a squirrel clung, to
watch him; a cock pheasant delicately stretched his shimmering neck from a brake of thorn to peer at him. There was a
goat of uncanny whiteness, gleaming like a goat of snow, who
turned her mild eyes towards me and bleated softly, so that he
knew I had arrived.

He smiles. He lays down his pipe, his elder bird call. He lays
upon me his irrevocable hand.

His eyes are quite green, as if from too much looking at the
wood.

There are some eyes can eat you.

The Erlking lives by himself all alone in the heart of the
wood in a house which has only the one room. His house is
made of sticks and stones and has grown a pelt of yellow
lichen. Grass and weeds grow in the mossy roof. He chops
fallen branches for his fire and draws his water from the
stream in a tin pail.

What does he eat? Why, the bounty of the woodland!
Stewed nettles; savory messes of chickweed sprinkled with
nutmeg; he cooks the foliage of shepherd's-purse as if it were
cabbage. He knows which of the frilled, blotched, rotted fungi
are fit to eat; he understands their eldritch ways, how they
spring up overnight in lightless places and thrive on dead
things. Even the homely wood blewits, that you cook like
tripe, with milk and onions, and the egg-yolk-yellow chanter-
elle with its fan vaulting and faint scent of apricots, all spring
up overnight like bubbles of earth, unsustained by nature,
existing in a void. And I could believe that it has been the same
with him; he came alive from the desire of the woods.

He goes out in the morning to gather his unnatural treasures, he handles them as delicately as he does pigeons' eggs, he
lays them in one of the baskets he weaves from osiers. He
makes salads of the dandelion that he calls rude names, "bum
pipes" or "piss-the-beds," and flavors them with a few leaves
of wild strawberry, but he will not touch the brambles; he says
the Devil spits on them at Michaelmas.

His nanny goat, the color of whey, gives him her abundant
milk and he can make soft cheese that has a unique, rank, am-

niotic taste. Sometimes he traps a rabbit in a snare of string
and makes a soup or stew, seasoned with wild garlic. He
knows all about the wood and the creatures in it. He told me
about the grass snakes, how the old ones open their mouths
wide when they smell danger and the thin little ones disappear
down the old ones' throats until the fright is over and out they
come again, to run around as usual. He told me how the wise
toad who squats among the kingcups by the stream in summer
has a very precious jewel in his head. He said the owl was a
baker's daughter; then he smiled at me. He showed me how to
thread mats from reeds and weave osier twigs into baskets and
into the little cages in which he keeps his singing birds.

His kitchen shakes and shivers with birdsong from cage
upon cage of singing birds, larks and linnets, which he piles up
one on another against the wall, a wall of trapped birds. How
cruel it is, to keep wild birds in cages! But he laughs at me
when I say that; laughs, and shows his white, pointed teeth
with the spittle gleaming on them.

He is an excellent housewife. His rustic home is spick-and-
span. He puts his well-scoured saucepan and skillet neatly on
the hearth side by side, like a pair of polished shoes. Over
the hearth hang bunches of drying mushrooms, the thin, curling kind they call jew's-ears, which have grown on the elder
trees since Judas hanged himself on one; this is the kind of lore
he tells me, tempting my half-belief. He hangs up herbs in
bunches to dry, too—thyme, marjoram, sage, vervain, south-
ernwood, yarrow. The room is musical and aromatic and there
is always a wood fire crackling in the grate, a sweet, acrid
smoke, a bright, glancing flame. But you cannot get a tune out
of the old fiddle hanging on the wall beside the birds because
all its strings are broken.

Now, when I go for walks, sometimes in the mornings when
the frost has put its shiny thumbprint on the undergrowth or
sometimes, though less frequently, yet more enticingly, in the
evenings when the cold darkness settles down, I always go to
the Erlking and he lays me down on his bed of rustling straw,
where I lie at the mercy of his huge hands.

He is the tender butcher who showed me how the price of
flesh is love; skin the rabbit, he says! Off come all my clothes.

When he combs his hair that is the color of dead leaves,
dead leaves fall out of it; they rustle and drift to the ground as
though he were a tree, and he can stand as still as a tree when
he wants the doves to flutter softly, crooning as they come,

down upon his shoulders, those silly, fat, trusting woodies with the pretty wedding rings round their necks. He makes his whistles out of an elder twig and that is what he uses to call the birds out of the air—all the birds come; and the sweetest singers he will keep in cages.

The wind stirs the dark wood; it blows through the bushes. A little of the cold air that blows over graveyards always goes with him; it crisps the hairs on the back of my neck but I am not afraid of him; only afraid of vertigo, of the vertigo with which he seizes me. Afraid of falling down.

Falling as a bird would fall through the air if the Erlking tied up the winds in his handkerchief and knotted the ends together so they could not get out. Then the moving currents of the air would no longer sustain them and all the birds would fall at the imperative of gravity, as I fall down for him, and I know it is only because he is kind to me that I do not fall still further. The earth with its fragile fleece of last summer's dying leaves and grasses supports me only out of complicity with him, because his flesh is of the same substance as those leaves that are slowly turning into earth.

He could thrust me into the seedbed of next year's generation and I would have to wait until he whistled me up from my darkness before I could come back again.

Yet when he shakes out those two clear notes from his bird call, I come, like any other trusting thing that perches on the crook of his wrist.

I found the Erlking sitting on an ivy-covered stump winding all the birds in the wood to him on a diatonic spool of sound, one rising note, one falling note; such a sweet piercing call that down there came a soft, chirruping jostle of birds. The clearing was cluttered with dead leaves, some the color of honey, some the color of cinders, some the color of earth. He seemed so much the spirit of the place. I saw without surprise how the fox laid its muzzle fearlessly upon his knee. The brown light of the end of the day drained into the moist, heavy earth; all silent, all still, and the cool smell of night coming. The first drops of rain fell. In the wood, no shelter but his cottage.

That was the way I walked into the bird-haunted solitude of the Erlking, who keeps his feathered things in little cages he has woven out of osier twigs and there they sit and sing for him.

Goat's milk to drink, from a chipped tin mug; we shall eat the oat cakes he has baked on the hearthstone. Rattle of the rain on the roof. The latch clanks on the door; we are shut up inside with one another, in the brown room crisp with the scent of burning logs that shiver with tiny flame, and I lie down on the Erlking's creaking paillasse of straw. His skin is the tint and texture of sour cream, he has stiff, russet nipples ripe as berries. Like a tree that bears bloom and fruit on the same bough together, how pleasing, how lovely.

And now—ach! I feel your sharp teeth in the subaqueous depths of your kisses. The equinoctial gales seize the bare elms and make them whiz and whirl like dervishes; you sink your teeth into my throat and make me scream.

The white moon above the clearing coldly illuminates the still tableaux of our embracements. How sweet I roamed, or rather, used to roam; once I was the perfect child of the meadows of summer, but then the year turned, the light clarified and I saw the gaunt Erlking, tall as a tree with birds in its branches, and he drew me towards him on his magic lasso of inhuman music.

If I strung that old fiddle with your hair, we could waltz together to the music as the exhausted daylight founders among the trees; we should have better music than the shrill prothalamions of the larks stacked in their pretty cages as the roof creaks with the freight of birds you've lured to it while we engage in your profane mysteries under the leaves.

He strips me to my last nakedness, that underskin of mauve, pearlized satin, like a skinned rabbit; then dresses me again in an embrace so lucid and encompassing it might be made of water. And shakes over me dead leaves as if into the stream I have become.

Sometimes the birds, at random, all singing, strike a chord.

His skin covers me entirely; we are like two halves of a seed, enclosed in the same integument. I should like to grow enormously small, so that you could swallow me, like those queens in fairy tales who conceive when they swallow a grain of corn or a sesame seed. Then I could lodge inside your body and you would bear me.

The candle flutters and goes out. His touch both consoles and devastates me; I feel my heart pulse, then wither, naked as a stone on the roaring mattress while the lovely, moony night slides through the window to dapple the flanks of this innocent who makes cages to keep the sweet birds in. Ear me, drink me; thirsty, cankered, goblin-ridden, I go back and back to him to have his fingers strip the tattered skin away and clothe me in his dress of water, this garment that drenches me, its slithering odor, its capacity for drowning.

Now the crows drop winter from their wings, invoke the harshest season with their cry.

It is growing colder. Scarcely a leaf left on the trees and the birds come to him in even greater numbers because, in this hard weather, it is lean pickings. The blackbirds and thrushes must hunt the snails from hedge bottoms and crack the shells on stones. But the Erlking gives them corn and when he whistles to them a moment later you cannot see him for the birds that have covered him like a soft fall of feathered snow. He spreads out a goblin feast of fruit for me, such appalling succulence, I lie above him and see the light from the fire sucked into the black vortex of his eye, the omission of light at the center, there, that exerts on me such a tremendous pressure, it draws me inward.

Eyes green as apples. Green as dead sea fruit.

A wind rises; it makes a singular, wild, low, rushing sound.

What big eyes you have. Eyes of an incomparable luminosity, the numinous phosphorescence of the eyes of lycanthropes. The gelid green of your eyes fixes my reflective face. It is a preservative, like a green liquid amber; it catches me. I am afraid I will be trapped in it forever like the poor little ants and flies that stuck their feet in resin before the sea covered the Baltic. He winds me into the circle of his eye on a reel of birdsong. There is a black hole in the middle of both your eyes; it is their still center; looking there makes me giddy, as if I might fall into it.

Your green eye is a reducing chamber. If I look into it long enough, I will become as small as my own reflection, I will diminish to a point and vanish. I will be drawn down into that black whirlpool and be consumed by you. I shall become so small you can keep me in one of your osier cages and mock my loss of liberty. I have seen the cage you are weaving for me; it is a very pretty one and I shall sit, hereafter, in my cage among the other singing birds but I—I shall be dumb, from spite.

When I realized what the Erlking meant to do to me, I was shaken with a terrible fear and I did not know what to do, for I loved him with all my heart and yet I had no wish to join the whistling congregation he kept in his cages although he looked after them very affectionately, gave them fresh water every day and fed them well. His embraces were his enticements and yet—oh, yet!—they were the branches of which the trap itself was woven. But in his innocence he never knew he might be the death of me, although I knew from the first moment I saw him how Erlking would do me grievous harm.

Although the bow hangs beside the old fiddle on the wall, all the strings are broken so you cannot play it. I don't know what kind of tunes you might play on it, if it were strung again; lullabies for foolish virgins, perhaps, and now I know the birds don't sing, they only cry because they can't find their way out of the wood, have lost their flesh when they were dipped in the corrosive pools of his regard and now must live in cages.

Sometimes he lays his head on my lap and lets me comb his lovely hair for him; his combings are leaves of every tree in the wood and dryly susurrate around my feet. His hair falls down over my knees. Silence like a dream in front of the spitting fire while he lies at my feet and I comb the dead leaves out of his languourous hair. The robin has built his nest in the thatch again this year; he perches on an unburnt log, cleans his beak, ruffles his plumage. There is a plaintive sweetness in his song and a certain melancholy, because the year is over—the robin, the friend of man, in spite of the wound in his breast from which Erlking tore out his heart.

Lay your head on my knee so that I can't see the greenish, inward-turning suns of your eyes anymore.

My hands shake.

I shall take two huge handfuls of his rustling hair as he lies half dreaming, half waking, and wind them into ropes, very softly, so he will not wake up, and softly, with hands as gentle as rain, I shall strangle him with them.

Then she will open all the cages and let the birds free; they will change back into young girls, every one, each with the crimson imprint of his love bite on their throats.

She will carve off his great mane with the knife he uses to skin the rabbits; she will string the old fiddle with five single strings of ash-brown hair.

Then it will play discordant music without a hand touching it. The bow will dance over the new strings of its own accord and they will cry out: "Mother, Mother, you have murdered me!"

The Elphin Knight

Traditional Scots Ballad

There were three sisters fair and bright
Over the hills and far away
And they three loved an Elphin Knight
The cold wind blows thy plaid away

The eldest sister let him in
Over the hills and far away
And barred the door with a silver pin
The cold wind blows thy plaid away

The second sister made his bed
Over the hills and far away
And placed soft pillows under his head
The cold wind blows thy plaid away

The youngest sister fair and bright
Over the hills and far away
Resolved to wed this Elphin Knight
The cold wind blows thy plaid away

"Married with me if thou wouldst be
Over the hills and far away
A courtesy thou must do to me
The cold wind blows thy plaid away

"Sew for me a cambric shirt
Over the hills and far away
Without any seams or needle-work
The cold wind blows thy plaid away

"Wash it then in yon spring-well
Over the hills and far away
Where water n'er rain nor yet rain fell
The cold wind blows thy plaid away

"And dry it then on yon hawthorn
Over the hills and far away
Where sun n'er shone since Adam was born"
The cold wind blows thy plaid away

She said "If I do this for thee
Over the hills and far away
Then ye must do something for me
The cold wind blows thy plaid away

"Find for me an acre of land
Over the hills and far away
Between the salt-water and the sea strand
The cold wind blows thy plaid away

"Plow it with thy blowing horn
Over the hills and far away
And sow it with a pepper corn
The cold wind blows thy plaid away

"Reap it with a sickle of leather
Over the hills and far away
And bind it up with a peacock's feather
The cold wind blows thy plaid away

"When ye have done and finished thy work
Over the hills and far away
Ye can come to me, love, for thy cambric shirt"
The cold wind blows thy plaid away

"My curse on those who learned thee
Over the hills and far away
For I've a wife and babies three"
The cold wind blows thy plaid away

"My maidenhead I'll keep then still
Over the hills and far away
Let the Elphin Knight do what he will"
The cold wind blows thy plaid away

Rhian and Garanhir

By Grail Undwin

From the beginning, Garanhir knew that his love for the Lady Rhian could most accurately be described as hopeless. He was a wandering elf-knight (virtually a mercenary), in possession of neither an ancient name nor wealth nor holdings, while she was an heiress of the noblest lineage in all of Annwyn, as the Welsh elves call their kingdom. Her father, Lord Gwyion, was of the Tylwyth Teg, descended from the Children of Llyr through the line of Prince Edeyrn, the King's brother; his house was, therefore, of the most illustrious and upon her marriage his daughter would inherit the barony, at least in time.

Yes, it was all quite hopeless; nevertheless, Garanhir dared to hope. There was no particular reason he could give for his optimism. Love, it seems, has its own arguments which are so potent that cool Reason can seldom, if ever, prevail. And upon thinking it over, the knight was not entirely certain that his suit was totally devoid of promise. Although his lineage was obscure, he had served with distinction in the north, when Earl Fuatha made war on the Fomorian giants; he had become a famous jouster at the court of Queen Tanaquil in the realm of the British elves; and he had once fought the dreaded Muirdris which had formerly inhabited Loch Rury—a feat still celebrated by the *jongleurs,* and for which he had been praised by none other than King Gwyn ap Nudd himself.

Then, too, Gwyion's house had fallen upon hard times. During the troubles over potential secession, Lord Gwyion

had backed Duke Arawn's party in defiance of the Crown; not
only had this imprudence served to dissipate the family fortune but it had cost him his place at court. And when, later, he
went a-wooing, he had found the princely houses of Annwyn,
Sorcha, and Logres cool to him, and had taken to wife a lady
of the Pellings—these were a rather bourgeois clan of Welsh
elves who dwelt in and about Corwrion and were descended
from one of the Ladies of the Lake who had wed a mortal
knight of the Round Table ages before. They were hence half-
elfin and half-mortal, and were not exactly to be considered of
the *haut monde*; so perhaps there was hope for Garanhir yet.

He had fallen in love with Lady Rhian during a tourney held
in celebration of her father's victory against the Muryans, a
troublesome tribe of Cornish fays whose forest land bordered
upon Lord Gwyion's demesne. He had bested several famous
champions in the lists, including Prince Madon and the gallant
Sir Kynon. In fact, he had been fortunate enough to win the
victor's chaplet of oak leaves from Rhian's own hand. It was
slim and soft and white, that hand, and her hair was smooth
and palely golden. Of her face, he was aware only of her eyes,
which were like sapphires in the shadow: they so bedazzled
him that it was not until later that he noticed the softness and
the sweetness of her lips. He rode from the jousting field filled
with an immense and heady joy, and very happy that her
father had enlisted him among his knights for the battle with
the Muryans.

Since then he had seen her often, but generally from a
distance. And they had spoken never, although he was sure
she knew him at sight, for usually she sent a cool, sweet smile
in his direction when he doffed his cap. Perhaps she remembered how valiantly he had unseated the famous Madon, or
how Sir Kynon had shivered his lance against Garanhir's
shield as against a mighty boulder.

He was very much in love, was Garanhir. He dreamed of
saving his lady fair from some monster or other—a pool-
dwelling Addanc, perhaps, such as Sir Peredur overcame, or a
terrifying Cyhyraeth which wails like the banshee, or a shaggy,
monstrous Pwcca. But, to his displeasure, no Addanc or
Cyhyraeth or Pwcca ever wandered into these parts of Annwyn. Occasionally the Spriggans came reaving down the
border, and from time to time the Muryans burned or pillaged
outlying farms, and once a hairy Urisk strayed far from the

woods of Scotland and caused a bit of trouble. But no danger of *essentially chivalric* nature presented itself, so that Garanhir could defend his lady love in a genuinely knightly manner. It was most annoying when you stopped to think of it.

As for Rhian, she went Maying when it was May, and went to balls when there were balls, and to fashionable weddings and garden parties, and was even presented at court by an obliging aunt who remained in the Royal Favor. She did not visibly pine or become wan and listless, as ladies do in the approved romances. And, surrounded by gentlemen and courtiers, she scarcely seemed to notice Garanhir, that grim-faced and husky mercenary who lingered about her father's castle long after his service had ended, finding one pretext after another to stay. If she loved him it seemed to him that it certainly did not show; her manner was affable but aloof, gracious at best, more distant than familiar. And they never spoke to one another.

Now it must be noted that the malady from which Sir Garanhir suffered was rare among the elves. They are, in general, a cold and heartless race; they are capable of tenderness and affection, it is true, but more often they are inclined to cruelty and to a certain sly, malicious humor. While they know passion, they rarely feel love: but Garanhir loved, and you would have thought that it was he who shared half-elfin, half-mortal descent, rather than Rhian.

One day in spring it was bruited about that the elf-baron had agreed to his daughter's marriage with one Cathlar, an elfin laird whose castle stood on the edges of the Wood of Celidon in the north. A pang went through Garanhir's heart when the whispered rumor reached him: it felt like an arrow of chill ice. His vision blurred and he had to hold onto the back of a chair to catch his breath. He hoped that it was not truly so, and that night he did not sleep.

But it was indeed so, and before long preparations began for the wedding, which was to be in Scotland. The women were all a-twitter, like a flock of busy sparrows: there was a bridal veil to be woven of fragile lace, a trousseau to be gathered, endless plans and arrangements to be decided upon. Garanhir was sick at heart but said nothing.

And, in time, the husband-to-be arrived from the Seelie Court, accompanied by an entourage of the Sluagh (as the warrior elves of Scotland are known). He was tall and lean, with dark red hair and an uncouth way of dressing in tartans—at least, it seemed uncouth to Garanhir. The women gossiped about his height and his dark eyes and his languourous smile, which set many a heart to fluttering. Garanhir loathed him on sight, and avoided his presence, even to pretending illness when the visitor reviewed the troops.

As the time for Rhian's departure came nearer, wild thoughts went through Garanhir's brain and he became distraught. He dreamt of killing her suitor and of carrying his love away into the forests of Annwyn—of becoming a *gunna*, as the elfin exiles and outlaws are called; a lone and solitary pair, they would live in a rude hut and he would hunt all day while she wove and spun. He knew this was madness, of course. In real life, such things do not happen.

And then, at last, the horrible day came. Mounted on a sleek and handsome Kelpie, Rhian rode through the gates of her ancestral castle for the last time, surrounded by her knightly entourage, her betrothed at her side. The morning should by all rights have been dark and gloomy, with lowering iron-colored clouds and, perhaps, drenching rains; incongruously, it was as bright and lovely a spring morning as Garanhir could remember.

Gay and laughing, Rhian rode past where he stood, her hand in Cathlar's, leaning to catch his joking whisper, the sunlight gloriously caught in her glorious hair, her face as fresh and filled with color as a flower. Garanhir's heart went dead as a stone as she rode by him without even a glance.

"Who is that fellow with the broad shoulders and the face like doom?" inquired Cathlar, glimpsing Garanhir in the crowd. Rhian turned in her saddle and looked back—looked full into Garanhir's face with an inquiring, unreadable expression that shook him to the roots of his soul.

"I do not know him," she said carelessly, for only Cathlar to hear. "Some knight of my father's, I presume."

And they rode on, taking to the air, circling the towers of the castle in a long train, then dwindling into the northern sky. And Garanhir turned away, blind and deaf with a strange, bitter joy, and he bore with him down all the many centuries of his immortality the bright memory of that one, brief, backward look—she had loved him all this time, after all, and could not bear to leave without one farewell glance into his face! Later, he told a troubadour at the King's court of it, and, later still, a song was made of their silent, unspoken love.

But that song never came to Rhian's ears, and she was never to know of the peculiar mistake by which "Rhian and Garanhir" were ever after to be remembered as among the famous lovers of the elves of Britain.

As for Sir Garanhir, he died in time—for the elves, although immortal, do sometimes die or can at least be slain—in a great battle against invading pirates from Lochlann in which he won lasting renown. They say he died happy, with Rhian's name on his lips. That is probably an invention of the poets. But not necessarily, for sometimes, as in the matter of that brief, backward look, Zurvan is kind even to lovers.

The Woodcutter's Daughter

By Alison Uttley

In an old thatched cottage deep in the forest lived the wood-cutter, Thomas Furze, and Margaret his wife. They were a homely couple, simple and hardworking. All they wanted was a child, and at last their wish was granted. Late in life, a little girl was born to them.

She was as pretty and dainty a little creature as they were plain and weather-beaten. They gazed upon her with rapture, as if a small angel had come to earth. Her cheeks were pink as the cherries in the wild wood, her skin was white as cherry blossom, and her lips as sweet as honeystalks. So the child was christened by the romantic name of Cherry-blossom, with Cherry for short.

The father was the romantic one of that family, for the mother was practical and matter-of-fact. Between them they managed not to spoil the little girl, and they brought her up very sensibly, considering all things.

Little Cherry helped her mother in the cottage even when she was very tiny. She went to the village school through the clearing in the wood, and her father took her part of the way, past the goblin trees and haunted dells. At night she sat by the fire, listening to the tales he told her while he carved strange beasts from the curiously shaped bits of wood he brought back from the forest. He always had an eye for odd things, and he noticed that some boughs were shaped like animals, and that faces sometimes seemed to peer from a crooked tree trunk.

The stories he told were very exciting and real to the little

257

girl. He spoke of dragons that once lived on earth, of fairies like brilliant winged people flying in the air, and mermaids dwelling in the coral sea. Cherry never wanted a book to read while she could hear such legends and folk tales. As her father talked in his low voice, and her mother's knitting-needles clicked, half-impatiently, the girl saw princes and peris, fairies and elves, inhabiting a world beyond the radiant moon, yet close to her own forest home.

As she grew taller and older, and perhaps a little wiser, she hid the fairy tales in a corner of her heart, and she left the village school. She had to earn her living, but the good people did not want her to leave home. So she put a little card, printed in neat characters with her own pen and ink, in the front parlour window.

"Good plain sewing and ladies' stuffs made up," it said, for all the world to read. The only ones who saw it were the tawny squirrels who ran along the low garden fence, and the robin hopping by the door.

However, there was soon plenty of sewing to be done, for Cherry's mother spoke to her own friends in the town and they told their mistresses and patrons. Once in three months Cherry went to this town, walking many a mile, and sometimes getting a lift in the carrier's cart for part of the way. She stayed the night at her grandmother's, a very ancient woman nearing ninety. She collected sewing to be done from the ladies, who admired the neat tiny stitches of the forest girl. At any rate, they said, her mother had taught her to sew, down there in the backwoods.

They gave her chemises and petticoats to make from fine linen, to be tucked and gathered, feather-stitched and button-holed, ruffled and pleated, and the threads drawn in lovely patterns. There were handkerchiefs to be hem-stitched and lace caps to be made. Cherry packed her parcels in a bundle, bound them with a cord, and carried them on her back to the cottage.

Then she worked hard with her needle, stitching the dainty work for the fine ladies, sewing her hopes and desires and dreams into the linen, embroidering her fancies on the edges with many a smile at her inmost thoughts.

One night when her parents had gone to bed, the girl sat late finishing a piece of work. Her needle flashed in and out of the white linen, and she leaned close to see her stitches. The lamp flickered out, and as there was no paraffin in the barrel in the house corner, she lighted a candle and finished by its slender beam. Then she sat by the fire, staring into the depths, half-dreaming, watching the golden castles in the flames, the towers that glowed and smouldered and fell with a silent clatter of gilded walls. She gazed at the flames, jagged like the antlers of the stags in the forest. They were soft as fur, they blew together in pointed tongues. They changed before her eyes, and lo! there was a golden bear in the great cave of the fire.

The girl stared bewitched at the lovely wonder of it, fearing the beautiful beast would disappear like all the marvels of enchantment in the world of fire. But he stayed there, walking slowly through the gateway of the caves and under the arches of gold. Outside, the wind howled like a wolf, it snarled and snapped, and the forest whined back. The door shook, and the shuttered windows rattled and bumped as an icy blast swept through the crannies and caught up the flames.

Cherry was afraid the fire would break up, and the pattern of mystery dissolve, but the bear came down the glowing embers, stepping silently along a track in the flame. It grew larger, its fur quivered, it raised its head and walked out of the fire, and stood on the wide hearthstone, its shaggy feet on the sanded stone.

It shook itself and sparks flew about the room. Its golden eyes gazed at her, questioning her. The girl sprang to her feet in terror and started for the door, but the bear spoke softly to her. Its voice was deep as the wind when it rumbles in the hollows of caves. Its eyes were filled with supplication. Its head was lowered before her in submission.

"Woodcutter's daughter. Give me a drink of cold water, I pray you of your mercy," it said.

Cherry ran to the bucket of spring water standing on the slnk, and she carried it to the hearth. The bear drank and drank, and its colour ebbed and flowed, from gold to black, as the coldness of the water touched it.

"Woodcutter's daughter. Give me food, I pray you of your charity," said the bear.

She went to the cupboard and brought out a honeycomb and a newly-baked loaf, which she put on a platter for the bear. It ate with enjoyment, finishing every morsel, while she watched, fascinated.

"Woodcutter's daughter, what is your name?" asked the bear.

"Cherry, if you please," she answered. "Cherry-blossom I was christened, but they call me Cherry for short."

The bear looked around, at the little kitchen, at the young girl, at the white sewing heaped on the oak table near the guttering candle.

"Cherry-red, cherry-white, cherry-blossom on the tree. Will you make a coat for me?" asked the bear, chanting and swaying as it spoke.

"A coat?" she cried, surprised and puzzled.

"Make me a green coat from the nettles in the cherry grove in yon woods," said the bear.

"I know where you mean, but—but—I don't think I can sew nettles," she hesitated.

"Stitch it finely and closely and bring it here for me," said the bear.

"Well, I'll try," said Cherry, "but I've never stitched nettles before. Only linen and lace. Not nettles."

The bear was already moving back into the fire, stepping across the hearthstone, growing smaller, walking into the heart of the flames. Deep in the fire Cherry saw the bear with a thin chain round its neck led by a sprite to the cave. It faded away, the fire burned up with a fierce rush, and she waited. She took the poker and stirred the cave. With a crash it fell, and the cherrywood log lay over the place, hiding everything.

"Am I dreaming, or did I really see a bear?" she asked herself. The empty water-bucket stood on the hearth, and the platter beside it. There was a loaf missing from the cupboard, and the honeycomb gone. She packed up her sewing, took her candle, and went slowly up to bed.

"Father, I dreamed that a great golden bear came out of the fire," she said the next morning.

"Ah! That's a lucky omen. Such dreams come when you burn cherrywood. I've been cutting down some of those great wild cherry trees in the clearing among the nettles. They are very ancient trees and some of them are hollow. That's where I found that wild bees' honeycomb."

"Where is that honeycomb, Cherry? I can't find it. I thought we had four loaves of bread, too, and there are only three," cried Mrs. Furze, peering in the bread-mug.

"Mother, I gave them to the bear, in my dream," stammered Cherry.

"You gave them to a bear? Whatever do you mean?" exclaimed her mother.

"Don't ye bother her, Mother," said the placid woodcutter. "This is a strange happening. I've heard of it before, long ago, when I was a little 'un. It has happened afore, and it brings good luck, they say."

No more was said, for Mrs. Furze was a sensible woman. Cherry went out to the grove where her father was thinning old cherry trees. She gathered a great basketful of nettles, which was nothing unusual, for those simple people had nettle broth and boiled nettles as vegetables many days in the spring when their garden had no green stuff.

The woodcutter left his work and joined his pretty daughter.

"See here, Cherry lass," said he, taking her arm and leading her to a place where the nettles were thickest. "Look here. This carved stone has meant something once upon a time."

He showed her a broken pillar of marble, carved with grapes and leaves and strange outlandish beasts.

"There's an old story told that many many years ago a castle stood here, in this clearing. It is country talk that wherever the nettles grow, there was once a dwelling for man. Nowhere in this forest are there nettles save here, among these broken stones and cherry trees."

"Yes, Father. I know," said Cherry. "I used to play under these wild cherry trees when I was coming home from school. I found many a piece of marble carving. I love this spot, Father."

"The cherry trees must have been in the castle grounds," continued her father, poking about in the rubble. "Nobody living knows what happened, or remembers anything about it. Your grandmother knew the tale, but her parents could not remember the castle."

He returned to his work and Cherry took the nettles home. She began to stitch them together with some hesitation at first and then with an eagerness to succeed in the task. Nettles are thick and fibrous, covered with tiny hairs that sting, but a good grasp overcomes the sharp prickles of poison. The girl sewed every night when her parents were in bed. She dare not

let them see what she was making. A coat of nettles for a bear!
They would think she was crazed. Although her father would
perhaps understand, her mother would scold, so she kept the
work secret.

Each night she went to the oak press and took out the nettle
coat. She stitched more leaves to it, using tiny stitches, and
sewing with extreme care and delicacy.

Many a time she went back to the clearing for more nettles,
and as she gathered them she exposed the old foundations of
the castle. She could trace the rooms, the great hall, the hearth
which was under a yew tree, and the courtyard, where four
cherry trees grew. Beyond was the orchard, where the older
trees spread their aged branches, and gardens, all wild with
primrose and dog roses.

Although she made many inquiries when she went to the
town with her bundle of finished garments, nobody could tell
her anything of the dwelling that had once stood there.

Sometimes when she sewed the green coat, the golden bear
came out of the fire and lay on the hearthstone by her side.
Round his neck was a chain. He never spoke, except once
when he asked for food and water. He did not answer her
questions. He lay with his head on his paws, watching her, and
she felt strangely happy when he was with her. Then back he
lumbered into the fire, and the thin black sprite caught him
and led him into the golden caves.

The coat sleeves were finished, the lapels stitched, and the
two large hunting pockets were fixed to the sides. It was a
grand coat, fit for a real hunter to wear, with plenty of room
for game in those pockets. Cherry spread it out on the floor
and looked to see if anything were missing. There were no buttons, of course, and she wondered whether to put some bone
buttons from her mother's work-box down the front. She
made three large button-holes ready.

Then she took her needle and some threads of her own silky
gold hair and embroidered flowers of the dead-nettle down
the front. It was an extra, something special, for the bear's
pleasure.

That night she saw three golden buttons glowing in the heart
of the fire. She raked them out, and left them to cool on the
hearth. Then she stitched them on to the embroidered front of
the coat and waited, for she was certain the bear would appear.

Out of the fire he walked, getting larger and larger, till he stood, a great golden bear, by her side.

"It is well done," said he. "Put the coat away till the time comes. Keep it safe until I am ready."

"When will that be?" she asked, disappointed that nothing happened.

"A few more months," he replied. "Now you must make yourself a dress, beautiful as snow. Make a dress fit for a queen."

"How can I?" she laughed. "I have no stuff for a dress, and I couldn't wear one of nettles."

"Make it of cherry blossom, like your name," said the bear, and he went into the fire without another word.

The next day Cherry went to the woods for the flowers of the wild cherry. The trees were full of bloom, but the petals would soon fall, and there was little time left before they would all be gone. She carried a basketful of flowers home and set to work at her dress. As she could only work at night, she sewed all through the long hours. It was easier than the nettle coat, for the bunches of flowers clung together with a few stitches, and soon she had a complete dress, sweet-scented and exquisite. The flowers did not fade, they stayed fresh as when they were gathered. Cherry spread out the dress for the bear to see.

Out from the fire he came and praised her work. "A little longer," said he. "I must wait till winter comes, and the fire roars up the chimney. Keep the cherry-blossom dress and the nettle coat near you till I come again. Be ready for me. You can save me, and only you."

Many days passed and although Cherry looked into the fire each night there was no golden bear in the caves. The flames danced in the fireplace, the smoke, blue as a gentian, billowed among the trees. Cherry sat sewing her ladies' garments. Sometimes she went out to the woods, to visit the deserted castle, with its wild cherry trees, red-gold in the autumn.

"When winter comes I shall see my bear," she thought. "I shall be glad to see him. I miss his company. When he came from the fire and lay by my side, how happy I was! Is it possible to love an animal with all one's heart?"

One winter morning she got ready early to visit the town. Her work was completed, and it was time to take it back before Christmas.

"I wish I could come with you, my dear," said her mother. "It is too far for me to walk, but you can carry a basket of eggs to your grandmother, and give her our love. Take care of yourself, child."

Cherry kissed her mother, and walked away in deep content, with her basket and bundle, for there had been a sprinkling of snow in the night, and the woods were very beautiful. She passed through the grove of old cherry trees, and they seemed to be in blossom. Each tree had round bunches of snow hanging on the knotted boughs, in clusters like real flowers. The shape of the castle walls was clearly outlined by the snow, and she stayed a few minutes to rest there, before she went on her journey. Under the yew tree the ground was clean and dry, with a carpet of yew needles. She thought she saw a shadow pass, and there were footprints in the snow of some large animal. There were chippings of wood left by her father, and she drew them together in a spirit of make believe, and piled them on the hearth. She placed four carved bits of stone round the kindling wood.

"Father can boil his can of tea here, when he comes," she said to herself. "He will know I got it ready for him."

Then away she walked, with quick light step, laughing to herself as she thought of his surprise. She had brought the nettle coat and the cherry dress in a parcel to show to her grandmother, and this also made her light-hearted. Surely the gold bear would not mind if such an old woman saw what she had made. If she had seen him, she would have asked permission, but it was several months since he had appeared in the fire. Perhaps when she got back home, he would be there. Her heart was warm with the thought of him.

She wore a blue handkerchief tied round her hair, and a thick brown cloak over her old blue frock. Her clothes were shabby, but in the woods they seemed to be exactly right. The snow shadows were blue, and the misty distances were azure, and the tree trunks were brown. The girl went along like a living shadow, moving swiftly in and out of the beeches and oaks and hollies. The carrier's cart never appeared, and she had to walk the whole way to the town. That made her late, and she went straight to her grandmother's house, and rested there for the night.

She showed the old lady the delicate sewing she carried in

her pack, but she kept back the nettle coat and the cherry-blossom dress in sudden shyness. She told the news of the forest, how her father had built a new shed by the house, and a squirrel had come to live in it, and the deer had broken into the garden one night, and the pig had been killed to make bacon for the winter months. She gave her grandmother a little carved egg-cup her father had sent, and the eggs from her mother, and some brawn she had made and chitterlings. Still she hesitated to mention the nettle coat and the cherry-blossom dress.

"Did you see anything in the forest when you came through?" asked the grandmother in quavering tones.

"Oh yes. I saw many things, Grandmother. Green woodpeckers, and the deer, and red squirrels, and a white owl, half asleep in a tree, and—"

"Nay, not those things, child. Did you see any queer things? Any strange unco' things?" persisted the grandmother.

"Why yes, Grandmother. I saw the trees all silvered with snow, the dark faces in the trunk of that tree I know very well. Like a gnome it is, all wrinkled and large-mouthed. I saw a shadow move once, in the wild cherry grove. I stayed there a minute among the trees in the clearing where there are carved stones, and, do you know, the trees seemed to be covered with cherry blossom, even in the middle of winter!"

"There's something else," said the old woman slowly. "A bear has been seen. A golden bear, they say. The hunters are after him. Yellow-gold fur, and gold eyes he has. They are after him."

"I'm not afraid of a bear," said Cherry. "I saw one in the fire. A golden bear, right in the flames, and he came out to me."

"Ah! I saw a bear in the fire long ago. It was there in the middle of the fire, and there it stayed. It's a lucky sign, they say. A bear in the fire is a piece of good luck waiting for you, but it's different from one outside in the wood. It might catch you."

The old woman wandered on, and Cherry was half asleep. She decided not to show her nettle coat but only the blossom dress, to her grandmother.

"I made this, Grandmother," said she, turning the skirt and bodice of snowy petals on the rug and shaking out the folds.

"Do you like it?"

The grandmother touched the lovely blossom with a shaking finger.

"Is it your wedding dress, my child?" she asked.

"I don't know, Grandmother. I made it out of the cherry blossom growing on the wild trees in our wood," said Cherry.

"Who are you going to marry, Cherry?"

"Nobody has asked me, Grandmother."

"This must be your wedding dress, my Cherry," said the grandmother. "I was asked to make a flower-petal dress when I was a girl, but I never made it."

"Who asked you, Grandmother?" asked Cherry, softly.

"One in a dream, I think. I heard a voice as I sat by the fire, and I never forgot. Life would have been different if I had hearkened and made it, I reckon."

She shook her head, and went off to sleep.

The next day Cherry called at the houses of the rich ladies, the goldsmith's wife, the clergyman's wife, the banker's lady, and the brewer's lady. She received her payment, and the new sewing to be done. They thanked her in their high hard voices, they shook their silken skirts, and sat in their fine rooms as she stood before them in her shabby clothes and took their orders.

"Mind you sew neatly. Take care you don't spoil this silk. This is soft as a flower. You have doubtless never had such fine materials, girl," they said.

"Once I sewed flower petals," said Cherry, curtsying.

"Nonsense. Nobody can sew flower petals," they scolded. There was quite a heap of linen and silk with gold threads woven in it, and soft wools, fine as cobwebs. Cherry's fame had spread and many ladies wanted the woodcutter's daughter to make their clothes, to stitch her pretty patterns on their shifts and nightgowns and petticoats.

It was late before Cherry had collected all the work to be done, but she knew her mother would be anxious if she stayed another night. She wrapped her money in her handkerchief, and stored it in her bosom. She carried the bundle on her back, tied up in layers of cloth to keep the stuffs clean. In her hand she had a lantern and the small packet with the nettle coat and the cherry-blossom dress.

"You won't get home till after dark, Cherry love," sighed the grandmother, and she gave her a loaf of bread and cheese for the journey, and a pannikin of tea.

"I shall be safe, Grandmother," said Cherry, kissing her on her withered soft cheeks.

"Mind that golden bear. Don't let him catch you. God be with you."

"And God be with you, Grandmother," said Cherry.

She waved the lantern and started off down the road. When she got to the forest she lighted the lantern and walked through the beech trees on the narrow track she knew so well. But the lantern threw strange deceiving shadows as she got deeper into the woods, the trees seemed to be moving this way and that, advancing and retreating to confuse her, and the pathway was hidden in snow. She went on for some miles, then the snow began to fall again, dancing flakes rushed to meet her, blinding her eyes, catching in her hair, lying on the pack till it was heavy as lead.

She struggled on, tired and sleepy, finding her way by the stars, until the snow hid the sky. She realized she was lost, and the only thing to do was to find a shelter and wait till morning. She went on, bewildered by the snow, seeking a tree where she could rest. She was unafraid, for she had often been in the forest at night, and she knew there was nothing to harm her. Then she saw the dark branches of a yew, and her feet stumbled against the stones on the ground. She knew where she was, and this could be no other place than the ruins of the old castle, two or three miles from her home.

Her lantern light fell on the heap of wood she had collected the day before, when she started off for the town. In a minute she had lighted it, and was warming her frozen hands at the blaze. She sat down in the warmth and shelter of the ancient yew tree, and spread out her wet cloak and scarf to dry. The yew needles were soft as a bed under her feet, and she leaned against the red scaly trunk of the tree, and unfastened the bundle with the nettle cloak and the cherry-blossom dress. They were crumpled and flattened, but she shook them so that the petals were fresh, and the nettles were stiff and shapely. Then she hung the two garments in the yew tree, and busied herself, warming her tea in the little pannikin, throwing more wood on the blaze.

The crackle of the fire was so cheerful, she laughed aloud with pleasure.

"Here I am, drinking tea in the ruined castle, and soon I shall be at home. I know my way blindfold from here. What a tale to tell!"

She was startled by the distant sound of shots, and in a minute a great golden bear came towards her, his side bleeding, his eyes half glazed with pain.

"My bear. My golden bear," she cried, running to him. She tore up her scarf and bound it round him. She opened the linen pack and took the choicest pieces to wrap on his wound.

"Drink this," she said, and she poured out the rest of her tea, and offered him food. He shook his head, and lay down by her side.

Then she heard the noise of approaching hooves, and shouts of men. They had seen the light, and were coming, nearer, nearer.

"Into the fire! Quick, or they will catch you," she cried.

"I escaped from the fire, Cherry-blossom, and now you send me back," he said.

"It's your only chance," said Cherry, urgently.

The bear stood by the crackling flames for a moment, and his blood made a pool on the ground. Then he entered the fire, and even as the flames touched him, he became smaller and disappeared in the leaping tongues.

The huntsmen galloped up, surrounding the tree.

"Which way did that bear go? He must have passed quite close. See—his blood is here. He might have killed you, for he was wounded and dangerous," they shouted.

"He went out of sight. He disappeared," said Cherry, standing with her back to the fire.

"And what are you doing here, a young girl alone in the forest at night?" asked one of the men, as the others galloped off.

"I am Cherry, the woodcutter's daughter. This is where my father has been cutting wood. I got lost coming from the town, and I am going home," explained Cherry.

"Then get on my horse and ride with me, Cherry, for you are a pretty girl, and I shall enjoy taking you home," said the young man.

"No, sir." Cherry thought of her bear, caught in his woodland fire.

"What? You don't want to go home? Then I shall stay here and take care of you. It isn't safe with a bear in the woods," he said impudently, and he flung himself from his horse, tied to it a branch of the tree, and sat down by the fire. He threw fresh boughs on it, and Cherry stood looking anxiously at him. Far away they could hear the horses galloping.

"Now tell me what you are doing here in the forest," he continued. "That wounded bear came very close to you. Here is its blood."

Even as he spoke, pointing to the ground, Cherry could see the golden bear moving in the flames. She went towards the man, lest he should notice, but the horse was aware of the presence of the wild beast. It reared and plunged in terror, neighing shrilly.

"What's the matter with you?" called the man, but he went to calm it. "The bear must be somewhere near, he's so frightened."

"Oh, golden bear! Come out and rescue me," whispered Cherry, leaning to the fire.

Out from the flames stepped the bear, growing tall and splendid as he left the fire, but already the horse had broken away and the man ran after it.

"Throw the nettle coat into the fire," commanded the bear. "Throw it into the flames, now."

She tossed the green coat upon the burning wood expecting to see it shrivel up. The leaves were burnt away, but the strong fibres of the nettles remained. It became a coat of gold, a web of gleaming threads like a coat of mail. The bear picked it from the embers and put it on his shoulders. Immediately he changed to a man, tall and fair, strong and valiant.

"Now throw your cherry-petal dress on the fire," commanded the bear-man, pointing to the white dress hanging in the yew tree.

Cherry obeyed, and the dress became white as silver with every petal clear and bright.

"Wear it, Cherry. It is for your wedding. Now look around."

Then Cherry saw that she was standing in the hall of the castle, and the yew tree was the wide chimney stack, growing up, with dark boughs curving to the roof. The fire glowed on the hearth, shining up to the great timbers of the roof, to the lovely branches of the tree. The floor was covered with the carpet of yew needles, and seats of carved stone and rugs of fur were in their places. Through the high windows of the spreading yew tree Cherry could see the stars, and at the far end there was a great door of carved wood.

"All this was destroyed hundreds of years ago," said the bear-man. "My enemy broke the castle walls and enchanted me, so that nobody knew what had happened. In a night all disappeared, and the memory of the place went. Into the flames I was cast and I was held there until a girl should release me. I became a bear of fire, doomed to lie in the gold cave, from which I could come forth at times to seek a rescuer. I tried to escape, but nobody helped me, until I found you. You made me the burning coat of nettles which had sprung up from the bones of my home. You brought me home to life again by lighting this fire on the hearthstone, from which it had been banished for centuries. You sat in the hall and played in the castle when you were a little child, among the broken stones. I loved you then, as I watched you with the cherry-blossoms falling upon your hair. I saw you unafraid, playing your childish games in my house."

"Yes," said Cherry, staring round in wonder and delight. "I used to play here. I always thought there was somebody watching me, sharing my games. I never felt alone."

"Woodcutter's daughter, will you marry me?" asked the bear-man.

"Yes, golden bear," said Cherry. "I will marry you."

"We will go back to your father and mother and bring them here to the castle. For long years I have been like one dead, held within the fire by the spirit of evil. Now I am alive and I love you, Cherry-blossom."

"And I love you, golden bear," answered Cherry, holding up her face to his.

He put his arms around her, and down upon their heads fell a shower of snow which was cherry petals. The cherry trees in the grove were in flower again that winter's day. The turtle dove cooed in the boughs of the yew tree, and a charm of goldfinches flew across the open chamber. Together the bear-man and Cherry-blossom walked out into the moonlit wood, to the thatched cottage of the old people. They looked back, and in the place of the cherry wood stood a great house, white as snow, shining like fire, with a yew tree rising from its walls.

The Famous Flower
of Serving Men

Traditional Scots Ballad

My mother did me deadly spite,
for she sent thieves in the darksome night:
they put my household all to flight,
they robbed my bower,
they slew my knight.
They could not do to me more harm
so they slew the baby in my arms
and left me nought to wrap him in
but the bloody bloody sheets
my love lay in.
They left me nought to dig a grave
but the bloody bloody sword that slew my babe.
All alone the grave I made.
All alone the tears I shed.
All alone the bell I rung.
All alone sweet psalms sung.
I leant my head against the block
and there I cut my lovely locks—
I cut my locks
and I changed my name
from Fair Elise to Sweet William,
and went to court to serve a King
as the Famous Flower of Serving Men.
So well I served my lord the King
that he made me his chamberlain;

271

he loves me as his own son—
the Famous Flower of Serving Men.
But all alone in my bed asleep,
it's there I dream a dreadful dream:
I see my bed swimming with blood,
and I see the thieves
gathered round my head. . . .

Our King has to the hunting gone;
he's ta'en no lords nor gentlemen.
Our King has left them all behind,
and the Famous Flower of Serving Men.
Our King has rode the woods all around,
and all the day has nothing found.
He's turned onto the road to home—
and it's there he's spied
the milk white hind.
The hind she ran, the hind she flew,
the hind she trampled the brambles through.
First she'd melt, then she'd shine,
sometimes before,
sometimes behind.
"Oh what is this? How can this be?"
Such a hind as this he ne'er did see!
Such a hind as this was never born—
he feared she meant him deadly harm.
All in a glade the hind grew nigh,
the sun grew bright all in his eye.
He sprang down,
his sword he drew—
and she vanished ever from his view. . . .

All around the grass was green,
and in the glade a grave was seen.
He sat him down upon the stone;
great weariness it seized him on.
Great silence hung from tree to sky,
the woods were still,
the sun on fire,
as through the woods a white dove came,
as through the woods it made a moan.

The dove he sat down on the stone;
so sweet he looked, so soft he sang:
"Alas the day my love became
the Famous Flower of Serving Men."
The blood red tears fell as rain,
and still he sat,
and still he sang:
"Alas the day my love became
the Famous Flower of Serving Men."
Our King cried out and he wept full sore,
and loud unto the dove did call:
"Oh pretty bird, come sing it plain.
Come tell me of this serving man."
"It was her mother's deadly spite.
for she sent thieves in the darksome night.
They came to rob, they came to slay.
They made their sport.
They went their way.
And don't you think that her heart was sore
as she lay the mold in her love's bright hair?
And don't you think her heart was woe
as she turned her back, away to go?
How she wept as she changed her name
from Fair Elise to Sweet William,
and went to court to serve a King
as the Famous Flower of Serving Men."
The bloody tears lay all around.
Our King has mounted up and gone,
and one thought is in his mind:
that he does love a serving man.
And as he rode himself alone,
a dreadful oath he there has sworn:
that he would hunt her mother down
just as he'd hunt the wild wood swine. . . .

There's four and twenty maidens all
and they are playing at the ball—
but fairer than all of them
is Sweet William the serving man.
Our King has ridden to the hall,
he's ridden in among them all

and he's lifted her to his saddle brim,
and there he's kissed her,
cheek and chin.
The nobles stood and they stretched their eyes;
the ladies took to their fans and smiled:
such a strange home-coming
no gentleman had ever seen.
Our King has sent his soldiers all
unto her mother's stately hall.
They've ta'en her who's caused such woe
and made her to the prison go.
Loudly did her mother cry,
the tears were standing in her eyes:
"Alas the day that she became
the Famous Flower of Serving Men."
And softly then our King did say,
as in his arms Sweet William lay;
"God bless the day that you became
the Famous Flower of Serving Men."
To put an end to further strife
he's ta'en Sweet William for a wife;
the like before was never seen—
a serving man to be a Queen.

Touk's House

By Robin McKinley

There was a witch who had a garden. It was a vast garden, and very beautiful; and it was all the more beautiful for being set in the heart of an immense forest, heavy with ancient trees and tangled with vines. Around the witch's garden the forest stretched far in every direction, and the ways through it were few, and no more than narrow footpaths.

In the garden were plants of all varieties; there were herbs at the witch's front door and vegetables at her rear door; a hedge, shoulder-high for a tall man, made of many different shrubs lovingly trained and trimmed together, surrounded her entire plot, and there were bright patches of flowers scattered throughout. The witch, whatever else she might be capable of, had green fingers; in her garden many rare things flourished, nor did the lowliest weed raise its head unless she gave it leave.

There was a woodcutter who came to know the witch's garden well by sight; and indeed as it pleased his eyes he found himself going out of his way to pass it in the morning as he began his long day with his axe over his arm, or in the evening as he made his way homeward. He had been making as many of his ways as he could pass near the garden for some months when he realized that he had worn a trail outside the witch's hedge wide enough to swing his arms freely and let his feet find their own way without fear of clutching roots or loose stones. It was the widest trail anywhere in the forest.

The woodcutter had a wife and four daughters. The children were their parents' greatest delight, and their only delight, for they were very poor. But the children were vigorous and healthy, and the elder two already helped their mother in the bread-baking, by which she earned a little more money for the family, and in their small forest-shadowed village everyone bought bread from her. That bread was so good that her friends teased her, and said her husband stole herbs from the witch's garden, that she might put it in her baking. But the teasing made her unhappy, for she said such jokes would bring bad luck.

And at last bad luck befell them. The youngest daughter fell sick, and the local leech, who was doctor to so small a village because he was not a good one, could do nothing for her. The fever ate up the little girl till there was no flesh left on her small bones, and when she opened her eyes she did not recognize the faces of her sisters and mother as they bent over her.

"Is there nothing to do?" begged the woodcutter; and the doctor shook his head. The parents bowed their heads in despair, and the mother wept.

A gleam came into the leech's eyes, and he licked his lips nervously. "There is one thing," he said, and the man and his wife snapped their heads up to stare at him. "The witch's garden . . ."

"The witch's garden," the wife whispered fearfully.

"Yes?" said the woodcutter.

"There is an herb that grows there, that will break any fever," said the doctor.

"How will I know it?" said the woodcutter.

The doctor picked up a burning twig from the fireplace, stubbed out the sparks, and drew black lines on the clean-swept hearth. "It looks so—" And he drew small three-lobed leaves. "Its color is pale, like the leaves of a weeping willow, and it is a small bushy plant, rising no higher than a man's knee from the ground."

Hope and fear chased themselves over the wife's face, and she reached out to clasp her husband's hand. "How will you come by the leaves?" she said to him.

"I will steal them," the woodcutter said boldly.

The doctor stood up, and the woodcutter saw that he trembled. "If you—bring them home, boil two handsful in water, and give the girl as much of it as she will drink." And he left hastily.

"Husband—"

He put his other hand over hers. "I pass the garden often. It will be an easy thing. Do not be anxious."

On the next evening he waited later than his usual time for returning, that dusk might have overtaken him when he reached the witch's garden. That morning he had passed the garden as well, and dawdled by the hedge, that he might mark where the thing he sought stood; but he dared not try his thievery then, for all that he was desperately worried about his youngest daughter.

He left his axe and his yoke for bearing the cut wood leaning against a tree, and slipped through the hedge. He was surprised that it did not seem to wish to deter his passage, but yielded as any leaves and branches might. He had thought at least a witch's hedge would be full of thorns and brambles, but he was unscathed. The plant he needed was near at hand, and he was grateful that he need not walk far from the sheltering hedge. He fell to his knees to pluck two handsful of the life-giving leaves, and he nearly sobbed with relief.

"Why do you invade thus my garden, thief?" said a voice behind him, and the sob turned in his throat to a cry of terror.

He had never seen the witch. He knew of her existence because all who lived in the village knew that a witch lived in the garden that grew in the forest; and sometimes, when he passed by it, there was smoke drifting up from the chimney of the small house, and thus he knew someone lived there. He looked up, hopelessly, still on his knees, still clutching the precious leaves.

He saw a woman, only a little past youth to look at her, for her hair was black and her face smooth but for lines of sorrow and solitude about the mouth. She wore a white apron over a brown skirt; her feet were bare, her sleeves rolled to the elbows, and her hands were muddy.

"I asked you, what do you do in my garden?"

He opened his mouth, but no words came out; and he shuddered till he had to lean his knuckles on the ground so that he would not topple over. She raised her arm, and pushed her damp hair away from her forehead with the back of one hand; but it seemed, as he watched her, that the hand, as it fell through the air again to lie at her side, flickered through some sign that briefly burned in the air; and he found he could talk.

"My daughter," he gasped. "My youngest daughter is ill—she will die. I—I stole these"— And he raised his hands pleadingly, still holding the leaves which, crushed between his fingers, gave a sweet minty fragrance to the air between their faces—"that she might live."

The witch stood silent for a moment, while he felt his heart beating in the palms of his hands. "There is a gate in the hedge. Why did you not come through it, and knock on my door, and ask for what you need?"

"Because I was afraid," he murmured; and silence fell again.

"What ails the child?" the witch asked at last.

Hope flooded through him and made him tremble. "It is a wasting fever, and there is almost nothing of her left; often now she does not know us."

The witch turned away from him, and walked several steps; and he staggered to his feet, thinking to flee; but his head swam, and when it was clear the witch stood again before him. She held a dark green frond out to him; its long sharp leaves nodded over her hand, and the smell of it made his eyes water.

"Those leaves you wished to steal would avail you and your daughter little. They make a pleasant taste, steeped in hot water, and they give a fresh smell to linens long in a cupboard. Take this as my gift to your poor child; steep this in boiling water, and give it to the child to drink. She will not like it, but it will cure her; and you say she will die else."

The woodcutter looked in amazement at the harsh-smelling bough; and slowly he opened his fists, and the green leaves fell at his feet, and slowly he reached out for what the witch offered him. She was small of stature, he noticed suddenly, and slender, almost frail. She stooped as lithely as a maiden, and picked up the leaves he had dropped, and held them out to him.

"These too you shall keep, and boil as you meant to do, for your child will need a refreshing draught after what you must give her for her life's sake.

"And you should at least have the benefit they can give you, for you shall pay a heavy toll for your thievery this night. Your wife carries your fifth child; in a little time, when your fourth daughter is well again, she shall tell you of it. In seven months she shall be brought to bed, and the baby will be big and strong. That child is mine; that child is the price you shall forfeit for this night's lack of courtesy."

"Ah God," cried the woodcutter, "do you barter the death of one child against the death of another?"

"No," she said. "I give a life for a life. For your youngest child shall live; and the baby not yet born I shall raise kindly, for I"—she faltered— "I wish to teach someone my herblore.

"Go now. Your daughter needs what you bring her." And the woodcutter found himself at the threshold of his own front door, his hands full of leaves, and his axe and yoke still deep in the forest; nor did he remember the journey home.

The axe and yoke were in their accustomed place the next morning; the woodcutter seized them up and strode into the forest by a path he knew would not take him near the witch's garden.

All four daughters were well and strong seven months later when their mother was brought to her fifth confinement. The birth was an easy one, and a fifth daughter kicked her way into the world; but the mother turned her face away, and the four sisters wept, especially the youngest. The midwife wrapped the baby up snugly in the birth-clothes that had comforted four infants previously. The woodcutter picked up the child and went into the forest in the direction he had avoided for seven months. It had been in his heart since he had found himself on his doorstep with his hands full of leaves and unable to remember how he got there, that this journey was one he would not escape; so he held the child close to him, and went the shortest path he knew to the witch's garden. For all of its seven months' neglect, the way was as clear as when he had trodden it often.

This time he knocked upon the gate, and entered; the witch was standing before her front door. She raised her arms for the child, and the woodcutter laid her in them. The witch did not at first look at the baby, but rather up into the woodcutter's face. "Go home to your wife, and the four daughters who love you for they know you. And know this too: that in a year's time your wife shall be brought to bed once again, and the child shall be a son."

Then she bowed her head over the baby, and just before her black hair fell forward to hide her face, the woodcutter saw a look of love and gentleness touch the witch's sad eyes and mouth. He remembered that look often, for he never again found the witch's garden, though for many years he searched the woods where he knew it once had been; till he was no longer sure that he had ever seen it, and his family numbered four sons as well as four daughters.

Maugie named her new baby Erana. Erana was a cheerful baby and a merry child; she loved the garden that was her home; she loved Maugie, and she loved Maugie's son, Touk. She called Maugie by her name, Maugie, and not mother, for Maugie had been careful to tell her that she was not her real mother; and when little Erana had asked, "Then why do I live with you, Maugie?" Maugie had answered: "Because I always wanted a daughter."

Touk and Erana were best friends. Erana's earliest memory was of riding on his shoulders and pulling his long pointed ears, and drumming his furry chest with her small heels. Touk visited his mother's garden every day, bringing her wild roots that would not grow even in her garden, and split wood for her fire. But he lived by the riverbank, or by the pool that an elbow of the river had made. As soon as Erana was old enough to walk more than a few steps by herself, Touk showed her the way to his bit of river, and she often visited him when she could not wait for him to come to the garden. Maugie never went beyond her hedge, and she sighed the first time small Erana went off alone. But Touk was at home in the wild woods, and taught Erana to be at home there too. She lost herself only twice, and both those times when she was very small; and both times Touk found her almost before she had time to realize she was lost. They did not tell Maugie about either of these two incidents, and Erana never lost herself in the forest again.

Touk often took a nap at noontime, stretched out full length in his pool and floating three-quarters submerged; he looked like an old mossy log, or at least he did till he opened his eyes, which were a vivid shade of turquoise, and went very oddly with his green skin. When Erana first visited him she was light enough to sit on his chest as he floated, and paddle him about like the log he looked, while he crossed his hands on his breast and watched her with a glint of blue between almost-closed green eyelids. But she soon grew too heavy for this amusement, and he taught her instead to swim, and though she had none of his troll blood to help her, still she was a pupil to make her master proud.

One day as she lay, wet and panting, on the shore, she said to him: "Why do you not have a house? You do not spend all your hours in the water, or with us in the garden."

He grunted. He sat near her, but on a rough rocky patch that she had avoided in favor of a grassy mound. He drew his knees up to his chin and put his arms around them. There were spurs at his wrists and heels, like a fighting cock's, and though he kept them closely trimmed, still he had to sit slightly pigeon-toed to avoid slashing the skin of his upper legs with the heel-spurs, and he grasped his arms carefully well up near the elbow. The hair that grew on his head was as pale as young leaves, and inclined to be lank; but the tufts that grew on the tops of his shoulders and thickly across his chest, and the crest that grew down his backbone, were much darker, and curly.

"You think I should have a house, my friend?" he growled, for his voice was always a growl.

Erana thought about it. "I think you should *want* to have a house."

"I'll ponder it," he said, and slid back into the pool and floated out toward the center. A long-necked bird drifted down and landed on his belly, and began plucking at the ragged edge of one short trouser leg.

"You should learn to mend, too," Erana called to him; Erana loathed mending. The bird stopped pulling for a moment and glared at her. Then it reached down and seized a thread in its beak and wrenched it free with one great tug. It looked challengingly at Erana and then slowly flapped away, with the mud-colored thread trailing behind it.

"Then what would the birds build their nests with?" he said, and grinned. There was a gap between his two front teeth, and the eyeteeth curved well down over the lower lip.

Maugie taught her young protégé to cook and clean, and sew—and mend—and weed. But Erana had little gift for herblore. She learned the names of things, painstakingly, and the by-rote rules of what mixtures did what and when; but her learning never caught fire, and the green things in the garden did not twine lovingly around her when she paused near them as they seemed to do for Maugie. She learned what she could, to please Maugie, for she felt sad that neither her true son nor her adopted daughter could understand the things Maugie might teach; and because she liked to know the ingredients of a poultice to apply to an injured wing, and what herbs, mixed in with chopped-up bugs and earthworms, would make orphaned fledglings thrive.

For Erana's fifteenth birthday, Touk presented her with a stick. She looked at it, and then she looked at him. "I thought you might like to lay the first log of my new house," he said, and she laughed.

"You have decided then?" she asked.

"Yes; in fact I began to want a house long since, but I have only lately begun to want to build one," he said. "And then I thought I would put it off till your birthday, that you might make the beginning, as it was your idea first."

She hesitated, turning the little smooth stick in her hand. "It is—is it truly your idea now, Touk? I was a child when I teased you about your house; I would never mean to hold you to a child's nagging."

The blue eyes glinted. "It is my idea now, my dear, and you can prove that you are my dearest friend by coming at once to place your beam where it belongs, so that I may begin."

Birthdays required much eating, for all three of them liked to cook, and they were always ready for an excuse for a well-fed celebration; so it was late in the day of Erana's fifteenth birthday that she and Touk made their way—slowly, for they were very full of food—to his riverbank. "There," he said, pointing across the pool. Erana looked up at him questioningly, and then made her careful way around the water to the stand of trees he had indicated; he followed on her heels. She stopped, and he said over her shoulder, his breath stirring her hair, "You see nothing? Here—" And he took her hand, and led her up a short steep slope, and there was a little clearing beyond the trees, with a high mossy rock at its back, and the water glinting through the trees before it, and the trees all around, and birds in the trees. There were already one or two birdhouses hanging from suitable branches at the clearing's edge, and bits of twig sticking out the round doorways to indicate tenants in residence.

"My house will lie—" And he dropped her hand to pace off its boundaries; when he halted he stood before her again, his blue eyes anxious for her approval. She bent down to pick up four pebbles; and she went solemnly to the four corners he had marked, and pushed them into the earth. He stood, watching her, at what would be his front door; and last she laid the stick, her birthday present, just before his feet. "It will be a lovely house," she said.

Touk's house was two years in the building. Daily Erana told Maugie how the work went forward; how there were to be five rooms, two downstairs and three above; how the frame jointed together, how the floor was laid and the roof covered it. How Touk had great care over the smallest detail—how not only every board slotted like silk into its given place, but that there were little carven grinning faces peering out from the corners of cupboards, and wooden leaves and vines, that at first glance seemed no more than the shining grain of the exposed wood, coiling around the arches of doorways. Touk built two chimneys, but only one fireplace. The other chimney was so a bird might build its nest in it.

"You must come see it," Erana said to her foster-mother. "It is the grandest thing you ever imagined!" She could only say such things when Touk was not around, for Erana's praise of his handiwork seemed to make him uncomfortable, and he blushed, which turned him an unbecoming shade of violet.

Maugie laughed. "I will come when it is finished, to sit by the first fire that is laid in the new fireplace."

Touk often asked Erana how a thing should be done: the door here or there in a room, should the little face in this corner perhaps have its tongue sticking out for a change? Erana, early in the house-building, began picking up the broken bits of trees that collected around Touk's work, and borrowed a knife, and began to teach herself to whittle. In two years' time she had grown clever enough at it that it was she who decorated the stairway, and made tall thin forest creatures of wood to stand upon each step and hold up the railing, which was itself a scaled snake with a benevolent look in his eye as he viewed the upper hallway, and a bird sitting on a nest in a curl of his tail instead of a newel post at the bottom of the staircase.

When Touk praised her work in turn, Erana flushed too, although her cheeks went pink instead of lavender; and she shook her head and said: "I admit I am pleased with it, but I could never have built the house. Where did you learn such craft?"

Touk scratched one furry shoulder with his nails, which curled clawlike over the tips of his fingers. "I practised on my mother's house. My father built it; but I've put so many patches on it, and I've stared at its beams so often, that wood looks and feels to me as familiar as water."

Even mending seemed less horrible than usual, when the tears she stitched together were the honorable tears of house-building. Maugie was never a very harsh taskmaster, and as the house-fever grew, quietly excused Erana from her lessons on herblore. Erana felt both relieved and guilty as she noticed, but when she tried half-heartedly to protest, Maugie said, "No, no, don't worry about it. Time enough for such things when the house is finished." Erana was vaguely surprised, for even after her foster-mother had realized that her pupil had no gift for it, the lessons had continued, earnestly, patiently, and a trifle sorrowfully. But now Maugie seemed glad, even joyful, to excuse her; perhaps she's as relieved as I am, Erana thought, and took herself off to the riverbank again. She wished all the more that Maugie would come too, for she spent nearly all her days there, and it seemed unkind to leave her foster-mother so much alone; but Maugie only smiled her oddly joyful smile, and hurried on her way.

The day was chosen when the house was to be called complete; when Maugie would come to see the first fire laid—"And to congratulate the builder," Erana said merrily. "You will drown him in congratulations when you see."

"Builders," said Touk. "And I doubt the drowning."

Erana laughed. "Builder. And I don't suppose you *can* be drowned. But I refuse to argue with you; your mother knows us well enough to know which of us to believe."

Maugie smiled at them both.

Erana could barely contain her impatience to be gone as Maugie tucked the last items in the basket. This house-feast would outdo all their previous attempts in that line, which was no small feat in itself; but Erana, for once in her life, was not particularly interested in food. Maugie gave them each their bundles to carry, picked up her basket, and looked around yet again for anything she might have forgotten. "We'll close the windows first; it may rain," she said meditatively; Erana made a strangled noise and dashed off to bang sashes shut.

But they were on their way at last. Maugie looked around with mild surprise at the world she had not seen for so long.

"Have you never been beyond your garden?" Erana said curiously. "Were you born in that house?"

"No. I grew up far away from here. My husband brought me to this place, and helped me plant the garden; he built the house." Maugie looked sad, and Erana asked no more, though she had long wondered about Maugie's husband and Touk's father.

They emerged from the trees to the banks of Touk's river pool. He had cut steps up the slope to his house, setting them among the trees that hid his house from the water's edge, making a narrow twisting path of them, lined with flat rocks and edged with moss. Touk led the way.

The roof was steeply pitched, and two sharp gables struck out from it, with windows to light the second storey; the chimneys rose from each end of the house, and their mouths were shaped like wide-jawed dragons, their chins facing each other and their eyes rolling back toward the birdhouses hanging from the trees. And set all round the edges of the roof were narrow poles for more birdhouses, but Touk had not had time for these yet.

Touk smiled shyly at them. "It is magnificent," said his mother, and Touk blushed a deep violet with pleasure. "Next I will lay a path round the edge of the pool, so that my visitors need not pick their way through brambles and broken rock." They turned back to look at the water, gleaming through the trees. Touk stood one step down, one hand on the young tree beside him, where he had retreated while he awaited his audience's reaction; and Maugie stood near him. As they were he was only a head taller than she, and Erana noticed for the first time, as the late afternoon sun shone in their faces, that there was a resemblance between them. Nothing in feature perhaps, except that their eyes were set slanting in their faces, but much in expression. The same little half-smiles curled the corners of both their mouths at the moment, though Maugie lacked Touk's splendidly curved fangs.

"But I did not want to put off this day any longer; for today we can celebrate two things together."

"A happy birthday, Erana," said Maugie, and Erana blinked, startled. "I had forgotten."

"You are seventeen today," Maugie said.

Erana repeated: "I had forgotten." But when she met Touk's turquoise eyes, suddenly the little smile left his face and some other emotion threatened to break through; but he dropped his eyes and turned his face away from her, and his hand trailed slowly down the bole of the tree. Erana was troubled and hurt, for he was her best friend, and she stared at his averted shoulder. Maugie looked from one to the other of them, and began to walk toward the house.

It was not as merry an occasion as it had been planned, for something was bothering Touk, and Erana hugged her hurt to herself and spoke only to Maugie. They had a silent if vast supper around the new-laid fire, sitting cross-legged on the floor, for Touk had not yet built any furniture. Maugie interrupted the silence occasionally to praise some detail she noticed, or ask some question about curtains or carpeting, which she had promised to provide. Her first gift to the new house already sat on the oak mantelpiece: a bowl of potpourri, which murmured through the sharper scents of the fire, and the richer ones of the food.

Into a longer silence than most, Erana said abruptly: "This is a large house for only one man."

The fire snapped and hissed; the empty room magnified the sound so that they were surrounded by fire. Touk said: "Troll. One troll."

Erana said, "Your mother—"

"I am human, yes, but witch-blood is not quite like other human blood," said Maugie.

"And I am my father's son anyway," said Touk. He stretched one hand out to the fire, and spread his fingers; they were webbed. The firelight shone through the delicate mesh of capillaries.

"Your father?"

"My father was a troll of the north, who—"

"Who came south for the love of a human witch-woman," said Maugie gravely.

Erana again did not ask a question, but the silence asked it for her. "He died thirty years ago; Touk was only four. Men found him, and . . . he came home to the garden to die." Maugie paused. "Trolls are not easily caught; but these men were poachers, and trolls are fond of birds. He lost his temper."

Touk shivered, and the curling hair down his spine erected and then lay flat again; Erana thought she would not wish to see him lose his temper. She said slowly, "And yet you stayed here."

"It is my home," Maugie said simply; "it is the place I was happy, and, remembering, I am happy again."

"And I have never longed for the sight of my own kind," said Touk, never raising his eyes from the fire. "I might have gone north, I suppose, when I was grown; but I would miss my river, and the birds of the north are not my friends."

Erana said: "My family?"

"You are a woodcutter's daughter," Maugie said, so quietly that Erana had to lean toward her to hear her over the fire's echoes. "I—did him a favor, but he, he had—behaved ill; and I demanded a price. My foster-daughter, dearer than daughter, it was a trick and I acknowledge it. . . ."

She felt Maugie's head turn toward her, but Touk stared steadfastly at the hearth. "You always wanted a daughter," Erana said, her words as quiet as Maugie's had been, and her own eyes fixed on Maugie's son, who swallowed uncomfortably. "You wish that I should marry your son. This house he has built is for his wife."

Maugie put out a hand. "Erana, love, surely you—"

Touk said: "No, mother, she has not guessed; has never guessed. I have seen that it has never touched her mind, for I would have seen if it had. And I would not be the one who forced her to think of it." Still he looked at the flames, and now, at last, Erana understood why he had not met her eyes that afternoon.

She stood up, looked blindly around her. "I—I must think."

Maugie said miserably, "Your family—they live in the village at the edge of the forest, south and east of here. He is the woodcutter; she bakes bread for the villagers. They have four daughters and four sons. . . ."

Erana found her way to the door, and left them.

Her feet took her back to the witch's garden, the home she had known for her entire life. She had wondered, fleetingly, once she understood that Maugie was not her mother, who her blood kin might be; but the question had never troubled her, for she was happy, loving and loved. It was twilight by the time she reached the garden; numbly she went to the house and fetched a shawl and a kerchief, and into the kerchief she put food, and then went back into the garden and plucked a variety of useful herbs, ones she understood, and tied the kerchief round them all. She walked out of the garden, and set her feet on a trail that no one had used since a woodcutter had followed it for the last time seventeen years before.

She walked for many days. She did not pause in the small village south and east of the witch's garden; she did not even turn her head when she passed a cottage with loaves of fresh bread on shelves behind the front windows, and the warm smell of the bread assailed her in the street. She passed through many other small villages, but she kept walking. She did not know what she sought; and so she kept walking. When she ran out of food, she did a little simple doctoring to earn more, and then walked on. It was strange to her to see faces that were not Maugie's or Touk's, for these were the only faces she had ever seen, save those of the forest beasts and birds; and she was amazed at how eagerly her simple herbcraft was desired by these strangers. She found some herbs to replace the ones she used in the fields and forests she passed; but the finest of them were in the garden she had left behind.

The villages grew larger, and became towns. Now she heard often of the king, and occasionally she saw a grand coach pass, and was told that only those of noble blood rode in such. Once or twice she saw the faces of those who rode within; but the faces looked no more nor less different than any of the other human faces she saw, although they wore more jewels.

Erana at last made her way to the capital city; but the city gates bore black banners. She wondered at this, and inquired of the gate guard, who told her that it was because the king's only son lay sick. And because the guard was bored, he told the small shabby pedestrian that the king had issued a proclamation that whosoever cured the prince should have the king's daughter in marriage, and half the kingdom.

"What is the prince's illness?" Erana asked, clutching her kerchief.

The guard shrugged. "A fever; a wasting fever. It has run many days now, and they say he cannot last much longer. There is no flesh left on his bones, and often he is delirious."

"Thank you," said Erana, and passed through the gates. She chose the widest thoroughfare, and when she had come some distance along it she asked a passerby where the king's house lay; the woman stared at her, but answered her courteously.

The royal gate too was draped in black. Erana stood before it, hesitating. Her courage nearly failed her, and she turned to go, when a voice asked her business. She might still have not heeded it, but it was a low growly kind voice, and it reminded her of another voice dear to her; and so she turned toward it. A guard in a silver uniform and a tall hat smiled gently at her; he had young daughters at home, and he would not wish any of them to look so lost and worn and weary. "Do not be frightened. Have you missed your way?"

"N-no," faltered Erana. "I—I am afraid I meant to come to the king's house, but now I am not so sure."

"What is it the king or his guard may do for you?" rumbled the guard.

Erana blushed. "You will think it very presumptuous, but —but I heard of the prince's illness, and I have some—small— skill in healing." Her nervous fingers pulled her kerchief open, and she held it out toward the guard. The scent of the herbs from the witch's garden rose into his face and made him feel young and happy and wise. He shook his head to clear it. "I think perhaps you have more than small skill," he said; "and I have orders to let all healers in. Go." He pointed the way, and Erana bundled her kerchief together again clumsily, and followed his gesture.

The king's house was no mere house, but a castle. Erana had never seen anything like it before, taller than trees, wider than rivers; the weight of its stones frightened her, and she did not like walking up the great steps and under the vast stone archway to the door and the liveried man who stood beside it, nor standing in their gloom as she spoke her errand. The liveried man received her with more graciousness and less kindness than the silver guard had done; and he led her without explanation to a grand chamber where many people stood and whispered among themselves like a forest before a storm. Erana felt the stone ceiling hanging over her, and the stone floor jarred her feet. At the far end of the chamber was a dais with a tall chair on it, and in the chair sat a man.

"Your majesty," said Erana's guide, and bowed low; and Erana bowed as he had done, for she understood that one makes obeisance to a king, but did not know that women were expected to curtsey. "This—girl—claims to know something of leechcraft."

The whispering in the chamber suddenly stilled, and the air

quivered with the silence, like the forest just before the first lash of rain. The king bent his heavy gaze upon his visitor but when Erana looked back at him, his face was expressionless.

"What do you know of fevers?" said the king; his voice was as heavy as his gaze, and as gloomy as the stones of his castle, and Erana's shoulders bowed a little beneath it.

"Only a little, your majesty," she said; "but an herb I carry," and she raised her kerchief, "does the work for me."

"If the prince dies after he suffers your tending," said the king in a tone as expressionless as his face, "you will die with him."

Erana stood still a moment, thinking, but her thoughts had been stiff and uncertain since the evening she had sat beside a first-laid fire in a new house, and the best they could do for her now was to say to her: "So?" Thus she answered: "Very well."

The king raised one hand, and another man in livery stepped forward, his footsteps hollow in the thick silence. "Take her to where the prince lies, and see that she receives what she requires and and—do not leave her alone with him."

The man bowed, turned, and began to walk away; he had not once glanced at Erana. She hesitated, looking to the king for some sign; but he sat motionless, his gaze lifted from her and his face blank. Perhaps it is despair, she thought, almost hopefully: the despair of a father who sees his son dying. Then she turned to follow her new guide, who had halfway crossed the long hall while she stood wondering, and so she had to hasten after to catch him up. Over her soft footsteps she heard a low rustling laugh as the courtiers watched the country peasant run from their distinguished presence.

The guide never looked back. They came at last to a door at which he paused; and Erana paused panting behind him. He opened the door reluctantly. Still without looking around, he passed through it and stopped. Erana followed him, and went around him, to look into the room.

It was not a large room, but it was very high; and two tall windows let the sunlight in, and Erana blinked, for the corridors she had passed through had been grey, stone-shadowed. Against the wall opposite the windows was a bed, with a canopy, and curtains pulled back and tied to the four pillars at its four corners. A man sat beside the bed; three more sat a little distance from it; and a man lay in the bed. His hands lay

over the coverlet and the fingers twitched restlessly; his lips
moved without sound, and his face on the pillow turned back
and forth.

Erana's guide said: "This is the latest—leech. She has seen
the king and he has given his leave." The tone of his voice left
no doubt of his view of this decision.

Erana straightened her spine, and held up her bundle in her
two hands. She turned to her supercilious guide and said: "I
will need hot water and cold water." She gazed directly into
his face as she spoke, while he looked over her head. He
turned, nonetheless, and went out.

Erana approached the bed and looked down; the man sitting by it made no move to give her room, but sat stiffly where
he was. The prince's face was white to the lips, and there
were hollows under his eyes and cheekbones; and then as she
watched a red flush broke out, and sweat stained his cheeks
and he moaned.

The guide returned, bearing two pitchers. He put them on
the floor, and turned to go. Erana said, "Wait," and he took
two more steps before he halted, but he did halt, with his back
to her as she knelt down by the pitchers and felt the water
within them. One was tepid; the other almost tepid. "This will
not do," Erana said angrily, and the man turned around, as if
interested against his will that she dared protest. She picked up
the pitchers and with one heave threw their contents over the
man who had fetched them. He gasped, and his superior look
disappeared and his face grew mottled with rage. "I asked for
hot water and *cold* water. You will bring it, as your king commanded you to obey me. With it you will bring me two bowls
and two cups. Go swiftly and return more swiftly. Go *now*."
She turned away from him, and after a moment she heard him
leave. His footsteps squelched.

He returned as quickly as she had asked; water still rolled
off him and splashed to the floor as he moved. He carried two
more pitchers; steam rose from the one, and dew beaded the
other. Behind him a woman in a long skirt carried the bowls
and cups.

"You will move away from the bed please," Erana said;
and the man who had not made room for her paused just long
enough to prove that he paused but not so long as to provoke
any reaction, stood up and walked to the window. She poured
some hot water into one bowl, and added several dark green

leaves that had once been long and spiky, but had become bent
and bruised during their journey from the witch's garden; and
she let them steep till the sharp smell of them hung like a green
fog in the high-ceilinged room. She poured some of the infu-
sion into a cup, and raised the prince's head from the pillow,
and held the cup under his nostrils. He breathed the vapor,
coughed, sighed; and his eyes flickered open. "Drink this,"
Erana whispered, and he bowed his head and drank.

She gave him a second cup some time later, and a third as
twilight fell; and then as night crept over them she sat at his
bedside and waited, and as she had nothing else to do she
listened to her thoughts; and her thoughts were of Touk and
Maugie, and of the king's sentence hanging over her head like
the stone ceiling, resting on the prince's every shallow breath.

All that night they watched, and candlelight gave the
prince's wan face a spurious look of health. But at dawn when
Erana stood stiffly and touched his forehead, it was cool. He
turned a little away from her, and tucked one hand under his
cheek, and lay quietly; and his breathing deepened and
steadied into sleep.

Erana remained standing, staring dumbly down at her
triumph. The door of the room opened, and her uncoopera-
tive guide of the day before entered, bearing on a tray two
fresh pitchers of hot and cold water, and bread and cheese and
jam and meat. Erana brewed a fresh minty drink with the cold
water, and gave it to the prince with hands that nearly trembled. She said to the man who had been her guide, "The
prince will sleep now, and needs only the tending that any patient nurse may give. May I rest?" The man, whose eyes now
dwelt upon her collarbone, bowed, and went out, and she
followed him to a chamber not far from the prince's. There
was a bed in it, and she fell into it, clutching her herb bundle
like a pillow, and fell fast asleep.

She continued to assist in the tending of the prince since it
seemed to be expected of her, and since she gathered that she
should be honored by the trust in her skill she had so hardly
earned. Within a fortnight the prince was walking, slowly but
confidently; and Erana began to wonder how long she was expected to wait upon him; and then she wondered what she
might do with herself once she was freed of that waiting.

There was no one at the court she might ask her questions.

For all that she had been their prince's salvation, they treated her as distantly as they had from the beginning, albeit now with greater respect. She had received formal thanks from the king, whose joy at his son's health regained made no more mark on his expression and the tone of his voice than fear of his son's death had done. The queen had called Erana to her private sitting room to receive her thanks. The princess had been there too; she had curtseyed to Erana, but she had not smiled, any more than her parents had done.

And so Erana continued from day to day, waiting for an unknown summons; or perhaps for the courage to ask if she might take her leave.

A month after the prince arose from his sickbed he called his first Royal Address since his illness had struck him down. The day before the Address the royal heralds had galloped the royal horses through the streets of the king's city, telling everyone who heard them that the prince would speak to his people on the morrow; and when at noon on the next day he stood in the balcony overlooking the courtyard Erana had crossed to enter the palace for the first time, a mob of expectant faces tipped up their chins to watch him.

Erana had been asked to attend the royal speech. She stood in the high-vaulted hall where she had first met the king, a little behind the courtiers who now backed the prince, holding his hands up to his people, on the balcony. The king and queen stood near her; the princess sat gracefully at her ease in a great wooden chair lined with cushions a little distance from the open balcony. It seemed to Erana, she thought with some puzzlement, that they glanced at her often, although with their usual impassive expressions; and there was tension in the air that reminded her of the first time she had entered this hall, to tell the king that she knew a little of herbs and fevers.

Erana clasped her hands together. She supposed her special presence had been asked that she might accept some sort of royal thanks in sight of the people; she, the forest girl, who was still shy of people in groups. The idea that she might have to expose herself to the collective gaze of an audience of hundreds made her very uncomfortable; her clasped hands felt cold. She thought: it will please these people if I fail to accept their thanks with dignity; and so I shall be dignified. I will look over the heads of the audience, and pretend they are flowers in a field.

She did not listen carefully to what the prince was saying. She noticed that the rank of courtiers surrounding the prince had parted, and the king stepped forward as if to join his son on the balcony. But he paused beside Erana, and seized her hands, and led or dragged her beside him; her hands were pinched inside his fingers, and he pulled at her awkwardly, so that she stumbled. They stood on the balcony together, and she blinked in the sunlight; she looked at the prince, and then turned her head back to look at the king, still holding her hands prisoned as if she might run away. She did not look down, at the faces beyond the balcony.

"I offered my daughter's hand in marriage and half my kingdom to the leech who cured my son." The king paused, and a murmur, half-surprise and half-laughter, wrinkled the warm noontide air. He looked down at Erana, and still his face was blank. "I wish now to adjust the prize and payment for the service done me and my people and my kingdom: my son's hand in marriage to the leech who saved him, and beside him, the rule of all my kingdom."

The prince reached across and disentangled one of her hands from his father's grip, so that she stood stretched between them, like game on a pole brought home from the hunt. The people in the courtyard were shouting; the noise hurt her head, and she felt her knees sagging, and the pull on her hands, and then a hard grip on her upper arms to keep her standing; and then all went black.

She came to herself lying on a sofa. She could hear the movements of several people close beside her, but she was too tired and troubled to wish to open her eyes just yet on the world of the prince's betrothed; and so she lay quietly.

"I think they might have given her some warning," said one voice. "She does have thoughts of her own."

A laugh. "Does she? What makes you so sure? A little nobody like this—I'm surprised they went through with it. She's not the type to insist about anything. She creeps around like a mouse, and never speaks unless spoken to. Not always then."

"She spoke up for herself to Roth."

"Roth is a fool. He would not wear the king's livery at all if his mother were not in waiting to the queen. . . . And she's certainly done nothing of the sort since. Give her a few copper coins and a new shawl—and a pat on the head—and send her on her way."

"She did save the prince's life."

A snort. "I doubt it. Obviously the illness had run its course; she just happened to have poured some ridiculous quack remedy down his throat at the time."

There was a pause, and then the first voice said: "It is a pity she's so plain. One wants a queen to set a certain standard. . . ."

Erana shivered involuntarily, and the voice stopped abruptly. Then she moaned a little, as if only just coming to consciousness, and opened her eyes.

Two of the queen's ladies-in-waiting bent over her. She recognized the owner of the second voice immediately from the sour look on her face. The kindlier face said to her: "Are you feeling a little better now? May we bring you anything?"

Erana sat up slowly. "Thank you. Would you assist me to my room, please?"

She easily persuaded them to leave her alone in her own room. At dinnertime a man came to inquire if she would attend the banquet in honor of the prince's betrothal? She laughed a short laugh and said that she felt still a trifle overcome by the news of the prince's betrothal, and desired to spend her evening resting quietly, and could someone perhaps please bring her a light supper?

Someone did, and she sat by the window watching the twilight fade into darkness, and the sounds of the banquet far away from her small room drifting up to her on the evening breeze. I have never spoken to the prince alone, she thought; I have never addressed him but as a servant who does what she may for his health and comfort; nor as he spoken to me but as a master who recognizes a servant who has her usefulness.

Dawn was not far distant when the betrothal party ended. She heard the last laughter, the final cheers, and silence. She sighed and stood up, and stretched, for she was stiff with sitting. Slowly she opened the chest where she kept her herb kerchief and the shabby clothes she had travelled in. She laid aside the court clothes she had never been comfortable in, for all that they were plain and simple compared to those the others wore, and dressed herself in the skirt and blouse that she and Maugie had made. She ran her fingers over the

patches in the skirt that house-building had caused. She
hesitated, her bundle in hand, and then opened another,
smaller chest, and took out a beautiful shawl, black, embroidered in red and gold, and with a long silk fringe. This she
folded gently, and wrapped inside her kerchief.

Touk had taught her to walk quietly, that they might watch
birds in their nests without disturbing them, and creep close to
feeding deer. She slipped into the palace shadows, and then
into the shadows of the trees that edged the courtyard; once
she looked up, over her shoulder, to the empty balcony that
opened off the great hall. The railings of the ornamental fence
that towered grandly over the gate and guardhouse were set so
far apart that she could squeeze between them, pulling her
bundle after her.

She did not think they would be sorry to see her go; she
could imagine the king's majestic words: *She has chosen to
decline the honor we would do her, feeling herself unworthy;
and having accepted our grateful thanks for her leechcraft, she
has withdrawn once again to her peaceful country obscurity.
Our best wishes go with her. . . .* But still she walked quietly, in
the shadows, and when dawn came she hid under a hedge in a
garden, and slept, as she had often done before. She woke up
once, hearing the hooves of the royal heralds rattle past; and
she wondered what news they brought. She fell asleep again,
and did not waken till twilight; and then she crept out and
began walking again.

She knew where she was going this time, and so her journey back took less time than her journey away had done. Still
she was many days on the road, and since she found that her
last experience of them had made her shy of humankind, she
walked after sunset and before dawn, and followed the stars
across open fields instead of keeping to the roads, and raided
gardens and orchards for her food, and did not offer her skills
as a leech for an honest meal or bed.

The last night she walked into the dawn and past it, and the
sun rose in the sky, and she was bone-weary and her feet hurt,
and her small bundle weighed like rock. But here was her
forest again, and she could not stop. She went past Maugie's
garden, although she saw the wisp of smoke lifting from the
chimney, and followed the well-known track to Touk's pool.
She was too tired to be as quiet as she should be, and when she
emerged from the trees, there was nothing visible but the

water. She looked around and saw that Touk had laid the path around the shore of the pool that he had promised, and now smooth grey stones led the way to the steep steps before Touk's front door.

As she stood at the water's edge her eyes blurred, and her hands, crossed over the bundle held to her breast, fell to her sides. Then there was a commotion in the pool, and Touk stood up, water streaming from him, and a strand of water-weed trailing over one pointed ear. Even the center of the pool for Touk was only thigh-deep and he stood, riffling the water with his fingers, watching her.

"Will you marry me?" she said.

He smiled, his lovely, gap-toothed smile, and he blinked his turquoise eyes at her, and pulled the water-weed out of his long hair.

"I came back just to ask you that. If you say no, I will go away again."

"No," he said. "Don't go away. My answer is yes." And he waded over to the edge of the pool and seized her in his wet arms and kissed her; and she threw her arms eagerly around his neck, and dropped her bundle. It opened in the water like a flower, and the herbs floated away across the surface, skittering like water bugs; and the embroidered silk shawl sank to the bottom.

The Boy Who Dreamed of Tir na n-Og

By Michael M. McNamara

It was in the hollow of the year when Seanin Beag found himself so dreadfully poor in the farmhouse beyond Green Wood. Many years had passed since the death of his father, Sean Mohr, a grand, round and jovial man, whose laughter had filled their little house and spouted itself up the chimneys and into the starry night. But more recently, the small boy's mother had passed into the Darkness. He remembered only the grayness of her face. He lived alone with the red cows and the fawn-tailed chickens and the donkey, Ned, as his companions.

Having eaten the last bowl of mush from the pot on the hob, Seanin pulled his jersey over his head and walked in the direction of the stable. If the donkey were to shoulder the heavy burden of kelp to the market, he would have to be fed the few remaining fistfuls of oats. The chickens would devour the leftovers. Seanin was grateful that the cows, at least, were capable of sustaining themselves without much attention. He had often heard his father say, "The cows could go on forever on the same half acre of grass and never know that the sun had fled or the moon had taken its place. They are like the Faeries, knowing no one or thing and caring the less." But Seanin rather doubted his father's estimation of Nuala, Deirdre, and Ulna. He had felt their warm breath on his neck. He knew that all three were envious of his touch.

As he fed the brown donkey, Seanin rubbed the rough oats into the saliva of the animal's mouth. It whinnied in gratitude,

and he suspected that there was an old tooth in there somewhere that needed soothing. He rubbed all the more.

From where he stood under the thatch of the stable, he
could see the waters of Kinvara Bay below him, and he
watched the mists drift inward from far out in the Other
Place. They danced across the crystal face of the bay, touching
ever so delicately its margin of sand and stones. He knew that
they came from that part of the sea that was forbidden to even
the bravest fishermen. Their long fingers were like fine threads
of silver. He longed to touch them.

Soon he would lead the donkey to the beach and begin the
piling of the kelp. But before that, as was usual to him, he
would dream for a moment. "Oh," he whispered, "that the
tables of our township might be full of wonderful things to
eat, that the churns overflow with cream, that the fires blaze
high with wood." And at last, with some guilt, he added,
"that there be a little more time for pleasure and not so much
work." But the dream had to be put aside. The chill and
dampness of the night brought him back to his senses as he
faced into them.

On his way to the strand, Seanin ran afoul of his neighbor's
two boys, Taig and Paud, eagerly playing rugger in the
pasture. "Come on, Seanin," they shouted. "Come and play
with us."

He hated to refuse the rambunctious lads, but their responsibilities were at an end for the day. His had merely begun.
"No. No," he called to them. "I'll play a match or two with
you on Saturday, after the fair. There'll be plenty of time."

The boys seemed disappointed. Seanin knew that in their
hearts they relished the time he spent with them, as he savored
the many nights he had spent by the hob with their father,
Seamus Dubh. He was a man of many whiskers and as many
stories. Seamus had cried like a child at the death of Seanin's
father. And since his mother's death, Seanin owed much to
the willing man who helped him daily with the heavy work of
the farm.

"Ah, come on," the boys said. "We'd love you to play."

It bothered his heart that he was obliged to wave and pretend that he had not heard their pleas.

Once on the strand, Seanin began immediately the torment-
ing labor. He strained to raise the heavy pitchforks of kelp
above his head and into the wicker basket on Ned's shoulders.

It was a grueling task, but he kept up the ritual, singing a schoolroom song as he worked:

> Oh, my little boat,
> That brings the fish to shore . . .

He had not finished the verse when he heard a voice from below him call out in alarm.

"Ocon! Ocon!" it lamented.

He dropped his pitchfork and ran in the direction of the sound. Perhaps it is a child who is afraid of the waves, he thought. Or a lad bitten by a silent jelly-fish. He would know for certain when he mounted the remaining rise of sand and seaweed.

To his surprise, he faced, instead, a young girl of less than his own age. Her face shone like the evening star. Her long golden curls danced in the late breeze from the bay, and her clothing was of a cut that he had never seen before.

"Who are you?" he asked in amazement.

"I am Ainne Ni Glorin," the young girl said, "and I have become entangled in these vines. I fear that they will be my downfall."

"Here," he said. "I will help you."

"No. No," she insisted. "I am fully capable of helping myself."

Seanin was not used to such curtness. He stood back and watched. It was curious to him that she made no physical effort to unleash herself. Instead, she merely cried out, "Free me! Free me!"

"Aw, that will do you no good," he said at length. "The kelp will not hear you. It obeys only the word of the fingers."

"No. Please do not assist me. I must free myself. Otherwise, I will be in your debt. I cannot have that."

"You will be in no one's debt," Seanin said, and with that he bent down and loosed the black kelp from her ankle.

She was dumfounded. "You should not have done that," she said. "Now I am deeply obliged to you. You have saved my life."

"From the clutches of a vicious seaweed," he laughed aloud. "There is no compliment." He made to return to his work.

"Oh, no, you do not understand. With the falling of the sun

and rising of the moon into its heaven, I would have perished here on this shore. You see, I am from Tir na n-Og.''

"The Land of the Young,'' he translated.

"Yes. And it is forbidden for me to remain in this place beyond nightfall.''

"And so you would rather have perished than be helped?''

"No. I must secretly admit that I am glad that you came along. But, you see, in Tir na n-og, there is no need of help from anyone else. All desires are granted, all wishes fulfilled.''

"If you have no power here, why did you risk coming?''

"Because of my foolishness, I strayed from my companions and rode the enchanted mists too close to this Land of Tears. And now I must go before the moth-hour falls upon the fields and I am destroyed by my carelessness.''

"Must you,'' Seanin said without thinking, for he had warmed to her in their short encounter.

"I must, for I already hear the sparrows chirp their warnings. But why not come with me and spend your days in Tir na n-Og?''

Seanin looked back towards the farm. He saw the house silhouetted against the dark clouds, the barn dilapidated against its shoulder, the living things clinging desperately to its margins. And it seemed to cry out to him to remain, to light its fires, to shield its breaches against the wind, to scatter seed on the face of its earth, to pass gentle words to its few kind neighbors and friends. But in his heart, also, he knew the loneliness of the place. He could not forget the bite of frost when there was no fire, or the clutch of hunger in his belly. At last, he said, "I will go, if Ned may come, too.''

Ainne looked down at the donkey, who was nuzzling the sleeve of her tunic. "I think that Ned will have no objections,'' she laughed.

Where, at first, they ventured, Seanin could not later recall, but he knew that he and Ned and the golden-haired girl tumbled through clouds of mist and fog. At times, he caught glimpses of green plashy places and heard the laughter of many children. When, at last, the velvet brume withdrew, they sat together in an open field of daisies. Seanin touched the flowers with his fingers. He knew that their season had come and gone in the Land of Tears.

"And now,'' Ainne said, "you are on your own, for in Tir na n-Og, you will have little use of friends.''

"But," Seanin cried, "I have never been without friends. I will be lost on my own."

Ainne merely smiled and was then gone.

For a moment, Seanin was bewildered. Then he noticed that Ned had strayed towards the open gate of the field, and he ran through the house-high grass to halt him before he became lost. But Ned knew his own whereabouts. He had wandered towards something familiar to him. Seanin saw what it was as he neared the donkey. It was the sea—a great sea of billowy waves and before it an expanse of iridescent sand. It was as though the stars of the heavens had been gathered and spread out before the surging face of the sea. On this strand played many children, their voices raised in merriment.

Seanin stood apart from it all and leaned on Ned. He looked down at his ragged clothing and felt ashamed. Stroking the animal's fur gently, he confided, "If only we were as they are."

Immediately, his wish was granted. His dull clothing was replaced by a gaily colored tunic much like that of Ainne's. About his neck hung a medallion of pure gold. Ned, too, had undergone a transformation. His fur was brushed to a silvery sheen. His mane was clipped short.

Seanin grasped Ned's collar and led him down the path of stones, which did not bruise the feet but felt like so many downy feathers. When he reached the shore, the Faeries called out their greetings and invited him to participate in their game. Then they became absorbed again in the ritual of the sport. Seanin watched with interest. It seemed that the entire frolic consisted of heaping the sweet-smelling kelp into great mounds and then diving into its depths. But the kelp was of a texture that Seanin had never seen before. It neither stung with its sharp bristles nor tore the flesh, burning it with its brine. In great delight, he threw himself into the game.

After a time, he became hungry and decided to try some of the fare which was spread out on tables adjoining the beach. He had never seen so much to eat! Cakes, tarts, pies, and cordials were neatly arranged on tablecloths of pure white. He sampled one and then another and still another, and yet there were more not tasted. "What a wonderful feast," he said to a boy next to him who was stuffing a raspberry tart in his already gorged mouth. "Who is the host of this celebration and who are the workmen who gathered the seaweed? I would like very much to give them my thanks.''

The Faery boy laughed. "Host? Workmen? Are you mad? There are no such things in Tir na n-Og."

"But who. . . . ?"

"We are all and everything. We merely wish and our desires are immediately realized. It is a game that goes on forever. Watch."

Seanin looked on in amazement as the Faery closed his eyes and said aloud, "I wish this instant for a polished seashell, so that I may listen to the sea when it is not in sight."

Almost at the same moment, his wish was granted. He held in his hand the most beautifully formed shell that Seanin had ever laid eyes on.

"There," said the Faery. His eyes showed no awe or astonishment.

Seanin, when he came out of his stupor, began to explain to the boy the lack of such wonderment in the Land of Tears, where, he said, each thing had to be earned, each pleasure drawn at the cost of labor and hardship. But after a few minutes, the Faery turned his heel and walked slowly away.

Suddenly, Seanin heard a loud thrashing of water and a voice raised to a high pitch. He looked towards the sea. There, not twenty feet from him, was a small child, bobbing up and down in the great waves. But nobody else seemed to hear the cries. The other Faeries continued to dive into their mountains of kelp or to sample the pastries of the table.

Seanin threw his food to the ground and rushed into the deep water. With a few powerful strokes, he reached the now unconscious child. He bent his arm about the pale neck and struck out for shore.

By the time he reached shallow water, the Faeries had abandoned their diversion and were gathering at the edge of the sea. Their faces were perplexed and questioning. But no one moved to help him. Seanin laid his burden on the sand and began to press with all his strength on the child's chest. He had seen his own father do this when fishermen had been hooked from the sea.

The Faeries drew nearer. One said, "Why did you rescue him?"

"He was drowning," Seanin said between strokes. "He must have hit his head and was knocked senseless."

"But now he will be your servant in some degree because of what you have done."

"Servant?"

"Yes. Here it is frowned on to receive aid. It is an admission of weakness. You see, we are a most perfect race."

"But he was unconscious. He had no time to save himself. . . ."

The Faeries would not argue further. Each in his turn backed away and drifted silently along the water's edge. It was as if they refused to look upon the child for fear that they would in some way be contaminated by him.

Though Seanin could not clearly see their reasoning, he felt, nonetheless, that his staying could only help to complicate matters. He looked down at the boy. He was beginning to regain consciousness. It would only be a matter of minutes before he was fully in control and capable of wishing himself perfect again. It was time to be gone. The boy would surely imagine that he had been buffeted ashore by the gentle waves.

As Seanin reached the summit of the rise above the strand, he noticed the thatched roof of a farmhouse, much like his own, protrude over the black reeds. His curiosity was aroused, and he decided to pay the farmer a visit.

He reached the barnyard and tied Ned to a trough which overflowed with grain of every color of the harvest. The donkey sniffed at the feast. Seanin wandered off towards the brightly lit building that was situated to the north of the cobblestoned yard. Before entering, he called aloud to the farmer, but nobody came. He decided to enter.

What met his gaze dazzled the eyes in his head. Not on the richest farm of his homeland had he seen such plenty. Bins spilled over with grain. Lofts spread their straw in fine showers of gold. Great wooden pails dripped with the thickest cream. Seanin fell to his knees and scooped up several fingerfulls. It tasted as fresh as the green clover of the hillock above his house. He ate until his stomach touched his throat.

A blazing fire burned in a hob that was as immaculate as the cream itself. To its right stood a deep chair stuffed like a kind of soft old grandfather. And Seanin, wishing only at that moment to dream of all that was past and yet to come, fell into its cozy arms. The wind was coming up outside. He could hear its raucous voice in the gables. He would sleep for a while.

When he awoke, a strange sound met his ears. At first, he mistook it for the wind, but then he recognized its melody. It was the music of fiddles and melodeons. The energetic notes soothed his mounting fears. Ned, too, had noticed. As he un-

chained the donkey, its great woolly ears perked with in-
quisitiveness.

Seanin and Ned began walking through the dew-wet grass.
Their feet seemed not to touch the ground, and the air was
filled with the scent of lavender and wild bulrush.

Before them lay a clearing which was flooded in brilliant
light. Within the blinding circle danced row after row of Faery
children. Each of them spun desperately around the raised
platform at the center, where several musicians tore out their
music from ancient instruments. On and on the music played.
Seanin himself was bewitched by its cadence. He pushed
cautiously forward and into the swaying crowd.

How long he danced he was not sure. Sometimes he stepped
to the music for three reels in succession. At other times, when
the constant whirling became monotonous, he merely waited
out the set, and took refreshment at one of the tables on the
perimeter of the clearing. Dance. Rest. Dance. Rest. Dance.
Rest. So it went. He seemed incapable of breaking the ritual
and leaving the place.

Towards midnight, as the great yellow moon peeked over
the horizon, he noticed a commotion at the other end of the
crowd. At first, he decided to ignore it, being absorbed in the
rhythm of his dance, but he thought that once or twice he had
seen Ned's ears above the heads of the Faeries. He moved
lazily in the direction of the hysterical laughter.

Sure enough, it was Ned. The donkey had been trapped in
the center of the small group and spun round and round in
confusion. The Faeries were enthralled with the animal's
dilemma and cheered in delight. Seanin watched the donkey's
head follow its tail. Or was it the other way around? How
foolish Ned looked. He began to laugh.

Suddenly, Ned lost his balance and fell heavily to the
ground. He whinnied in great pain, unable to rise again on his
feet. The Faeries clapped their hands in glee.

In the shutting of an eyelid, Seanin was beside his companion. He looked into the old eyes. They were filled with terror
and sadness. The Faeries crowded in upon them, suffocating
them both with their chant, "Down boy, down donkey. Down
boy, down donkey. Down . . ."

Seanin threw his arms about the cherished woolly head.
"Oh, Ned, I am sorry to have neglected you," he said. "I was
thinking only of myself. I wish that we were far from this hor-
rid place."

In an instant, the bright clearing had fled, and they sat together in the heart of a seamless meadow. The darkness of night enveloped them as they huddled close against each other. Seanin was dreadfully lonely. "I may conjure up all that one can imagine," he said, "and yet I am unhappy."

He turned to Ned and said, "Look!"

No sooner were the words out of his mouth than before them lay plates of sweets and custards and other delights. He had attended to Ned's wants, also. A stack of fresh hay took shape out of the night. And, yet, neither of them had a mind to touch a morsel.

Seanin began to cry, his tears running down his face and onto the fur of the donkey. He wished for the company of Seamus Dubh and Taig and little Paud and the old shattered faces of the township, for the warm hands across the hearth, for the kettle singing on the hob, for the chatter of loving voices.

Ainne Ni Glorin stood before them. "Seanin," she said, "have you found your heart's content?"

Seanin bowed his head. "No," he answered.

"Have you thought of home?" she continued.

"Yes."

"All is well there. Only a few short hours have elapsed since you left."

"But I have been gone for such a long time."

"Our time is not like yours."

"Has my absence caused anyone distress?"

"Yes. An old man with a crooked stick searches for you on the strand."

"Seamus Dubh."

Ainne looked across at him. "And so you wish to leave Tir na n-Og," she said.

"Yes."

"I do not understand your displeasure. Here there is so much, and there lies nothing but sadness and strain with few moments to enjoy uninterrupted pleasure."

Seanin was silent.

"There is no persuading you to stay?"

"No."

Ainne sighed deeply. "Well, then," she said, "I must say goodbye. I will not forget that you saved my life."

"Goodbye, Ainne Ni Glorin."

"Goodbye, Seanin Beag."

Before he could count the fingers on his hand or the buttons on his tunic, Seanin and the donkey were thrown gently into the air, all vision of Ainne gone, all compass of place and time withdrawn. It was as though a heavy sleep fell upon him, a sleep of troubled dreams. When he opened his eyes, he found himself and Ned on the strand below the farmhouse. The sun was rising in its path. The cold morning air drifted mercilessly across the waters of the bay.

Suddenly, a voice shouted, "Seanin! Heaven save us, I found you. The whole township has not slept a wink, worrying about you."

It was Seamus Dubh. As the old man rushed down the strand, Seanin could see the tears in his eyes and the laughter on his lips. He threw his arms about the boy. "Where on earth have you been?" he said. "I searched all night for you. Someone reported having seen you walk far out into the tide. It was by sheer luck that I chanced to find this little cove and you asleep in it."

"I had a vision of Faeryland."

"Ah, don't we all dream of Faeryland. It's what keeps us going."

"Maybe you're right."

"Well, let's be about getting that kelp up on the donkey, or we'll never get you to market. Were to God that the rotten old weeds were gold. They're saying that there's no knowing to the price of *that* princely stuff, these days. But sure, what would we know about such fancy goings on, we, poor kelp gatherers?"

Seanin remembered. He reached inside his ragged jersey. The gold medallion was still there, close against his heart.